RENEGADES
LORD OF EXCESS

RENEGADES
LORD OF EXCESS

RICH McCORMICK

BLACK LIBRARY

A BLACK LIBRARY PUBLICATION

First published in 2024.
This edition published in Great Britain in 2024 by
Black Library, Games Workshop Ltd., Willow Road,
Nottingham, NG7 2WS, UK.

Represented by: Games Workshop Limited – Irish branch,
Unit 3, Lower Liffey Street, Dublin 1,
D01 K199, Ireland.

10 9 8 7 6 5 4 3 2 1

Produced by Games Workshop in Nottingham.
Cover illustration by Manuel Castañón.

A CIP record for this book is available from the British Library.

ISBN 13: 978-1-80407-671-2

See Black Library on the internet at

blacklibrary.com

Find out more about Games Workshop
and the worlds of Warhammer at

warhammer.com

Printed and bound in the UK.

For Katherine: my own Saviour.

For more than a hundred centuries the Emperor
has sat immobile on the Golden Throne of Earth.
He is the Master of Mankind. By the might of his
inexhaustible armies a million worlds stand
against the dark.

Yet, he is a rotting carcass, the Carrion Lord of
the Imperium held in life by marvels from the
Dark Age of Technology and the thousand souls
sacrificed each day so his may continue to burn.

To be a man in such times is to be one amongst
untold billions. It is to live in the cruelest and
most bloody regime imaginable. It is to suffer an
eternity of carnage and slaughter. It is to have cries
of anguish and sorrow drowned by the thirsting
laughter of dark gods.

This is a dark and terrible era where you will
find little comfort or hope. Forget the power of
technology and science. Forget the promise
of progress and advancement. Forget any notion
of common humanity or compassion.

There is no peace amongst the stars, for in the grim
darkness of the far future, there is only war.

they were around his throat, needle-sharp nails as pinpricks on exposed skin, ready to pierce.

She squeezed, hard, and pleasure became pain.

Xantine came into reality choking. He felt hands around his neck, skin soft but the grip ceramite-strong. Nails penetrated skin, and he felt the trickle of blood, cooling as it slipped past the gorget of his Mark IV armour and stained the collar of his bodysuit.

He threw his own hands to his throat, fighting through narrowing vision to claw the attacker away. But he found nothing there. He gulped hard, and the air finally came, rushing down his throat, satiating his burning lungs. He breathed, shallow at first, his armoured chest rising and falling to a frantic rhythm, his twin hearts offering a syncopated backbeat. He consciously slowed his physiology. He was millennia removed from his indoctrination, but he still remembered how to use his body as an instrument.

He sucked in a long, deep breath. The air tasted rich and sweet on his tongue, like overripe fruit left in the sun. Like home. His elongated pupils contracted slowly, adjusting to his reality.

There was cacophony. Sirens blared, their music discordant and, to Xantine's extreme tastes, delightful. He would have loved nothing more than to revel in their sound, but he knew their troubling meaning: the frigate *Exhortation* had been hurled from the warp much earlier than expected. He and his warband – the Adored, made up primarily of Emperor's Children Space Marines deemed Traitoris Extremis by the Imperium – had been set on a course to meet with other remnants of the III Legion. The journey was long and difficult, and was scheduled to take weeks, if not months of travel.

A spike of adrenaline hit his bloodstream, the chemical's effect boosted in potency by Apothecaries of the Emperor's Children millennia before. His reality sharpened.

From his throne in the pleasure chamber of the *Exhortation*, Xantine saw colour. Gold, in the chandeliers that hung from the high ceiling, impurities in the metal rotting green over centuries in the void. Blues, fading to black, in the darkened corners of the vast space, hidden places that the sultry orange glow of candles and lumens couldn't pierce. The tan, beige, ochre, and brown of human skin, flayed from dying bodies and stretched between diamond-tipped hooks set overhead. Faces in the leathery material lay open in wordless screams that had lasted centuries.

Beneath the throne, in a space that resembled an orchestra pit, he saw spurts of turquoise and cyan, magenta shot through with yellow, white or silver. The colours danced across the armour of his warriors. His Adored sparred with razor-sharp duelling sabres, or cradled foaming, steaming bowls of narcotics that filled the air with their heady scent.

And he saw red. So much red. Red of all shades: crimson, vermilion, ruby and wine, splashed against cogitators and across frescoes. Encrusted on tapestries that dangled from above, swaying lightly as a discordant melody disturbed the air, and stained onto huge, heavy curtains that framed the room's window to the void.

Between those curtains, through a vast viewport, a pearl. Pastel pink and perfect, it hung in black space as if it had been placed on a velvet cushion. Shiny, beautiful and new. Of all the locations in the galaxy, the *Exhortation* had been flung from the warp within touching distance of a new world.

A jewel, said a voice at the nape of his neck. A voice not heard, but felt. In his fingers, in his muscles and his bones – in all of the body that they shared. The one who held him like a lover; the one whose hands had slipped around his throat.

S'janth.

A pretty bauble, but a distraction. You promised me, my love.

She had no form – not on this plane of base pleasures, anyway – but Xantine knew she was staring at the world, feline eyes hungry. He felt her desire, always so close to the surface. It was an ache, an all-encompassing thing. As it ever was.

She was desire incarnate, once one of Slaanesh's favoured companions, who, despite her privileged seat at the Dark Prince's side, had taken leave of the comfortable confines of his palace to savour the tastes of the galaxy.

He had taken her – or she had taken him – on the planet of Kalliope. She had wandered too far, too naive in her desperation, and had been imprisoned by aeldari captors, locked away from sensation, satisfaction, and all that made her whole for millennia, until Xantine had freed her, had shared his physical form with her, in exchange for her power. She was weakened by thousands of years in captivity, but her strength was intoxicating.

The Lord of Excess waits for me. He needs me. He needs us.

Her power had given him his own warband, his Adored, and his own ship. It had given him the strength to break free from Abaddon's yoke, tearing off the black of the Warmaster's Children of Torment for the royal purple and riotous pink of his own Emperor's Children. It had clarified his purpose.

We must continue, my love. Do not allow yourself to be consumed by base pleasure. Slaanesh can offer you so much more.

The world floated in the viewport. He watched it, hungrily.

PART I

CHAPTER ONE

The censer swung like a metronome. Arqat stared at it, transfixed. Fashioned in ornate silver and trailing cloying grey smoke, it would disappear for a moment into its own wake, before reappearing once again, a stinking comet in reverse course. The smell stung Arqat's nostrils, and he rubbed at his nose, taking his eyes from the book he was copying.

Arqat heard a thwack, and the pain came a second later: sharp and stinging across his shoulder blades.

'Concentrate, boy!' Gospeler Lautrec shouted, tucking his cane back into hands folded behind his back. Arqat watched, anger fomenting on a face too young to hide its effects yet, as Lautrec continued his interminable pacing, walking the pews of the Cathedral of the Bounteous Harvest.

Arqat muttered a curse under his breath, and refocused his eyes on the page in front of them. It was so *stupid*. He was in his nineteenth cycle, he was a Ministorum adept in training, he was a *man*, but he was being treated like a child by an old gargoyle.

Arqat hated the older priest's hands. The skin, spectre-pale and so thin that it split over his knuckles like torn paper, leaving little punctuation marks of blood on the parchment he handed his students. Serrine was a blessed world, his father said, where the worthy could bathe in the youthful waters of rejuvenat treatment. Why did Lautrec spurn that blessing?

And, more importantly, why did Arqat have to listen to him?

'Tradition, Arqat,' his father had said, reciting the rules for vassal children before Arqat could stop him. *'First son to his master, second son to the masters, third son to the Master of all.'*

His oldest brother had left home before Arqat could hold on to memories, his duties as an aide to the undersecretary of planet-side logistics arranged between Arqat's great-great-grandfather and the hereditary holder of the noble title generations before. Arqat wasn't envious of his existence, if only because on the few trips he made back to the family table – when his master was on hunting expeditions across the grass ocean, or recovering from one of his clandestine visits to the seedier establishments in the undercity – it sounded like his brother had to do just as much copying of documents as he did.

But his middle brother, Telo, ah, there was an experience to be envied. He was *doing* something with his life: keeping the peace in the planetary militia. Arqat had listened, rapt, as his brother regaled him with tales of training that made him sharp, strong and brave. Of journeys below the haze line and into the darkness of the undercity to corral filthy smugglers and shut down their illicit trade.

His brother, always bigger and stronger than Arqat, had been made bigger and stronger still by the militia's chemical regimen until he – only two cycles older than Arqat – stood a head and a half taller than even their father.

And here Arqat was, stuck in a musty cathedral, copying

scripture for the tenth time for the Emperor knew what reason.

He could recite the story from memory, anyway. He and his brother would request it from Nanny every bedtime – at least until Telo started to get hair under his arms and decided he didn't like hearing children's stories any more. Arqat got his own hair soon after that, but he still liked the story, and sometimes, when Telo was out playing war with the other boys at the academy, he would ask Nanny to tell it to him. He would lay his head on her shoulder as she sat in her wheeled chair, her curly grey hair tickling his cheek, as he mouthed the words of the tale along with her.

It was their most basic story, and it told of the foundation of their world. He saw it now in the book he copied, laid out in both words and pictures so that even a child could understand. The parchment was ancient and the ink was fading, but the image was still vibrant and clear.

'*Once there was a world,*' Nanny would start, '*where pain could be found.*'

A grey circle lay on the page, bleak and perfectly empty.

'*From his golden throne, our lord came to the ground.*'

A blazing figure, descending from heaven, his long hair forming a billowing halo around his perfect features.

'*He brought salvation, bounty for us all.*'

Golden light shone from above, illuminating the four ceremonial offerings that represented Serrine: the sheaf of grass, the threshing blade, and the two cups – one of water, one of Solipsus sap. Four offerings, held in four arms. Father had said that the Saviour should only have had two arms, but Nanny's book featured a perversion of the human form that had increasingly been adopted by members of the faith.

'*Return'd to us if dark times should befall.*'

The figure stood vast, astride the world, wrapped in armour the colour of Serrine's main export. The colour of kings and emperors.

A deep, imperial purple.

The grass told its secrets at night.

Cecily had learned its language when she was young, on the precipitous border between true childhood and the age at which she was assessed to be just tall enough, just strong enough, just educated enough to work the threshing machines or tend the irrigation pipes. She would steal out at night, during the precious few hours assigned for sleep, and lie at the edge of the fields where grass rose like a wall, each soft-pink blade as strong as a cable and as wide as a man's head, listening to the waft and wave of the fronds on the wind.

It told of beasts and barbarians that spent their lives nestled in its bosom, and places, special places far from the cities and the reach of the threshing machines, where visitors could even see the sky. The grass stretched the length of existence, her grandpa had told her – from this horizon to that horizon, and back again. She had never seen the horizon – she'd never even been above the haze line – but the grass told her that the old man was right.

It whispered of the threshing machines, the huge harvesters that carved miles-long furrows through its depths, slicing and slashing at growth old and new. These injuries changed its tone, making it weak, scared or angry. It whispered of the water, the thousands of miles of irrigation pipes that trickled a steady stream of fertiliser-enhanced liquid into the parched soil. Her cousin Sol had worked these pipes, monitoring their status from his glider, checking for breaks in the line with patched-up magnoculars that he would report back to base for others to fix. Grandpa said that Sol was a born pilot, and she thought for years that was how it worked: that your life was chosen for you when you were put on this world. That the Emperor, in His infinite wisdom, watched over all the billions upon billions of babies born in His Imperium, and picked a job for them as they came into the world, all wet and squealing. Grandpa had laughed when she told him that, and said that wasn't how it was, but she wasn't so sure. She still wasn't so sure.

She asked the grass about Sol, a week after the warm day that he hadn't come home. She wanted to know if he'd been taken by one of the hovering monsters – those flat, rippling things that hung in the sky and scanned the grass with rows of belly-set eyes – or if he'd been speared by a dive-bomber, its three-foot beak severing his spine as it carried him to the soft dirt. Had his glider failed, a wing shearing off through overuse? The mechanics of the undercity did their best, but supplies were always limited, and anything that did make its way down the pipes from above usually came clapped out. Or had he just crashed, the joy of flight addling his mind and taking his life? She put all these suggestions to the grass, but it ignored her, continuing its song of itself.

It whispered of the city. The city was clanking, steaming, whirring – a blight that marred its immaculate pinkness. It wanted to envelop the city like a white blood cell, to eat at its cancer until all was quiet, nothing left but the soft hiss of wind on grass. But for now, it made do by encircling the city, growing back even when it was cut down, forcing the tiny things that lived inside to build upwards, ever upwards, until they were above the clouds. She wondered if they could see the Emperor's light up there.

Yes, the grass had always spoken, and she had listened, but tonight – tonight it was different. Tonight it was speaking directly *to* her. She could hear it all the way down on the third sub-basement of her refinery hab-block, through solid ferrocrete and soft dirt. It woke her as she danced on the edge of sleep, pulling her from her bunk, teasing her out of her threadbare blanket, and leading her past the sleeping forms of her shiftmates. She walked the route she'd walked as a youth, out past the barricades that marked the edge of the undercity, past thresher machines, their engines slumbering until they took tomorrow's toll, to the edge of the grass ocean.

She stood for a moment, a hand outstretched, palm against a fibrous stalk. The grass was thick and strong, ripe for harvest. Once, it would have already been taken, sliced at the root by whirring blades before being deposited into vast containers held at the back of the threshing machines like the abdomens of vicious beetles. From there, it would be mulched, pounded, and pulverised in the refineries at the heart of the undercity. Their chimneys spewed a pastel mist as the grass was rendered down to its constituent parts – a cloying, sweet-smelling fug the same colour as the clouds above that blocked out the sky.

And when it was done, it was grass no more. It was thick, pungent, the purple of a mouldering bruise – the drug that gave her world purpose. Her grandpa said it helped make people young again, that the fancy types who lived up above the clouds would lie, cheat, and even kill for it. She didn't understand why they would have to do that. Why didn't they just come down here? There was so much grass – enough for everyone.

A soft susurrus pulled at her attention, and she stepped forward, into the field. The waving fronds surrounded her, each taller than a man and then half as tall again. The city lay just behind her, she knew, vast in scale, but cloying mist made it into a vague shape, and she felt her bearings slip away. The mist teased her nostrils and slid down her throat, tugging at her lungs. She gulped hard, looking for the breath that would slow her racing heart. The grass spoke to her.

Calm, it whispered. She breathed again, and felt the staccato rhythm in her chest start to stabilise. *Forward*, the grass said, and she walked, pushing springy fronds aside as she ventured into the perfectly uniform pinkness. *Keep going, that's it*, the grass urged, the tone reassuring, like a mother to an infant. *You're close.*

She was close. She didn't need the grass to tell her that now. She could hear voices, cheated by the wind and dampened by the fog, but still powerful, their owners raising them in unison. She could hear the resonant boom of a drum, the skin of one of the canid predators that prowled these grasslands in packs pulled taut over a length of pipe or a part of a threshing machine's engine. And she could hear the grass, still, over all this, guiding her to her future.

It's time.

She pushed the fronds aside and saw a hole in the world. A great depression had been carved into the earth, wide and deep enough to hold a thousand people. Hundreds were already there, standing in groups on shaped dirt steps, and as she stood at the lip of the makeshift amphitheatre, she saw more filter in: grizzled threshers, sallow-faced washers, refinery mulchers. Even in the milky moonlight, she could see that many had a purple tinge to their skin and the peculiar hairlessness that her grandpa had put down to proximity to the chemicals produced by the grass.

She recognised faces among the crowd. There was Doren, whose daughter she had played alongside as a child, until she was old enough to join a thresher gang and the grass claimed her. There was Pount, scrap dealer, who would trade parts surreptitiously lifted from threshing machines or the network of pipes that connected the undercity to the world above for little vials of the refined grass sap. The hit made you feel a decade younger, her more adventurous friends had said, but she saw the comedown first-hand – headaches, memory loss, and skin so tight that it would split around the eyes – and decided that it wasn't for her.

But the vast majority she didn't know, a mass of humanity that had spilled out into the depths of the grass on this night for... something. Had they been called from their beds as well? They carried tools of their trade: blades, spanners, wrenches and heavy hammers. They must have come straight from their shifts, she thought with a twinge of idle sympathy, walking the long walk through the grass without time to even return to their bunk or hab-block, to wash or change their clothes.

And they were all silent. No conversation flowed in the loose groups they stood in; instead, their attention was fixated on the centre of the amphitheatre, and the spectacle that was unfolding there. There stood a makeshift stage, built from engine parts, rusted pipes, and battered panels seemingly stolen from the side of thresher machines. Around it, she saw the source of the drumbeat: four giants, easily as tall as the grass she had walked through, brought bleached bone clubs down onto huge drums. The figures were robed, their faces hidden in the heavy gloom, and as their arms rose and fell with each strike, she saw that their skin had been swaddled in rough-looking bandages. She was perturbed to see that one of the drummers – seemingly their leader – had three arms.

A figure stood at the centre of the stage. Like the drummers, it wore a long robe, its head hooded and its arms hidden by billowing sleeves. It stood onstage a moment longer, captivating in its pure stillness, before a hand rose from one of those sleeves, silencing the drums. In their absence, even though she stood shoulder to shoulder with strangers, surrounded by thousands of the undercity's residents, she could hear the whisper of the grass, so perfect was their rapt attention.

'My brothers and sisters,' the figure on the stage began. Its voice was beautiful: mellifluous and light, but imbued with such force that Cecily could hear it as if the figure was standing next to her. As if it was in her mind. It sounded like the grass speaking to her.

'We are told that the Emperor protects. That He sits on the Golden Throne on far-off Terra, and watches over His subjects, over our toils and our troubles, salves our aches, and heals our wounds. We are told that this world pleases the Emperor, and that our harvest belongs to Him – that *we* belong to Him.

'We grow, and water, and harvest, and mulch, sending shipments to the city above. But the fruit of our toil rots in the sun that we cannot see. Terra does not answer our call. The Emperor does not answer our call.'

The figure continued, its beautiful voice rising in register.

'Look inside yourselves. I tell you what you already know. We do not belong to the Emperor on Terra' – it paused for a breath – 'because the Emperor is dead.'

The figure on the stage almost spat the word, and Cecily gasped at both its tone and meaning. Her hand shot to her mouth, and she felt her stomach lurch like a glider pilot falling from the sky. This was blasphemy, heresy, counter to the reality she had been raised in. But somehow more shocking was that none of the people around her seemed shocked at all. They stood, unmoving, jaws set, or swaying slightly as if in a trance, hammers, blades, and clubs dangling limply from arms by their sides.

'We are a poisoned people,' the figure went on. 'We are born below the clouds. We toil below the clouds. We die below the clouds. We waste our bodies for those who dwell above. We are sliced and slashed, gassed and choked, stunted and warped, and most of us will never see the sky.'

The figure gestured upwards with both arms. In the gloom of deep night, the haze line above was rendered in grey, giving it an artificial glow – as though a plasteel bubble had been lowered over the amphitheatre.

'But I *have* seen the stars. Our salvation lies within them. We can reach for them together, but we must rise, as one, above the cloud that blinds us. We deserve this world, we deserve the sky' – both arms were raised now, long and willowy, exposing pinkish skin – 'and we deserve the stars!'

The crowd found its voice, suddenly, and all at once. There was a roar of assent, uniform and perfect, before the figure spoke again.

'Only in those stars will we find salvation. Our Emperor has forsaken us, but rejoice, for a better master rises to take His place. We will rise from below the clouds, and we will take this world!'

As the figure tipped its head back, the hood fell, and Cecily saw the owner of the voice clearly. She had the stained pink skin of the refinery workers, but where their work made their bodies haggard, their eyes sallow, and their skin sag, she was the most beautiful creature Cecily had ever seen. Her skin was so perfect as to be luminous, and her green eyes shone bright in her hairless head.

Cecily would follow her. She would obey her. She would die for her.

'Tonight, children of Serrine,' the luminary on stage shouted. 'Tonight, we take this world for ourselves, and for our future!'

CHAPTER TWO

The mound of flesh stank. Even for Xantine, who had stood unbowed in the galaxy's most depraved charnel houses, the smell made his lurid turquoise eyes water.

For the *Exhortation*'s mortal crew, it was too much. Most of them clipped their nostrils closed with pincers of gold or silver, breathing through gauze-wrapped mouths. Others had appended nosebags over their faces, each filled with narcotic herbs and pungent spices, giving them the appearance of large flightless birds as they manoeuvred around the cramped bridge.

It impeded the crew's work, but they were necessary steps. After all, the mound was far more important than any of them. It was called Ghelia, but in truth, it *was* the *Exhortation*: the ship's brain and body, the muscle that gave it the impetus to run, and the imperative to fight. It had the cognition to make careful and complex jumps, allowing the ship and its master to sail the warp without a living Navigator on board.

That wasn't technically true. It had been a Navigator once,

Xantine knew. Ghelia was born the youngest daughter of Resh Irili, one of many scions of Navigator House Irili. The house had long been a solid and dependable source of Navigators for Terra's small-scale shipping enterprises, but the lady Resh's epicurean tastes would not be sated by a life considered merely comfortable. Seeking pleasure, she had disguised herself and departed the Throneworld, using her talents to eventually reach the fringes of the Eye of Terror. Xantine had not met Resh Irili – the lady had died in the employ of a long-departed warlord whom he didn't care to recall – but she had left a crowd of daughters. Ghelia was one of these, more or less baseline in appearance before she had turned her name and her body over to become the pulsing, stinking blob of matter whose tendrils now ran the full length of the *Exhortation*.

It was a difficult business, maintaining a Navigator on board a vessel of the Emperor's Children. Some simply went mad, the cacophony of sound and sensation too much for their delicate psychic capabilities. Others became distracted, their minds turned from the minutiae of piloting a vast warship through the eddies and tides of unreality by earthly pains and pleasures.

Xantine had seen this happen first-hand. Deploying his silver tongue – and the gift of a few hundred slaves – he'd once managed to orchestrate an audience with the Dancer-in-Silks, once a brother of the III, and now choirmaster of his own warband: the Souls of Splendour. Conscious of the Dancer's infamously fickle nature, Xantine had ordered the *Exhortation* to the rendezvous point with weapons on standby and void shields to full, but of the rival warband, there was no sign.

Weeks later they discovered their ship – the *Splendour's Vision* – half embedded in a moon on the outer edge of the system. Investigation of what was left of the stricken craft turned up several dozen transhuman bodies and vox-records that indicated the ship's Navigator had been inspecting his reflection in a nearby mirror when his talents were called upon to navigate safely out of the warp. Indeed, the records suggested he had been admiring himself in the same mirror for the previous standard month, forcing the recently transferred slaves to feed and bathe him so he would not have to avert his eyes from his own form.

Xantine found it difficult to understand what the Navigator saw in the reflected form that bewitched him so, but then, it had been hard to see much of the man by then: the majority of his face had melded into solid rock.

Even Navigators still enthralled to the Imperium tended to mutate as their careers went on, but those that found themselves in service to warbands like Xantine's own tended to change more rapidly, in more exotic ways, the currents of the warp colliding and coalescing to make them something truly special.

This was Ghelia. Xantine didn't remember the woman, in truth. She had been sequestered in her chambers at the heart of the ship, communicating primarily with the warlord Euphoros and his bridge crew. He, in turn, had been but one of Euphoros' warriors at the time. A trusted and respected warrior, he told himself, but one whose focus was on his own betterment, rather than the vagaries of running a vast voidship. As he took S'janth into himself and wrested control of the warband, and with it the *Exhortation*, from Euphoros, he found Ghelia already in her flowered state.

He had investigated the possibility of removing Ghelia from the ship, intending a clean break from Euphoros' previous regime, but the creature was like a tumour that had wormed its way into every vital organ of a body, and it could not be excised without killing the host. Instead, he simply accepted the reality, and in the process discovered the sublime power of the creature.

It did stink, though.

Rhaedron, the statuesque shipmaster, had a more elegant way of dealing with the problem: she had simply removed her nose. New flesh filled the centre of her face where the offending organ had previously stood, puckered and pink against the sallow skin surrounding it. It made her look permanently surprised, Xantine thought, an effect compounded by the large and complex hairpiece that she wore atop her head. Ringlets and curls of shimmering gold were held in place with feathers of magenta and blue-green, their shafts piercing the skin of her scalp to ensure that the whole edifice didn't move.

She hoisted her silvered cane and prodded the mass of quivering flesh in its flank. It squealed, recoiling from her touch, before settling back with an annoyed harrumph. Rhaedron spoke to the awakened mass.

'We have suffered an unexpected translation from the warp. The magnificent Xantine demands to know what has brought us back to realspace.'

For a moment, there was no response, and she prodded Ghelia again. Another squeal, and from deep inside the creature's lumpen form, a vox-grille appeared. A voice followed, its words clipped and precise as a machine's, but punctuated by wet slurping sounds.

'Cause – unknown. Warp drive – offline. Navigational course – unplanned.'

'Bring the warp drive back online, and plot a course to the system's Mandeville point,' Rhaedron snapped.

'Impossible,' Ghelia slurped. 'Complex warp currents circle this region of the void, rendering this system's Mandeville point unusable.'

Rhaedron sniffed in annoyance. 'Where are we?' she asked, directing her question to the bridge crew, who sat close by, partially bonded to ornate cogitators. A flame-haired man turned, eager to provide an answer.

'Recent Imperial records have no mention of this world, my lady, but older data sources make reference to a planet named Serrine. It was an agri world. The records show that the world produced vital ingredients used in rejuvenat treatments. Population was confined to cities, split between the cloud line.'

'How old are these records?' Rhaedron asked.

'From centuries past, my lady.'

Rhaedron went to continue, but Xantine cut in, his deep voice quieting all other conversation. 'And that population. Are they still present?'

The flame-haired man's voice quivered, but he answered the warlord directly. 'At present, auspex scans show increased concentrations of fyceline and promethium in the local atmosphere.'

Rhaedron took up the explanation, keen for the praise. 'Telltale signs of explosions, your magnificence. The human population remains, and there appears to be some… unpleasantness among their number,' she said.

Xantine let a grin play across blackened lips. This world could be a rare prize indeed – juicy, sweet, and ripe with plunder. Certainly, it could offer more than their most recent jaunts.

Xantine and the Adored had been reduced to raiding mining colonies in recent years, and more often than not lately, they came across the carcasses of worlds already picked clean by their fellow renegades – their resources plundered, their weapons purloined, their people slaughtered, sacrificed, or taken into slavery. More than once, they found Imperial worlds that had beaten them to the kill and immolated themselves.

Bax III, where a brave Titan Legio splintered and fought itself to a standstill in the rubble of the only continent's largest city. Evenly matched and unable to accept defeat, both factions elected to detonate their Titans' plasma reactors, killing millions and irradiating the settlement far beyond habitable status. The two princeps senioris responsible for the destruction, sisters by birth, had but one fundamental disagreement: whether the Emperor was dead, or had simply forsaken His Imperium.

Horsk, whose planetary governor had sabotaged their void shielding, asphyxiating the world, preferring a quick and silent death to the oblivion promised by the Cicatrix Maledictum. Xantine had kept the governor's journal, and found it made pleasurable reading to chart the perverse logic that led one man – a mortal one, at that – to take the lives of millions with a single action. The governor's writings remained level-headed to the last, the man never giving in to the ravings and madnesses that many in his situation might have spewed when presented with such a vision into unreality. Xantine couldn't fault the man's argument; he only wished he had been there when he took the shields down to watch the spectacle first-hand.

Each offered a morsel of misery, but for a warband low on the harsh realities of their trade – ammunition, weapons, slaves and narcotics – these were wasted journeys that further depleted their stockpiles.

Xantine stood on the dead ground of these worlds and wept, knowing that their spoils had gone to lesser beings. Shrieking lunatic followers of the Blood God; dour, droning devotees of Nurgle; or the endlessly tiresome lackeys of the Changer of the Ways. Worse still, they sometimes found the telltale brands of a Black Legion presence. Abaddon's gaggle of morons, barbarians, and cowards had been attempting to follow the Adored for decades now – Xantine had lost track exactly how long.

It was a chase that would continue until either Xantine or Abaddon were dead, he knew. The Warmaster of the Black Legion could never forgive the murder of both a lieutenant and a favoured pet, and Xantine's subsequent flight from the Children of Torment – and the formation of his own warband – rubbed salt in the wound of a being whose subjugation of the galaxy hinged on subjugating his fellow renegade Astartes first. That Abaddon had yet to find the Adored, Xantine took as a confirmation of his own brilliance. The alternative – that the Warmaster simply did not care to look, or even know who Xantine was – did not cross his mind.

Fortunately, Abaddon's brutes were easy to feint, always moving in straight lines while Xantine allowed the whims and predilections of his crew to guide the movements of the Adored. Vavisk, the Noise Marine, his closest brother, forever chasing the song of Slaanesh. Qaran Tun, the diabolist, once a Word Bearer but now as consumed by his passions as any of Xantine's gene-brothers, tireless in his search for exotic Neverborn to test and catalogue. Sarquil, the orchestrator, his obsessions more practical than any of his ragged Legion, ensuring that the Adored obtained men and materiel.

And they were low on both. This was a risk, Xantine knew: to invade a world of the Imperium, even one in the midst of an uprising. But Serrine was too tasty a morsel to give up, a chance for the Adored to live on scraps no longer.

I can give you so much more, S'janth purred.

He ignored her, and savoured the moment. A world, a whole unsullied world, with its soft belly exposed. How delicious.

Truly, a boon from the Youngest God.

Xantine traced his long tongue around blackened lips and spoke.

Oh, how Pierod hated running. His knees complained as he pumped legs rendered weak through lack of use, and felt sweat turning the silk of his trousers rough. Elise hadn't even oiled his dry heels this morning, he remembered, an extra huff of air escaping with the realisation. If he made it out of here alive, he was going to have very cracked skin tomorrow morning.

He missed Rogirre. How could he be expected to run with such abject grief weighing him down? Abject grief, and the multi-course breakfast that his manservant had prepared for him.

The explosions had been coming closer since first light, and as the sun rose in the sky, they had been joined by a chorus of screams. After he served breakfast to the roused Pierod, Rogirre had taken to pacing the polished floor of his master's chalet, and no attempts to reassure him seemed to salve his frustration.

'Rogirre,' Pierod called, sweetly at first. 'We're safe here, my friend!' Like everything in his chalet, the walls were beautiful, rendered in green marble layered with veins of gold. But they were functional, too. A core of ferrocrete kept out the cold of the night high above the ground, and would serve to stop most armaments short of a battle cannon shell. A foundation stone stood above the doorway, an heirloom that his father told him had been brought from Terra itself, mined from the ancient quarries of Franc.

And he had guards. They were tough, small-eyed men who patrolled the perimeter of his chalet, sturdy lasguns held at the ready. He saw them sometimes through the building's double windows as they completed their rounds, their bald heads bobbing slightly as they walked. It must have been a ritual, that severe hair-style, or perhaps some kind of challenge. Or maybe it was just the new fashion? Pierod had resolved to check – he never wanted to miss a trend.

But he couldn't see the guards now, and he was really getting quite worried.

'Rogirre!' he called again, injecting a little steel into his voice. His manservant didn't look up, continuing his pacing. Irritation boiled over into rage in Pierod's prodigious gut, an ugly emotion stoked by fear and a lifetime of having his own way. 'Rogirre! Get over here this instant!' he screeched.

Rogirre looked up, and Pierod was sure, for a moment, that he had reawakened the man's sense of duty. But for the first time during their long association, his manservant did not obey his order. Instead, Rogirre turned on his heels and flung open the chalet's ornate hardwood door – a beautiful piece commissioned by Pierod's father – and prepared to run from his master's well-appointed domicile.

Rogirre took but a single step before he was bisected by a saw blade the size of a Taurox hatch. It slammed through his midsection and embedded itself deep in the antique wood of the door frame. Pierod saw him die from a position propped up on cushions on a seven-seater couch. He watched as Rogirre's legs slumped lazily to the floor, separated from a torso that still stood atop the blade, proud and tall like one of the cakes Lady Salomé served at her midnight banquets, and he winced as red blood, thick and wine-dark, leaked from Rogirre's wet insides. The pool expanded until it soaked against the thick rug that bore Pierod's family crest. He'd wanted to weep, then – that rug had been woven by the child artisans of Diltyn – but abject panic had forced him from his comfortable couch, his pudgy legs manoeuvring his bulk towards the hatch in his wine cellar that concealed one of the chalet's multiple escape tunnels.

The whole thing was such a shame, Pierod thought as he waddled past faintly glowing lumen bulbs towards an exit he hoped was closer than it appeared. Though, if he was honest, he did think it rather served Rogirre right for opening the door in the first place, rather than tending to his master.

What was he shouting about, anyway? Pierod wondered for a moment whether the manservant had a family – he'd never thought to ask – but he realised he didn't really care. All that mattered was that it wasn't *his* name, and that his faithful attendant of the last seventeen years had forced Serrine's esteemed vice treasurer to *run*.

'The indignity of it all,' Pierod blustered to himself, as he stumbled, sweating, to a halt against the tunnel's exit hatch. His chest heaved, but over the sound of laboured breathing, he could hear the noises of battle. The regular crack of autoguns, the boom of explosions, and screaming, rising and falling in waves. But there was another sound, too, the one he was desperately relieved to hear: the whine of engines. Serrine's void port was close, and still functional. He would make his way to a ship, use his connections, and escape into the comfort of the void while the planetary militia dealt with this unpleasantness. He would survive this day, he resolved, cracked heels be damned.

It was never quiet on board the *Exhortation*. Squeals and moans, shrieks and howls penetrated even its darkest corners: the engine decks, where grinning once-humans danced between arterial cables that pumped viscous and stinking red liquid; the hold. Even the bilges vibrated with sound, as sleek, smooth-skinned creatures swam through centuries of accumulated narcotic run-off, sending ripples and tides through the sloshing effluent. Behind it all, a discordant drone set the metre, the sound of the universe itself, of all the beauty and all the pain it contained within.

To a mortal, these sounds were terror given voice. To Xantine, they were music, and he hummed along as he walked the *Exhortation*'s thickly carpeted hallways on his way to visit his brother Vavisk.

Why must we converse with your kin? S'janth asked, as Xantine strode towards Vavisk's chamber.

'Because they are brothers of the Emperor's Children, and I desire their counsel.'

Lies. You court their approval because you fear that they will betray you.

Xantine laughed. It was a hollow sound. 'You share my body, daemon, but you will never understand my kind.'

I know your soul, S'janth said. *You seek to turn your brothers to your cause. It is a foolish aim, and a foolish cause. We are so powerful, my love. We need not this world, nor your duplicitous brothers.*

'Not powerful enough,' Xantine admitted. 'You wish a return to your former glory? Then we require weapons, supplies and slaves. This world will have each in abundance.'

You are wrong, the daemon said. *This world is diseased. I know it.*

'Then I will be its cure. I will hear no more on the matter.'

Xantine turned his attention fully to the artworks displayed on the walls of the *Exhortation*'s central corridors. Many of the pieces on show were his own: a representation of Canticle City before its destruction by the Black Legion, completed in crystal and bone shards; a careful study of aeldari physiology, created by pressing one of that perfidious race between two panes of transparent plasteel until they were microns apart, presented in a gold-leafed frame.

His gene-father had been an artist. Xantine felt he reflected his primarch's talents in the field, but where Fulgrim had worked in traditional media, Xantine yearned for new canvases, new materials. He could rarely predict when inspiration would strike, and so had left his right pauldron unadorned, at odds with the complex and ornate patterns, colours, and images rendered upon the rest of his armour. The pearlescent surface was a blank slate, and he often turned to it during the chemical rush of battle, painting with the raw materials of combat: blood, excrement, and the countless other bodily fluids of the galaxy's species – fluids of which Xantine had an encyclopaedic knowledge. By now, it was a palimpsest of excess, scrubbed almost clean after each sortie, but redolent with the memories and stink of wars once savoured, of enemies once slaughtered.

His other shoulder bore a trophy from one such foe: the long-snouted skull of some exotic xenos creature, its lower jaw removed, its brightly feathered skin still attached to the white bone in patches. Xantine had broken the Silken Spear on its hide, shattering the ancient aeldari weapon that had once served as the key that locked S'janth in her arcane prison. A shard of that spear now formed the blade of Xantine's rapier – a weapon he called simply Anguish – set into a guard fashioned from carved aeldari bone.

He often wore his full plate, even while aboard the *Exhortation*, enjoying the suite of sensations that the ceramite transmitted to his supple skin. It was a show of power, to walk the decks of his own ship so conspicuously armoured – a message to his underlings that he would accept challenges at a moment's notice. He had wrested the frigate from its previous owner, his former commander, Euphoros, in lethal combat, and S'janth was at least partially correct: there were those among his current crew that undoubtedly eyed a similar line of succession. Keeping them in line required not just raw strength – something that S'janth assisted with – but symbols, too.

This symbology was the reason why Xantine had donned his full armour now. It was an amalgam of parts scavenged from burning battlefields and taken as trophies in single combat, but it was built around the core of his original war plate, earned as a member of the Emperor's Children under the command of Primarch Fulgrim. He knew the breastplate, even with its winged claw warped so that its talons curved into the symbol of Slaanesh, would spark fealty and honour in the twin hearts of his most trusted brother.

He met Vavisk in the Chamber of Exultation, at the rear of

the *Exhortation*. His brother was choirmaster to the Adored's host of Noise Marines, and although Xantine could not see the warriors, he could certainly hear them. They were singing louder than he had ever heard them, the secretive clade having raised their volume and tempo since the frigate had arrived in-system. The sound reverberated through the bones and the fluids of his body, exciting the blood in his veins, the acid in his stomach, the humour in his eyes.

They were orchestrated by Vavisk, who conducted the unseen choir from the Organ of Bliss. The vast edifice was a contraption of Vavisk's own design, requiring the obsessive work of decades to find the most beautiful voices in the galaxy – or at least the most talented singers unfortunate enough to find themselves in the path of the Adored – before bringing them into the fold.

Xantine had seen the organ countless times, had even diverted the *Exhortation*'s course to help his brother complete his opus, but the device still impressed him. Vavisk stood in the centre, singing into a gently quivering orifice that connected to a forest of golden pipes. These pipes curved up and around each other like bundles of nerves, before plunging deep into the neck of a human mortal. Other tubes burrowed into the humans' barrel stomachs, passing through enough nutrient paste to keep them well fed and ensure their voices had sufficient power. Larger tubes carried waste away from their lower intestines and bladders, while finer cables connected to wrists and ankles, capturing read-outs on their vital functions. Vavisk was protective, reacting quickly to sickness or other malaise in any of the individual humans that made it up.

The results were quite mesmerising. As Vavisk sang, his voice was amplified a hundredfold, taken up by row upon row of these human instruments. Their jaws worked in perfect time with each other, reproducing the same notes and tempo, but imbuing the composition with their own specific timbre. Xantine lingered a moment, allowing his brother to continue his current overture without disruption.

It was Vavisk who called a halt to the song, quieting the Organ of Bliss and hauling his warp-wracked body to its feet. Xantine greeted him as he rose.

'Quite the composition, Vavisk,' he said, inspecting the blades that jutted from his greaves with an air of practised nonchalance. Once, he would have embraced his brother, savouring the touch of a cultured warrior, but even in the relative privacy of the chamber, it wouldn't do to show such deference to a subordinate.

Still, part of his body longed for the contact. Vavisk was his oldest friend, so much as that term still had meaning in a Legion of pleasure seekers and hedonists. At the very least, of all the beings in the galaxy, it was Vavisk who had done the most for Xantine. Not the Legion selectors who plucked him from the noble schools of Chemos, nor his sergeants and captains of the Emperor's Children, nor even his dilettante primarch, the Phoenician's attentions turned from his own children to pleasures beyond comprehension.

It was Vavisk who was inducted into the Emperor's Children alongside Xantine, Vavisk who fought alongside him during the Great Crusade. Memories of fighting for the Corpse-Emperor left a taste like ash in Xantine's mouth, but Vavisk's bravery and loyalty was a true prize from that conflict.

It was Vavisk who had pulled him from the wreckage of Canticle City as Abaddon hurled the warship *Tlaloc* down on the world of Harmony. Were it not for his brother's intervention, Xantine would have been incinerated along with thousands of his fellow Emperor's Children and millions of mortals, his remains joining the vast field of melted glass, rock, and biological matter that was all that remained of the once-beautiful civilisation on the planet.

It was Vavisk who stood alongside him as Xantine turned on his warlord, using the strength of the daemon sharing his body to decapitate Euphoros – also once of the III Legion, before he'd become Abaddon's lapdog. Xantine had taken the *Exhortation* and run from the Black Legion, striking out on his own with his dearest brother at his side.

And that was why it hurt to see Vavisk so addled.

'Yes, Xantine. They sing because we are close. Closer than ever before to finding our primarch and uniting our Legion once more.'

Xantine fought hard not to roll his turquoise eyes. He revelled in Vavisk's brotherhood, but the Noise Marine always wanted more. The flight from Abaddon's band of barbarians and thugs had rekindled the spirit of unification in Vavisk's breast, and he longed now to bring the disparate and capricious warbands of the Emperor's Children back together under the patrician gaze of their ascended primarch. Guiding him on this mission was a song that Vavisk claimed to hear: an undulating, primordial rhythm that he desperately attempted to capture in the hope of finding the palace of Slaanesh, whereupon their primarch would be convinced to return to his children. Xantine, for his part, could only hear the random and chaotic howls of a galaxy of pain and pleasure – beautiful to his ears though it was.

Xantine indulged his brother in this fantasy, even facilitated the creation of projects such as the Organ of Bliss, but Xantine was a scholar of culture. He knew the Emperor's Children could not truly reunite as a Legion: after ten thousand years of indulgence in the Long War, his brothers were far too mercurial and preoccupied for that. More importantly, even if they could somehow be persuaded to put their countless differences aside – the return of an attentive Fulgrim as a catalyst, for example – then it meant a return to subordination for Xantine.

Vavisk continued, warming to his subject. 'We will be whole, Xantine. A Legion once more, singing together in worship.' He wheezed as he spoke, the sound like damp air forced through an ancient accordion.

Xantine stepped alongside his oldest friend. 'We have been presented with a new opportunity, brother – a world upon which we can sate ourselves,' he said with a forced breeziness. He began pacing the stage, dark wood beams bending slightly with each armoured tread. 'It is a world unsullied by our cousins, yet cut off from the septic glare of the Corpse-Emperor.' He turned to the Noise Marine. 'We can take it and make it ours, Vavisk.'

Vavisk said nothing.

'Imagine,' Xantine went on, 'a cathedral built in your name, with you as the conductor, guiding thousands – millions – of worshippers in song. Join me, support me, and I can give you that.'

'I need no cathedral, Xantine, and I need no worshippers,' Vavisk said, still staring out across the chamber. 'Neither do you, brother. The song leads us on to divine pleasure, and every missed step takes us further from these distractions.'

'But think of the hall, Vavisk, grander than this meagre hold. Think of the instruments, the voices you could raise...'

'And what happens while we build this folly? The song keeps its rhythm without us.'

Xantine reoriented his approach. 'This is a sweet opportunity to refuel, to rearm, to reacquaint ourselves with the tastes of the galaxy. My Adored need sustenance, Vavisk. Pleasure shared is pleasure doubled – do not stand in their way.'

'I have spoken with Sarquil. I know we have sufficient wargear, consumables, and slaves to last until we reach the Eye and rejoin with our brothers.'

Another angle.

'How many battles have you joined with me, Vavisk? What is one more, for the sake of our brotherhood? Our blades flashing, together, in glorious combat!' Xantine waited a beat in the hope that this cut would land.

'I am no fool, Xantine,' Vavisk said, his blood-red eyes flashing with a moment of anger. 'I understand well enough your machinations. This is no courtesy – you *need* my support to convince our brothers to prosecute this attack. If you have chosen to speak to me now, ahead of the vote, then you suspect that we may not win. We are Emperor's Children, we do not fight if we cannot win.'

'We can always triumph, brother! With you at my side, we can win any day.'

Vavisk turned then, finally, and stared back at his warlord, his millennia of strained experience worn hard on a wreckage of a face.

He had never been beautiful. Where so many of the Emperor's Children had taken their rarefied features from their gene-sire – their high cheekbones, their narrow nose, their violet eyes – Vavisk had a squarer jaw that betrayed his birth in one of Chemos' factory families. He had always looked, Xantine thought after first serving alongside the Iron Hands during the Great Crusade, like one of Ferrus Manus' brood.

That resemblance had been noted by their brothers in the Emperor's Children – jealous of their bond, no doubt – who had teased them for their similarity to Fulgrim and Ferrus: Xantine, with his delicate features and shoulder-length hair, and Vavisk, with his pugnacious mien and straightforward attitude.

The good nature had evaporated from that teasing when

41

Fulgrim lopped his brother's head off on Isstvan V, but still it persisted as brothers became rivals in the warbands that metastasised from the stricken body of his Legion.

It had only stopped for good in recent years, now that Vavisk looked like he did.

The resemblance was long gone now. He barely resembled a human. His once-square jaw had collapsed, subsumed into a vox-grille that made up the lower part of his face. Xantine was not sure whether the grille was a relic of Vavisk's Mark IV helmet, or whether it had simply sprouted unbidden from inside the legionary's lumpen form, but after millennia spent plying the tides of the warp, he knew better than to try to obtain a solid answer.

The skin above it hung loose, falling from buried cheekbones like tallow from a burning candle. Sparse tufts of desiccated white hair grew in clumps on a liver-spotted head, framing engorged ears that had grown fluted to better catch sound, and eyes so bloodshot that the irises were stained red. They were always so tired, those eyes.

'Why do you think I follow you, Xantine?' Vavisk asked.

'Because I am powerful,' Xantine replied, the self-evidence of the statement obvious.

Vavisk sighed. 'You could be the greatest of us, Xantine,' he said, his tone suddenly as tired as his eyes. 'But you have shackled yourself to this thing that wears your skin. This form of command doesn't suit you.'

It was Xantine's turn to anger. 'Watch your tongue, *brother*, lest I pull it from that ruin of a throat and watch it myself,' he warned.

He felt S'janth rouse in his breast at the spike of rage he had inadvertently fed her, circling his consciousness like a sea beast that had tasted a drop of blood in the water.

He is insolent, my sweet, she purred as she coiled herself around him. *He will turn against us.*

No, Xantine shot back. *Not him.*

'I ask for your counsel, Vavisk, because you have shown yourself to be wise. But wisdom comes in many forms. The wisdom to know when to fight, and the wisdom to know when to retreat, when to acquiesce to the desires of your betters.' Xantine felt S'janth's presence pulse in his body as his anger blossomed. 'This is my ship, and the Adored are my warriors. *You* are my warrior. When I call on you, I expect you to answer me, or else I will return you to Abaddon myself to answer for your crimes.'

Vavisk, for the first time in millennia, was silent. Even the mouths on his neck had ceased their incessant whispering. Red eyes stared in hooded sockets, the gloom rendering them almost black.

Strike him, S'janth whispered. *No one can stand against us.*

Xantine turned and strode from the room. His right hand was clenching and unclenching, forming a fist and releasing it, without his control.

CHAPTER THREE

Pierod hated Serrine's void port. The structure was a rarity on the planet: functional, rather than fashionable, built from bare ferrocrete and decorated with few of the statues, frescoes, or ornamental parks that were common in the wider overcity. This was in part due to its age – its creation from STC was referenced in the planet's dustiest collections of millennia-old prophecies and proclamations – and in part due to its function.

As a designated agri world, responsible for producing a drug vital in some of the more forceful rejuvenat treatments, Serrine had played host to a vast collection of ships since its reintro-duction to the Imperium. These ships would arrive in the skies above the planet every month, their schedule as reliable as the Astronomican, before disgorging a fleet of big-bellied ferry craft. The ferries, themselves larger than even the planetary governor's personal frigate, settled their huge hulls down in Serrine's void port just long enough to be pumped full of precious liquid cargo before lifting off again.

This bounty had given the planet power and influence in the Imperium, and meant that his father could pull strings as far away as Terra. Pierod had never let the other boys in the scholam forget it. He had wielded that influence to convince Ysaac, two years his junior, to forge the numeracy tests required for him to take his current position, on pain of being taken away by the Adeptus Astartes. When Ysaac grew wiser and that threat lost its teeth, he turned to bribery instead, offering rare goods from his father's visits to the Throneworld, as well as the promise of a good word in the ear of some high-up Administratum major-domo. That good word would never be uttered, but Pierod didn't care by then; he'd played the game, passed the tests, and was in theory set up for a life as comfortable as his father's.

But then came the opening of the Great Rift, and life on Serrine changed. The collection ships had stopped coming when he was a young man, their bulk replaced in the sky by a yawning scar, red raw and painful to look at. It was a decade before the next ship arrived, and when it did, it hung in orbit for a week, silent, before the decision was made to send a scouting party from the planet's surface to investigate the craft. They never returned, but rumour had it that they managed a few garbled transmissions before their communications were cut, gibbering descriptions of hunched, half-human monsters, and the debris of a devolved society that suggested years lost in the warp.

After that, the collection ships simply stopped coming. Serrine, a world built and maintained solely for the growth and harvest of a single drug, continued its routine of growth and harvest regardless, society too calcified to shift to a new reality.

In his position as a government functionary, Pierod had seen the stockpiles of Solipsus sap – vast tankers of spilled and spoiled purple liquid, sequestered in the darkest corners of the overcity so as not to spook the wider populace. They represented Serrine's loss: loss of millennia of purpose, loss of contact with the wider Imperium, and – worst of all for Pierod – loss of prestige in the galaxy. So he had come up with an effective way of managing the problem, a luxury for a man used to luxury: he simply wouldn't think about it.

Serrine's former wealth meant the planet had been blessed with food supplies and water purification facilities. For Pierod and the other families that made up Serrine's complicated web of noble houses, major and minor, change was anathema. If the grass kept growing and the harvest kept coming, then Pierod could live out his lifespan – artificially extended through rejuvenat treatments, of course – in the fashion his noble birth demanded. And that certainly didn't include running.

He could still feel his heartbeat in his throat, thick and unsteady. He swallowed to chase it back down into the meat of his body, and prised the tunnel's exit hatch open a crack. His pink face pressed close to the cold metal of the hatch, he risked a look outside.

The void port was even more hideous than it was before, he thought with resigned sadness. Pierod had tried to convince himself there had been beauty in its brutalism, the perfectly flat grey surface stretching out like a calm, man-made ocean. Now it was marred with gouges and divots, lumps and bumps. Taken as a whole, the void port reminded him of Ysaac's teenage face, the ravages of adulthood pockmarking something that had once been unblemished (but still terribly dull).

The largest of these disfigurements were huge cylinders – the remnants of elevator shafts that had once been used to move Solipsus sap onto the vast loader ships. Three still stood on the horizon, but the others lay across the void port like toppled trees, their trunks creating makeshift corridors and barricades where previously there was open space.

The smaller bundles were bodies, he realised with horror, clad in the pale pink robes of Serrine's militia. They lay alone, or in groups of two or three. They appeared to have been shot in the back as they ran, their weapons lying in front of them as if thrown from their hands towards the huge, square building that served as the void port's central command tower.

That was not good. Serrine could always provide more militiamen – the death toll wasn't the issue – but if the void port garrison had been routed, Pierod thought, then there would be nobody to protect *him*.

Who was responsible for this attack, anyway? Off-worlders, jealous of their fortune? Filthy xenos, come to befoul the most civilised society in the galaxy? He'd heard tales told of such things in the plush council smoking houses. Or, infinitely more likely, was this the work of another house attempting to put itself in the ascendancy?

If it was, then it was a grander affair than he was used to. Such coup attempts came around every few years, and things usually worked themselves out with a handful of palace scuffles, a few jewelled knives buried in a few noble backs, and a subtle rearrangement of the lines of succession. They didn't tend to wheel out the heavy artillery.

For now, the point was moot. There were people killing other people, and while he didn't know if the void port tower still held, he certainly wasn't getting off-world hiding in this tunnel like some kind of common rat.

Breath slowly returning to his lungs, he steeled himself and poked his head out of the hatch, preparing to run again.

He ducked backwards just in time as three figures sprinted past, close enough that he could see the worn tread on their identical boots. They were clad in grubby overalls that were once white, but now stained with an array of browns, blacks

RENEGADES: LORD OF EXCESS

and purples. All three figures had the telltale pastel-pink skin of the undercity's denizens.

'Refinery workers?' Pierod questioned aloud. 'What are they doing up here?'

As vice treasurer, he had dealt with beings – he preferred not to use the word 'people' – who lived below the haze line before, but only in the structured confines of the cabinet. He never liked these meetings to go on for more than a few minutes, leaving any subsequent discussion on harvest dates, thresher machine repair, or pay outs to family members lost in the grass for his subordinates to handle. They had a peculiar smell, these under-city dwellers, one that wrinkled Pierod's nose and offended his delicate sensibilities.

As he watched, two of the three figures wrestled a long cannon from the ground, mounting it on a tripod set up by the third against a chunk of broken ferrocrete. A belt of ammunition was hefted into the firing chamber, and the third worker aimed the weapon across the void port towards the central tower, squeezing the trigger as the barrel swung into alignment.

The weapon spat light and sound, and Pierod flinched, ducking back away from the cacophony.

'Throne!' he hissed. He pulled the hatch almost closed, leaving only a slit open as the mounted cannon rattled through its first full belt of ammunition.

Fire lanced back from the direction of the tower as the gun wound down, the telltale fizz of las-bolts superheating the air. They slapped into the ferrocrete barricade, scoring small, uniform holes into the blackened masonry. That was good, at least, Pierod thought. That meant Serrine's militia were still in this fight, and when they were confronted with a better, they would put their lives on the line to get him off this world.

Their backs against the ferrocrete, the workers rooted around in ragged sackcloth bags, pulling out ribbons of ammunition and boxy magazines like intestines and organs from fabric corpses.

As soon as the fusillade slowed, they were up, one feeding the mounted gun its next bullets, another connecting wires between lumps of a waxy substance that Pierod didn't recognise.

He wished he had a weapon. No, that wasn't right. He wished he had Rogirre, and that Rogirre had a weapon. He didn't want to get his hands dirty, and besides, what if he missed? Much better to have a man do your dirty work for you.

The one with the waxy lumps finished his complicated wiring job, and nodded to the other two. His eyes were deep-set and beady, cast with a yellow tinge that Pierod could see from his hiding spot. They sat beneath a heavy brow and a bulbous, hairless skull.

Pierod ran a hand through his own shaggy, ash-blond hair now as the figure clutching the wired object thumbed a button on an attached control unit. The button flashed on, turning a bright red, and the figure raised his hand in a closed fist.

Ammunition replenished, the worker on the heavy cannon opened up again, aiming a withering salvo of fire at the command tower. Cover provided, the figure with the object – Pierod had assumed by now it was a demolition charge – tucked it to his chest, peeled out from behind the barricade, and began crouch-running across the open ground.

The first las-bolt hit him in the knee, and he crumpled, mid-shuffle, to the ground. His leg had been destroyed – that much was clear from the blackened and smoking hole in his jump-suit, but the worker didn't seem to care. Beady eyes lit with grim determination, he was clawing himself along the pock-marked ferrocrete when the second and third bolts hit, lancing into his back and the left side of his head. For a grim second

Pierod thought the figure would keep moving forward, some kind of animated corpse from millennia-old legend, but its wiry arms slackened, and it lay motionless, come to rest on top of the bundle it had been carrying. A moment later, Pierod heard a *wumph* of detonation, and ducked back into his hatch as the constituent parts of the unfortunate worker pitter-pattered back to the ground as grisly rain.

The explosion disoriented the figures remaining behind the barricade, sending them stumbling backwards, and giving the snipers in the tower clear shots. Las-bolts converged on the two men, burning skin and muscle down to the bone. Secondary shots slammed into their lifeless forms even as they fell, sending their limp bodies skittering along the ferrocrete.

Silence descended on the scarred apron of the void port, and for a moment, Pierod considered staying put, hiding out in his hole until this whole grisly business was over, or until some ruffian put a bullet in his brainstem – whichever came first. But he was so close. With the cachet that came with his rank, he could demand access to a ship; he could get off-world, at least for a time, living out the remainder of this – whatever *this* was – in the confines of a luxury yacht. Once the shooting had stopped, he could return to Serrine as a leader-in-waiting, his noble bloodline and obviously superior genetics granting him a role at the very pinnacle of whatever government would be erected.

Pierod manoeuvred a sweaty leg over the edge of the hatch, placing his bottom on the ledge as he made to swing his other leg over. He caught his trailing foot halfway through the movement and tumbled out onto the open ferrocrete. He tucked into a ball, trying to make himself small, and whimpered as he waited for the sniper's shot to finally end this most miserable of days.

No shot came. The only assault was from the pungent smell

on the air: of smoke, ferrocrete dust and fyceline. There was something else, too, like the smell of Rogirre's kitchen. It was the smell of the dead men, he realised, their flesh cooked by explosive flame and las-bolt.

He thought of sausages and fat meat rashers, the sizzle and spit of animal juices, and the char of a perfectly cooked roast. His stomach rumbled, and he baulked, pink face turning ashen.

He vomited then, noisily, body expunging Rogirre's final gift to his master. The chunky liquid arced from his open mouth and hit the scarred ferrocrete with a playful splash, pieces of half-digested fowl and fruit seeds still recognisable amongst the mess.

Pierod hadn't cried since his father had beaten him bloody at the age of fourteen for talking to the son of a butcher in the city, but as he sat in the besieged city, chased from his own home, covered in his own sick, he fought back tears.

His eyes felt hot, stinging, as though they too were being pierced by tiny las-bolts, just as those disgusting workers had been. They had come up here, from whatever undercity hovel they lived in, bringing their sweat and grime and stink into his city – his cultured, ordered, pristine city. How dare they?

No. No! This would not do! What would Father say? Father would stand, Father would lead, Father would survive. He was Pierod, scion of the Vaude family, and vice treasurer of Serrine. He would not be felled by some jumped-up ruffian in a dirty jumpsuit who didn't know his place.

Pierod unfurled himself, bracing a quivering leg against the ferrocrete, before drawing himself unsteadily to his feet. Steadily, pointedly, he raised both his hands and his face to the building. 'Throne help them if they shoot *me*,' he muttered under his breath. And then louder, he shouted: '*I am Vice Treasurer Pierod, and you will give me safe passage!*'

A shot rang out from the top of the tower.

CHAPTER FOUR

Living chairs groaned under the weight of their occupants, their spines stretched and ribs splayed open to form seats large enough to house transhuman warriors.

Five such warriors occupied these seats, their genetically enhanced bodies draped in simple togas of white silk. The sixth and final chair played host to a much smaller figure, barely half the height of the others in the chamber, and so slight as to be a child in comparison. She, too, wore a slip of white material, but any claim to simplicity was undone by the amount of jewellery she accented the robe with. She was festooned in gold and silver, bracelets and rings lining her arms and fingers so that they jangled together noisily at the slightest movement of her body. Rubies and emeralds the size of eyeballs dangled from her neck on platinum pendants, pulling her head forward with their weight. They gave her the appearance of an exotic bird.

Xantine idly traced a silk-gloved finger around the knuckle

of his own chair. The skin twitched in response to his touch, a shiver of either pleasure or revulsion – he wasn't sure which.

'My friends,' he began, pleased to hear the conversation in the room die immediately. 'My council. Thank you for joining me here today. I call you because before us lies a difficult choice, so I turn to my most trusted, wise and esteemed peers.' Xantine inclined his head to each of the figures in the room in turn. 'Vavisk, my composer. Sarquil, my quartermaster. Qaran Tun, my collector. Torachon, my champion.' He turned to the woman last. 'Phaedre, my muse.'

She bobbed her head in acknowledgement. Xantine had seen that head bob when he first found her: stinking, clad in rags, forced to steal snake eggs and trap insects to survive. She had lived in a choking swamp on the edge of a world that had been fought over by warlords whose armies used wooden catapults and blunt iron swords as their weapons, crushing their people into rigid social classes and forcing them to die for miniscule gains in territory.

This society cast Phaedre out when she was young, calling her a witch, or a monster.

They were right.

She was old already back then, much older than she looked now after countless rejuvenat treatments and flesh transplants. The Adored had ravaged her world, and with the battle fought, Xantine had taken to wandering the planet, his soul swollen with excess. He had been grateful of an audience when he found Phaedre, and he revelled in the detail of the destruction.

He expected anger, righteous and delicious, but she had laughed. Her laughter ignited the air, and as the dim sun rose the next morning, as they stood in the burnt ruin of her hovel, Xantine knew he had found his latest muse.

It was these six that Xantine would convince of Serrine's value, and with these six that he would plan an invasion of the world. The decision had been made, of course. Serrine was too precious, too perfect, to pass up, and besides, after the last disastrous raid – where the Adored had been chased away by Black Legion forces arriving in-system – the planet represented the only realistic choice they had.

More than that, he *wanted* it. This world could be liberated, its people freed from the drudgery of their lives, with Xantine as their guide.

He began.

'Our path has led us to Serrine, a planet only recently revealed to us by the weft of the warp. It is, I am delighted to say, a hidden jewel' – he used the word S'janth had used for it – 'in the Corpse-Emperor's crown.'

The youthful figure in the chair opposite spat at the reference, a gobbet of thick fluid launching from his mouth to land on the polished stone floor, where it spread out into a domed puddle, fizzing gently.

Xantine's glance was withering. 'Quite, Torachon,' he said, with mild exasperation. 'But could we hold such emanations until we are outside of these rarefied halls?' Torachon lowered his head in a short bow, and Xantine shook off the interruption, raising a hand to Rhaedron.

The shipmaster stepped forward, coughed lightly, and spoke.

'Serrine is an agri world. Multiple defence lasers surround the void port in its largest city, and the planetary militia – its soldiers taken from the planet's noble families and made up primarily of their retainers – is well equipped. An elite corps of these soldiers are recorded as being chemically enhanced. Despite auspex scans showing little orbital activity over the past century, these defences appear to be intact.' She paced as she addressed them, her high-heeled boots tapping out a staccato rhythm. 'The world's primary produce is Solipsus, a potent chemical used most commonly in rejuvenat therapies across the Imperium. It also finds common use as a base for many sanctioned stimulants, as well as several of the galaxy's more popular, and most illegal, narcotics.'

That would get their attention, Xantine thought.

'Thank you, shipmaster.' He spread his hands wide, palms open, a gesture that he hoped would display humility. He could never be sure – he had forgotten the feeling. 'Your thoughts, my senate?' he asked the room.

Torachon replied first, as he always did. 'We must take it, your magnificence!' he shouted, rising slightly from his seat. He was the largest of them, huge even among the genetically enhanced and warp-touched transhumans that made up the warband. Broad pectoral muscles rippled under his white toga as he strained in his seat.

'My boy,' Xantine said, forcing good-natured bonhomie into his tone, 'this is a place of equals! You do not need to address me as such. A simple "lord" will suffice.'

'Of course, my lord,' Torachon said. 'My desires are yours. As you will it, this world must be ours. I simply wish to taste its splendour.'

Torachon had no deference for etiquette. It was a by-product, perhaps, of youthful exuberance, but it was a trait that Xantine found peculiarly irritating. A newcomer to the Long War, Torachon had not fought at Terra, nor during the Legion Wars, after Horus' death and the end of his Heresy. He had not fought at Canticle City, where the Black Legion cast a black knife into the heart of the Emperor's Children, destroying the galaxy's most beautiful city in a monstrous and unforgivable act of desecration.

He had not even seen the beginning of the Warmaster's Thirteenth Black Crusade, as Xantine's former warlord Euphoros threw away his loyalty to the glory of the III Legion to ride

Abaddon's coattails, joining the wider Black Legion as members of the Children of Torment.

Torachon had come to the Adored later, fresh from Fabius Bile's gene forges, the stink of the Clonelord's arcane biology raw on his perfect skin. He was a reward, bestowed by Fabius himself for work well done by Xantine's warband, and as far as prizes from such a creature went, Torachon was a good one. Strong, loyal, and rapid as starlight, he took to the debaucheries of the Adored as a sword to its scabbard: a natural fit for his regal form.

Long white-blond hair framed a symmetrical face that was split by an aquiline nose and embedded with two eyes of deep violet. They were Fulgrim's eyes, and it thrilled Xantine to command such a perfect reflection of his primarch.

It unsettled him, too, to see such deference from those eyes. Torachon was loyal to a fault. Xantine didn't know if Bile had bred that loyalty into his creations, or whether it was simply his gene-seed's natural deference to a superior, but while he may have had his primarch's eyes, he had none of Fulgrim's deviousness. Xantine found the younger Space Marine's guileless acquiescence cloying, like the attentions of a slobbering pet.

But he was useful. Torachon was young – far too young for a warrior to be admitted to the senate, typically, but Xantine had hastened his ascent, engineering his placement as the sixth member of the group after the death of Talon Yannos at the Shrieking Chasm. Power was always held in a light grip amongst the remnants of the III, and Xantine was conscious of the usefulness of a good yes-man in his decision-making body.

Some of the others had grumbled at the appointment, but Xantine – at pains to conceal his involvement in the procedure – pointed to Torachon's unblemished record and popularity amongst the rank-and-file of the Adored's hedonists for his martial prowess and good humour.

'Of course, my boy,' Xantine said. 'I will count your vote as cast, making one of our esteemed conclave in favour. An auspicious opening. Who will speak next?'

Ever the cynic, Sarquil cleared his throat.

'Hah,' he coughed. Sarquil was never seen out of his Tartaros Terminator plate – not even by his closest allies amongst the Adored's Terminator cadre – and the dark skin of his head was the only part of his flesh-and-blood body still visible. With one arm, he drummed the fingers of his massive power fist, while the other hung slack, surgically grafted to the firing mechanism of his beloved chaincannon. The top of his skull was covered in rippled silver, the result of the Space Marine's practice of dripping the molten remnants of his enemies' wargear onto the bare skin of his head after the close of battle. After generations of raiding, Sarquil now seemed to wear a silver skullcap that shone in the candlelight of the conclave chamber. A hawkish face sat beneath his metal pate, his mouth set in a permanent sneer.

'A well-equipped army,' the creature said. 'Are we well-equipped, Xantine? Are we even acceptably equipped?'

Sarquil's upper body had been shredded in conflicts long since passed, and his augmetic replacements were sterile and ugly in aesthetic. Meaty pistons in his neck worked as he spoke, their movement exposing raw muscle and veins. Xantine wished his quartermaster would have them replaced with something a little more appealing to look at.

'We have three thousand four hundred and twenty bolter shells, one hundred and sixty-five lascannon power packs, and seventeen canisters of promethium remaining after our last sortie.' Sarquil ticked each of these counts off on his splayed hands. 'In the court of the Dark Prince, could we even call ourselves "equipped" at all?'

Coward, S'janth hissed in Xantine's head. *He has no passion. Let me taste his agony.*

Xantine clenched, a bodily pulse of irritation that he aimed at the daemon, its meaning clear: *Let me handle this.* The Terminator hoarded his materiel like a dragon, and prising it from his grasp demanded a lighter touch.

'My friend,' Xantine said, his hands open across his chest as if he was welcoming a favoured pet home. 'These are joyless numbers. What matters is our skill in using such wargear. And on that matter, our armour is impregnable and our weapons never miss, because we are of the Third. Just one of our warriors is the equal of ten thousand mortals.'

'Tell that to Yannos,' Sarquil said. 'He was one of us, and he died just fine.'

'Yannos was a preening fool, Sarquil, you know that better than all of us.' The two had almost come to blows when they shared a seat in the Adored's council, Yannos' wasteful recklessness and taste for theatrics clashing with Sarquil's material obsessions.

'That he was, Xantine, that he was.' Sarquil chuckled, leaning back in his chair. He flicked his hand as if batting the matter away, but Xantine pressed the issue.

'Besides,' Xantine said, turning the topic to the wider conclave, 'the spoils of this world will stock our armoury for years to come.'

'If we win,' Sarquil said. 'We are not equipped for protracted battle, and every shell we expend on this wastrel world must return to us fivefold in order to justify the penetration of my stockpile.'

My stockpile, Xantine thought, working his blackened mouth into a smile to avoid the frown of annoyance that had picked at his facial nerves. 'Yes, my friend. Serrine promises us riches unlike those we have feasted upon before,' he said.

Sarquil snorted, and started counting. 'I need seventeen thousand one hundred bolter shells, eight hundred and–'

'Not just our armoury.' Xantine cut him off, aware that Sarquil, if he had his way, would talk about his hoard until all the stars of the galaxy blazed out. 'Our slave decks will know once more the crush of mortal flesh, our storage hold will be swollen with new and exotic narcotics, and our decadence will call forth wondrous Neverborn for our archives.'

Xantine turned to Qaran Tun with this last promise. The diabolist sat motionless in his living chair, his back straight and his gaze even. His shaved head was covered in spidery tattoos that seemed to shift in the weak light of the chamber, forming symbols and shapes before fading back into skin the colour of bronze. Once of Lorgar's XVII Legion, Tun had been compelled to travel far from his brothers, his need to research and catalogue the strangest and rarest daemons driving him to depths of debauchery that even his fellow Word Bearers found unsettling. Now he served with the Adored, his loyalty assured as long as Xantine ensured his obsession was fed.

'My lord,' Tun said, his hoarse voice hesitant. Xantine knew his attentions lay elsewhere. Serrine had survived the opening of the Rift – the galaxy-spanning tear in reality the corpse-worshippers called the Cicatrix Maledictum – in relative calm, the whims of the warp clouding it from view and decreeing that this world escape the horrors visited on others who had been less lucky. Xantine, with Tun alongside him, had heard stories of a planet whose billion-strong population had fused together in one agglomeration, so large that it breached the atmosphere. On other worlds the sudden influx of warp energy sent mortal populations into such ecstasies and agonies that entirely new clades and classes of daemon were vomited into existence. Tun was pragmatic, especially compared to the mercurial Emperor's Children, but he was also an egotist, and ached to be the first to study such esoteric beings.

'This world will offer a bounty of base attractions to those so inclined.' Tun looked pointedly at Torachon, but the younger Space Marine appeared not to notice, preoccupied instead by measuring the span of his bicep with a gigantic hand. 'But I believe our journey must take us into the depths of the Great Rift, where we may better escape the attentions of our former slavemaster' – Xantine snarled at the reference to Abaddon – 'and we will find more scintillating pleasures.'

'More interesting pets for your menagerie, you mean?' said Xantine, a teasing edge to his question. 'The Adored do not sally forth to glorious combat purely to fill your vases and amphorae with tattered scraps of monstrosity, Word Bearer.'

Tun blustered, and his tattoos seemed to swirl faster as his hissed responses caught in his throat. Xantine raised a hand to forestall his defence, his choler falling as quickly as it had risen.

'No, my friend, no matter. I asked for your counsel, and in accordance with our honour, I value it.'

Tun settled into his seat, back rod straight.

'Two votes for, two against,' Xantine said. He turned to the only mortal amongst his advisers – though he wondered if she could truly be considered mortal now – and opened his palm in an invitation to speak. 'My muse, Phaedre. Your counsel, please.'

She took long moments to answer, and when she did, it was with a voice that sounded like the wind through reeds. The crystals and chimes that hung from her ears swayed gently as she spoke, producing a sound like soft rain.

'How do they live, the people of this world?' she asked.

'In luxury, my dear,' Xantine said in response. 'They live above the clouds in cities of polished stone and shaped marble, and their children want for nothing.'

She sighed in pleasure. It sounded like a soul escaping at the moment of death.

'I should like to see this world, Xantine,' she said, her milky eyes staring into the middle distance as if picturing the treats that awaited them. Her gnarled hands grasped gently at the air as she spoke, reaching for something Xantine couldn't see.

'Of course, assuming that my dearest brother concurs with our course of action. Vavisk? Tell me, will we take this prize as our own?'

The sixth and final member of the conclave sat slumped in his living chair, breathing heavily. Each rise and fall of Vavisk's chest was accompanied by a musical wheeze that jangled Xantine's nerves and set his jewel-studded teeth on edge. Buzzing, brassy and electric, the life rhythm of the Noise Marine filled the air with static.

Vavisk's body, so rarely removed from his baroque armour, was a ruin. The wet little mouths along his neck and upper chest opened and closed, their palpating tongues and pursing lips visible under the silk of his already stained toga. It was a cracked reflection of the man Xantine remembered – a warped vision of the most noble of their number.

The Noise Marine heaved another musical breath, and his bass voice burred. 'No, Xantine,' he intoned. 'This world is a distraction.'

Xantine's hearts fell. He had expected Sarquil's reticence, even banked on it. Tun, too, was conservative, a natural voyeur rather than a participant. But Vavisk's denial threw his calculated gambit – engineering the conclave's vote of approval to offer legitimacy to his plans – into disarray.

Some warlords ruled through vulgar force or displays of power; others stocked their warbands with dullards and dimwits, unthinking slabs of muscle that shouldered the load for their masters.

That was not the way of the Emperor's Children. Theirs had been a collective of artists and aesthetes, the most cultured of all the Legions. The most cultured beings in all the *galaxy*. Xantine thrived in company that stimulated him, but such an arrangement brought with it more practical concerns of control. His grip on power amongst the Adored was light, like a rapier held in a fencer's stance, and Vavisk's support – typically unwavering – was the foundation on which he could legitimise his demands.

'My choirs have taken voice, following the song of Slaanesh. It guides us, back to our Legion, and back to our primarch. It leads us beyond this little world.' Vavisk heaved another sigh. 'To stop its cadence means death.'

Do you see? S'janth whispered in the depths of his soul. *He has forsaken us.*

'Vavisk,' Xantine said, his honeyed voice betraying something of the genuine hurt he felt. 'We can make this world sing a new and glorious song. Millions, liberated from the tyranny of the Corpse-Emperor, living free and unfettered, with equal ability to indulge their every whim. All in the name of the Youngest God. All in the name of *us*.'

'There is only one song, Xantine,' Vavisk said, affixing him with a red-eyed glare. 'It is the song of joy and agony, and it leads us to our brothers.'

Xantine indulged the Noise Marine's desires as long as it suited him, promising the dream of the unification of the III, but he would only seek out his brothers if he could command them, and there was little chance of that happening as long as Eidolon drew festering breath. The promise of unification, the threat of the Black Legion, his pledge to his dearest brother Vavisk that he would follow the strains of his mindless song – these were all truths of convenience, wielded by Xantine to destabilise and distract, to head off any organised resistance to his command with enemies both real and conjured.

'My brothers are *here*, Vavisk. Look around you. A surfeit of sensation for them to gorge on, and you deny them their feast for your dour asceticism? Must we prolong the satisfaction of today for tomorrow's fleeting promise?'

Vavisk was drawing away from him, from reality, with each passing year, becoming insensate to earthly pleasures as his entire body attuned to the music of the universe – music that only he could hear. His warband, his brothers, Xantine – he was forgetting and forgoing them, becoming a receiver for a truth beyond comprehension.

Xantine opened his palms again. The right hand, he noticed, was once again clenching a fist. 'How can I convince you, brother?'

'You cannot, Xantine.'

He folded his hands together, a gesture of finality designed in part to stop the involuntary motion in his right hand.

'Very well.'

Three votes for. Three against. Time, then, for the hidden blade.

'In this collective of equals,' Xantine said, 'I am your superior. But I am a fair leader, and I respect your judgements, flawed as they may be.' He shot dark glances at the dissenters as he spoke. 'But in this moment, my conclave, we are at an impasse. And so we turn to the final member of our group.'

Sarquil spoke up. 'No! She has no voice here,' he yelled, outrage in his voice.

Vavisk, too, rumbled his displeasure at what was to come. The mouths on his neck sucked and slathered, the wet sound of a nervous beast breathing hard.

'Silence!' Xantine cut them both off. 'She is perfection given flesh – *my* flesh – and we will listen to her.'

Qaran Tun, his mood the counterpoint to his cousins', broke his rigid posture to sit forward, self-control lost as he rubbed his hands together greedily, hunger in his eyes at the daemonic spectacle about to unfold. 'Let her speak, my lord...' he whispered.

My darling, Xantine asked inwardly. *My body is yours to take.*

There was a sensation, like fingers uncoupling from the embrace they shared, and he allowed himself to fall. As he fell, he saw S'janth ascend through a shimmering veil – a barrier that grew thicker and more opaque as he descended below the tides, down, down to the depths of his consciousness.

Xantine's eyes rolled in his head as he gripped the arms of his chair with transhuman force. The bones broke under his grip, and he heard a scream of agony. It was distant and fading, like a wave on a beach drawing back out to sea, quieter and quieter, until he heard nothing but silence, and saw nothing but darkness.

Those in the room saw Xantine sit forward again, his motions smoother and more graceful than before, his turquoise eyes now shining purple. A long tongue worked blackened lips, and S'janth spoke through Xantine's mouth.

'You tarry too long, mortals,' she said, her influence making their master's voice more sibilant, more ethereal than Xantine's deep tone. *'The Prince of Pleasure aches for my return. Take me to Slaanesh.'*

'It is decided, then,' Sarquil said, his tone exultant. 'Xantine's own pet has turned against him.'

She opened Xantine's mouth to speak again, but her words were drowned out by a bang that rocked the *Exhortation*. The slaves staggered, almost falling to the ground, and the chairs wailed as their huge occupants steadied themselves.

Xantine felt the impact, even from his liminal space, and took advantage of S'janth's surprise to gain a foothold in his own body, dragging his consciousness back to the forefront. He closed his eyes, and when they reopened, they were turquoise again.

'Ghelia, report,' Xantine said.

The mound of flesh quivered for a moment, its tapered end

slapping the bier that it lay upon as it cogitated. Eventually, it spoke. 'Combat analysis – incoming fire from surface-to-void defence batteries on the planet below. Damage report – major damage to plasma reactor, major damage to primary engines, major damage to secondary engines, major damage to warp drive, significant damage to weapon systems. Situational report – reactor leak contained, engines inoperable, warp drive inoperable, main weapons inoperable. Recommendation – disable source of incoming fire.'

CHAPTER FIVE

The sky was more beautiful than she had imagined. Cecily had grown up in the undercity, where the uniform pink haze blocked out the stars entirely and reduced sunlight to a weak glow. Now the sun blazed in a cobalt-blue sky, impossibly bright and primally gorgeous. She tried to stare at it, and was surprised when her eyes hurt.

She stared at the ground instead. Even that was beautiful, made up of thousands of fragments of glass, streaked with flecks of gold, forming streets and thoroughfares that dazzled as they caught the bright sunlight. Those streets were lined with statues and sculptures of muscular men and women, of soldiers and saints, of cavorting children and strange hybrid animals, rendered in marble, bronze and gold.

What a wonderful world she lived on, and she had never known.

Did she belong here, above the clouds?

She had been shepherded into one of the great elevators that carried machinery between the under- and overcities of the planet, she remembered. It had been bitterly cold inside the elevator shaft. The utilitarian structure was designed for the transit of huge threshing machines, not fragile human bodies, and there was no roof or walls to the platform, no heating to keep out the elements. There had been fifty of them, give or take, in her group. She looked around as they made the journey upwards. The luminary on the stage had gone; instead, she saw only focused men and women, their deep-set eyes locked on crude weapons, on battered data-slates, or fixed into the middle distance. She was surprised she hadn't seen any of them before.

The door slid open, and her compatriots debarked from the elevator en masse. Most of the group moved with purpose, but others, like her, hung back, disoriented by the unfamiliar surroundings and confused as to their aim.

They caught the attention of the largest men, who moved among these stragglers, pointing at objectives, distributing weapons, and cajoling the reluctant. One of them had spied her and pressed a small and battered autopistol into her hand. She had taken it without question. She looked down at it now, seeing it properly for the first time. She was surprised to find it was so heavy. She'd never held a weapon before and had no idea how to load it, but she knew enough that she should keep her fingers away from the trigger, and instead wrapped them tightly around the ragged material that covered its grip. She hoped she would never have to use it.

What was she doing here, anyway? She had been in bed in her hab-block when she walked out into the grass and saw... something.

Move forward. Stay with the group.

She was further from the surface of her world than she'd ever been before, but she still heard the grass. It tickled at her mind, leading her onwards, away from the industrial detritus of the elevator loading platform and into the city itself, past huge statues and glittering spires. She saw unfamiliar people as she moved, wearing clothes of gaudy colours: oranges, purples, greens and blues. They were well fed, even rotund, and clean. Their faces were free of the dirt and dust of the undercity, and they were contorted. Not in fear at the invading mass from below, but in disgust – sneering faces that disappeared behind locked doors and down side streets, putting physical distance between themselves and the interlopers from below.

There was confusion, too. Men and women stopped and stared, open-mouthed at a sight as alien to them as the overcity was to her. Those that stood too close were shoved aside; others who stood in the way and tried to question the group's intentions were beaten to the ground with rifle butts, their brightly coloured clothes disappearing under work boots as the mass kept moving.

The hive is strong. The individual is weak.

The grass spoke differently now. It had spoken only at night before, and with a voice feather-light, as sinuous and flowing as the pink blades themselves. Now with the sun she had never before seen high in the sky, it spoke with a hard edge. It commanded her.

They had reached an open area, some kind of central square decorated with statues, fountains and even trees. She had only ever seen the grass before, rendered in pale pink, and found it staggering that plants could be so vibrantly green. Hundreds of overcity dwellers milled around, standing in small groups or sitting at outdoor cafes, eating, drinking and talking. They wore jewellery: rings, bracelets, and necklaces of gold and silver, the kind of luxury that only the wealthiest gang bosses and smugglers could afford in the undercity. She met the gaze of one moon-faced woman in an elaborate yellow robe, who scanned her up and down, narrow eyes widening as they came to rest on the pistol she held in her hand.

Across the square, she saw another group of undercity workers, their drab clothing incongruous in such a riot of colour.

Take your weapon. Kill the prey.

There was a monstrous cracking sound, and the moon-faced woman flew backwards, arms windmilling before she landed in a heap on the floor. Her eyes were still open, still wide, as her yellow robe stained red with her lifeblood, leaking from ragged holes in her body.

Cecily spun to find the source of the sound – louder than anything she had ever heard before – and saw a worker in pink-stained overalls a few paces in front of her, a rifle cradled in his arms. He grimaced as he levelled the weapon again, finding a new target in the mass of people in the square.

Some, the sharpest amongst them, ran. Several of them were shot in the back as they fled, falling forward into splayed shapes of bright colours like exotic birds. Others stood still as they died, dumbstruck by the incongruity of the situation. Those that had the capacity to escape did so, and humanity flowed out of the square like blood out of a wound. Still, her new-found comrades kept firing, a barrage of light and sound disrupting the previous tranquillity of the square.

Kill, kill, kill.

She raised her pistol, lifting it towards the back of a man who had stumbled as he tried to run. He scrambled now, half crawling, tripping over his robe in pure panic. The gun shook in her hand as she tried to steady her aim, to kill for the voice in her head, to do as she was told. Her finger moved to the trigger as the man turned, mouth pulled into a rictus of terror.

Kill for the hive.

She squeezed her finger to the cold metal, and the gun bucked in her hand. The bullets flew high and wide, and the man stood up, shaping to run.

'No...' she gasped. She tried to drop the gun, its barrel smoking, to the ground, but her fingers would not release their grip.

'Keep shooting,' the man next to her hissed, as he loosed off a burst of fire at the fleeing figure. The first bullet took the stumbling man in the neck, and he crumpled to the floor, lost in the folds of his clothing.

Kill for the hive, the voice in her head commanded again. It was louder now, a buzzing, grinding voice that overloaded her senses and seemed to control her body. Involuntarily, she raised her pistol again, her shaking hand moving without her guidance. She saw a sea of fleeing humans, and found them in the autopistol's sights. Her finger curled around the trigger, and she squeezed. The shots went wide, to her relief, and the strident sound of their exit from the gun shook her out of her daze.

'No, no, no, *no!*'

With her off hand, she pushed the muzzle of the autopistol to the ground, squeezing the trigger over and over, until the weapon stopped its booming report, and offered only a clicking sound. With a mental effort that left sweat beading on her brow, she forced the voice down in her consciousness, drawing back to reality. This was not the grass, she realised as she met the dead-eyed stares of those workers around her. This was something else, and it was speaking to her brothers and sisters from the city below, guiding them to maim and kill for its pleasure.

'Stop,' she whispered, suddenly aghast with her senses returned. 'This isn't right!'

The man closest to her turned, sharp teeth flashing in a sneering mouth. 'Look how they live,' he snarled. 'See what they hoarded while we rotted and died below! Kill them, or we will kill you!' He cuffed her across the back of the skull, and she pitched forward under the weight of the blow, ears ringing and vision tunnelling as she fell onto her hands at the feet of the group.

It was no idle threat, she realised. Another man in the group, easily into his sixth decade by the sag and wrinkle of his stained skin, was also wavering. His cassock, sewn together from grass storage sacks and marked with the unmistakable pink of Solipsus sap, denoted him as a preacher.

'Stop this madness!' he shouted as he dropped his own pistol to the floor, a plea for mercy amid the bloodshed.

Without a word, one of the workers turned and shot him through the chest. The old man raised a quivering hand to the hole in his body, looking down quizzically at the ruin of blood and meat and bone, before slumping slowly to the floor.

She gasped, covering her mouth with a dirty hand. She wanted to scream, but the brute stood over her still, his rifle raised for a backhand swing. This one was aimed at her head, and his corded muscles – freakish in their size – meant that the blow would crack her skull like a bird egg.

She raised an arm to defend herself, and centred her thoughts around a single message.

She tuned herself not to the grinding, buzzing voice that was palpating at her consciousness, but to the wind, to the trees, to the essence of Serrine. After years of listening to the secrets of the grass, she could speak the planet's language, so she spoke.

Let me go, she said.

The man's angry eyes clouded for a second, his grimacing mouth slackening. His rifle drooped in his grasp, and he looked up for a moment, towards the sky, trying to find the source of the image in his mind. He stared back down, confusion writ large on his face – a receiver cut off from the signal.

She took her chance. She pulled herself into a crouch, pushing through legs and past bodies until she reached the edge of the group, before barrelling into a sprint. She ran for debris, for chunks of twisted metal and uprooted trees, ducking behind splintered wooden benches, waiting for the bullet that would sever her connection to this world for good.

The las-bolt fizzed through the air so close that Pierod could smell the burned ozone, flying over his left shoulder. He turned to look, and saw a body slumped half-out of the hatch exit, smoke wisping from a hole in the side of its neck. The body hung there for a moment, almost comedically relaxed, before it was thrown forward by some unseen force, its legs flipping forward over its hairless head until it came to rest in a heap. Behind it a gun appeared, pointed fingers squeezing against the trigger.

Pierod didn't wait to see what came next. He ran again, sprinting forward as fast as his underutilised legs could carry him, towards the command tower. Las-bolts tracked over his head from the snipers in the building, and he turned back to watch the first few converge with their targets, catching glimpses over his shoulder of workers that seemed to be rising up from drainage tunnels and maintenance shafts – an endless stream of ugly humanity, each bearing crude weapons and clad in tattered robes.

He saw where these figures had fallen before: dozens of bodies littered the apron of the void port. The majority of the corpses he passed were workers, their provenance clear by their filthy clothes and peculiar skin tone. He had heard that those in the undercity were tainted by their proximity to Solipsus sap, but these figures had a waxy, purple sheen that was alien to any human Pierod had ever met.

He saw mutants, too. Huge, dead things, twice the height of some of the more stunted workers, their brows so heavy as to be ridged with bone. Chitinous armour seemed to be grafted to their purple skin, and in some unsettling cases, their silhouettes were perverted by the growth of an extra arm, an unnatural addition that jutted out from their armpits. Even in death they clutched huge blades and hammers – crude weapons that were stained with worrying amounts of blood.

One of these giants seemed to coalesce from the smoky air itself as Pierod drew within the shadow of the command tower. It was lumbering into a run towards Pierod until it took a las-bolt in the side of the head. The shot seared half its skull away, but still it kept coming, the dull light in its eyes no less dimmed for having a sizeable chunk of its brain cooked off. A second shot took its legs out from underneath it, while a third removed the rest of the skull, the massive body left twitching and jerking where it fell.

The scale of death and destruction was staggering, but Pierod noticed the corpses changing around him as he ran. These were not the bodies of workers, mutants, or whatever in the Emperor's name these things were. These figures were clad in the lurid magenta robes of Serrine's planetary defence forces.

The dead men and women were big, and even in death they were beautiful. Serrine's elite militia made use of the planet's surplus of rejuvenat drugs, putting their soldiers through intense treatment regimens to prolong their lifespan and enhance their growth. This, coupled with a lack of any major threat to the overcity, meant that even shackled to a soldier's spartan existence, service was a qualified honour on Serrine: a prize for the semi-nobles and the upper middle classes, who would send their second sons and daughters to the forces.

Only occasionally were these soldiers pressed into service, asked to delve below the haze line that separated Serrine's society – to weed out some smuggler, or to eliminate a gang leader who had managed to whip up the disparate worker clans into something approaching revolutionary fervour. Most of the rest of their time was spent at guard posts in front of the city's huge number of monuments, statues and artworks, or performing in elaborate parades.

They had clearly not been ready for this. The dead men and women wore their mortal injuries like fashionable makeup, the trickles of blood that ran from open mouths and the pale skin of bloodless faces seeming to copy trends that Pierod had seen in boutiques and salons across the great overcity. Only their unnerving stillness hinted at the truth.

Scores of these bodies were draped over the imposing steps that led up to the command tower door. Pierod picked his way past the corpses as small-arms fire cracked and pinged against the building's reinforced frontage.

He slammed his bulk against the door, hammering his fists as he tried to finally catch his breath. 'Let me... in,' he wheezed, his heart thumping so hard in his throat that he thought he would be sick again. Then he shrieked, 'Let me in, you morons!' as an autogun shell slammed into the plasteel of the door a few feet above his head, gouging out a small circular hole.

He heard a crunching sound on the other side, and a small slit opened in the door. A pair of cold eyes looked out, scanning the killing field ahead before coming to rest on the vomit-covered figure of Pierod, cowering below. The eyes widened in surprise.

'Pierod?' the owner of the eyes said. 'Dear Throne, man, I thought you of all people would certainly be dead.'

He had been shot at more times than he could count already today, but Pierod still found time to bristle at the remark.

'Frojean, let me in!'

'Yes yes, of course. Let me just find someone to help...'

Pierod heard the voice tail off as the slit slammed shut.

Somewhere not so far away, he heard a boom, and turned to see a boxy tank trundling towards the command tower. The war machine was a relic – one of a handful still functional on the planet, taken out of the museum it inhabited only for parades and festivals. Pierod didn't think it had ever fired a shot in anger.

It was firing now, though. The tank's cannon belched white smoke, and a fireball blossomed against the armour of the last craft on the void port's apron. There was a secondary boom as something inside the lightly armoured ship – designed for high-atmosphere jaunts, rather than the rigours of combat – exploded. Pierod threw his arm across his face as pieces of crystalflex came raining back to solid ground with a melodious tinkling sound.

'*Frojean, let me in!*' Pierod screamed. There was another scraping sound, louder this time, and the huge doors opened a crack. Pierod pushed himself through the gap, sucking in his stomach as he went, and spilled out onto the synthetic floor of the void port's central control centre.

'Oh Pierod, my good man,' Frojean said, towering over him. Frojean always towered: the man was rail thin and almost as tall as Serrine's grasses. He would've been even taller were he not locked in a permanent stoop. It gave him an air of perpetual disapproval that he only exacerbated by perpetually disapproving of everything and everyone he came across.

'What's going on?' Frojean asked. 'Are we being invaded?'

'They are our own,' Pierod said. 'Rebels from the city below.'

'Oh, how frightful!' Frojean gasped, involuntarily throwing a long-fingered hand to his mouth. 'What malady has affected them so that they would turn against their own kin?'

'Never mind that!' Pierod snapped, hauling himself to his feet. They were unsteady – he was crashing from his adrenaline spike, and he had run faster and harder than the last time old Master

Tuille made him run the length of the parade ground for stealing an extra sweetcake. 'Get me to the vox! We must call for aid.'

Frojean looked confused. 'Aid?' he said, hands once again folded together. 'I share your worry, but Pierod, my good man, who would provide us aid? We haven't had a harvest collection in thirty years, and even our finest astropaths have been unable to communicate with Terra. Come, the nastiness outside must have been dreadful – join me and our esteemed colleagues in the shelter below, and we can wait for our forces to put down these dogs.'

Frojean loomed over him with an expression of such perfect smugness that Pierod had to fight not to hit him in his beak-like nose.

'I am not your good man,' Pierod snapped. 'I am your superior, and you shall address me as such. Even if these rebels do not breach our defences, we do not have the supplies for a siege, and with lines cut to the factoria and refineries below, we have no way of obtaining more. There will be no waiting this out, and there will be no counter-push from our militia – scores of them lie dead outside this very door!'

The robe-clad soldiers in the room shared worried glances. At least, Pierod assumed they were worried; their wrinkle-free skin was pulled so taut against their perfect jaws and cheekbones that there was barely any expression at all on their faces.

'I will get off this world, even if I have to launch *you* into the atmosphere, Frojean. Now take me to the central vox-unit.'

Frojean recovered his composure with a speed that drew some grudging respect from Pierod. 'Of course, vice treasurer. Follow me – these good fellows will lead the way.' He pointed at a small group of uniformly beautiful soldiers, their magenta robes splayed open at the waist to display tightly wound leather strapping around their legs and midsections. The robes marked them out as members of the Sophisticant Sixth: Serrine's elite military unit.

The men and women looked stunned to be addressed in such a manner, but, again, Pierod couldn't tell if they were genuinely surprised to be called upon by a member of the middle nobility, or if that was just their default expression. To their credit, they began to move into formation: two at the front, leading their party up the large staircase in the middle of the huge foyer, and two at the rear, covering the double doors warily with ornate lasguns.

The bullets sang as Cecily ran, high-pitched notes that descended in tone as they flew past her shoulders and over her head. Her fellow citizens had noticed the deserter in their midst, and were now trying to bring her down.

She cleared the edge of the park and reached a side avenue off the main square. Even this minor thoroughfare was lined with statues of all sizes, their white stone gleaming in the midday sun. She saw men and women, children and cherubs, figures holding swords, quills, containers and coins.

Her legs kept pumping, carrying her past buildings of glass and tempered metal. She could hear the crackle of gunfire not only from the square, but from elsewhere in the overcity too, and knew that her group was just one of many that had come up on the huge elevators – an invasion force from within.

Her own pistol hung heavy in her hand, and she thought about tossing it away, when three figures appeared at the end of the street. She skidded to a halt, throwing herself against the plinth holding the closest statue aloft, praying for the invaders to pass.

She tilted her head back as she mouthed pleas to the Emperor and saw the statue she had chosen, silhouetted against the cloudless blue sky. Its muscular body bore four arms, and in each hand, it carried the objects she and her people toiled for: the threshing blade, the grass, the sap, and the water that gave life to the world.

This city was alien to her, but she knew this figure. Grandfather had told her the stories of an angel from the sky who had descended on wings of fire, who had cleansed the land and planted the grass, who would return again when Serrine had its most dire need. 'The Saviour', he had called this angel.

She risked a peek over the plinth. The men at the end of the road had moved on.

'Incoming vox request from the surface.' The mound of flesh spoke again.

'Put it through,' Xantine ordered. 'They can answer for their desecration of my glorious ship.'

Immediately, a male voice filled the bridge, breathing hard with exertion. He had clearly been attempting to contact the *Exhortation* for some time.

'...*for the Emperor's sake, vessel of the Imperium! We are loyal citizens of the Imperium! Help us!*'

'Help you?! How dare you...' Rhaedron began, before Xantine held up a silk-gloved hand, cutting her off.

The mortal on the vox spoke again, panic and anger dragging his voice into new registers. '*I am Pierod Vaude, vice treasurer of Serrine, vital agri world of the Imperium, and we humbly request your aid! We are under attack from our own citizens, rebels who have turned against their Emperor. Our city is falling, and our government is in hiding. We will not survive much longer. Please, help us!*'

Rhaedron looked to Xantine, but the Space Marine's hand remained raised, offering only silence. The human voice grew more strained, trying a different approach now.

'*My father had friends on Terra, you know. I demand you send forces to assist us on the double, or they will hear of your scurrilous cowardice.*' Another beat. Pierod screamed, equal parts frustration and fear. '*You cowards! Help us!*'

Xantine finally spoke. 'Human, do you know to whom you speak?' he said, his voice soft, but his tone iron-hard.

Pierod gulped, audibly, his bluster evaporating. '*I apologise, my lord, I do not. I know only that we speak to a vessel of the Imperium! Our auspex scanners are having trouble picking up your ship's signifiers.*'

'You require help? Make your report, then, so that my forces understand how best we may assist,' Xantine said, relishing the chance to play a part in this production.

'*We are under attack from within. Traitors and rogues have destroyed half the city, captured the central palace, and worst of all, they killed Rogirre!*'

'And where are the soldiers to defend your city? Are they so cowardly that you must call upon the Adeptus Astartes to assist?'

'*Astartes? Did you say Astartes?*' Pierod asked, incredulous. '*Are you Space Marines?*'

'Yes, mortal. You speak to the pinnacle of the species.'

'*Then… then the Emperor Himself must have sent you! Oh, of course, of course. Father said that Terra had turned its back on us, but Terra would never forsake a world as important as Serrine. Oh Throne, thank you!*' Pierod laughed, giddy with relief.

'Your soldiers?'

'*Oh, yes! Our Sophisticant elite guard still stand – they are here, defending the planet's most valuable individuals, myself included. The remnants of our militia must also stand, but they are under heavy attack, and I have no idea of how many remain.*'

'Very good, Pierod, very good,' Xantine said, licking his lips. 'And what else can you offer us?'

'*Offer you?*' Pierod's astonishment was clear even over the distortion of Ghelia's vox-output. '*My lord, please, we are a simple agri world – what could we offer to the true children of the Emperor?*'

Xantine let a smile play out across his blackened lips. 'Oh, believe me, Pierod, we are true Children of the Emperor. But you have seen the Great Rift that blankets the sky. Do you think yours is the only world that suffers, that calls out into the void for aid? The Emperor helps those who help themselves, and we must reach an accord before we are able to provide our services.' He waited a beat. 'So, I ask again – what can you offer us?'

'*Anything! Anything you desire,*' Pierod responded. '*We have ammunition, we have fuel, we have medicine. Take it, and afterwards, when the day is won, I personally will lead the procession in your honour. Just help us!*'

'Then the stage is set. Pierod, tell your world to prepare for our arrival. The Emperor's Children are coming to save you.'

CHAPTER SIX

The first boom shook dust from the ancient stone ceiling above. Arqat brushed it away from the page, irritated by the thought he might be caned again for an interruption that wasn't his fault. Even the second boom – louder, closer, and powerful enough to send the golden candelabra skittering off the altar of the Emperor – didn't dissuade him from his studies. It was only with the third boom, the one that shattered the twenty-foot-tall glassaic image of an angel in purple descending from a golden sky, that Arqat looked up.

He decided to risk breaking the imposed silence on the Ministorum adepts, and turned to the young man sitting next to him. 'Hey, Roque – what do you think is going on?' he asked.

Roque met him with a bemused expression, before a fourth boom forestalled any chance of a reply. This one came with the sound of splintering, and as Arqat turned, he saw the cathedral door bow inwards, the ancient wood splitting open like a monster's mouth to reveal jagged teeth. Another explosion and the door became so many splinters, filling the air inside the entranceway with missiles. The midday sun shone through the doorway, illuminating smoke in the air, and framing the silhouettes of dozens of men and women as they streamed through the hole they had created.

They were shouting, guttural challenges and cries of rage that Arqat could barely recognise as Low Gothic. They were all filthy, and brandished rusted weapons that they brought to their shoulders, before firing indiscriminately in his direction.

Bullets tore through stacked holy texts and pinged off intricately carved columns, sending puffs of marble dust into the air with each shot. More windows shattered, the shards of coloured glass cascading to the ground like flowing water.

Arqat threw himself under his pew, immediately incensed at the destruction. Who were these low-born heretics, to force their way into this most sacred of places? To desecrate the Emperor's image, and spit in the face of the planet that had birthed him. How *dare* they?

Not for the first time today, he wished his brother was here. Telo would have put these traitors down without a second thought. He felt a tingle of excitement as he imagined it: a carbine levelled at soft bodies, its bullets tearing through skin and muscle until there was nothing left but chunks of ragged meat, and Arqat, the hero.

But Telo wasn't here, and Arqat had no weapons – just a children's storybook and a quill.

He looked to the old priest Father Tumas for direction, but he saw not anger in his milky eyes, but fear. Tears ran down his wrinkled face, and he raised his hands into the air. Arqat hated him more than ever before in that moment.

'*Do* something,' he whispered under his breath, as the old priest whimpered in surrender.

Arqat wasn't waiting any longer. He slid from his seat, reaching forward to tuck his copybook under his arm as he moved to a ducking run, keeping low and behind the pews, out of sight of the people streaming through the door. Other youths sat and watched, dumbfounded. They were close to their twentieth year, all of them, but their sheltered lives and oversized cassocks made them look impossibly young. Arqat hissed at them, trying to get their attention, beckoning them to follow. They too slipped out of their pews, joining him in a procession away from their attackers, towards the back of the cathedral.

They had been taken by surprise, but he knew this church, knew its secret corners and passages. He led the boys past the nave and the altar, pushing gently on the tapestry of Saint Desade to reveal a short tunnel that led precipitously down into the cathedral's undercroft. He lifted the heavy tapestry with one arm and beckoned the other boys through, half guiding and half pushing them down the short slope to reach comparative safety below. Once he was sure he had rounded up all of his compatriots, he skittered down the worn stone after them.

The gunshots were quieter down here, filtered through layers of ancient rock, but they still weren't safe. The crypt, with its heavy adamantine doors, was his aim.

Serrine's grand cathedral was the patronage of many of the planet's noble families, and though he rarely saw any of their number at worship, they competed to outdo each other with elaborate gifts bestowed upon the Ecclesiarchy.

Some took pride of place in the cathedral itself, but there was only so much room, and as the fortunes of the planet's families waxed and waned, more and more of these gifts ended up in the undercroft, their lustre dimmed by years in the dark. Arqat led the boys past marble statues of winged figures, golden lecterns in the shape of Imperial eagles, and more representations of

Serrine's four-armed Saviour of legend than he could find the energy to count.

Finally, they reached the imposing double doors that marked the entrance to the crypt. Ignoring their complaints, Arqat ushered the youths through the door, shoving the more hesitant of their number into the gloom.

'Is this the only way?' one boy asked, his face pained. 'Won't they find us down here?'

'It's better than up there,' Arqat said, brooking no argument as he pushed the boy past the threshold and into the crypt.

A face reappeared out of the darkness.

'What do we do, Arqat?' Voulet asked. He was one of the youngest of the boys, and inordinately proud of the wispy moustache he had grown over the last winter. It was full of wet snot now, and Voulet sniffed deep, before wiping away the remnants with the sleeve of his cassock.

'Stay here, and stay quiet,' Arqat replied, putting a comforting hand on the boy's shoulder. 'Lock the door, and only open it if the Emperor Himself comes knocking.'

'Where are you going?' Voulet asked.

'I'm going back up there to show these base-born scum what happens to people who attack the Emperor's chosen.'

His route back to the cathedral's nave took him past treasures, and he paused in front of one idol, rendered in polished black stone. The figure was the one from his picture book: a four-armed figure, clutching two bowls and two blades. The blades were ceremonial, but looked wickedly sharp, glinting even in the dim light of the undercroft. Arqat gave the closest blade a testing tug, and was pleased to see that it was held in a loose grip. He tested the weight of the sword in his hand, and realised he would need two hands to hold it, let alone swing it. Still, it was a weapon, and he trusted his righteous fury to guide it true.

'Sorry,' Arqat said to the mythical founder of his world. 'I think I need this more than you.' Hefting the sword over his shoulder, he turned back to the idol. 'I'll bring it straight back, I promise.'

The curtain material was soft on her skin. Cecily ran her hand down it, hoping to find an opening, but found it springy and firm, like the grass she had pushed through before she arrived here. It felt like a lifetime ago, but it must have only been a few hours. She found a seam and shouldered through, stepping out of the open door and onto a balcony that overlooked the city.

She saw it arrayed in front of her for the first time. From street level, Serrine's overcity had been beautiful; from up here, it was stunning. She saw mansions of glass and pillars of marble, towers of silver and gold, and between them all, forests of statues, their shapes human and beast and all stages in between. She took it all in, all the exotic beauty so utterly alien to her, until her eyes landed on something familiar. A church.

It appeared as if dredged up from her memory. It was far more grandiose than any of the sheet-metal chapels and pipework shrines she had come to know in the undercity, but the trappings of faith – the huge golden aquila high on the wall, the depictions of the Emperor in glassaic windows two storeys high, and the vast statue of Serrine's founding angel set into a niche on the building's south-facing side – gave away its purpose.

There were taller buildings clustered around it, spires and towers encrusted with ornate decorations and the ubiquitous statues, but even they seemed to bow in deference to the church, the path clear for all nearby to see this masterpiece and appreciate its beauty. A vast pipe rose from its centre, used to carry Solipsus sap from the surface to this city above the clouds. Long and dark, it resembled the proboscis of some vast insect, sucking the lifeblood of the city below to feed the city above.

The church's double doors were made of dark wood and inlaid with metal that, from her vantage point on the balcony, reflected the sunlight back into her eyes. She winced, and cast her gaze down, across the marble stairs that led up from the street level.

They were decorated with bodies. There were dozens, maybe hundreds, dead, killed as they fled or fought. Figures draped over steps in their resting places as if they were lounging in the bright sun, their perfect stillness and the pools of red that stained the white marble below the only indication as to the truth of the matter.

'Throne...' Cecily gasped, taking in the scale of the massacre. 'Why did they do this?'

A human shape lay on the balcony itself, white in the midday sun. 'Hello?' she called, hoping that the figure would stir, but it remained unnervingly still. Summoning her tattered bravery, she crept towards the body, until it revealed its true form: a statue, toppled from one of the many platforms and plinths that decorated the overcity. Below, too, statues lay alongside the flesh-and-blood humans that they depicted, their perfect faces serene, their complexions so pure a white in the midday sun that they appeared to be the negative form of the people that had died around them: a perverse imitation of death by an object that played at life.

To see such death and destruction pained her spirit. Wetness welled in the corner of her eyes as she scanned them across dead men and women in brightly coloured robes, their mouths open to take in the horror of their last moments.

No, it pained more than just her spirit. There was a physical pain in her head, too – a gnawing, buzzing sensation as though her skull was being constricted in one of the refinery's pulping machines.

'No,' she groaned, pushing the heels of her hands into her eyes for a moment of respite, and gasped as they came away dotted with bright spots of blood. 'Get out of my head!'

The stillness was broken by movement as figures appeared from a side street. They moved like a swarm of insects, circling and falling back together as they headed towards the steps. She steadied herself, her head still swimming, and peeked over the edge.

Outriders on the edge of the group moved quickly between the corpses, some picking up objects that she couldn't see, others firing bullets into fallen men and women to ensure they were truly dead. The next ranks scanned the rooftops and walkways of the marble city for targets, training autoguns and lasweaponry upwards even as they moved. She pressed herself closer to the low wall as they turned in her direction, her vantage point giving her unique oversight of the group.

At their centre, held up on a palanquin carried by hulking figures, was the beautiful woman. Her robe had been cast off, revealing a pale pink jumpsuit, similar to those worn by those she commanded. Even with such mundane clothing, she was luminous in the sunlight, a dazzling figure whose edges seemed to fray and warp as Cecily watched her guide her troops. Behind her, carried between metal poles by similarly huge figures, was a container, its contents hidden from view, but clearly both massive and revered by the throng.

The buzzing in her head became a roar as her eyes passed back and forth between the woman and the container, the pain pressing against her head like a vice. She thought she could hear words in the maelstrom – like someone whispering over the sound of a threshing machine's engine – but couldn't work out their meaning.

She wanted to stand, to reveal herself, to wave her arms and apologise for her weakness – anything as long as she could join the leader and her collective. Cecily would kill for her, she would die for her, she would do whatever this luminous figure deemed necessary, for as long as she wanted. The sound in her head blocked out any other thoughts, and she started to rise from her hiding place, arms raised.

No. *No.* She pulled her right arm down with her left, and when they started to rise in unison, plunged them both into her work suit's ample pockets.

She felt a small object, and – grateful of a physical distraction to the mental barrage – pulled it out. It was a bundle of dried grass, shaped roughly into human form, albeit with four arms instead of two.

She knew it immediately. Of course she knew it: she had carried it with her for the last six years, her ever-present companion for every shift cycle, every bunk rotation. It was her own Saviour. Grandpa had woven it for her thirteenth birthday, the same day that she had been drafted into the refinery labour detail.

'He'll protect you,' Grandpa had said. When she'd asked what specifically the object would protect her from, with the cynicism of a child on the cusp of adulthood, he had simply closed her hand around the icon. *'Anything you need him to,'* he had told her, and left it at that.

She looked up at the church, at the figure of the Saviour. It looked nothing like her own icon. Hers was woven from dried grass banded together with cast-off bundle wire. It had none of the beautiful features depicted on the church – no thin nose, no pursed lips, no wide-set eyes. It had no face at all, but it was unmistakably the same figure, and it connected her from this unfamiliar place to her own past.

She could feel the blood on her cheeks now, her vision reddening as the pressure in her head built. She held the icon in two hands and pulled it into her body, making herself a home for her protector, just as the church was a home for its own icon. She saw its four walls, strong and high, and built them in her mind. She put her protector front and centre, and studded it with more of her own icons: of her grandpa and her brave cousin, of the grass and the Solipsus sap, of the Emperor Himself.

The maelstrom swirled still. The voices, indistinct before, were growing louder, speaking words of command and control. They pressed against the walls she had built in her mind, and when they couldn't break them outright, felt around instead, searching for a weak point in the foundations that they could slip through. But she had built these walls with her own faith, and knew their strength.

'Throne, protect me,' she whispered, as the pressure built until she thought her head would burst.

And then it was gone.

She risked another glance over the wall. The woman was gone, so too was her cargo, the last stragglers from her group disappearing through the church doors – doors that appeared to have been blasted open.

'Thank you,' she whispered to the four-armed figure. Beyond it, in the blue sky, she saw a moving light, like a star falling from the heavens.

The bridge of the *Exhortation* rang with a cacophony of sound. Sirens blared, klaxons wailed, bridge crew and servitors screamed in mindless panic as the frigate rocked again under explosive force. Thick curtains swayed as Xantine pushed through them, taking up position in his command throne.

'Damage report,' he demanded as he settled into the golden seat.

'We have taken a massive hit to the *Exhortation*'s core ganglion cluster,' Rhaedron responded, turning smartly to address her Space Marine warlord from her position in the crew pit. 'The decks are impassable, so we can't assess the damage ourselves, and reports from the Navigator are... incoherent.'

Ghelia's droning voice was just one sound amid the orchestra of chaos. Xantine focused on her robotic tones as the ship-spanning entity called out a garbled status report.

'Lower decks breached, venting flu-fluids. Engine decks breached, reactor mis-mis-misfiring.' The Navigator's voice was halting, staccato, hitched as if with a laboured breath that it didn't have. 'I can't fe... feel my...' And then, with an audible gasp: 'The void sinks into my bl-blood...'

Pain hung thick in the air, so dense that Xantine could taste it. The mound of flesh convulsed, writhing as if in agony.

Rhaedron stared at him, gauging his reaction.

'What was that?' Xantine asked.

There was a short delay before Rhaedron responded. 'I don't know, my lord,' she said. 'The ship has been returning garbled responses to my status requests. It seems to be... confused.'

Ghelia continued her grim report, her voice once more robotic in tone. 'Weapon systems inactive, require immediate maintenance. Void shields inoperable. Void shields cold. The void is cold.' There was a sucking sound, like a gut-shot man catching his last breath, and then the voice came back. It was softer now – still loud enough to be heard across the bridge of the *Exhortation*, but the harsh mechanical tone had softened, and it was now wavering in pitch and timbre. It sounded almost human.

'Hello?' the ship whimpered. 'Are you there? I'm so cold.' There was panic in the voice now, audible through the distortion. Alarms swelled with each word, the suffering building until the ship was screaming in agony, howling its final coda.

'Help me!'

The alarms reached a crescendo, klaxons and horns and sirens, the full complement of sounds on a ship that had never known silence, all firing at once. They harmonised to build a single, screaming tone that burst the eardrums of human bridge crew unlucky or unwise enough not to plug their ears. Men and women banged their skulls against cogitator consoles, driven insensate by the violence of the sound as blood and lymph fluid ran from their heads.

And then the sound stopped. There was silence. Absolute silence, for the first time on the bridge of the *Exhortation* since the ship entered the service of the Emperor's Children.

'Report,' Xantine hissed. Something in his subconscious suggested that he keep his voice low. Reverence, perhaps.

'I… I don't know, my lord,' Rhaedron said. She steadied herself against Ghelia's central support dais, shaky from the sonic ordeal. Members of her crew moaned in pain, the sound almost comically quiet in the wake of such noise. 'Core cogitators are down, servitors not responding, and the Navigator is…' She prodded Ghelia with her silvered cane, and received nothing in response. The mound of flesh didn't even recoil from the touch, and Rhaedron tailed off. 'I'm sorry, my lord. I know nothing more than you.'

'I demand answers!' Xantine screamed, drawing a mewl of panic from Rhaedron. She caught a breath, but any response was swallowed up by the sound of a new voice over the bridge vox-channel, sibilant and dry.

'She is dead,' Qaran Tun said matter-of-factly.

Xantine let out an involuntary growl. 'You lie, Word Bearer,' he said, disbelief and anger swirling together.

'I tell the truth,' Tun said. The Word Bearer had no particular malice towards Ghelia, but observing her passing had been of

particular scholarly interest to the collector. Xantine could hear the smile on his tattooed lips.

'She was quite the soul, you know. She had grown into a creature like no other, and her passing left a rent in the warp. You should see the Neverborn, Xantine. They writhe and cavort as we speak. I have weeks of cataloguing ahead of me.'

'You disgust me,' Xantine said. He dearly wished he could strike the Word Bearer through the vox. 'Ghelia *is* the *Exhortation*. My ship. She cannot simply die. She would not do this to me.'

'My lord, if I may,' Rhaedron cut in. 'I can only imagine the depths of sensation you must be feeling at this moment. But if what Lord Tun says is true, then we have no Navigator.'

'I know this,' Xantine snapped. 'Make your point or you will join her in death.'

'Without our Navigator, we cannot leave this system. The... thing–'

'Ghelia,' Xantine corrected.

'Ghelia,' Rhaedron said, swallowing the word like rancid meat, before trying again. 'Ghelia was so embedded into the *Exhortation*'s systems that the warp drive, and the ship itself, will not be functional without her.'

'What do you propose?' Xantine asked.

'I do not know, my lord,' Rhaedron said.

Tun spoke again, his voice still even despite the dire predicament the Adored were in. *'There may be a way,'* he whispered with a voice like shifting sands. *'Just as Ghelia's body entwined with the ship, her soul grew closer to the warp. Should we find someone with specific psychic compatibilities, our chirurgeons may be able to intervene, connecting the ship's organic systems with the mind of a pliant psyker.'*

'But where would such an individual be found?' Rhaedron said.

'We have a planet at our disposal,' Xantine said. 'I'm sure we can procure something – someone – to meet our needs.'

CHAPTER SEVEN

Two blades, always, for the Emperor's Children: the open, and the hidden. The hidden, the blade responsible for the killing cut, would be wielded by Xantine himself. It always was, Torachon thought, with a stab of annoyance. He was more accomplished than his warlord in all of the ways that mattered to the Emperor's Children – a more seasoned tactician, a more skilled duellist, and a finer artist – but Xantine would not cede honours to his warriors, no matter how strong they clearly were.

But at least he had been chosen to command the open blade, his squad now hurtling down to strike at Serrine's void port, where the fighting was the thickest, tasked with sowing panic and confusion into the heart of the enemy position. This visible show of force would draw out the enemy's leaders; Xantine would decapitate them.

'Perhaps Xantine would allow me the honour of the killing strike?' Torachon wondered aloud in the darkened confines of the Dreadclaw. 'I have proven my strength many times.'

'Hah,' Orlan said in response, spite in his voice. 'Not a chance.' Torachon ascribed his attitude to jealousy – Orlan was significantly smaller and weaker than he was.

Torachon ignored the slight, and focused instead on more fundamental questions. He could never decide which sensation he enjoyed more: the anticipation of battle, or battle itself. It was a question he asked himself often, and he'd yet to find a satisfactory answer. He yearned for both, but when he had one, he invariably wanted the other, leaving him unable to truly savour the afterglow of combat.

He sighed and pushed such existential questions aside, concentrating for now on the delicious tension in the minutes before his drop pod made planetfall. He closed his eyes and stretched out as much as the cramped confines allowed, performing a mental inventory of his enhanced body, from his fingers down to his toes. Every nerve in his enhanced body was poised, ready to strike.

Good. He stroked the oiled leather handle of his power sword – a thin, thrusting sabre he had taken from a duelling master on Loucin IV – and felt a distinct kinship with the weapon. They were both killers: sharp, potent and lethal, and they were both thrumming with barely contained energy. Torachon flicked the sabre's power generator off, and then back on again, repeating the action a few times, enjoying the shuddering vibrations as blue lightning coruscated along the length of the blade. His fellow Adored sharing the Dreadclaw shot him irritated looks.

'Impact in ten, nine...'

The synthesised voice came over the Dreadclaw's vox, and Torachon felt tingles of sensation travelling the length of his limbs, just as the power field energised his blade. It was joined by a burst of pride, and he thanked his lord again for the honour. To have risen so far to be trusted with leading the attack on a new world, to be the spear-tip of the Adored's assault, to face such danger and taste the first glories – Xantine must think highly of him indeed.

'...*three, two, one, impact.*'

The final word was joined by a bass boom and a physical impact so forceful that it catapulted Torachon forward in his harness. He used the momentum, unclasping his restraints with one hand and leaning forward into a roll, an acrobatic man-oeuvre made trivial by his genhanced body and his modified armour. His Mark VII war plate had been taken from some loyalist Space Marine Chapter, one he'd never felt compelled to learn about. It did not matter. It only mattered what he did with it now. Like all of Bile's experiments, it had been dras-tically altered. The ablative plates had been cut so they were segmented, allowing for freer range of motion, albeit at the cost of pure defensive capability. That wasn't a concern for Torachon, though: he didn't plan on ever getting hit.

In other places, the suit had been cut away entirely, exposing naked skin. Torachon had decorated both his armour and his body with elaborate scarification, carving whorls and spirals that travelled between ceramite and flesh. The only part of his frame left untouched by these scars was his face, which was blessed with perfect skin and violet eyes the colour of his primarch's armour, and marred only by a natural sneer.

The Dreadclaw's doors descended with a hydraulic hiss and a burst of steam. The process took seconds, but Torachon couldn't wait that long. He placed an armoured boot on the side of the opening and leapt clear over the half-descended door, the elec-tric blue of his sabre's power field illuminating the cloud of hydraulic gases and impact detritus like an ancient thunder god.

He found himself in an open space, its ferrocrete surface large enough to land cargo vessels, and studded with refuelling stations. 'Good,' Torachon said under his breath, pleased that the Dreadclaw had not been jolted off course during the descent.

Something moved underneath his boot, and he looked down. Slitted eyes stared back, yellow and unblinking, set in a bulbous, hairless human head. The man had been bisected by the impact of the Dreadclaw, his bottom half either severed or destroyed so effectively that his body ended at its navel, yet he still lived. There was no fear in those strange eyes, just a cold anger. The absence of emotion turned Torachon's stomach, and he reached down, tightening his hand around the man's throat, and squeezing until he heard a dislocating pop.

Around him, he saw dozens more mortals. They were silhouettes in the slowly settling cloud of dust, coalescing but still indistinct as they drew themselves from the ground they had been thrown to. Across the void port, more figures turned in the direction of the new arrivals, hefting mounted heavy stubbers and training autoguns on the giant in pink armour in their midst.

He was surrounded, he realised, he and his squad having successfully arrived right in the midst of the foe's forces. A lesser warrior would have planned their retreat, but Torachon simply smiled. He was the open blade, after all – a thrust aimed deep into enemy lines. He was playing his role to perfection.

'Behold, mortals!' he proclaimed, raising his sabre high as he drew the cold eyes of his foes. 'Behold my beauty, and behold your death!'

Torachon whipped his blade down in a long, arcing cut, his long white hair spinning as he sliced open the stomach of one figure as it tried to rise. He was rewarded with a horrifying screech, and the smell of burning blood in the thick air. Bolters barked as the other warriors of the Adored's initial strike force made their way out of the Dreadclaw, their rhythmic chatter

RENEGADES: LORD OF EXCESS

forming a drumbeat. Mutants and cultists alike exploded as bolts buried themselves in bodies, the dust and blood caking the warriors' brightly coloured power armour, reducing the vibrant pinks and purples to dull grey and gore red.

Torachon could kill to this sound. He whirled between the injured figures as the dust settled, thrusting indiscriminately, putting them down as they tried to rise. He noticed again their peculiar physiology: there were entirely too many arms for these to be standard humans. Maybe it was the strange pink fog that separated the city from the ground beneath. They died the same though, he thought, as he stomped a boot through the chest cavity of a dirty man dressed in greasy rags.

'These wretches stink of xenos,' Orlan called over the open vox, at the same time as Torachon thrust his power sabre through the heart of a three-armed mutant. He let the beast sizzle for a moment on his blade, flailing and thrashing for an impressively long time as the charged edge burned out its internal organs, before bringing his weapon closer to better inspect the creature.

'Strange creatures, indeed,' he said. Black blood fizzled and spat, superheated by his weapon, and a peculiar smell filled his nostrils. It was bitter and alien, most unlike the pleasing aroma of human vitae. 'Like the void,' he noted with a sneer, and let the mutant slip from his sword to the ground.

Truth be told, Torachon had never looked too closely at humans. They had some key characteristics he could remember: they were small, easily scared, and very *wet*. He had an idle theory that there was a correlation between their fear and their moisture levels, but most of the humans he'd earmarked for serious research into the question died before he was able to confirm his suspicions.

These humans, however, were different to the normal varieties he'd seen on his travels around the Eye. These were not the gibbering maniacs of a world fallen to unguided worship of the

Pantheon. Nor were they simple peasants, disgruntled with the Emperor's insane rejection of pleasure.

The way they moved was unusual: coordinated, yet silent, as if they shared a mind. Torachon thought back to his youth and realised he'd seen such things before, in his creator's gene forges, though they looked very different there. They were skittering things, like vast insects, with hyper-specialised mutations. Some had claws as long as Torachon's own leg; others grew over-sized poison sacs and drooling proboscises that could launch gobbets of lethal goo with frightening accuracy.

Tyranids, Fabius had called the general clade, but there was a specific type that Fabius had mentioned as being particularly virulent on human-colonised worlds.

A four-armed creature pulled itself from a sewer grate in front of Torachon, slipping through a gap no wider than his handspan, before unfurling itself to its full height. It threw its four arms wide, black claws glinting in the sun, as it screamed. Tentacles on its face rippled with the sound.

Ah, that was it.

'Genestealers!' Torachon called, as the creature scythed its talons down in a blow aimed to tear open his ribcage. He pulled his sword to his chest and pirouetted, a turn that took him to the side of his attacker. Without a second glance, Torachon weighed a single cut, bringing his blade across the back of the beast. The sword cut through chitin until it hit the softer meat inside, and the genestealer split, carved completely in two. Both halves of the creature continued to thrash on the ferrocrete floor, its claws grasping upwards at Torachon as he towered over it. With a sneer, he kicked the genestealer's upper half, sending it slamming against a wall, where finally it stopped moving.

Fabius had tried to use the creatures in his experiments, to extract their most useful traits and incorporate them into his future projects, but they proved frustratingly resistant to the Clonelord's meddling. Filthy xenos they may be, but they had a perfection of form that even the arch-meddler Bile could appreciate.

A second genestealer rose from the same grate as the last, a third pushing behind it, its glossy black claws slicing at the air to reach its prey.

Torachon pulled his sword into a duelling stance, hilt drawn to shoulder level, point forward. He was ready to lunge, when a bass voice called out from behind.

'Stand back, boy,' Vavisk commanded, his voice staggeringly loud even over the din of battle. The Noise Marine was part of the open blade's second wave, and had arrived with his coterie on the other side of the void port. Now that both squads were linking up, they were due to push for the port's control centre.

Bile rose in Torachon's throat as the Noise Marine captain lay a gauntleted hand on his shoulder, pushing him out of the way. His sabre-arm twitched at the dismissive gesture, but even brash Torachon knew better than to challenge Xantine's right hand. He swallowed his pride and resolved to savour the oncoming spectacle instead.

Vavisk stepped forward, calling five of his Noise Marines into formation alongside him with a burst of screeched static. Each of his underlings had a body almost as warped as their captain's, but they moved with surprising precision, as if keeping to a rhythm that Torachon could not hear. As one, they levelled their sonic blasters – ornate golden things that were more ancient instrument than weapon – and began to call forth their infernal sound.

The air thrummed as the weapons spooled up, finding a shared frequency and harmonising their tone with the music of obliteration. The process took several seconds, and the genestealers, ignorant of the unholy onslaught about to be visited on their number, continued their headlong charge. Torachon unclasped his bolt pistol from its mag-locked position on his right leg and shot one of the closest creatures through the head. It launched sideways, its claws still grasping for air as it flew, skidding to a halt at Vavisk's feet. The Noise Marine let out a discordant roar of sound that Torachon chose to take as appreciation.

Autogun bullets pinged off the Noise Marines' acid-pink armour as genestealer cultists further back rose from firing positions to attack the new enemy. One of Vavisk's coterie took a heavy stubber shell to the throat, and the pitch of the chorus changed slightly as he staggered. The wound was deep, but Torachon watched in real-time as the wound closed over with fibrous strands, the stringy ligaments criss-crossing until they had formed a vox-grille in the Noise Marine's neck. He stepped back into formation, his newly altered physiology fully functional, joining the harmony with a horrific shriek of its own.

'Begin!' Vavisk roared, and the Noise Marines' sonic blasters erupted in turn. The wave of noise was so powerful that Torachon could see it: a visible bow shock that travelled the length of the void port at the speed of sound. It moved through bodies – both chitin and soft flesh – as if they weren't there, bursting eardrums and jellifying bones as it went.

Humans, or those close to human, threw their hands to their ears and opened their mouths. Torachon assumed they were howling in agony, but their cries were drowned out entirely by the blessed noise that tore across the void port's apron.

Purestrain genestealers, lacking the emotional processing capability to express pain, simply collapsed as they ran, their organs scrambled inside their exoskeletons, their lethal talons flailing aimlessly at the air as they died.

Vavisk called the cadence for his coterie, sending pulses and shrieks of sound in the midst of the sustained assault. These ripples forced cultists from cover, their eyes, ears, and other orifices pouring with their own blood. The hybrid genestealers' mutations worked against them, chitinous plates that would normally offer protection against ballistic weapons increasing the pressure on skulls squeezed from inside. Torachon watched as one giant mutant's head exploded, bony shards and brain matter ejected backwards across its wailing comrades.

The sonic blasters called forth the sound of the warp, and with their sustained fire, the distance between material existence and the empyrean narrowed. Tongues and tendrils poked and probed through tiny tears in reality, aching to find the source of this profane noise. Some slipped through entirely, wrapping themselves around the limbs of Vavisk and his Noise Marines as they maintained their volley of sound.

The music of the apocalypse made Torachon's vision blur, and he blinked. As he opened his eyes, he saw reality flicker, revealing a version of the void port wreathed in purple haze. The genestealers were gone, and the sound, while still present, had become a drone – the background noise of stars collapsing into black holes. Somewhere in this space, Torachon saw a pair of eyes – violet, like his own, but feline – turn their gaze to his. It was as if, through the skein in the empyrean, something was seeing him for the first time.

He blinked, and he was back. He felt his hearts flutter as the song drew to a crescendo, and then, with a final blast of unbearable noise, it was over. Fat little tentacles slapped to the ferrocrete floor, fizzling back into non-existence as the primacy of the material plane reasserted itself. Torachon was down on his knees, he realised, drawing heaving breaths.

From the huge building behind him, he heard a barked order, the voice impossibly small in comparison to Vavisk's orchestra, and then the soft crackle of lasgun fire, as human defenders mopped up the last of the genestealer cultists' failed assault. He heard the clunk of a lock, and then the creak of massive doors.

The smell of fear and sweat hit Torachon's nostrils as small men and women appeared in the opening, their frames weak and their eyes wet. To Torachon, they looked little different to the xenos creatures who were currently assaulting their position.

'Thank you, thank you!' a thin voice cried.

After three decades of silence, to find a warship of the Imperium – of the Adeptus Astartes, no less! – on manoeuvres in-system. It was a piece of fortuitousness from legend itself. As Pierod's father had always said, truly, the Emperor smiled on His favourites.

The details, he could work out later. The Adeptus Astartes – even thinking of their splendour brought a skip to his step – had arrived, blunted the enemy's major assault, and then mopped up the rabble. Soon he could get back to his mansion. Maybe he'd be awarded a *new* mansion. Yes, the cachet of being the saviour of Serrine, the one man who could call down the angels themselves to rescue his world from damnation, would be considerable.

Such power! Even to speak with one of the angels had weakened his knees and sped his heart, but he had done it, and he would not let his peers forget. Half of Serrine's noble class were likely lying with bullets in their backs; there needed to be someone to rebuild, to lead. Who better than he? Pierod the Decisive, Pierod the Brave, Pierod the Caller of Angels.

He'd have to replace Rogirre, first of all. And then he'd need some new clothes.

All in good time. First, he had to welcome the Astartes. He had never met one of their number before, but he had heard both their legend, and their battle outside. It was impossibly, illogically loud, and it had sent even the most seasoned of the Sophisticant Sixth sprawling to the floor of the control centre, their hands covering their ears. Pierod had joined them, screwing his eyes shut and groaning in pain until the noise stopped. He had sat on the floor for a moment, trying to rationalise what he had heard.

That was what they had called themselves: the Emperor's Children. Of course the Emperor's own sons would make war in such a terrifying manner, with force so destructive that no one could, no one *would* stand against the primacy of mankind and its master. He shuddered as he imagined what it must be like to face such Angels of Death on the battlefield.

He wondered what they would look like. He imagined muscular figures, broad-shouldered and smiling with benign grace, microcosms of the images and statues of the Emperor that adorned his city.

He would find out in moments. Pierod had ordered Frojean to open the command tower's great doors, and the thin man had delegated the task to members of the militia who were only now just picking themselves off the floor.

Pierod positioned himself at the top of the stairs, ready to receive his guests. It was a trick he'd learned in high society, to give oneself the height advantage during introductions. He coughed once, and prepared to project his voice. From the diaphragm, as Father had taught him.

'Welcome, Adeptus Astartes of the Emperor...'

A gasp of shock rippled up the stairs as the first of the warriors ducked to step over the threshold, and Pierod's welcome died in his throat. The Space Marine was clad in armour of shocking pink, its panels decorated with strange symbols and pierced with rings that held fetishes of gold and bone. Skins hung from his waist, swaying back and forth as he lumbered into the control centre's hallway. Pierod was sure he could make out the shape of a human hand in this grisly tabard, the fingers pointing at the ground.

But most shocking of all was the face. Pierod had initially assumed the warrior was wearing a strange helmet, perhaps to terrify his enemies on the battlefield, but he realised with horror that he was gazing upon the naked skin of a once-human face. To Pierod, the Space Marine looked as if he had melted, like a candle left to burn for too long unattended. The skin of his face hung sallow, barely clinging to cheekbones as if it had been nailed into place. His jawbone had collapsed entirely, subsumed into an oversized vox-grille that hummed and buzzed as the giant stepped forward. The sound continued as he came to rest, and Pierod realised it was the sound of his breathing.

Frojean was the first to overcome his shock, stepping forward to greet the newcomer. 'My... my lord? You are injured! P-please, let my men take care of your grievous wounds.'

The Astartes warrior cocked his head to the side, blood-red eyes narrowing as he regarded the rake-thin mortal in front of him. 'I bear no injury,' he said in a voice laden with static and distortion.

Pierod winced to hear him speak, physically recoiling from the sound and grasping at the banister. He gulped, steadied himself, and tried to reply. 'Xantine, of the Emperor's Children. I bid you welcome to Serrine.'

The giant turned to him and huffed a squeal of static that might have been a laugh. Pierod threw his hands to his ears before collecting himself, forcing his arms back to his side to present a statesmanlike appearance.

'I am not Xantine,' the Space Marine rumbled in a voice that sounded as if it came from the centre of the planet. 'He is in orbit, awaiting our initial strike.'

Pierod cringed in embarrassment. This wasn't going to plan at all. 'Then who, may I ask, do I address?' he asked, attempting to inject his voice with gravitas and authority.

A new figure ducked through the open door and into the hallway. This one was tall – taller even than his peers – and blessed with the angelic bearing that Pierod had initially expected from the Astartes of legend. He tossed long blond hair as he straightened himself, before fixing Pierod with a contemptuous glare.

'He is Vavisk, and I am Torachon. And you will address us each as "my lord", or I will dirty my blade with your blood.'

'Throne,' Pierod said under his breath, taking a step back up the stairs.

'Speak not that word here, mortal,' the handsome one said, placing his hand on the pommel of his sabre. Pierod took the gesture as the escalation in threat it was intended to be, and assumed that this one was the more pious of the two Astartes emissaries.

'We were told you had soldiers,' the one with the melted face continued, ignoring the posturing of his colleague.

'We do, my lord,' Pierod said. 'I place the Sophisticant Sixth at your command. They are the elite of the elite, and will serve you well, alongside any additional members of the militia still operating in the overcity.'

Both Space Marines looked him up and down. Suddenly self-conscious, Pierod tucked his hands behind his back, sucking in his gut and straightening his posture as best he could. He hoped they wouldn't notice the crusted vomit on his robes of office.

'*You* lead this planet's military force?' the beautiful one asked. 'Then you have failed, utterly. Your world would be destroyed if not for my arrival.'

Pierod felt his face flush, panic hardening into anger. He

channelled it, attempting to inject some steel into his voice. The effort was only partially successful.

'I am Vice Treasurer Pierod of Serrine,' he called, his voice wavering in the face of the terrifying newcomers. 'It was I who called you here, and with Serrine's ruling council now missing, most likely dead, I am the ranking noble on this world.'

He mustered the courage to meet the taller warrior's gaze. Purple eyes stared back, hard as gemstones, set in a face that was too symmetrical, too perfect. Fear gripped his stomach, and he looked away, casting his eyes across the other warriors of the vanguard.

There was no uniformity on show: they wore mismatched armour of pink and black, with panels and pauldrons daubed in dusky purples or luminous greens, seemingly at random. The tallest one was so handsome that he might have been chiselled from marble, but the others were elaborately mutilated, bearing facial scars or wounds presumably earned in their many battles.

They were, to Pierod's considerable concern, absolutely terrifying to behold.

'Speak, little man,' the handsome one said, his eyes flashing. Pierod twitched at the demand, and did his best to continue.

'Yes! As I was saying, that puts me in charge of not only this planet's military, but its logistics, its economy, and of all the major decisions its population makes.'

'Vice Treasurer Pierod?'

Frojean's interruption made Pierod wince. 'Yes, Frojean?' he asked through gritted teeth.

'The council. They're not all missing, or dead. Around half of them made it to safety. They're downstairs.'

'The council? They're *here?*' Pierod asked, incredulous.

'Oh yes,' Frojean said, as if the information was obvious. 'The Sophisticant Sixth extracted the governor the moment the attacks on the city began. All of the most important members of the council were identified and escorted here.'

'Take me to them,' the tallest Space Marine said, stepping forward so fast that Pierod had to lurch to one side to avoid being bowled over. He caught Frojean as the attendant attempted to follow, grabbing him by the wrist, hard.

'I received no such escort,' Pierod hissed.

'No…' Frojean looked down at him with a simpering gaze and placed a hand on his shoulder. 'Unfortunately it was decided that our resources were better used… elsewhere.'

Pierod slapped the hand away and stormed past the taller man, heading down the steps and after the Space Marines, towards the bunker in the command tower's basement.

'Still, you made it here in one piece!' Frojean called after him. 'Bravo to you!'

CHAPTER EIGHT

'You manipulated them, Xantine,' Sarquil said, his shiny silver head reflecting the red light of the Dreadclaw's interior lumen.

'Manipulate? Me?' Xantine replied, playful outrage in his voice.

'You thought I would not check the arsenal logs? You ordered the Dreadclaws primed and the armour slaves to begin the blessing rituals before the conclave had met for the vote.'

'Of course, my friend,' Xantine said. 'What manner of leader would I be had I not prepared for all eventualities?' He smiled inwardly. He hadn't needed to leave such an obvious clue to his intentions, but it was hard to resist such a flourish. Xantine knew that his fastidious quartermaster would go snooping into the *Exhortation*'s records – only he and his coterie of dour obsessives truly cared about such trivialities on board the ship – and by preparing for battle before the decision to fight had been made, he proved his ability to outmanoeuvre his peers. Had the *Exhortation*'s reactor not been crippled by the attack from Serrine's still-active surface defences, then they might have been moving on from the planet – the vote had gone against him, after all – but it was better not to think of that.

It was much more enjoyable to revel in Sarquil's impotent irritation. It was the little things.

'And as a result of my preparation, the Adored were able to reach combat deployment capability sixty-eight point two-five-nine times faster than would otherwise have been possible,' Xantine continued, revelling in the chance to employ Sarquil's statistics against him. 'The rapier's strike should be accurate, but it is nothing if it is not *fast*, Sarquil – I expect you to know that.'

'That's not the point, Xantine. And of course I know that. It is I who designed our combat-readiness protocols, I who drills our troops, applying principles of perfection to our rabble.'

And they hate you for it, Xantine thought. Sarquil's drills lasted days and were grindingly dull – so dull that more than one of Xantine's warband had asked for the right to take the quartermaster's head in a duel. Xantine had demurred, however, preferring to leave Sarquil in his current position of relative power, at least for now. He might have been a devastatingly tiresome individual, but Sarquil was easily placated with material gains, and Xantine had to admit that his obsession with military precision had turned the Adored into a more effective fighting force.

'Truly, your work is appreciated,' Xantine said. 'I look forward to seeing its effect on the battlefield.'

Sarquil grumbled, opened his mouth as if to speak again, then closed it. He cast his eyes down to his chaincannon instead, and pulled the ammunition belt from its chamber, counting the shells individually for the fourth time that day.

The Dreadclaw was designed to carry ten Space Marines, but Xantine and Sarquil shared the space with only a handful of the Adored's elite. Not that they would be able to fit ten in, anyway – not with Lordling on board.

The massive warrior had been a Space Marine once, but he had grown beyond his armour's capacity to contain him. He was swollen now, pink and pudgy, his pendulous belly hanging over Mark IV greaves that had split under internal pressure, and were now held together with leather straps of some unknown provenance. Knowing Lordling's predilections, Xantine guessed it was human. Atop his bulk sat a hairless head held up by rolls of fat. His eyes were dark, and his mouth was pulled into a permanent rictus grin.

He grunted now, little puffs of confusion emanating from his slit mouth as he fiddled with his restraint harness. The creature had been forced to loop harnesses from three seats – each designed to house a warrior as large as a Space Marine – around his limbs to hold him in place during the turbulent journey from the bay of the *Exhortation* to the planet's surface.

'I trust you are comfortable, Lordling?' Xantine asked, glad of the distraction.

The huge warrior looked up with excitement in his eyes as the Dreadclaw shook, saliva foaming at the corner of his mouth in anticipation of the battle to come. He wrapped monstrous fingers around his harnesses to better secure himself in his makeshift seat. 'Guh!' he said.

'Good to hear!' Xantine replied, grateful at least that he could use the brute to extract himself from conversation with Sarquil.

Xantine found Lordling useful in myriad ways, his apparently simple comprehension of existence and easy malleability making him a useful bodyguard, but he was hardly a conversationalist: in all the years Lordling had served with the Adored, Xantine had never heard him utter an intelligible word.

Fortunately, there wasn't much time for extended conversation on their descent to Serrine. Xantine had toyed with the idea of making his entrance in *Tender Kiss*, but the Thunderhawk would present a tempting target for the attacking forces on the ground. Xantine had his suspicions about the rebels' cause and origins, but it was an unnecessary risk to bring a landing craft into the middle of a warzone. One lucky shot with a missile launcher could bring it down, turning a heroic entrance into an embarrassment.

No, it was much more fitting to arrive by Dreadclaw. The drop pod assault had been a favourite of the Emperor's Children from the days of the Great Crusade, a successfully orchestrated strike offering a heady mix of surprise, skill, and more than a little panache. They were used often in the Legion's legendary Maru Skara strategy – a two-pronged attack that followed the open blade with a hidden blade designed to decapitate an enemy force by identifying and slaughtering its leaders.

But while they wore the Legion's armour, even Xantine had to admit that the Adored did not have the power of the Emperor's Children in their pomp. The Legion would deploy its scouts and sentries, identify lines of weakness, and strike with such applied force that the enemy was crippled within hours. For his part, Xantine still didn't know who they were fighting on this world, let alone where he would find its leaders. Garbled reports from the useless Pierod had only described an unwashed mass, appearing inside the city as if they crawled from the pipes that ran beneath it.

Strike fast and hard, S'janth whispered. The daemon had grown more and more restless in her physical cage as she drew closer to the planet, the proximity of millions of souls rousing her consciousness.

'Yes, my dear, I am aware of how to fight. This is hardly my first battle.'

'Guh?' Lordling asked, looking over at Xantine's comment as the giant struggled again with his restraint harness.

'Nothing, Lordling,' he replied.

I am hardly nothing! S'janth bristled. *I am the temptress of the maiden moon, the devourer of the light of Suldaen, the crescendo–*

Xantine was delighted when the daemon's list of conquests was drowned out by the sudden roar of burning atmosphere outside. That meant they had covered the distance from the *Exhortation*'s launch tubes to the planet, and would be hitting the ground soon. In a matter of moments, the Dreadclaw would split open and disgorge Xantine on the surface. He would soon see a new city, a new sky, a new world. He would make it perfect.

He had taken a moment to compose himself after he stomped down the winding staircase to the command tower's bunker, out of view of the terrifying Space Marines, the gormless soldiers of the Sophisticant Sixth, and the damnable Frojean. He'd straightened his robes, adjusted his belt, and forced a cheer into his voice that he certainly didn't feel.

The bunker door was huge, made of reinforced plasteel, and criss-crossed with hydraulic bars. Still, the tallest Space Marine nearly filled the entrance, his huge finger stabbing the call button on the bunker's vox-unit.

The voices that came back over the boxy device were tiny and faint, the signal weakened by layers of protective ferrocrete, but Pierod could make out their meaning. They were squabbling.

The Space Marine pressed again, so hard that Pierod feared the unit would splinter. Finally, a single voice came back, shot through with a hint of panic.

'Who is that?'

Pierod recognised the voice of Governor Durant. Most of the planet would have recognised it, he wagered, such was the governor's predilection for addressing his populace.

'Open the door, mortal. The glorious Adored demand your fealty.'

'I beg your pardon?' Durant spluttered.

Courage rose in Pierod's heart – a rare sensation – and he stepped forward. 'My lord,' he asked the tall Space Marine, not daring to meet his gaze, 'if I may?'

The Space Marine twitched, as if preparing to strike him, but paused, and opened his palm instead. 'You have but a moment, before I open this door myself.'

Pierod keyed the vox, and spoke quickly. 'Lord Durant! It is Pierod, council member, and your humble servant!'

There was a brief discussion on the other end of the vox, and Pierod pretended not to hear as Durant asked his fellow parliamentarians who exactly he was talking to.

'Ah yes, Pierod. Treasurer Tenteville's assistant. What are you doing here, man? This location is reserved for high council members only. We do not have the resources in here for a man of your... appetites.' Even over the vox, Pierod could hear the condescension dripping from Durant's tone.

'No, my lord,' Pierod continued, keeping his voice light. 'I bring glad tidings – I have saved us all!'

There was a snort over the vox. *'And how, pray tell, have you done that, Pierod?'* Durant asked.

'I have orchestrated the arrival of the Adeptus Astartes. Astartes of the Emperor's Children, no less. Terra sends their most noble to answer our call.'

'This is some rebel trick,' Durant said. *'We have had no contact with the Imperium for three decades. Why would they appear now, on the very day that we are attacked from within?'*

'I... I do not know, sir. But I do know that they were able to blunt the rebel assault. They have demanded command of Serrine's remaining military forces, so that they may complete our liberation.'

There was a static buzz, as if Durant was considering the idea. 'Sir,' Pierod said. 'I have brought us salvation. Open the door, that we may be saved.'

Serrine's planetary council of nobles presented a sorry sight as they trudged up the stairs of the void port control centre. Separated from their elaborate dresses, multilayered robes and complicated wigs, they were crumpled creatures, clearly roused from their late-morning sleep by servants and soldiers before being whisked away to the safety of the bunker below. They wore nightgowns and undershirts, wrapping themselves in rugged blankets to stay warm.

In a few cases, they wore the evidence of last night's excesses. Garish bodysuits and sleek bodices marked out those whose evenings had run long at Serrine's various drinking establishments, before their pleasure was cut short by the arrival of extraction teams. Pierod almost pitied these souls. Lord Armand had crumpled against a nearby wall, his head cradled in his hands. He was moaning softly. Pierod had smelt the amasec on his breath as he filed out of the bunker, liquor whose after-effects were no doubt making this *dies horribilis* even more horrible.

The council had not been willing to leave the bunker, initially, but soon changed their mind when the tall Space Marine started cutting through the door with his massive power sword.

Durant's sneering cynicism had died on his face as seven-foot-tall warriors of the Imperium in shocking pink power armour strode into the bunker. Shock gave way to fear, and then a quiet awe, as it became apparent that Pierod had been telling the truth: not only had Serrine had its first contact with the Imperium in thirty years, it had come in the form of the Emperor's greatest warriors.

The rest of the council milled about now, throwing poorly

concealed glances at the Space Marines, and then at Pierod. They had followed Durant out of the bunker, calmed eventually by the Space Marine's brusque confirmation that they had neutralised the attacking forces. Any question as to the veracity of this statement was answered when the command tower's great double doors swung open, admitting a tiny woman so festooned in jewellery that she resembled an exotic bird.

She stepped into the vast hallway so lightly that she seemed to hover, her bare feet making no sound as they padded against the control centre's polished floor. Nor did she speak, and while she wore as much jewellery as a noble of Serrine, the planet's council members saw the uncanny strangeness in the woman, and recoiled from her presence. In some, it was a physical revulsion – Lady Musetta visibly shuddered as the woman walked past, drawing her attention. The newcomer turned her stooped head to face the council member, a wide smile breaking across her face. She stepped towards Lady Musetta, bringing her face close and closer still, until they were inches apart. Her skin was taut and fresh, pink and puffy, as if under the surface it was permanently inflamed – the telltale signs of rejuvenat therapy.

She tilted her head to the side, the necklaces on her stooped neck jangling together, and sniffed at Lady Musetta's throat. Musetta stifled a cry. Still inches from her, the tiny woman finally spoke.

'Not this one,' she said, in a desiccated voice that seemed to come from outside the room. Her breath smelled like rotten meat and stagnant water. It was almost enough to make Lady Musetta throw up.

The woman turned back to the room, leaving Musetta sobbing quietly, and resumed her slow padding, craning her neck to look at the other council members arranged around the room.

'I say,' Durant said, shaking off his shock and stepping forward, 'who do you think you are?'

The tiny woman ignored him, and continued inspecting council members in turn. Durant stepped forward again, but found his way barred by a needle-sharp blade, levelled in front of his chest like a barricade. He followed the blade back to its owner, and saw the handsome Space Marine holding it level in a one-handed stance.

'You will not interfere with Phaedre's work,' the Space Marine said in the voice of one explaining simple mathematics to a child. 'This will go much faster if you just sit down and shut up.'

Durant opened his mouth to speak again, but thought better of it as the Astartes flicked the blade's power source on, sending humming energy and dancing spurts of lightning down its length. The Space Marine gestured with the tip of the sword, and Durant sat back down, frowning.

The tiny woman stopped again in the middle of the room, and raised a bony finger at a bald man who had been studiously avoiding her gaze. Pierod recognised him from the Department of the Harvest. As this was one of the few arms of the council that had to make regular visits to the undercity, Pierod had made great pains to avoid contact with such representatives, lest the stink of the underclasses transfer onto him.

The woman's demeanour changed as the bald man realised she was looking at him, and met her gaze. Her smile, previously beatific, developed a hard edge as an expression of pure malice settled on her face. More unsettling was her speed. She was next to the bald man in an instant, covering the ten yards between them so fast that she seemed to teleport. A gasp ran around the room as she cupped his chin and tilted his head back, exposing his throat. Once again, she moved her face close to his bare skin and sniffed.

'Ahh, this is the one,' she sighed, seemingly to herself.

'What are you doing?' the man asked, his eyes wide. He tried to shake his head free of her grip, but she was apparently too strong. He brought his own hands to her wrist, pulling down to try to break their connection, but even with the size difference, and with his obvious exertion, she maintained her grip on his face.

'There are secrets in there, I can smell them,' she whispered. Jewels and links of precious metals tinkled together as the man struggled, but the woman didn't seem to notice.

'My lord, help me! Call this vermin off, please!' he shouted. Governor Durant looked over to the Space Marines, assessing the situation. The handsome one had removed his left gauntlet and was inspecting his nails, his power sword still active and held loosely in his right hand. The deformed one just appeared bored.

'She's hurting me!' the man squealed.

'It would be so delicious to give in, would it not... Balique?' Phaedre said in a cruel voice. 'Just tell me what I need to know.' She clasped her long fingers around the man's chin, squeezing his lips together.

'I don't know what you're talking about!' he said, his voice distorted. 'How do you know my name? What do you want from me?'

'I want to know where your leader is hiding, Balique,' Phaedre said. She was whispering into the man's ear, but some eldritch effect meant that every soul in the room could hear her demands. 'Just tell me that, and you will be free.'

'My leader is here, you maniac!' Balique moaned, flailing an arm at Governor Durant.

'No no, not him, silly. *Your* leader. Where is the Patriarch?'

True panic danced in Balique's deep-set eyes now, a flash of understanding that suggested he knew how much danger he was in.

'I... I... I can't tell you...' he said, stuttering over his words. Heads that had been careful to avoid meeting the man's gaze during his interrogation now snapped to face him, his answer indicating his culpability in the attack.

'Oh darling, of course you can,' Phaedre said, tracing her other hand down his reddening cheeks.

'No, no, you don't understand – I *can't* tell you. I *can't*,' he said, slowly tapping his temple with his free hand. 'I want to, believe me, I do. But the words...'

'A shame,' Phaedre said, pushing his face away. Free of her grasp, Balique massaged his jaw, staring up at the tiny woman with a wary look on his face.

'No matter. If you will not give me what I want, then I will make you pull it out.'

Phaedre's bracelets bounced as she raised a hand. The man's eyes widened as his hand moved suddenly. His fingers pulled together, making a wedge shape, before they pushed against the opening to his mouth, nudging and probing like a worm trying to make its way into a burrow.

Phaedre flicked her long fingers, and Balique's mouth was pulled into a rictus grin by the same unseen force that was controlling his limb. He tried to shout something, but his words were muffled by his own hand as it scrabbled and clawed to make its way past his teeth and tongue and down his throat.

'What was that?' Phaedre asked sweetly. 'You're ready to tell me?'

There was a strained gurgling sound as he tried to scream, but the sound died as Balique started to push his hand down his own throat.

'Shh now,' Phaedre said, leaning close once more. She placed her forehead against the man's own, and put her two hands to either side of his head. The air in the hall seemed to shimmer around the two of them, as something invisible passed from the man's mind into Phaedre's own.

With a sigh, she pulled Balique's head forward – his hand still in his own mouth – and planted a light kiss on his forehead. 'You have already given me everything I need to know,' she said in a sing-song voice.

Tears streaked down the side of the man's face now. Blood vessels in his eyes burst, decorating the white sclera with blooms of bright red. He fell to his knees, but still he pushed deeper, using his left arm for leverage until he was buried up to the elbow in his own gullet. For a moment, there was silence, any sounds choked off by the obstruction in his airway, before – with a heave and a wet plop – Balique pulled, yanking a fistful of his own innards out of his mouth. They hung limply in front of him for a moment, swaying gently as they dripped blood and other fluids onto the polished wooden floor, before he toppled face first into the bed of his own extracted organs.

Phaedre examined the dead man for a moment, a shy smile spreading across her lips, before she turned and padded away, her footsteps still silent.

'The Cathedral of the Bounteous Harvest. That is where we will find our prize.'

CHAPTER NINE

The sword was so heavy that he had to cradle it like a child to stop it scraping against the cathedral basement's polished stone floor. It was a ceremonial weapon, designed for display rather than actual combat, but Arqat knew the amount of money that went into forging these gifts for the church, and knew the blade would cut well enough. It wouldn't need to last long, anyway. He had no expectation of making it back to the crypt, of making it out of here alive at all, but if he could just take a few of these defilers out before they got him then he'd feel as though his life had been worth something.

They had the weapons and the numbers, but he had two advantages of his own: surprise, and righteous anger. Both were powerful weapons.

He had rejected this place, had longed for a different life. But now it had been attacked, invaded and desecrated, he realised he would defend it to the death. He burned with a rage that made him feel good, made him feel strong.

He imagined this was how his brother felt all the time. A sanctioned anger, hard and jagged, deployed against targets who deserved no mercy. It was intoxicating.

Arqat shivered as he imagined the feeling of the heavy sword digging through soft flesh. How deep would it cut? The edge – still sharp, he felt with a probing finger – would slice through skin and muscle, but would it get stuck in bone? Would he need to pull it out of a shoulder or even a skull? Would he have the strength? Would his enemies gurgle as they died? Would they squeal? Would they beg, cry or wail? He felt contentment as he thought about their deaths.

There was noise from upstairs. Footsteps on stone, dozens of them. He laid the sword down onto the stone floor, careful not to let it clatter, and stood on tiptoes to look out of a street-level glassaic window. His view was coloured red and blue by the glass, but he could see towering figures carrying a litter into the cathedral: open-topped, bearing a woman.

She radiated an aura that made her outline shimmer in the midday sun, a conquering hero at the head of her horde. It hurt Arqat's eyes to look at her. It hurt his head, too. He heard a buzzing, thrumming noise rising as he watched her, seemingly coming from inside his own skull. He groaned in pain, and his hand slipped from the window frame. He toppled to the floor, landing next to his sword. The buzzing had stopped, and he clasped his hand around the hilt.

Arqat pulled himself to his feet. His head was quiet now – as quiet as the basement itself – but he was not alone under the cathedral.

A man in filthy overalls stood close by, the material stained as pink as his skin. He cradled a weapon of some kind in his arms. Arqat couldn't see what type: the man had his back to Arqat as he stepped carefully through the cathedral's basement.

He wouldn't have known the weapon from sight, anyway. His brother, he of the planet's elite guard, would be able to identify the make and model of the gun right away. He could name its ammunition, hazard a guess at its age, and most likely strip it down to its constituent parts in a few short moments.

But his brother wasn't here. It was only Arqat, his borrowed sword, and the advantage of surprise. He walked with bare feet now, stepping slowly to avoid the slap of skin on stone, keeping to the shadows where he could. There were lots of shadows down here.

He planned his route. If he kept to the wall, he could bring the sword down on the man, cleaving him from shoulder to stomach. Or he could swing horizontally, taking him across the spine, incapacitating him for a slower kill. Or he could...

He was shaking. It was the cold, he told himself, the stone walls and his bare feet making his extremities numb. But it was more than the cold. He was scared. The man was so much bigger than him, his arms and legs wiry with muscle. Arqat had fought with his brother, but never with a stranger, never to kill.

But he wanted to try. He was *excited*, shaking with adrenaline coursing through his bloodstream. To kill, to maim, to unleash his anger to save his planet and his people from these unwashed interlopers.

He hefted the sword in a two-handed grip, and moved slowly, walking on the sides of his feet. He would run the man through, he decided, hoping that the momentum of the strike would make up for his inability to bring the heavy sword down with any real power. He pulled the blade up and tried to catch it in his hand, bracing the flat edge against his palm, ready for the attack.

He missed. The blade was unwieldy, and it sailed past his open palm to slam against the stone floor with a sound like a bell being rung. The filthy man wheeled around, raising his weapon as he searched for the source of the sound. Small eyes alighted on Arqat's slight form, his cassock draped over his skinny teenage body. Pointed teeth appeared in the man's mouth as he grinned, the expression of a hunter that had found smaller and weaker prey.

Suddenly, Arqat heard the rat-a-tat-tat of automatic weaponry, impossibly loud in the echoing confines of the cathedral's basement. Arqat squeezed his eyes shut and waited for the bullets to tear through his body. He had been so close.

The bullets didn't come for him. The filthy man blinked, beady eyes now wide in his bulbous skull. His gun – a rusted rifle, wrapped in rags and bandages – slipped from his fingers and clattered to the ground. As blood slowly added to the stains on his overalls, the man slumped to his knees, before toppling forward onto his face, dead.

'Target neutralised,' someone behind Arqat said. Two figures, a man and a woman, their shoulders broad and voices deep, ran past. They moved with long strides, and wore flowing magenta robes that Arqat recognised immediately: his brother's own uniform. These were Serrine's elite soldiers, the Sophisticant Sixth.

'Sweep complete. The basement is clear. What are your orders, my lord?'

The voice on the other end of the vox was deep and mellifluous, even with the signal distortion.

'Secure the building,' it said. *'And prepare for the arrival of his magnificence.'*

Father Tumas was scared. He was tired too, and so very, very old. He didn't partake in the rejuvenat therapies so common to Serrine, unlike most of his congregation, but he had lived a long life anyway, his body strengthened by the finest foods and healed in times of sickness by the best physicians in the overcity.

His cathedral was the largest on the planet, the de facto focal point for the planet's noble families to show both their piety and their generosity – when it suited them.

His position had given him power and influence, but he didn't much want either. He just wanted to tend to the cathedral.

He had done that successfully for seventy years: sweeping its tiled floors, cleaning streaks from its glassaic windows, and – his favourite job of all – dusting its beautifully painted ceiling frescos.

The glassaic had been smashed, the tiles had been cracked, and the ancient wooden doors had been blown open by yellow-eyed men with guns. 'Monsters,' he whispered under his breath as he hid. 'How dare you desecrate this sacred place?'

They had walked the cathedral, those men, talking in hushed tones, setting up defensive positions with huge, tripod-mounted weapons. They were preparing for something, he realised, their quiet industry focused on making the space safe for someone, or something else.

They searched for survivors, too. He saw them find one of those unfortunate souls – a man he recognised, who had fled to the cathedral seeking succour when the attack started. He had been a pious man, a rarity for Serrine, but even he had been willing to renounce the Emperor when the men found him and dragged him from his hiding place. His desperate pleas hadn't done any good, though: they put their filthy boots on his neck and shot him in the head just the same. His blood splattered the pews, staining books centuries old and priceless in value.

Something else had come now – something horrific, something profane. 'Oh!' he whimpered as he heard it move, the clang of something huge climbing through the pipe that had given life to his cathedral, to his planet. It hurt his head and broke his heart to have to live through such desecration.

At least he still had the ceiling. He looked up and saw the Saviour, his likeness painted by an artist whose name had been lost to the millennia. He saw the most precious piece of art in the most precious building on all of Serrine. They could not take this from him.

And then he saw it explode.

He had no time to identify what it was that caused the destruction. A pod, rendered in Imperial purple and shining gold, landing claws extended like the talons of some great hunting bird.

He saw the ceiling irrecoverably shattered, and his old mind started to process the sensation. Synapses fired and chemicals in his brain swelled, preparing a cocktail of shock, fury, horror and abject sadness.

But, a small mercy on a dark day, Tumas never felt those emotions. Tumas felt nothing else after Xantine's drop pod landed on him, his mind – like the rest of his body – now little more than a smoky smear of matter streaked across the cathedral's broken floor. Nothing more than the total obliteration of self.

The Dreadclaw's doors opened all at once, falling to the cathedral's polished floor like the unfurling petals of an exotic flower. Dust and debris from the collapsed ceiling swirled, shrouding the pod's interior from view.

There was blessed quiet for a moment, the sound of close gunfire halted by the sudden arrival of a bolt from heaven. The cultists in the Cathedral of the Bounteous Harvest stared, needle teeth visible in mouths stunned into silence.

When the silence was broken, it snapped in two places at once. At the front of the cathedral there was a series of explosions, chased by the sound of shouts and screams. Two voices guided the tumult: one strident and clear, one bassy and low. They spoke the same command:

'Forward!'

In the middle of the cathedral, a raw chattering issued forth from the interior of the royal purple pod, a cacophonous sound joined by bursts of light that illuminated the settling smoke.

Cultists were torn apart as bolt-shells detonated inside their bodies, showering the ancient cathedral's interior with the profane taint of xenos blood. Behind this covering fusillade, a figure lumbered from the pod's interior. The blooms of light could only render it in silhouette, but even compared to the assorted cultists, mutants, and genestealers that had set up their base of operations in the cathedral, it was huge. It broke into a lolloping run as it cleared the cloud of debris, resolving itself into view just moments before it swung an electrically charged zweihander into the closest group of cultists.

Their bodies split, bisected cleanly by the force of the blow, and Lordling laughed as he brought the sword around for another swing. It was a high-pitched sound, cruel and clear even over the sounds of battle emanating from outside. From his position inside the Dreadclaw, Xantine savoured the shock of his arrival on the world, the sensation of the cultists' fear and confusion almost palpable in the musty air. He checked his weapons, languidly preparing himself for the combat to come. He twirled Anguish in a reverse grip, striking a staccato beat against the serrated blades that stood up along his purple greaves, each one carefully shaped to resemble an eagle's wing. At his hip, he carried his bolt pistol. Like many of the Adored, the weapon had changed after centuries sailing the Eye of Terror. Its handle was fleshy now, and warm to the touch. The pistol seemed to understand its purpose, too, sighing in apparent contentment as its bolts found the soft meat of Xantine's targets and blew them apart. He had taken to calling the weapon the Pleasure of the Flesh.

'They are regrouping, Xantine,' Sarquil said. The quartermaster stood at the lip of the Dreadclaw's ramp, his purple Tartaros armour almost obscuring the pod's opening. 'Are you quite ready?'

'The hidden blade stays sheathed until the perfect moment to strike,' Xantine replied. He had been poised to rise from his restraint harness, but after Sarquil's comment, decided to linger a moment longer. He adjusted the golden circlet that he wore around his head, ensuring once more that it would keep his long black hair in place. He stood, finally ready to taste the blood of this world.

'Children of Serrine!' the beautiful woman screamed as a detonation rocked the front of the Cathedral of the Bounteous Harvest. She stood in the apse of the huge structure, given pride of place at the top of worn stone steps in the building's north side. Behind her lay the point of worship for the congregation: the vast pipe that carried the Solipsus sap to the city's void port.

Hundreds of heads turned to regard her, momentarily distracted by the sounds of battle. There were humans in the crowd, their eyes glassy, and their crude weapons hanging limp in loose grips. They stood alongside beings that played at humanity. They shared the same general structure as their peers – two arms, two legs, two eyes and ears – but their genetic material was markedly alien, as their ridged foreheads and clawed fingers made clear.

Still others were more visibly xenos. Three-armed hybrids wore robes and stained overalls, the trappings of humanity – harvesting tools, autopistols, respirators and goggles – perverse in their clawed grips or strapped to bulbous, waxy heads. They coaxed and corralled aberrants: heavily muscled monsters with distorted heads and tiny, dim-witted minds, only truly capable of comprehending violence. In the shadows of the aisle, four-armed genestealers stood swaying, their fast-twitch muscles and alien synapses unused to a lack of motion. Some of their number climbed the walls, their talons digging into the ancient rock, making them appear as apocryphal gargoyles brought to life.

These genestealers were the fastest to react as a purple pod smashed through the cathedral's roof, slamming into the stone floor with a bone-shuddering impact. They moved in silence, joined by two groups of hybrid cultists who peeled away from the congregation, wordlessly responding to the need for additional troops to deal with this unexpected threat.

This moment had been chosen: the world had been seeded effectively, with genestealer hybrids present in all rungs of society, and the wider populations of the under- and overcities either too downtrodden or indolent to be able to defend against an armed insurrection. That they appeared to be putting up such a fight, and with such powerful weapons, was troubling.

No matter. They were so close now.

'Children,' she called again, attracting focused attention once more. 'We have risen from the dust and dirt of this world, and we stand now in its most holy place.' She gestured towards the curved apse of the cathedral, the huge glassaic windows now cracked and smashed. The pipe rose up from below, a conspicuously industrial presence in the ornate building. 'But this is a place of false gods,' she said, venom injected into her voice.

Soldiers had breached the cathedral now, the woman knew. She saw through the eyes of her acolytes as they fought and died to prepare the space for their master's arrival. She saw muscular humans in bright robes, with warriors in purple among their number, taller and far faster than their peers. Some of these warriors used strange weapons that seemed to fire concentrated bursts of sound, and she winced as she felt the acolytes' eardrums burst and their brains liquefy in their heads.

'The Imperium has forsaken us,' she continued, rushing now. Purple-armoured giants had stepped from the pod, and were carving through her brothers and sisters with furious speed.

'The Emperor is dead,' she said, projecting certainty and finality with her mind. Wails of sadness filled the cathedral, as those true humans under the woman's psychic spell reacted to this pronouncement, said as it was with such certainty.

'Do not weep, my children. You have been manipulated, lied to and abused, but you have risen now. Your tormentors were correct in their prophecies – Serrine will indeed have its saviour, but he will not come from the heavens.'

There was a noise from inside the pipe. A rhythmic thumping that seemed to be getting louder, audible even over the increasing sounds of battle from outside.

'No. Our Saviour comes from below!'

The creature had lain on this world for generations in the darkness. As countless harvests came and went, as families rose and fell, as the wider Imperium took less and less notice of Serrine, until, one night, the sky was torn open and the huge voidships stopped coming to collect their cargo. It watched. It waited. It survived.

It was not idle. It could not *be* idle; idleness wasn't something coded into its finely honed genetic balance. It was a forerunner, a precursor, built to live – and kill – alone, moving fast, striking faster. It was the survival of a whole species, distilled into one creature. One perfect creature.

Not quite perfect. It was not lonely, because, once again, such an organism could not comprehend such a sensation. But it *yearned*. It yearned for its brood. It had called for them, and they had answered. They surrounded it now.

That was still not enough. It wanted more, this near-perfect creature. It knew, somehow, on some base level, that it was only part of a whole. A thing, a consciousness, that spanned the whole galaxy. Spanned even further than that, across unimaginable distances, across the cold void between the agglomeration of stars, across the construct of time.

That time meant nothing to this consciousness. There was only hunger. There was only yearning.

Soon, this being would call for this consciousness. It would reach out with its mind, searching the spaces between the stars for the brood that birthed it. It would find them, after so many millennia, and it would transmit just one thought.

We are here.

But there was work to be done first. First it would take control of its brood, then, together, they would make this world their own; make it ready to be enveloped into the glorious whole.

Xantine stepped from the Dreadclaw and surveyed the scene. The pod had come down through the roof on the eastern side of the vast cathedral, placing the largest mass of genestealer cultists between the force led by Vavisk and Torachon currently breaching the cathedral through its front door, and his personal retinue.

'The perfect blade,' he said through a smile.

His Adored were beacons of riotous colour amongst the drab tones of humanity that had already swarmed them. Recovered now from the shock of the Dreadclaw's arrival, dozens of filthy cultists, mutants, and full-blown xenos creatures clawed at their pink-and-purple power armour, their fingers and talons trying to find purchase in perfection.

There was none.

Sarquil fired his chaincannon in staccato bursts, conserving his precious ammunition by selecting high-value targets. Less threatening foes – hybrids, acolytes, and humans won over to the cult's cause – he simply swatted with his power fist, sending crumpled and broken bodies to the floor.

Lordling pulled his sword back and forth through the throngs of people, grunting with effort. Unlucky cultists were split open where the sword's edge caught bare skin, their blood and organs cascading onto the warm stone. Others were simply batted aside, the huge weapon used as a club as much as a blade. Some remained where they lay, spines snapped and ribs broken, but others stood back up and tried to rush at their attacker, cradling gaping wounds.

Euratio and Orlan, the silver-masked twins, stood back to back, their bolters firing to the same rhythm. Filo Eros stood apart, calling forth challengers with a raised palm, before cutting them down with a swing of his heavy sabre.

Threats remained. Genestealers surged across broken masonry and along carved walls, serrated teeth gnashing; huge aberrants swung man-sized blades and heavy hammers; metamorphs lashed fleshy whips and flexed chitinous claws capable of crushing even a Space Marine's bones.

Xantine discounted them all. He scanned transhuman eyes across the interior of the ancient building, looking for the head of this particular serpent.

'There,' he whispered. She was small and slight in stature, but given her position – standing in front of the pipe that the cathedral appeared designed to venerate – and her deft control of the crowd, Xantine knew she was in command of this rabble.

Good. She would be an easy kill. Xantine would make it look harder, of course, for the audience.

Not in command, S'janth whispered.

'What?' Xantine asked, out loud, irritated by the suggestion that he had misjudged the situation.

Not in command, the daemon said again. *There is… something else.*

S'janth was wary – surprisingly so. As expected, the daemon's consciousness had risen in his body as he drew closer to the planet and its wellspring of souls. But he expected confidence, impetuous and imperious, married to her perpetual gnawing desire. Instead, she bristled in his body now, her soul jangling, on edge. Xantine had never felt such a sensation from the daemon.

He ignored her.

'I am Xantine, magnificence of the Adored, paragon of the perfect Third, and the deliverer of your blessed release,' he called, levelling Anguish at the woman on the stage. Grotesque heads turned, and xenos-tainted humans sprinted at Xantine. He drew the Pleasures of the Flesh and shot one, two, three as they ran. They fell into each other, driven back by the concussive force of the bolts. He spun the rapier with his other hand, carving through the kneecaps of a fourth. The mutant tried to haul itself up on its three arms, but Xantine twirled Anguish and jabbed it downwards, neatly sliding its monomolecular edge into the mutant's enlarged brainpan.

It is coming, S'janth said in his mind. She was still cautious, like a feline with its back against the wall, its fur on end. Strange.

From the woman on the stage, there was no acknowledgement of Xantine's spectacular arrival. She kept her gaze aimed at her congregation, her words too quiet for Xantine to hear over the din of battle both inside and outside the cathedral.

Her insolence irritated him.

'I challenge you, xenos scum,' Xantine called again, jabbing his now-blooded rapier in her direction. 'I have conquered worlds and savoured the fruits of the galaxy. It will be your pleasure to be destroyed by me.'

She turned then, fixing Xantine with slitted eyes. Her congregation turned, too, as one, beholding him as one organism.

He felt xenos eyes on every inch of his body. 'Good!' He smiled, twirling the rapier in his palm as he strode towards his foes. 'Good!'

She continued her ceremony even as he dispatched her outriders, gesturing at the huge pipe above her head. Her words were still inaudible, even to his transhuman hearing, but her lips kept moving. Thin and pink, they danced in her hairless head. Behind them, he saw pointed teeth and a tongue that forked, like a lizard's. Like an alien's.

He realised she was not talking at all. No sound left her mouth, yet the congregation listened, rapt.

He roared, his surgically augmented voice echoing forcefully from the cathedral's walls. 'I will cut off your head, snake, and your body will die. Thank your maker that you are to be killed by the glorious...'

He tailed off as a crushing pressure in his head constricted his vision. It had been a background hum, he realised, there from the moment he arrived in the cathedral, but it had been previously unnoticeable until it had risen in tone and tenor. It drowned his thoughts now. There were words amidst the cloud, but they weren't for him. They spoke in a language he didn't know, with a consciousness he couldn't comprehend.

It is almost here, S'janth said in a lilting voice, like a child's. He could barely concentrate on her meaning. *I can taste its power.*

A reverberation brought him back to the moment. He took in his surroundings: the gore and the broken glass, the stink of filthy humans, and the septic stench of xenos creatures.

There *was* something, moving in the pipe. S'janth had been right, Xantine realised with a pang of annoyance. The woman wasn't the commander of this rabble. She was just its envoy, guiding them to this place to call forth their true leader.

I warned you, S'janth said. **You cannot defeat this foe. Run, while we can.**

'It… is… nothing,' Xantine said through gritted teeth. 'I will kill it,' he swore, his voice rising in volume. 'And kill you all!'

A claw as long as a human forearm pierced the thick metal of the pipe with a terrible shearing sound. It stuck there for a moment, finding purchase, before it was joined by a second. The cathedral reverberated with the noise of their impact, the sound running the length of the pipe like thunder through the sky.

Then they pulled downwards. The claws tore through the inches-thick metal as if it was parchment, digging wide furrows in the millennia-old pipe, exposing a passageway that had only been used for the transfer of Solipsus sap to the planet's main void port since Serrine's compliance.

A hand appeared through the ragged hole. It was purple-skinned and long – too long – split by too many knuckles and with pointed black nails that looked to be as sharp and strong as the larger claws. They glinted like obsidian in the gloom of the cathedral.

Another hand appeared, and another, and another. The four arms braced themselves around the edges of the makeshift exit, and pulled, widening the hole with awful screams of tortured metal.

Eyes appeared in the black, shining yellow with a malevolent, alien hunger. Teeth followed, diamond-sharp and split by a long tongue that probed at the damp air of the stone cathedral like a snake tasting for prey. It pulled the rest of its head through the hole, exposing a swollen brain that pulsed in its alien skull, the ridges and fibres visibly contracting and expanding as it calculated its next move.

The creature – the Patriarch – pulled the last of its chitinous body out of the pipe. It unfurled, drawing itself up to a height twice that of a Space Marine, and screeched.

'Behold!' the beautiful woman called to a mass of humans, near-humans, and genetic hybrids over the din. 'Our Saviour!'

CHAPTER TEN

The creature killed Filo Eros first. He had been the closest of the Adored to the new threat, and, thrilled by his own luck, took the chance to claim the glory of the kill for himself. He had hefted his heavy sabre in two hands and sprinted straight for the Patriarch, battering cultists aside with the sheer concussive force of his transhuman charge.

The creature barely glanced in Eros' direction as it flicked its tail – long, corded with muscle, ridged with chitin, and ending with a curved barb – through the layer of ceramite that protected his stomach. It lifted him from the ground as it drove the barb deeper, tearing through abdominal muscles and intestines first before aiming upwards, puncturing his diaphragm, and settling between his lungs. There, it convulsed, pumping viscous black venom into Eros' chest cavity.

Xantine saw none of this detail. He simply saw his brother's mouth foam with dark spittle as he lolled, impaled on the creature's tail; saw him convulse, silently, as the beast deposited him to the cathedral floor slowly, almost tenderly.

Xantine watched as the poison worked with cold efficiency, as his brother of a hundred conflicts, of a thousand years of shared existence, twitched and sucked in his last gasp of damp air.

'I shall have to secure a sample of that,' Xantine said, under his breath.

At his shoulder, Sarquil raised his chaincannon, taking aim at the monster. 'No!' Xantine commanded, slapping the weapon down with an open palm. Its multiple barrels were blazing hot to the touch, even through Xantine's gauntlets. 'Have some decorum, Sarquil. This foe is mine.'

Sarquil opened his mouth, ready to argue, then thought better of it. He checked his chaincannon's ammunition counter and shrugged, his huge Tartaros Terminator plate whirring musically with the motion. 'So be it,' he said, turning to resight his weapon on a hunting pack of genestealers attempting to conceal their advance on the Dreadclaw's position.

The Patriarch scanned the cathedral, eyes unblinking. Its swollen skull pulsed, the beats in time with the waves of pressure in Xantine's mind.

There was another restless presence alongside it. S'janth prowled the edges of his consciousness, her wariness turned into full-blown terror.

Run, she urged. *Run, run while we can.*

No, he shot back, his transhuman system flooding with adrenaline and other stimulants of more exotic provenance, in anticipation for the battle to come. S'janth repeated the command, more insistent this time.

Run, she said. *Run, run, run.*

The word became a percussive drumbeat in Xantine's head as the monster's eyes alighted on his own, irises of turquoise and yellow meeting across a shattered world of dust grey and dirt brown.

He would not run. He would kill this abomination, on his own, and be worshipped for the feat.

Runrunrunrunrun...

Enough! he screamed in his own mind, loud enough to drown out the daemon's insistent demands. *I am Xantine, lord of the Adored, and there is no enemy I cannot lay low.*

He levelled Anguish once again, pointing it at the massive xenos creature. He hated to repeat himself, but there were standards to maintain.

'I am Xantine,' he began again, 'magnificence of the Adored, paragon of the perfect Third, and–'

The rest of his challenge became a strangled cry as the Patriarch leapt at him, its claws raking polished purple ceramite as it launched him backwards, sending him skidding into a pile of collapsed masonry.

Xantine's vision swam, the force of the impact exacerbated by the psychic pressure in his head from the proximity of the Patriarch. More by impulse than intent, he leapt to his feet, adopting a Chemosian duelling stance as he allowed his senses to examine his wounds. He found a catalogue of sensation.

Pain, in his fused ribs, dull and distant. Like storm clouds on the edge of a city. He tasted blood in his mouth, rich and ripe, like wine.

This is no xenos half-breed, S'janth said. *If you will not run, then I will. Let me in, lover. Share your flesh, give me your sensation, and together we can escape this doomed world.*

She was wheedling him now, her desperation leading her to cajole him in ways that only she knew. Ways that had worked many times before. He could feel her power – still not fully restored to her former glory, but *strong*. Standing in the wreckage of the Cathedral of the Bounteous Harvest, Xantine wanted to sink into her, to give himself to her, to feel her use his body with that power, that grace.

Vavisk's face flashed in his mind, his bass voice rumbling. *'You have shackled yourself to this thing that wears your skin.'*

The words were needles that pierced his pride. They stung worse than the pain in his ribs.

'No!' he roared. He was furious at S'janth for questioning his skill, at Vavisk for questioning his leadership, and at the xenos monstrosity that was currently raking its claws through his pink-clad Adored. Xantine bit hard into his anger, chewing it, tasting it, using it as fuel.

'I *will* kill you, beast,' he spat.

The cathedral was engulfed in a melee. Figures in the bright robes of the planet's elite guard were pushing their way into the vast space, ascending side stairs from unseen basements and scrambling through gaps in the broken windows. They were setting up firing positions, using crumbled columns and smashed statues as barricades, felling cultists by the dozen as they were able to bring their gold-inlaid lasguns to bear. Still they came, climbing over the corpses of their xenos-tainted brethren, giving their lives willingly to protect the huge beast that stalked between the pews.

'Help, my lord!' one soldier in magenta robes called. A gene-stealer talon was embedded in her leg, pinning her to the stone floor. She had crippled the creature, and its legs dragged limply behind it, a cauterised hole visible above the knee in each. But still it crawled forward, a cold light in its yellow eyes, sharp teeth gnashing.

'My weapon,' she gasped, scrabbling for a lasgun that lay among the detritus from the cathedral, just out of reach of her grasping hands. It would be a triviality to kick it to her.

Instead, Xantine allowed the creature to move closer – so close that it could almost reach the woman's incapacitated leg – before he brought his boot down on its skull. She looked up at him, a mixture of awe and terror written on her sweat-streaked face.

Pleasure: the thrill of death, so close, so final. A minuscule lurch in the stomach, unmoored, like flying.

His eyes were fixed on the Patriarch again. The creature had turned its back on him, and he would punish it for its impudence.

'Good!' Xantine called, forcing a snide humour into his voice, projecting it loud enough that it could be heard even over the din of battle. 'Good! Finally, I have been blessed with a worthy foe!'

The Patriarch turned, and Xantine thought he registered surprise in its alien eyes. The blow that knocked him to the ground would've bisected a typical human. But he was no typical human.

He started to circle the creature, his rapier held in a light grip, its monomolecular tip piercing the air.

'I am Xantine, magnificence of the Adored, and paragon of the perfect Third. You – well, you may have brute strength, but I have killed a thousand of your kind.' He spun the rapier, its power field thrumming. 'Come, that I may kill you, and make this world my own.'

The Patriarch stalked towards him, slower this time, taking a moment to size up this larger, more resilient prey. It was wary of him. That was good.

Pleasure: satisfaction rippling out from his prefrontal cortex, through his nerves and muscles. A wave of satisfaction, cold and delicious, like ice water, salving the pain in his chest.

The Patriarch leapt, its talons extended for a decapitating strike. Xantine knew it was coming this time, and ducked to the left, thrusting Anguish upwards in two hands to impale the monster through its throat. It was an ostentatious strike that would see the Patriarch doom itself: the most perfect killing cut of all.

'You are too...' he called as the Patriarch twisted in the air, wrenching its alien body in a way impossible for humans – impossible even for transhumans. 'Slow,' he finished, as the creature brought a huge talon down across his wrist, sending his rapier skittering across the cathedral floor.

Pain: sickly in its warmth and wetness, the result of a blow that would have severed his hand were it not for his armour. He is naked without his weapon, a moment of vulnerability.

Let me in, S'janth whispered, choosing her moment.

'No,' Xantine grunted, forced to parry an unexpected swipe from the Patriarch on his spiked gauntlets. The force of the blow sent him staggering backwards, skidding on the uneven floor of the damaged cathedral, away from the rapier.

Let me join you, my love. Share your body with me, so that we may live to savour the galaxy together.

Xantine brought the Pleasure of the Flesh up in one motion, pulling the pistol from its soft leather holster and pumping three shots in the direction of the Patriarch. The bolts struck their target, but the alien was bounding across the chamber, already too close, and its thick chitin sent the mass-reactive rounds pinging off into the depths of the cathedral. Xantine heard distant screams as they exploded amongst human and xenos bodies alike.

The Patriarch was on him again, and without Anguish, he was forced into a duellist's stance, arms held forward to either deflect or, better, avoid its blows. Xantine, like most of his Legion, had trained extensively in bladework, but the creature was relentless, its alien physiology rendering it seemingly immune to fatigue.

It brought its talons down again and again, scything at air until eventually, inevitably, Xantine mistimed a feint, and the Patriarch's talons found their target. They dug deep into his upper arm, slicing through the silver-and-gold chains that hung from his marbled pauldron until they reached transhuman flesh.

Pain: in his upper left arm, bone deep. Hot and sharp and localised, like exposure to a miniature sun.

Xantine yowled and rolled with the blow. The movement softened the impact slightly, ensuring his arm wasn't severed completely.

He was panting now. Bleeding, too, the gash in his arm deep enough to defy the enhanced clotting agents in his blood. He felt the blood on his skin, felt it as it cooled and became tacky, his advanced physiology trying to staunch the flow and close the wound. He felt S'janth in his soul, empowered and emboldened by the spike of agony she had tasted.

The Patriarch closed on him again. Xantine scanned the cathedral, searching for flashes of purple and pink amidst the mass. He was looking for help, but found none.

'Sarquil,' he gasped over the vox, trying to slow his breathing. His quartermaster opened his own channel, the rhythmic sound of his chaincannon audible in the background.

'Yes?' Sarquil asked. There was no pretence to decorum for the Terminator now, and certainly no honorific for his warlord.

'I have reconsidered my position,' Xantine said, spitting bloody saliva. 'Would you care to join me in felling this beast?'

'Not at all, my lord,' Sarquil replied. The smile on his face was evident even over the vox. 'I would not want to usurp your great honour.' Xantine heard the chatter of Sarquil's chaincannon as it chewed through mutant bodies. 'Besides, I am certain that you have the matter entirely in hand.'

'Bastard,' Xantine hissed, closing the vox-connection a moment later. He tried to attract the attention of Lordling, but the giant was lost to his bloodlust, shrieking as he dragged his massive zweihander through cultists, even as they dug claws and blades into his back like crampons and climbed his massive frame. He was shrieking from his slit mouth, his eyes rolling in his head. With pain or pleasure, Xantine could not be sure.

He opened the vox again, blink-clicking to his command-level frequency. 'Vavisk, Torachon, do you copy? Where *are* you?'

Torachon's voice came back a moment later.

'A thousand apologies, my lord,' the vat-grown Space Marine said. *'We are facing surprising resistance at the cathedral entrance. Something seems to have rallied these abject wretches.'*

Xantine had seen it too. The Patriarch's arrival had galvanised the cultists, who fought now with absolute disregard for their own lives. Theirs wasn't the wild, howling abandon of the Pantheon's cults, their morale as fickle as their loyalties. Instead, they battled with cold, alien efficiency, bearing trauma that would send a typical mortal into lethal shock with dead eyes and rictus snarls.

He was on his own.

Not quite true. He was never on his own.

Behind you, my love, S'janth said.

The Patriarch swung a balled fist into his back.

Pain: like an asteroid impact on a planet's surface. A spine, bent to almost breaking point, bruised ribs battered further.

Xantine was off his feet before he'd registered the pain. He skidded across the cathedral floor again, scraping pink and purple from his elaborate armour. He heard a machine whine and sputter, and realised the blow had been hard enough to shatter the ceramite casing of his backpack's power core. The sound was joined by a low rumble, like a carnodon purring. He looked around the cathedral, craning his abused neck, for the source of the strange sound, before he realised it was coming from inside his head. *So sweet,* she whispered, her caution and fear giving way to pleasure at his pain. She was swelling inside his body, using that pain as fuel.

Xantine looked up to see the Patriarch looming over him. Acidic saliva dripped from its needle teeth. It took his head in its hand. The fingers were cable-strong as they closed around his skull. For a moment, it held Xantine's head in place, cradling it carefully, like a mother would hold a baby.

Then it slammed his head down, smashing skin and skull against the stone floor.

Pain: in his head, sharp and loud, like an explosion in both of his ears.

SLAM

Pain: in his head, white and blinding, like a sun exploding.

Yes! S'janth says, ecstatic. *Yes!*

SLAM

Pain: in his head, the worst pain, the sickening pain of bone cracking and breaking.

More, more, MORE! she screams.

SLAM

The pain is overwhelming. It is absolute.

Xantine starts laughing. He looks up at this grossly proportioned thing, this walking nightmare, this disgusting attempt at perfection of form. It is hideous.

'Savour...' he cries, through foaming blood in his mouth.

SLAM

'Your...'

SLAM

'Last...'

SLAM

'Breath...'

LET ME IN! the daemon in his head cries.

He feels the pain, truly feels it, as only a transhuman can. He knows every inch of his body, every organ, every bone, every artery. They are aflame now, and he wants to remember this sensation: this perfect agony.

And then he lets her in. She is warm, and there is no pain. She wants to take his body, but she cannot, not yet, so they share it, joining their power.

They are powerful. So very, *very* powerful.

The Patriarch is fast, but he – they – are faster, now. He watches as the creature slashes for his throat with a taloned arm, and he catches the limb in flight, holding it with minimal exertion. He looks at the arm, and his eyes take in the creature in more detail than he thought possible.

He can see the ridges and whorls in its chitin, an individual fingerprint for a creature of a hive mind. He can feel the throbbing of corrosive blood under its skin, so chemically different from his own. He can smell its stink: of sewers and filth, both human and xenos.

He sees it as she sees it, in the framework of sensation. Rough and smooth, light and dark, pleasure and… pain.

He places the palm of his other hand around the Patriarch's arm, and gently, carefully wraps his armoured fingers around it. He tests the weight, the tensile strength of the xenos biology, sliding his hands along the limb to find the proper purchase.

Xantine breaks the arm. The chitin casing shatters, firing dark purple shards into the air where they hang for a moment, twinkling like stars. Blood fills the ragged hole, dark, thick, and stinking of ozone.

The Patriarch screams. The sound is a high-pitched screech to everyone else in the cathedral, but to Xantine, the sound is long and low, as stretched out as his reality. It is screaming in pain, in rage, in whatever emotion – or approximation of emotion – that it can feel. He drinks it in, and even with its potency dulled by distance and separation, it has a strange purity.

The Patriarch spins away, leaving its broken arm in Xantine's hands. It flails with its stump as it tries to balance on the uneven floor, and Xantine finds himself taking the chance to retrieve his rapier from the floor of the cathedral.

A wise choice, he thinks, where no one can hear him. This thing is wounded, and S'janth is growing stronger on a surfeit of pain, but it is still lethal, still an apex predator on this world of prey.

The Patriarch rushes him, slicing down with another taloned arm: its second of four. He dances out of the curve of the blow, and digs the rapier's tip in through the Patriarch's armpit. Even here, the armour is thick, but – grudging praise to those perfidious aeldari smiths – the slender blade slips through to the shoulder, cutting through tendon and bone, through nerves and whatever else these creatures hide under their outer shells.

The Patriarch's momentum is still carrying it forward, and Xantine wraps its arm around himself in a perversion of an embrace. Xantine finds himself cradled in the bosom of a xenos alpha strain for a millisecond, before he is spinning, tearing the second arm loose at the joint. The limb separates and Xantine sends it caroming into a mass of cultists, showering them with caustic gore. They scream, in pain and sadness, and it is a delightful sound.

The Patriarch stumbles, its missing limbs throwing off its preternatural balance, and its clawed foot slips in a slick of purple gore. It falls and splays out. Cultists rush to its side, placing their hands on its chitinous hide, trying to help it up. It flails with a bone talon and shreds the closest of their number, carving through bone and organs and gristle as it pulls itself back to its feet.

It turns and sprints towards Xantine now, loping like a canid, barrelling genestealers and mutants out of the way. Liquids are leaking from its damaged body – oily blood from the stumps of its arms, stringy saliva from its fanged mouth.

'*Xantine,*' he hears over the vox. The voice is faint to him, but he knows it is violently loud in reality, distorted and devastating.

It is Vavisk.

'*We have breached the cathedral,*' he says. There are no honorifics in his speech. There never are. '*We will be with you in a moment.*'

Ahead of schedule, but no matter. The kill will still be theirs.

Surgical augmentation has made his voice a weapon, and while he lacks the raw power of a devotee of noise such as Vavisk, it is still a hammer blow when projected with such force. The wave of sound hits the Patriarch as it leaps, and it overcorrects, twisting predictably in the air. Xantine slides smoothly to intercept it, holding his rapier in two hands. The tip of the weapon enters its fanged mouth. Xantine braces, power-armoured boots skidding on the cathedral floor, and feels as the monomolecular blade slips down the monster's throat, slicing through muscle, tissue, and major organs on its journey into the creature's guts.

The Patriarch's momentum arrested, Xantine lets the tip of the rapier fall to the ground. The creature drops with it, still skewered on the aeldari weapon. It is still alive, and it stares, yellow eyes wide, as blood bubbles up its throat to mix with its stinking saliva. It forms a dark foam along the length of the blade that sends a shiver of disgust through Xantine's floating consciousness.

He thrusts the tip of the rapier down, out through the Patriarch's stomach. It slides easily into the cathedral's stone floor, pinning the beast in place like an insect in a collection. It flails and claws at him, but Xantine watches himself avoid its grasping swipes expertly, so slow they seem to his divorced reality.

He knows the daemon's next move. She ignores the melee

around her, ignores the dying screams of humans and mutants alike. Their pain, their misery: these are crumbs of sensation to a sublime being such as S'janth. She wants something new, something exhilarating, something she has never tasted before.

Xantine takes up a long blade, discarded in the melee. It's rusty and well used, one end wrapped in dirty material that form a grip. It's a makeshift weapon, with no art to its construction, no balance to its heft. But it will cut. It will do.

He takes the Patriarch's leg in his armoured hands. The thing kicks frantically, as if its life depends on it. *It does*, he thinks, with detached amusement. He is stronger; more accurately, the daemon inside his body, gorged on pain and pleasure, is stronger. He rakes the eagle-wing blades on his vambraces across the Patriarch's inner thigh, gouging deep enough – he thinks – to sever nerves. Its kicking slows, and he pulls the leg outwards, bringing the rusty blade down, hard.

The first blow makes it halfway through the limb, so he applies a second, and a third. He hacks with a delicious insouciance, like a butcher at work, dispassionately carving meat, until the leg is held on only by strands of chitin and sinew. He pulls, and it detaches with a glorious pop.

He feels the wave of pleasure travel through the daemon. To him, it is just a ripple, an echo of her sublime sensation, but still it is powerful. Then he is moving again, applying his art to the Patriarch's other leg, sawing and slicing until this too comes loose in his hands.

It would be simple enough to kill this creature. He could put his pistol to its eye and pull the trigger, or slide his gilded paring knife into the seam between the chitinous plates that protect its swollen brain. But S'janth wants to prolong this pleasure. She doesn't want to just murder this xenos monstrosity; she wants to *ruin* it entirely, destroying everything it is and everything it represents to demonstrate her own superiority. Her own perfection.

Xantine watches as slowly, carefully, lovingly, she tears the Patriarch down, drinking its alien pain like nectar. She leaves a shell of a thing: mewling, bleeding, weak.

The effect of the torturer's art is transmitted to the Patriarch's flock. Their resistance, so galvanised by the arrival of their lord, breaks. Mutants and monsters hold their skulls and scream as their brood leader is torn apart. Mad from the transmitted pain and spiritually bereft, they hurl themselves at Xantine and his coterie. They run shrieking, wild-eyed, lashing out with crude clubs and blunt blades. Others stagger around the cathedral as if waking from a nightmare, their eyes wide, their mission forgotten. They are easy kills for the Space Marines of the Adored, who tear them apart with claws, disembowel them with blades, or smash them into the ground with fists.

S'janth is feasting on the pain. She is a crescendo, rising, rising, rising, until she is a single scream of ecstasy, burning brighter than any star. And then, like a star that has used its fuel, she starts to contract, to collapse in on herself.

He takes his moment. He has shared his body with the daemon for long enough now that he has learned to keep the faintest touch of consciousness on his body, and he uses these fingerholds now to claw himself back into his flesh-and-bone form. She barely resists, rendered almost insensate by her banquet, and he asserts his primacy within his own skin.

He catalogued his pain once more, the sensations suddenly brought into sharp focus. His cracked skull had already started knitting itself back together, the slow motion of bone becoming a deep throb in his ears. The torn skin of his shoulder had scabbed over, new skin forming underneath the protective layer, pink and itchy. His muscles were burning, pushed to limits beyond even his transhuman physiology by the daemon's influence.

It felt *wonderful*.

'*They are breaking,*' Vavisk rumbled over the vox. '*Survivors are running into the sewers and pipes under the city.*'

'Let them flee,' Xantine said, his voice projecting in the ancient cathedral as the last of the dying insurrection bled out through doors and broken windows. 'Let them return to their holes to tell their squalid vermin of me – of my magnificence.' He stepped to the top of a pile of corpses and raised his arms aloft. 'I am Xantine,' he bellowed, loud enough to rattle the broken glass in what was left of the huge windows. 'And I have saved this world!'

He could hear cheering from outside.

CHAPTER ELEVEN

Arqat scurried after the Sophisticants, sword dragging behind him, all attempt to muffle its clanging against the stone floor now forgotten.

'Wait!' he called at the back of a magenta-robed figure as it started up the well-worn staircase to the cathedral's nave. 'Is my brother with you?' he asked, and when he received no reply, he called out again. 'I can help you!'

'Stay back, boy,' a broad-shouldered woman said over her shoulder as she made her way up the steps, keeping her body close to the wall and tracking an ornate lasgun back and forth.

Arqat slowed slightly, surprised that the muscular figure had even responded to him, but he kept coming. 'My brother is in the militia! He taught me how to fight! I can help you,' he shouted. He cringed as he heard his voice bounce back off the ancient stone walls. Reedy and nasal, a child compared to the strong, vital woman in front of him.

'I'm serious, boy. Leave this to the Sixth, we've got the angels on our side now.' Arqat didn't know what she meant, but she laughed as she said it, so he didn't question further: what if she took him for an idiot?

'Run along now, there's a good lad,' she said in a patronising tone that sent a spike of rage into Arqat's brainstem. He protested, wanting to fight his corner, and stepped forward, only to find himself face to face with the lethal end of a lasgun. 'I'll shoot you myself, I mean it,' the woman told him, her voice hardening. 'We have lost a lot of people today. What's one more body to add to the pile?' Arqat stopped his advance, but held his ground, his breath heaving in his pigeon chest.

They stared at each other for a moment, separated by circumstance, gene enhancements, and many years of rejuvenat treatments, but both still children of Serrine.

The woman broke eye contact first. She tutted and jerked her head to the side – one final attempt to send the boy to safety – before turning up the steps and disappearing out of sight.

'She wouldn't have shot me,' Arqat whispered to himself, drawing a deep breath to stabilise his shaking hands. He waited a time, allowing the adrenaline to move through his system, listening carefully until he heard the woman's boot steps fade, heard her squadmates' voices dwindle as they communicated with unseen figures over the vox. And he followed her.

He climbed the stone steps, as he had countless times before in his young life. He knew the places they were most worn down, knew the markings carved into them over the generations by the most rebellious of Serrine's priests-in-training. He knew what was at the top: more rote learnings, more interminable study, more lectures from doddering old fools.

But not today. Arqat crested the stairs and saw something wondrous, something from legend.

An angel, resplendent in pink armour, imperious amidst a

melee of dead and dying monsters and mutants. He was tall – taller even than the rejuvenated and genhanced soldiers of the Sophisticant Sixth – and beautiful, with an alabaster face that seemed to be carved from living marble.

He was perfect. Serrine's salvation, given flesh.

The angel moved faster than Arqat thought possible. Its two arms scythed so swiftly they seemed to blur into four, a long blade carving furrows through the cultists that dared to approach such a holy creature. The blade rose and fell, swirled and arced, moving through the press of flesh around the angel as if the people were wisps of cloud. They clawed and scratched at the luminous purple plate as they died, but their talons left no mark on the perfect armour, and the figure stepped over their corpses as if they were not there. After all, what were devils to an angel of such beauty?

A mask covered the lower portion of the angel's face, hiding any grimace of exertion or anger and creating a picture of pure serenity as it fought. Its eyes were bright and full of life, almost smiling despite the carnage it waltzed through.

Only its hair belied its sheer speed. Lit by the midday sun through the broken door, it trailed after the angel like the tail of a shooting star, bright and beautiful, a memory of motion.

One of the lumbering three-armed monsters came for the angel, swinging its huge saw two-handed in a wide arc that aimed to split him across the stomach. The angel caught the blow between two sharp blades protruding from his wrist, and seemed to smile as he twisted into a spin. With one bladed arm, he pulled away from the creature, pulling its three arms forward in the process as if in supplication. He brought the other arm across the proffered limbs, severing all three at the elbow.

The creature bellowed in agony and fell forward onto bleeding stumps. The angel lifted a long leg and placed a pointed boot on the back of its head, driving down with such force that Arqat heard the creature's skull crack, its bellow become a wet gurgle.

Arqat's sword fell from his hand to the stone floor. Tears fell too, tracing lines in the dirt smeared on his face before they dropped to the ground.

He had wrestled with doubts, but here was incontrovertible evidence of the divine: an angel that had stepped from the pages of his picture books, a statue of a god given life.

What Nanny had said. What his father had said. What his brother had said. Even what the doddering old Tumas had said. It was all true. The Saviour wasn't just a story, a way of imagining the Emperor, far off on His Golden Throne on Terra. It was a prophecy. It was *reality.*

'Throne on Terra...' he whispered to himself, and the puffed-up bravery of adolescence burst like a pricked balloon. His righteous fury disappeared in a moment, replaced by the fear and awe of a child.

The angel finally stopped moving. It cast a glance around the cathedral, at the dozens of invaders, mutants, and xenos that it had slain. Satisfied, it inspected its weapon, and took a moment to flick blood from its blade.

It begged to be worshipped. More than worshipped: something so perfect should be adored. Arqat moved without thought. Before he was aware of his own intentions, he was on his feet, his eyes transfixed on the creature of legend.

'I knew, I *knew,*' he called as he walked towards the angel, thin voice echoing in the charnel house of a cathedral. He ignored the stinking corpses piled high, enraptured only by this figure of legend. It regarded him with those bright, shining eyes, its body finally, perfectly still.

He raised his arms as he came close, to touch this being of light, to feel its earthly form, reaching for his salvation to prove it was real. He believed – oh Throne, did he believe. He had wanted something else from his life. How naive! How wrong! He was born to believe, to be a priest, to proselytise. He knew that now. How could he not believe? He had seen his Saviour in the flesh, seen its perfection.

Arqat heard the cut first – the slice of the blade through the air like a sudden gust through Serrine's Park of Princes on a blustery day – then the soft pitter-patter of blood onto the marble floor like rain.

He smelt it next, the iron tang of his life, gushing from the ruin of his shoulder, and tasted it soon after: the chemical bloom of adrenaline, the panicked flush of saliva.

He felt it last. It was a clean agony, pure and vibrant, hitting him all at once as if he had stepped into a new reality. It came with a new sensation: absence. He tried to move his arm, but how could he move something that was no longer there? He saw the limb on the church floor, skin the colour of his skin, wearing the sleeves of his robe. Presented whole, like an offering.

As he fell to the ground, Arqat realised that he never saw the cut that removed his left arm just below the shoulder. The angel had been too quick.

For the first time Cecily could remember, it was quiet in her head. The commanding voice that had driven her up to this strange city above the clouds had fallen silent, and in its place was a stillness, utterly disorienting in its perfection.

She heard nothing, not even the wind, as it travelled through the arms and legs of the countless statues. They didn't talk, these white-faced men and women. They just stared, smiling, blank-eyed. This city was built for them, she decided: a world of opulence and expense that wouldn't be stained by the filth and fluids of flesh-and-blood humans.

She did not belong in the overcity; she should never have come here. She wanted to go back below, she wanted to go back to familiarity, she wanted her bunk and her shift and her family, and – oh Throne – she wanted to go home.

She listened for the voice of the grass, aching to hear once more the tales it told between the soft swish of its blades. It had been a rhythm to her whole life, she realised, but its voice was dead to her now, too faint and too far away to hear from this lofty perch.

The thought was too terrible for her to comprehend, and she strained harder for any kind of comforting sound from home, searching her senses for some mote of familiarity. She heard nothing.

No, not nothing. There was a sound: feeble and fading, but it was there. She closed her eyes and felt with her mind, feeling blindly towards the weak sound as if she was returning to her bunk in the dead of night.

She found it. It was pain.

The steps that had been lined with the dead now bore the weight of the living. Tired and dishevelled soldiers hefted sandbags and barricades into place, dismantling hastily erected firing positions. Others began the morbid work of removing corpses, groups of twos and threes carrying the bodies of their compatriots and their mutant invaders, hefting them by clawed limbs and throwing them into ugly piles.

They had been joined by the braver members of the civilian populace. Faces appeared alongside the placid countenances of the planet's statues, popping up on balconies or peering from behind pillars as the tide of the insurrection had turned. They were desperate for a glimpse of the angels, the rumours of whom had spread through Serrine's powerful gossip networks.

The planet's ruling families were scared for their own safety, but worse still would be the face lost if they were seen to have hidden while the Emperor's own returned from the stars.

They had been rewarded for their bravery, catching sight of lurid figures in pinks and purples as they marshalled Serrine's soldiery. Torachon, Vavisk, and the other Adored from the initial assault at the void port were granted control of the Sophisticant Sixth, the elite force forming the thrust of the advance towards the cathedral. The telltale magenta robes of these broad-shouldered, rejuvenat-enhanced soldiers were spots of colour amongst the more drab colours of the city's regular planetary defence forces. The Space Marines had bolstered their assault with these shattered soldiers as they moved through the city, finding poorly trained men and women who had previously only dealt with minor inter-family conflicts and infrequent worker demonstrations quivering in their opulent barracks, before press-ganging them back into the fight.

Together, they had been the open blade: the visible attack that, while powerful and well directed on its own, was designed to distract the foe from the true danger. That was the killing cut, and of course, that honour had gone to Xantine.

The appearance of this combined force, operating not only with the cooperation of the planet's best-known elite unit, but under the control of the Emperor's own Angels of Death, inspired an audible response amongst the civilian populace. It was a low sound at first, like the babble of a distant river, but it rose quickly as it became apparent that the insurrection had been driven off.

As Xantine stepped out into the blazing midday sun of Serrine's city above the clouds, it had become a roar – a city showing its appreciation. He basked in it, allowing the adulation to salve his wounds and soothe his strained muscles. He raised his right arm, palm to the sky and, like a conductor in an orchestra, cut the sound with a sweep of his hand. Silence reigned.

'Good citizens of Serrine,' Xantine shouted, the sonic projectors in his modified Mark IV armour working to transmit his booming voice to the mass of humanity that lined the steps of the Cathedral of the Bounteous Harvest. 'Your ordeal…' – he let the moment hang, building suspense – 'is over.' He beckoned behind him, and Euratio and Orlan brought forward the woman from the stage. Phaedre followed at a distance, the slight figure somehow still bathed in shadow, despite the blazing sunshine.

Whatever glamour the woman had employed had been stripped by the presence of a psyker as potent as Phaedre. In her place was a woman, no different in appearance to the hairless workers that she had commanded. She struggled pathetically in the grip of the transhuman warriors, her skinny wrists held tight in pink gauntlets, her legs buckling as she was pulled forward. Xantine could not see the twins' faces – they were always hidden by silvered, mouthless masks – but their pleasure radiated off the both of them like a stench.

The alien hissed as she was hauled out into the bright sunlight of Serrine's midday, her slitted yellow eyes constricting as she was dumped to her knees in front of the assembled hundreds. She flailed clawed hands towards the sky in a futile attempt to ward off both Xantine and the sun itself, but to no avail; he simply batted them away, and picked her up by the scruff of the neck, showing her to the crowd like a game bird.

'Gaze upon your would-be conqueror,' he shouted. The crowd booed and hissed.

'This wretch has laid low your great city,' he continued, derision in his voice. 'This xenos filth, this monstrosity, this… weakling.' He turned the creature around in his grip, looking into her alien eyes. They were wide with terror.

'Pathetic,' Xantine said to the alien, and spat in her face. He turned his attention back to the crowd.

'Many thousands of you have laid down your lives today,' he called, letting the xenos fall to the floor and beginning to pace the great marble steps. 'But I command you – do not remember this day as one of death, nor of sadness, nor of grief.' He spun and cast a gloved finger at the crowd, commanding them. 'No! You must remember this day as one of rebirth!' He raised his arms again, a conspicuous attempt to copy the pose of the vast statue on the frontage of the cathedral behind him. 'This world will rise from the ashes!

'Remember this day as one of power, as together we excised and destroyed the cancer at Serrine's heart. And remember this day as one of glory.' Xantine threw his arms wide, Anguish clutched in one huge hand. 'Because this day brought *me* to Serrine.'

Torachon proffered his sabre, and Xantine brought it down on the alien's neck. Her hairless head bounced as it hit the marble, staining the white stone red.

The cheers were loud enough to shake the ground that Xantine stood upon.

The church was far too big and far too pretty to be compared to the places of worship in her city below, but it was still a church, Cecily was sure of it. The woman had gone inside, but this place was dedicated to the Saviour. The Saviour would protect her.

Keeping low to avoid the soldiers on the stairs below, she scurried along the balcony, squeezing past the countless Throne-cursed statues that seemed to be trying to block her path. She found a walkway that led to the cathedral's second storey, one of many connection points between the old stone building and its newer neighbours. She found a door leading into the interior, and tried the handle – a knobbly, ornate thing of shiny black metal. It wouldn't turn.

'Come on, come on!' she hissed to herself, putting a foot on the frame of the door as she pulled hard on its handle, but to no avail.

She looked down at the pistol in her hand, and covered her eyes as she pointed its muzzle at the crystalflex panel in the centre of the door. Squeezing the trigger, she was rewarded with the bark of a single shot, and the tinkle of breaking glass.

She squeezed through the gap, avoiding the coloured shards, and stepped into a darkened space. Her eyes acclimatised to the relative gloom, and she realised she was on a deserted mezzanine that looked out across the interior of the cathedral. The plaintive sound was closer now. She couldn't hear it, not with her ears, but she knew it was coming from below, even as it faded fast. She moved to the edge of the mezzanine, placing her hands against an intricately carved wooden balustrade depicting the cycle of the harvest: planting, tending, slicing, refining.

There was a stink in the air, both sour and sweet. Incense, she could recognise, infused into the wood and stone of the ancient cathedral. It reminded her of her own worship, though this was much richer, more potent than the thin sticks the priest would light at her chapel. Even so, it was drowned out by another smell, one that also reminded her of the city below.

It was the smell of butcher houses. She had visited just a few of the blood-soaked chambers in the undercity before, but she wouldn't ever forget the smell. They existed outside the law, black-market spaces where workers could barter trinkets, blades, or bottles of refined Solipsus sap for hunks of unspecified meat – something to add some variety to the endless grass-starch rations that barely filled hungry bellies.

The cause of the smell was obvious. There were so many of them, and they were so still, that she had mistaken them first for fallen statues, but the reek of dead meat made it clear that the cathedral was packed with corpses. Dozens of them, hundreds of them, forming a macabre flesh carpet on the floor of the church.

And then, among the mass of dead things, she saw movement. The smallest flicker of motion, like a twitch. The voice in her head nothing but a whisper in the dead silence.

She followed the motion. She made her way down stone steps, picking past lifeless bodies and shards of broken glass as long and sharp as threshing blades. She was grateful for her hard-wearing worker boots. Grandpa had given them to her.

She found the boy between two dead things. She didn't recognise them, didn't want to recognise them. They had too many arms, claws like something from a nightmare, and glassy yellow eyes that stared through her even in death.

The boy's face was as grey as his cassock, the white material made ashen by the masonry dust and smoke that wafted into the cathedral from the explosions that breached the door. An arm lay by his side, the fingers curled, leaking blood from where it had been removed from its owner. It was *his* arm, she realised.

Something was happening outside. She could hear the sounds of gunfire, wild and loud. She wanted to run, to hide, to get away from the murderers and monsters that were terrorising this dark mirror of her own existence.

But she couldn't leave the boy. His eyes were fluttering and he drifted in and out of consciousness. She looked at the wound on his shoulder. No, 'wound' was the wrong word. This was too perfect a cut, too precise. This was a dissection.

He needed help. She had seen amputations like this before, when a threshing blade broke free, or when an inexperienced refiner stuck a hand into machinery to clear a blockage. She knew the shock might kill him soon, and even if it didn't, the blood loss certainly would.

She made a decision. She tore a strip from his cassock, exposing bare feet and calves that were almost hairless, and wrapped it tight around the bleeding stump of his arm. She picked him up. She had always been strong – you didn't get by in the refinery if you couldn't haul the sap barrels – but she was surprised how light he was. Truly, just a boy.

She wondered for a moment if she should take the arm as well, but thought better of it. He would be lucky if he survived the next few hours in a city under attack by mutants; the chances of finding a chirurgeon capable of reattaching the limb were next to zero.

Outside, she heard cheering.

Xantine had been near carried to Serrine's senate, swept along by a tide of grateful humanity.

'Please, lord,' one old man gasped as he struggled to keep up with the crowd. 'What is your name?'

'I am Xantine,' the warlord said, and the word carried like a virus through the herd, until it was screamed by dozens, hundreds. Xantine had heard his name on the lips of mortals before: they had cursed it, or screamed it, or groaned it as they died by his hand. It had been a long time since he had heard it spoken like this. The people of Serrine whispered his name like lovers confiding in one another. They chanted his name, affirmations of survival and supremacy. They screamed his name in ecstasy, that their saviour had finally arrived, just as prophesied.

He revelled in the sensation, accepting the adulation like a narcotic. Just like a narcotic, it dulled his senses.

A young woman grabbed for his bladed vambraces, and S'janth hissed at the touch. He turned with murder in his eyes, but he pulled the blow when he realised she was holding out a bouquet of flowers. Her eyes were wide with terror, but Xantine could only see the colours of the flowers: pink and purple bloomed from vivid green stems, a vision of delicacy set against the day's savagery.

'For you, my lord,' she whimpered, hands shaking. 'My father grows them for the nobles, but I think you should have them because you… you…' She tailed off, flowers still outstretched like a weapon.

Xantine accepted the bouquet with a bow.

The woman melted back into the crowd as they moved through streets lined with fallen figures, many missing limbs, or blown into their constituent chunks. The white dust of destroyed masonry and marble covered every surface, and Xantine could only tell statue from corpse by the distinctive coppery tang of blood in his nostrils as he was ushered past. He felt tiny spikes of sensation as he moved amidst this human wreckage. It was pleasure – to be so close to death always ignited a flash of excitement in his soul – but it was also pain, he realised: the pain of something beautiful destroyed.

It was a pain he knew all too well. Serrine was a cracked reflection of Harmony, a shadow of that beautiful place, but being here still conjured images of the adopted home of the Emperor's Children. That home was gone now, destroyed when Abaddon, the vulgar brute, had cast a spear into the heart of Harmony's Canticle City. In doing so, he had robbed the galaxy of its cultural and artistic pinnacle.

Chemos had been that pinnacle before Harmony. Fulgrim had spoken to his sons of his home world, describing a drab, dull place with a population of dead-eyed drones. His coming had elevated the planet, the application of his singular genius making it not only an effective and efficient manufacturing world, but also a cradle for artists and artisans. Chemos was a paradise, standing alone as a jewel in the nascent Imperium.

And then Fulgrim's wandering attentions had ensured that the gift of Chemos was squandered. The planet had been destroyed by those with no understanding of perfection. Just as Canticle City had been.

Xantine could not save his adopted home, just as his father could not save his. But Xantine could save Serrine. He *had* saved it.

Eventually, they arrived at the great wooden doors of a building of such opulence that it rivalled some of Canticle City's more drab districts. They swung open for him and his warriors alone, the throng of people behind him barred entry by the Sophisticant Sixth's soldiers in their magenta robes. Of Serrine's human population, only nobles and their coterie of servants were permitted to remain inside the chamber, and those that did try to chance their arm were beaten with lasgun butts or threatened with sabres until they fell back.

Xantine trailed a hand behind him as the doors closed, his last connection to the crowd that had buoyed him and fed him their adulation. He could hear them outside still, their raucous celebrations only now starting to die in volume as the great wooden portal of the senate was shut upon them.

The nobles inside provided a much more reserved welcome, many of them having seen first-hand the unsettling appearance and uncanny abilities of the Adored. Nonetheless, their presence as guests of honour demanded that the Space Marines have pride of place at the huge banquet table that ran along the centre of the chamber. Xantine had been seated close to the head of the table in a chair that would have been ostentatiously huge for a standard human occupant, though it managed to just about support his armoured frame.

By human standards, the victory feast was lavish. Centuries-old bottles of amasec were uncorked, ceremonial songbirds were slaughtered by the hundred for inclusion in elaborate pastries, and serfs in Serrine's customary brightly coloured robes danced for so long that many of their number slumped to the floor mid-song, too exhausted to continue.

For Xantine, whose stretched neuroreceptors had taken in a whole galaxy of sensation, it was all quite dull.

'I hope this is to your liking, my lord?' a pinched man asked from over Xantine's shoulder, handing him a goblet of wine. Xantine took it. As guest of honour, he had been assigned a gaggle of cupbearers, food tasters and other serfs. The pinched man appeared to be their leader.

There had been an obvious interest in Xantine and his chosen escorts – Torachon, Vavisk, and the twins – as they entered the chamber. The presence of the huge Angels of Death in pink, purple, and golden armour filled the room with a strange charge that hovered between excitement and terror. To compensate for the sensation, the lords and ladies reverted to the preferred pas-time of career politicians the galaxy over: gossip. They stood in huddles together, or leaned conspiratorially between their seats, discussing the power vacuums left in the wake of the uprising while they eyed the terrifying newcomers.

One larger man stepped forwards. He had climbed the stairs to the senate's upper levels, and his blond hair was stuck to his pink forehead with sweat. He was trembling, Xantine noticed, both from exertion and from fear. Nonetheless, he threw forward a hand.

'I am Pierod, your humble servant,' the man said.

Xantine looked at the hand for a moment, like a snake sizing up a meal, before inclining his head slightly.

Pierod coughed and withdrew the hand, sliding it backwards through his mop of blond hair with feigned nonchalance. 'My lord Xantine, I am honoured to have had the pleasure. We spoke earlier today – it was I who called you to this world.'

'Then I should express my thanks,' Xantine said. 'It is quite the jewel.'

Their attention was drawn by sound, as the great chamber doors were flung open. From outside, Xantine could hear the cheers of the populace, previously aimed at him, finding a new target. The sound rose like a wave as the governor entered the room, flanked by sixteen members of the city's elite guard. Like them, he had changed into a magenta robe, but his had been trimmed in gold, denoting his position. He was met with a standing ovation from the assembled council members.

Lord Durant waved to the room with feigned humility and placed a hand on a soldier's shoulder, steadying himself as he stepped up onto a cushioned litter. Four of the robed soldiers stepped forward, bent at the knees, and picked up the litter, moving up the senate stairs with practised grace. The governor accepted the adoration of the senate as he moved towards his seat at the pinnacle of the chamber, offering patronising nods or placing his hand to his heart as senators called his name and expressed their joy at his safe return.

'Pierod, was it?' Xantine asked the man, who jumped as he heard his name spoken.

'Y-yes, my lord?'

'The governor – I wish to speak to him.'

'Of course, my lord. Let me speak with his attendants, we can arrange a formal introduction.'

'No, you misunderstand me,' Xantine said. 'I wish to speak to him now.'

Pierod blustered for a moment, falling over his response. He found this warrior giant terrifying, but he had not been able to secure his own meetings with Governor Durant, even after years of bribes and favours.

But that was then, when he had been simply Pierod. Now,

he was Pierod, Caller of Angels. He cleared his throat and tried to fill his voice with a confidence he did not feel. 'My lord,' he said, 'if you would follow me?'

'Lord Durant, may I present Xantine of the...' Pierod turned to the Space Marine, unsure of how to introduce him.

Even with Durant sitting in his colossal throne, Xantine loomed over the governor. He met the man's gaze, offering no motion that might be construed as subservience.

'I am a Child of the Emperor,' Xantine replied. His smile didn't reach his eyes.

'Xantine, a Child of the Emperor,' Pierod finished.

'How delightful to meet you, Xantine,' Durant said. 'I had the distinct pleasure of being introduced to your fellow warriors earlier today. A terrible shame that they should have the opportunity to meet me during such unpleasant times – I do hope you'll convey my apologies.'

Xantine said nothing, sizing the governor up. Durant continued.

'I also met the *enchanting* woman who travelled with them. Will she be joining us for dinner?' he asked. Xantine could smell his trepidation.

'Phaedre has retired to pursue other interests tonight,' Xantine said.

'Splendid!' Durant said, with obvious relief. 'Splendid. Well, I believe a toast is in order.'

The governor clapped his hands together, once, twice, three times. By the third clap, conversation in the room had fallen to a murmur.

'Ladies and gentlemen,' he shouted to the assembled crowd. 'A toast! A toast to our guests, and their timely intervention.' Turning to Xantine, he raised his goblet. 'A thousand thanks for your efforts today, Xantine, Child of the Emperor. Truly, the

Emperor smiles on us to send His most...' He looked the Space Marine up and down, eyes lingering on the shaggy head of the alien beast on his pauldron. 'His most... exotic warriors to our aid. These are dark times, when mankind is riven across the stars, but your blessed presence reminds us of Serrine's importance to the Imperium.'

Durant drained his glass, holding it out for a cupbearer to refill.

'Do you know,' he continued, the corners of his lips stained red from the amasec, 'there is a legend, on this world, of a Saviour who will return from the heavens in our hour of need to lead us to glory. Superstition, of course – our only Saviour is the Emperor on Terra – but your arrival reminds me of the story, and warms my heart. Truly, you have saved us.' Durant waited for the applause to die down. 'Please,' he said, bowing slightly, 'convey our thanks to the lords of Terra when you leave.'

'Leave,' Xantine whispered, echoing the governor. It became a question as it rolled over his tongue.

He opened a vox-channel to Vavisk with an imperceptible movement. His old friend's voice vibrated the bones of Xantine's ear, and Xantine pictured Vavisk with his cadre of Noise Marines, standing ready to level key structures in the city. He was just waiting for the signal.

He thought also of Lordling, leading his slavemasters into the city's warren of residential streets, licking his slit lips at the thought of corralling thousands of humans into the *Exhortation*'s pens. Of Sarquil, already dispassionately counting the spoils of this ransacked planet, its art and culture and beauty rendered down into their constituent parts for mindless consumption.

And he thought of the fallen figures outside, toppled things of masonry and human meat. The remnants of a world trying, striving, for some appreciation of perfection in an ugly galaxy. A world that appreciated *him*.

He would not make the same mistakes again. He would make it right this time; make it perfect.

Xantine turned to Lord Durant, eyes wide in mock surprise. 'Why would we leave?'

The governor smiled for a moment, waiting for the joke to unfurl. When the punchline did not come, his mouth worked, forming shapes without sound. Eventually, words came. 'What do you mean?'

Xantine addressed Durant directly, but projected his voice, using his surgically augmented throat to ensure that all banquet attendees – from kitchen porters to Durant himself – could hear his words. 'Why, my decision to stay on this world should come as no surprise to you, my good man. Your story was prophecy, one that I now fulfil. I have come from the heavens to your world, and I have found it lacking. But I will not destroy it. I will save it. Rejoice, for Xantine has come!'

'But, my lord…' Durant said, a confused smile still flickering on his lips. 'These statues… The Saviour… These are myths!' The statement drew gasps from some of the banquet's attendees. Most present saw the Saviour as a foundational legend rather than a real figure, but to deny his existence remained gauche, even in Serrine's most rarefied circles.

Durant continued. '*I* am the governor of Serrine,' he said, voice finally hardening as he realised the gravity of the situation. 'My family was chosen by our blessed Emperor to serve His interests. We alone have the right to rule the citizens of this most valuable world.'

'Tell me,' Xantine said, open palm pointed at the governor's throat like a duelling rapier. 'If your rule is absolute, how did your own people rise up against you?'

'P-p-people?' the governor stammered, wrong-footed by the direct question. 'They were not my *people*. They were dwellers of the

undercity, citizens in name alone. They are fit only to grow and harvest the grass, they lack the sophistication and intelligence to rule.'

'They seemed to disagree,' Xantine said.

'They were in thrall to a monster!' the governor said.

'Yes… A peculiar malady, among your sort.'

Xantine cast a pointed glance around the room, his turquoise
eyes taking in the accumulated mass of hereditary nobles and
power-hungry social climbers.

'I have decided to stay on this world, to guide it into perfection. Serrine has been failed by its leaders. Its people deserve a
leader of character, of honour, of skill. You are a decadent and
ineffectual collection of dilettantes who deserve nothing more
than the glory of death at the tip of my sword.'

There was a ripple of sound among the attendees, an intake of
breath that clearly titillated Pierod, who stifled a giggle. Xantine
gestured at the large man.

'Only Pierod here had the presence of mind and quickness
of wit to aid his planet, his people. As such, he will serve as
my governor – my representative in matters of state as I preside
over the creation of a just society.'

'Him?!' Durant spluttered, incredulous. 'He is nothing! A
puffed-up secretary! You cannot replace me. I will simply not
allow it.' Durant pointed a trembling hand at the giant. 'Guards!
Arrest this… thing!'

The soldiers started to move from their positions at the side
of the chamber. Without looking in their direction, Xantine
raised the Pleasure of the Flesh and shot them: one, two, three,
four. Four skulls opened in turn, brain matter and bone fragments spreading like flower petals before they splashed over
the robes and gowns of the banquet attendees, burgundy on
white, pink and magenta. There were screams from the guests,
piercing sounds that caused S'janth to stir from her restful state.

Is it to be pain, my love? she breathed, softly.

It is, Xantine thought back.

Good, she sighed, contented.

Xantine traced a gauntleted hand down Durant's cheek. It had drained of colour. He affected a theatrical whisper, loud enough still that the chamber could hear his every utterance.

'My dear, your own people have turned against you. A ruler must be loved. Listen to the crowds outside. They do not love you. They love *me*. How could I let you remain in power?'

Durant quivered as the huge hand stroked his cheek. The touch was surprisingly light.

'You, rule us? This is madness! Why would you come from the heavens to save us, just to subjugate our world?'

Xantine backhanded Durant across the face. The blow twisted the man's head so fast that it ripped loose from the meat of his neck, launching upwards from his shoulders as if it was taking off for orbit. Only the connective sinew of the spine kept the skull from flying free, arresting the travel of his head and allowing gravity to work its effects. Durant's head came to rest on his own shoulder, cocked to the side. The dead eyes regarded Xantine with a quizzical look.

He turned to the senate, all whispers silenced.

'Open the doors!' he shouted, pointing towards the grand wooden doors at the far end of the chamber. The image of the four-armed Saviour was carved into their dark surface, its perfectly blank face offering no judgement. The remaining soldiers hesitated, and Xantine raised the Pleasure of the Flesh again. 'Open the doors,' he said once more, the demand spilling from his augmented throat and warp-tuned vox-unit as a squeal. The gun pulsed in his hand, its warped innards thumping a thrilled heartbeat. There was no delay from the humans this time: several soldiers stepped forward, shaking hands working locks and sliding bolts until the ornately carved doors cracked down the centre, revealing the deep blue sky of the early evening.

With the colour came sound – the cacophony of hundreds, screaming their pleasure at their continued existence into the sky. The volume rose further as the mass realised the doors were opening, and not just opening but opening for *them*. Xantine used his gifts to project his voice once more, to welcome his people into a chamber once reserved for those who put themselves above them.

'Citizens of Serrine!' Xantine roared. 'I throw open the doors of this celebration to you! Please, join us in our feast.'

A cheer convulsed through the crowd, and Xantine was pleased to hear his name was still on their lips. It moved organically through the mass, like a disease.

'XANTINE!' they bellowed, as word of their invitation spread to the dozens in the first rows.

'XANTINE!' they whooped, as others picked up the call, a rallying cry for hundreds; for thousands.

'XANTINE!' they wailed, as they pressed forward as one entity, towards the slit in the door. The mass, finding the soldiers that had barred their way before too shocked to block them now, wrenched the wooden doors wide. The sight of the luxury inside drove the crowd into a frenzy, and they crawled and climbed over each other in desperate attempts to put themselves close to power, to say that they too had been there when their world had been saved. Bones broke and skin split as smaller and weaker members of the mass found themselves trapped under boots or against walls, but their cries were drowned out by the pulsing cheer of their friends and neighbours.

'XANTINE! XANTINE! XANTINE!'

The mass burst through the doors and ran like water into the spaces of the senate chamber, filling corridors and walkways, climbing stairs and overturning tables as they went. They reacted to their surroundings with wide eyes but adapted quickly. Some picked at golden bowls piled high with pastries, grabbed for trays of amasec goblets, or stopped worried-looking serving staff carrying plates of roasted meats. Others tried to engage senate members in boisterous conversation, or sat in luxurious chairs designed for occupants of high breeding.

The gathered nobles reacted as if these interlopers were vermin, hoisting their robes and standing on chairs, in case one of the common folk should come near them or, Throne forbid, touch them. Some ran screaming for the exits, but found their way barred by yet more of the mass who had entered through side doors and emergency escapes. Others had been rendered stunned by the death of the planet's governor, and sat blinking, ill-equipped by lives of luxury to deal with their new reality.

Xantine pulled Durant's corpse by the hair and lifted it from his throne. He held it up with one hand, investigating the dead man's face. A weak chin. A bulbous nose. The almost imperceptible scars of a chirurgeon's scalpel, along the hairline. Inelegant. Ugly. Xantine threw the corpse down the stairs, watching with disdain as it tumbled over itself, limbs contorting, until it came to rest on its back, broken neck hanging loosely over a step, lifeless eyes regarding the people that Durant used to rule.

Xantine sat in the vacated throne and addressed his new subjects.

'The people of Serrine deserve a better world. You deserve a better world. I will deliver it to you.' He paused, drinking in the silence. It was born of reverence, perhaps. Or fear. Either was acceptable to him. He continued, the whole crowd in the palm of his hand. 'Strength, skill, and talent will be rewarded. Any man or woman may challenge any other for their place, provided that they can best them in an agreed challenge.'

He stood now, aping the vast statue of the Saviour that hung over the chamber, arms raised to the side to accept their adulation.

'I will preside over these challenges, and guide Serrine into a new era.'

'Xantine,' the crowd murmured, the chant from before picked up again.

'Weep today for your pain, but be glad that your pain brought me to Serrine, because I will bring a new society. A just society. A *perfect* society.'

The chorus began anew, and it filled his hearts to hear it.

'XANTINE! XANTINE! XANTINE!'

PART II

CHAPTER TWELVE

'Here commences the four hundred and seventeenth Council of the Most Wise.' The voice rattled windows in the top-floor chamber, loud enough that the room's human residents threw hands up to cover their ears. 'Observe, all ye citizens of Serrine – Governor Pierod, our august Barons Vavisk, Sarquil, Torachon, the lady Phaedre, and the most just, Lord Xantine. Long may they rule!'

The woman who had spoken fell to her knees, panting, each heaving breath leaving her body with a burst of static. She had no choice: her mouth and nose had been removed, replaced by a circular golden vox-unit that popped and whined, even when she was at rest. The unit was piped into her neck, gold and silver cabling meeting and then disappearing underneath the sagging flesh of her throat, where it plumbed into her augmented lungs. A belt of nutrient bags hung around her waist like a bandolier of ammunition, piping sustenance directly into her stomach.

Anjou D'urbique was Xantine's personal speaker. The role

was a high honour, but the woman was old when her family had challenged for the position, and the extensive surgeries required to adequately fill the position had taken their toll on her body. She needed more than a minute to compose herself, eyes bloodshot and chest still heaving from the effort, before she could draw herself up to her full height. She was short for a citizen of Serrine – a world where gene therapy and rejuvenat treatments were so common – and it took her several more minutes to totter from the chamber, assisted by muscular women in white silk robes.

Xantine watched her go, and grimaced. He didn't like starting his days with displays of weakness. 'The good Lady D'urbique may have outlived her effectiveness,' he muttered to a hulking figure in a golden mask to his right. 'See if we can't engineer a challenge in the coming days. I hear that House Gillone want to advance their stock.'

'Yes, lord,' the figure rumbled, and withdrew to make the arrangements.

Xantine was in a foul mood. S'janth had grown restless of late, and she bucked in his soul now, agitated and restless. The daemon was swelling with power, feeding on the suffering and pleasure of the millions of souls in Serrine's tiered city, and she exerted her will more frequently. He often lost hours at a time, as she took control of his body by force, stalking through the alleys and streets of his world, slaking her dark desires on his people. This loss of control gnawed at his thoughts. His mood darkened further when Sarquil spoke first.

'Emergency point of order,' the silver-headed giant said. 'Our slave stock is diminishing faster than we can replenish it, even with enhanced breeding programmes. Two hundred and twelve slaves only remain with the *Exhortation*, from the initial three thousand, four hundred and seventeen that made planetfall on this world.'

Sarquil offered a cold smirk. 'On the positive side, the number of deaths diminish the impact of our food supply problems.'

'What do you propose?' Vavisk growled.

Xantine shot his old friend a venomous look, hoping to stop him from encouraging the quartermaster. It was in vain.

'I propose that we overturn this sham of a civilisation, enslave the bulk of the city's population, redouble our repair efforts on the *Exhortation* and put out a call for aid to our brother warbands. The Flawless Host have been known to raid in this sector. They may hear our call.'

Xantine closed his eyes for a long moment, and drew in a slow breath. Sarquil had always been single-minded, but he had become truly monomaniacal since the Adored's forced grounding on Serrine.

'Brother,' he sighed, 'how many times have we had this conversation? I ask because I am certain you have kept records – meticulous records – of my responses to this line of questioning. The answer is always the same. What makes you think that I will change my mind now?'

'I hope that you will see reason,' Sarquil said.

'You speak not of slaves, but of my people. I offer them a fair society, a just society. The Corpse-Emperor subjugates the unenlightened, grinds them to gruel to feed His inane war machine. But I have seen the truth – the galaxy is full of pain and pleasure. I have unshackled humanity and let them taste it.'

Sarquil slammed his massive hand on the arm of his chair. It yelped in pain. 'They are slaves, Xantine, and nothing more! You are blinded by their indulgence, but I see the course clear – we must use the bounty of this world to rearm and rebuild, and rejoin our brothers in the Black Legion.'

He wants your power, my love, S'janth said, surprising Xantine. Her words were like a finger traced along the nape of his neck.

'Torachon,' Sarquil said, turning to the young Space Marine. 'You see this, surely?'

Torachon's face flickered in confusion, and he looked to Xantine, gauging the correct response. Xantine met him with a small shake of the head.

'No, Brother Sarquil. Lord Xantine's rule is absolute. If he bids that we remain on this world, then we remain.'

'The ignorance of youth.' Sarquil turned, searching for allies in the council. He locked eyes with Phaedre, and the witch returned a cruel smile. He would find no common ground with Xantine's muse. He turned instead to Vavisk.

'Vavisk. The song of Slaanesh calls to you, I know. Your Noise Marines are restless – I hear their chorus across the city. They long to share their musics with the stars.'

The mouths on Vavisk's neck spoke in response, whispering affirmations and disagreements. Xantine wondered if they spoke for his brother, or for themselves, but he knew better than to accept their answer. He waited.

Bloodshot eyes cast at the floor, Vavisk spoke through his vox-grille mouth. 'We endure.'

Xantine closed his eyes and breathed deeply, a theatrical gesture of frustration. When he opened them, he fixed Sarquil with a murderous glare. 'Are you finished, quartermaster? You will find no allies here.'

He stood, his gauntlets clasped around the fine hilt of Anguish. 'You wish to usurp me?' he asked. 'You wish to take this paradise that I have created?'

'I have no desire to rule this backwater cesspit,' Sarquil answered, incredulous. 'I want to *leave!*'

He is lying, S'janth whispered.

'I know your machinations, Sarquil. I see how you scheme and plot to take this jewel from me, how you try to win the favour of our loyal brothers. You think my rule so weak that you – a small-minded pedant, a dull-witted materialist, a glorified bean counter – that *you* could wrest control from one such as I?' He brought the rapier into a two-handed grip, and assumed a stance once favoured by his Legion's Palatine Blades. A clear gesture of threat. Sarquil would back down.

Good, my love, good! S'janth was drinking from the deep well of his anger, he knew.

But the Terminator didn't back down. 'Enough!' Sarquil roared. The giant rose from his chair, his usually calm demeanour upended. 'Eight years on this blighted world, and for what? So that you can build a squalid monument to Fulgrim's Chemos? Look around yourself, Xantine – you seek the worship of addled mortals and our Legion's cast-offs. This world is rotting, and you are the cancer at its heart.'

'I am loved.'

'You are despised. Abaddon had the true measure of the Third…'

'Do not speak the Betrayer's name in my presence!' Xantine thundered. He lunged forward and brought Anguish around, two gloved gauntlets aiming the weapon at Sarquil's gorget. The weapon vibrated in his grip, inches away from the Tartaros plate protecting his brother's neck.

Sarquil stared him down, unflinching. Without a word, the giant sparked the energy field of his power fist. Green flares danced between his fingers as they uncurled.

'You are no prince, Xantine, and I will no longer follow your command.' Sarquil turned and strode from the room.

CHAPTER THIRTEEN

The attack came in the night. Sarquil knew that Xantine would spend his evening in repose in his chamber, knew that he would partake in the latest delicacies from Qaran Tun's collection, and that this would be the best time to strike, while his leader was drifting in the spaces between the souls that inhabited his body.

It was easy for Sarquil to reach Xantine's chamber. There were fewer than fifty of the Adored on Serrine, and as massive, warp-touched transhumans amongst comparatively feeble mortals, most were afforded the freedom of the city. Sarquil, as a particularly well-known member of both the warband and the planet's government, was only challenged when he reached the stairs to Xantine's chamber, his way barred by two genhanced guards almost as tall as he was. He had simply crushed their skulls, one in his power fist, one with the barrel of his chaincannon, before making his way to the spire of the building.

Even in his Terminator panoply, Sarquil moved quietly. Xantine had always appreciated that about his brother. He appreciated other things, too. Sarquil was strong, stubborn and focused – to a fault. His brother could not see outside of his own plan, could not countenance any shift to routine. Xantine played into that idiosyncrasy.

As expected, Sarquil found Xantine weakened, ripe for execution. The warlord was slumped in his throne, black bile trickling from the corner of his mouth. He had consumed another daemonic morsel – a squat, undulating thing that Qaran Tun had winnowed from the warp during their previous raids. It had squealed as he devoured its essence, and wailed as he severed it from its own reality.

The battle had been short, but it left Xantine drained, his body and soul exhausted from metaphysical digestion. He could barely raise an arm as his brother stepped into his chamber, tilting his head instead to track the Terminator's entry. Lank black hair fell over his left eye. Still, he broke the silence first.

'At least you have the decency to raise the blade yourself,' Xantine said, his voice reduced to a croak. Black liquid fell from his lips to the purple ceramite of his breastplate, where it bubbled and hissed.

Sarquil raised his chaincannon, wary. The servos of his Tartaros armour hummed quietly with the strain. He panned the weapon left and right, and stepped into the room. It was long, and had been ostentatious even before Xantine took up residence. The Space Marine had only made it more so. Sculptures and statues stood freely between plinths and daises topped with golden eggs, chattering homunculi, and other such oddities, standing in front of huge windows that ran the length of the room.

Assured that they were alone, Sarquil spoke. 'You left me no choice.'

'You were always fated to betray me,' Xantine whispered through a slackened jaw. 'Just a matter... of when.'

'You fool. I followed you. You promised our Legion would be restored to its glory, standing in our rightful place as the vanguard of the Long War. You promised me an army, a fleet, a war worth fighting.' Sarquil sighed. It was a strangely human sound. 'Pretty words with shallow ends. You are the same as the rest of them. Eidolon and Lucius, Kaesoron and Fabius.'

He took a step forward, chaincannon still raised.

'Petty.'

Another step.

'Shallow.'

One more step.

'Weak.'

He stood ten yards from Xantine now, at the bottom of the carpeted ramp that led to the Lord of Serrine's throne.

'I hate this world, Xantine. I hate its mewling, snivelling mortals. I hate its four hundred and nine million square yards of fertile grassland. But most of all, I hate you. I hate you for confining us to this dead planet, while the galaxy is ripe for plunder.'

He raised the chaincannon. The gilded maw at the tip of the barrel glinted in the chamber's candlelight.

'Torachon. Qaran Tun. Vavisk. They can't see yet, but they will. You are nothing but a pale imitation of our father. A child, desperate for approval.'

'I... am... not... Fulgrim,' Xantine said, his voice barely a whisper.

'You try so very hard to play the role, but no, you are not even close to his majesty.'

Xantine pulled his blackened lips into a grin. 'I am better.'

'Hah!' Sarquil barked a laugh. Xantine realised that in millennia of shared service, and decades of fighting side by side with the man, he'd never heard the sound. 'Do you know what Father said about you?'

'I confess… I do not,' Xantine said.

'Nothing,' Sarquil spat. 'Fulgrim never even knew your name.'

Xantine laughed, but the barb cut deeper than expected. It dug through his memories, to a time before S'janth stepped into his body, to a time before the demise of Canticle City, to something moving, shifting. Like sand.

Is it time now? S'janth said, bringing him back to the present.

'Yes, my sweet.'

The words tumbled from his mouth, and he fell with them, out of his body. Colours dulled, sounds faded out, taste, smell, and touch became memories. He saw his body through a shadowed frame as the daemon grew to inhabit it, took it for herself.

S'janth rose to her feet, armoured knees bent, Anguish tucked into a backhand grip, the Pleasure of the Flesh in her off hand.

'I can assure you, little man,' the daemon said, *'that he knows mine.'*

CHAPTER FOURTEEN

Sarquil depressed the chaincannon's trigger, and the ancient barrels started to spin. The whine was musical – Sarquil was meticulous in his maintenance of his weapon – but it took a few moments to build to its crescendo.

It was all S'janth needed. The transhuman body she dwelled within was not as perfect as the form she had once held, but it was still fast and strong. They found themselves at odds on occasion, but when their purposes aligned, they could will Xantine's Space Marine form to feats of strength and skill that no flesh-and-blood consciousness could ever achieve.

She leapt from the throne and rolled as the first shells spat from the muzzle of the chaincannon. They tore through thick carpet, sending tufts of material into the sweet-smelling air of the chamber. She kept moving, her armoured legs pumping, her black hair whipping behind her head, until she reached hard cover: a huge symbol of Slaanesh crafted from aeldari bones. She dropped, squatting on her haunches, her back pressed against the relic. The Pleasure of the Flesh thrummed in her hand, and she felt a brief connection with the daemon that inhabited the weapon.

The chaincannon began its dirge once more, and the symbol exploded, sending splintered bone fragments bouncing off her pauldrons. More suffering for that benighted race. Delicious. She moved again, firing the daemon-possessed pistol as she ran. Each shot hit, and the gun quivered as it waited to smell hyper-oxygenated blood on the air, but Sarquil's thick Tartaros plate absorbed the impact of the mass-reactive shells, and she felt the weapon's disappointment. *'Don't pout, little one,'* she said, as she halted again, this time behind an enlarged silver effigy of Xantine himself. *'There is always more pain.'*

Sarquil padded forward, quiet as ever. 'Is this how the glorious Xantine leads? Allowing your Neverborn to fight on your behalf?' He injected poison into his voice. 'Do you feel like you're in control?'

It was almost imperceptible, but she heard a quiver in his voice. It wasn't fear – the Anathema had cruelly bred that most delectable of emotions out of these insipid creations – but it was something close. Uncertainty. This was not going as Sarquil expected.

It was not as Xantine expected, either, she knew. She felt his consciousness moving gently within her, agitated and confused. They had made an arrangement, but she was prolonging the pleasure, toying with her prey.

It felt wonderful. Her daemonic form had been utterly oblit-erated by her aeldari captors, and the subsequent millennia of captivity had rendered her too weak to take her new host's body outright. But the city had nourished her – so close she could taste its suffering and its misery, its pleasure and its joy.

She had hidden her strength from everyone, even her host, and used it now in this vital, pulsing, muscular form. Her twin hearts beat with hot blood, her muscle fibres bunched in anticipation, her senses rang with scents and tastes, images and sounds.

She turned and dug her shoulder into the pedestal of the statue. The pink ceramite of her armour scraped against the metal, and she pushed. The statue swayed, tipping forward, then back towards her. She rode the momentum, and pushed again – an almighty heave that sent the depiction of Xantine toppling towards Sarquil. The Terminator swung his power fist at the artwork, caving in its inanimate chest with an almighty crack, and redirecting its bulk to slam harmlessly against the chamber floor. The statue's head dislodged, and rolled lazily, until it came to rest, face frozen in a beatific smile.

S'janth used the distraction, planting one armoured boot on the toppled pedestal, before launching herself forward, her weight braced against the sharp point of her rapier. She aimed the weapon at Sarquil's breast, aching for the kiss of blood and bone as it tore through the Space Marine's fused ribcage and enlarged organs.

She was denied. Sarquil was off balance, and couldn't bring his power fist to bear, but the Terminator reacted with admirable speed. He lifted his chaincannon instead, putting the bulky weapon between the trunk of his body and the tip of the blade. It was just enough. The rapier raked through the weapon's casing, before sliding up Sarquil's right arm, carving a deep furrow in the purple ceramite. The gouge sparked and hissed, venting gases. Sarquil roared with pain and frustration.

Her blackened lips shaped a smile at the sound. It wasn't the pain that she craved – she wanted the raw, wet agony of a slow-killing wound – but the Space Marine's reaction showed that she'd hit something deep, something important. That was good.

S'janth rolled and came up in a lithe fighting stance, firing the Pleasure of the Flesh from the hip. The mass-reactives blossomed against Sarquil's chest, where they dug holes in the pristine plate. Pinpricks of pain spiked in the ether again, but nothing substantial enough to fell the warrior. She would need to get closer, to feel his hot breath on her face as he died.

S'janth fell forward, her fingers disappearing halfway into the thick carpet, and ran like an animal, four limbs pumping to close the ground between the two figures. Her eyes flicked between power fist and chaincannon as she ran, anticipating the parry, waiting to see which way to feint before burying the rapier in her prey.

She didn't see the boot. Sarquil swung his tree-trunk leg forward, catching her as she charged. Her own velocity – unnatural, impossible, inhuman – counted against her, and she crumpled, winded, to the floor. She was wheezing curses to her temporary mortal weakness when Sarquil pressed the boot against her chest, and she felt the solid bone cage of her ribs creak under the incredible weight of both the giant and his ornate armour.

'Not so fast now, are we?' Sarquil said. 'It is a shame to destroy one of Slaanesh's creations, but you cannot be trusted, daemon.'

He raised the chaincannon, and aimed it at her forehead. She took in its snarling jaws, traced the six blackened barrels back to the depths of the ancient weapon. A Space Marine would not beg for their life, but she was no Space Marine. She was a creature of desire, pleasure and pain, of obsession and indulgence, and the concept of oblivion – a plane of no sensation – horrified her.

She offered Sarquil slaves, weapons and soldiers. She offered him Slaanesh's favour, even though it was not hers to give, and promised to bring him to his father, even though Fulgrim would not grant him audience. She offered him anything, everything, that he could ever want.

When that failed – when Sarquil simply stared back with his dark eyes – she clawed and scratched and raved, black foam frothing from black lips. It was all for naught.

Sarquil depressed the trigger of the chaincannon.

The weapon exploded.

The rapier had cut deep, severing key arteries inside the cannon's bulky frame, causing a catastrophic failure when it was finally fired. Its barrels erupted outwards, bending and bowing like a flower blossoming; its trigger, receiver and ammunition cycler simply ceased to exist, atomised by the detonation.

Light and sound filled her senses. There was pain, too. Hot shrapnel tore through the meat of her face, glazing her cheeks with blood that ran like tears.

But there was more pain in this room. Sarquil's right arm was missing, vaporised to the elbow. What remained of the limb hung limp against his side, pink-white bone degloved by the force of the blast. Explosions continued up the chaincannon's ammunition feed as it hung limp at his waist, staccato detonations leading towards the reactor on the back of the Tartaros armour. He stumbled, power fist clutching at his missing arm, as he tried to steady himself, howling in agony.

Sarquil staggered between portraits and landscapes, smashing sculptures and knocking over busts, destroying the cultural wealth of this world in his pain. He stopped, finally, massive feet splayed wide, his face a mask of rage. He was framed against the window, framed against the purples and pinks, blacks and golds of the Great Rift. She thought of that place. A shifting tide of sensation where she could shed this mortal frame and rejoin her patron and prince, by his side after millennia alone.

But not yet. There was pleasure to be had first. Improvising, she hurled Anguish, full force, at Sarquil's central mass. The warrior reacted too slow, blinded by pain, or frustration, or both, and the blade, perfectly thrown, bored through his stomach armour. It found skin and muscle, blood and organs as it travelled, soft and yielding. It passed through them all, tearing and ripping, until it reached something hard: bone – the bone of Sarquil's spine – where it finally stopped its course.

The starlight reflected in his metal pate as he staggered backwards, carried by the momentum of the thrown rapier, towards the window. His shoulder touched glassaic and it shattered, allowing the cold of the city into the chamber. It touched her skin like a caress. He started to fall into the void.

She moved faster than she thought this body could, and caught the hilt of the rapier in one hand, arresting the fall. Her glove was already sticky with gore, the white of the silk now stained red with Sarquil's innards. The giant teetered at the window, his feet on the ledge, his body suspended above a precipitous drop into the lower reaches of the overcity. His eyes met hers. His wide, pleading; hers slitted, feline. For a moment, a perfect study in opposites.

It could not last. The blade was buried deep in muscle and bone, but Sarquil was too heavy in his Tartaros plate. The monomolecular blade of Anguish dislodged from its home amongst his thoracic vertebrae, and the huge Space Marine slid backwards. Blood and bone fragments burst from the wound as the ancient weapon left his body completely, a bloom of red and white that the warrior seemed to wear on his chest like a flower as he fell from the council tower, past massive hab-blocks, vast agglomerations of pipes, and statues the size of skyscrapers.

The speck of purple and red shrank until it was so small that even her augmented, transhuman eyes could no longer track it. She reached out with her other senses – ones only her kind possessed – but could not locate Sarquil's soul amongst the millions that called Serrine their home.

She could delve into the city's depths to find her prey. She imagined Sarquil, weak and dying, his bones broken, his body pulverised. She would enjoy placing her sword between his shoulder blades, leaning on the weapon until it drew out the last of his lifeblood. But she might not find him, or worse, he might be dead already. Such a tiresome possibility – no pleasure at all.

She looked out into the city, its lights dimmed, its souls flickering like candles as they slumbered. Others burned brighter, engaging in the pleasures that Slaanesh encouraged. She would join them, she decided. She could show them such delights.

PART III

CHAPTER FIFTEEN

She cradled him like a child.

Carefully. Firmly. He was secure as she carried him, her body powerful against his. He was weak compared to her, small and fragile. But he was content. So content. He could just close his eyes, just sleep here. Sleep here forever, in her arms. In this warmth, in this darkness. In this safety.

But something was wrong. Something wrong with his body. He knew his body. It was his body after all – his alone – the body he had been born in and grew in and lived in. He knew its freckles and scars and hairs and lumps better than he knew any other place, and something was *wrong*.

His weight was off. That was it. His weight was off. He was slipping within her embrace and – oh Throne, it *hurt!* – he was listing to one side, the absence of something, something so painful, causing him to howl in agony, to unbalance, and to fall, fall, fall…

Arqat woke with a scream on his lips.

There was a hand, too. Tough and leathery, it had stopped him from calling out.

'Shh,' Sanpow hissed, his voice a low whisper, urgent. The old man's deep-lined face loomed over Arqat, eyes white even in the gloom. He slowly removed his hand and pressed a finger to his own lips, miming silence.

'Who?' Arqat mouthed.

'Gassers,' Sanpow responded, the sound of his lips parting the only noise inside the pipe.

'How many?'

Sanpow held up three fingers.

Arqat nodded. The adrenaline had hit his system now, and he was wide awake, the memory of the nightmare already fading. He had it every night he slept in the pipes, and he knew how to shake it off. He had to recover his wits quickly when he kept watch on the edge of the territory, especially when there were Gassers about. They couldn't be reasoned with, couldn't be bought off. They might not kill you immediately like a lot of the other gangs fighting for Refinery Cedille-Five, but if they took you, then you'd wish you were dead. They'd choke you out with their gas, until the pink of the world became grey, then carry you back to their secret places. There they'd snip a bit here, slice a bit there, until a person wasn't a person any more.

Sanpow's eyes bugged. Arqat knew that look: it meant the old man was listening hard. Arqat joined him, focusing on a corroded bloom of rust on the pipe wall as he waited for the telltale slap of bandage-wrapped foot on metal.

Nothing yet. Just the slow drip of liquid somewhere, condensation mixing together with old sap residue to ring out the ever-present sound of Serrine's refinery complexes. That drip had infuriated Arqat when he first arrived in the undercity; now it was a comforting sound, the background rhythm of the arterial system of pipes that made up his new home.

The old man raised a hand. 'There!' he mouthed.

Arqat could only hear drips, the tap-tap-tap on rusted metal. Maybe the old codger was hearing things, decades in the pipes addling his brain meat. Maybe they'd have to retire him from outings.

'You sure?' he mouthed back, raising an eyebrow. They'd been careful: they'd scuffed away their footprints as they walked through the miles of pipes that made up Serrine's vast under-city refinery complexes, and when they'd found their sleeping spot for the night, Sanpow had kicked away the spent power-cell they'd used to climb into the maintenance hatch.

Sanpow nodded furiously and cupped his ears. Still nothing.

Wait. Between the taps, a gentle sound.

They moved quietly, the Gassers. They didn't like a fight, much preferred to knock you out without getting their hands dirty. They were immune to their poison, of course, or as close as it was possible to get. They wore old refinery suits, patching them up with bandages, tape, and anything else they could get their grubby hands on. It made them look like nightmares, Sanpow said, all saucer eyes and long noses. The youths said that was what they'd turned into, spending so long in the gas, but Arqat knew better: that was just their masks. At least, he told him-self that.

All of Serrine's undercity residents lived below the haze line, but the Gassers had gone deeper still, into the bowels of the refineries. They were the first down after the filtration units failed, the most ragged and most desperate of the undercity's rats, willing to trade their bodies and their brains for an oppor-tunity to thrive. It was full of poisonous gas, sure, but there was real estate down there too, the kind of room that would make a gang boss green with envy – the kind of room that would spark full-scale gang warfare in the upper reaches of the undercity.

But you had to pay the price. The first gangers who ventured down there came out *wrong*, they said. Arqat had been too young to see them himself, too new to the undercity, but Sanpow had told him about monsters that had stumbled out of the depths – howling, gibbering things. They'd been stretched, squeezed by the gas they sucked in.

There was a new sound: a hiss. Wisps of green smoke crept from a grate in the base of the pipe, about fifty yards away, close to where they'd entered for the night.

'Gas!' Arqat shouted, and reached for his mask. He fumbled for the scavenged rebreather with one hand, trying to loop the strap around the back of his head in a single motion. He missed, and the mask slid sideways, bouncing uselessly in his grasp. He tried again, panic rising in his chest as the thick smoke blotted out the far end of the pipe. He missed again. His hand was shaking, and he forced himself to breathe. He felt he could taste the gas on the air already.

He felt rough hands on his wrist, and Sanpow helped him pull his mask into position, clamping it tightly over his mouth and nose before closing the clasp at the back.

The old man slapped him on the shoulder, and Arqat nodded shakily. The scavenged rebreather wouldn't protect his lungs from the thick green substance for long, but it would buy him valuable seconds.

'We have to go,' Sanpow said, and set off down the pipe in a half-crouch. Arqat followed him. Sanpow was built for this: the old man had grown up in the undercity, and even before the angels came, he had already spent a life scuttling around in its secret places. Arqat was a head taller and far broader, the narrow shoulders of his youth having expanded with age and training. He ducked, awkwardly shuffling after his guide until he almost bumped into the back of the old man. The pipe was narrow, but he could see why he had stopped over Sanpow's stooped shoulders. More gas, in clouds as thick as those that blocked out the sky, barring their way. The Gasser crew had herded them in, and now they were trying to smoke them out.

The old man turned, caught Arqat's gaze. Together they looked down at the maintenance hatches beneath their feet. They ran the length of the pipes, these hatches, installed so that work crews could inspect every inch of the thousands of miles of pipework that carried Serrine's precious sap to the surface for export off-world. Now many were rusted shut. They nodded at each other, plan agreed wordlessly.

Sanpow moved to stand over one grate, pointing his younger companion to another. They'd practised this before. 'Multiple points of exit to sow maximum confusion, limited application of violence, and then make good your escape.' That was how Galletti had explained it, during her drills.

'Why "limited"?' Arqat had asked once, raising the stump of his arm. 'Why don't we stick it to 'em? We're strong – stronger than the Gassers, even the Screamers.' He'd drawn a chorus of approval from the other youths, but Galletti had rolled her eyes and explained. They hadn't got to where they had by picking fights with other gangers. 'That's why we ain't got anywhere,' he had mumbled under his breath.

Sanpow caught his wandering gaze with a wave, and reached down between his feet. He pointed, then cut his hand down on his palm, the message clear: *drop and run*. They would meet at the pre-agreed location, close to their own turf. Arqat nodded, reached down, and pulled the grate with his hand, ready to drop into the maintenance corridor below.

There was a face below him. Huge eyes shone in its featureless surface, their shiny blackness reflecting the wan light of the last flickering glow-globe illuminating the corridor. The Gasser cocked its head, quizzically. There was something in its hands – something dull silver, shaped like a bottle.

Arqat dropped onto the Gasser. His boots connected with his target's torso, and they both crashed to the floor with a thud that echoed along the corridor.

He heard the old man drop a few yards further down: a thud, and then a crunch. Sanpow must have landed on something, Arqat realised, as he saw his mask skitter out of his hand and away across the floor. He watched it slide, until its movement was arrested by a bandage-wrapped boot. The owner of the boot turned to look at the old man, splayed out on the floor, and brought its foot down on the rebreather, crunching the glass faceplate.

Sanpow tried to rise, but his leg buckled under him. The lower portion was bent at an unnatural angle. Arqat was no healer, but he knew even from here it was broken. There was only one way out for the old man: he would have to be carried.

Arqat drew himself up to his feet, shaking off the impact of the collision, and started to move towards his downed friend. He barely made it a step before thin arms snaked around his body, holding him in place. He struggled, but the Gasser's arms were cable-strong, and he heard a wheeze in his ear. He realised with disgust that it was a laugh.

The first Gasser brought itself to its feet, jerky movements and huge black eyes making it look like one of the huge refinery spiders that lived in the darkest tunnels down here. Arqat had been terrified of the creatures when he was first brought to the undercity. He didn't like them much more now.

It knelt across the back of the old man's legs and wrapped an arm around his neck, presenting his face to Arqat. Sanpow's eyes, always so sharp and composed, looked frantic as they glinted in the gloom.

The Gasser pulled a small silver bottle from its bandolier, and placed it just below Sanpow's chin. Keeping its bug eyes on Arqat, it removed the stopper from the bottle with a careful motion. There was a small hiss, and thick purple smoke crawled from its depths and up over the old man's face.

Sanpow aged a decade in a moment. His skin, already drawn and leathery from decades underground, puckered further as the gas touched it.

'Run,' Sanpow gasped, his tongue shrivelling in his mouth as he tried to speak. 'Ruuun...'

'No!' Arqat screamed, struggling in the arms of his attacker. The wheezing laugh in his ear was louder now.

The flesh of Sanpow's face died in front of Arqat's eyes, blackening and dissolving to reveal the white bone of his old friend's skull beneath.

Arqat screamed again, howling through his rebreather mask in an impotent rage as he struggled in the Gasser's grip. Sinewy fingers reached over his face, unseating his rebreather as they tried to stifle his screams.

Suddenly, he could smell the air of the tunnel: damp, cloying and ripe. His consciousness lurched, and a memory surfaced – of swaying censers, of sickening incense, and of Tumas, the old priest. He had been so weak, unable to save his flock. Arqat *hated* him.

He took his chance. He grabbed for his machete with his good arm, and reached over his shoulder, stabbing and stabbing and stabbing at air until he found a target. There was a scream, and the Gasser's arms fell from his torso. Arqat spun to find his attacker with its hands to what was left of its face, blood gouting through bandaged fingers.

The other Gasser let Sanpow's shrivelled head fall from its grip, and reached into the folds of its protective suit, pulling out an autopistol. It raised the weapon and pulled the trigger, but the gun, like most of the Gassers' equipment, was poorly maintained, and it clicked, the round jammed in its chamber. The Gasser slapped the weapon against its free palm, and raised it again, but this time, it didn't have the chance to squeeze the trigger. Arqat tackled the figure, wrapping his good arm around the Gasser's waist as he brought it to the slimy tunnel floor.

They wrestled next to the corpse of his mentor. His friend. Arqat glanced at the ruin of Sanpow's face. The sight drove him on, and he fought with a feral rage, raining blows down on the Gasser's torso, neck and head. This one was much like the other – wiry and powerful – and it gave as good as it got, Arqat's grunts of exertion and anger met by the Gasser's infernal, inhuman hissing. The Gasser pulled a knife from somewhere inside its robes, and slashed wildly, catching across the skin and muscle of Arqat's stomach.

Arqat had expected the wound to slow him, but the pain was white hot, and he used it, a furnace at his core, driving him on. He slammed his elbow into the Gasser's neck, grinding cartilage and constricting airflow. The Gasser gurgled, and Arqat smiled a cruel smile. He had killed before – everyone had, down here – but he would enjoy this one. He rolled, hooking his legs around the laughing Gasser until he was on top of his masked enemy, knee across its throat. He slammed the heel of his fist against the insectoid face mask, hard enough that he could feel something crunch. The blank glass eyes remained indifferent to the blows.

Still the Gasser hissed.

'Stop *laughing!*' Arqat screamed, and dug his fingers into the rubberised seal at the side of the mask. He pulled with his new-found strength, tearing the mask from the Gasser's face.

Part of its nose came with it. Blood gouted from the hole, inky black against the ghost-pale skin of the man beneath. Hazy pink eyes regarded him with amusement – at least he thought he saw amusement, beyond the blood – and he roared with anger.

'Stop it, stop it, *stop it!*'

Arqat used the gaping hole in the Gasser's face as a target, slamming his fist down again and again and again into the man's skull. He stopped only when there was no longer any skull to speak of, just a wreckage of meat and bone, and looked up. The final Gasser had watched the decapitation of its colleague in mute horror. Now it hissed in panic and turned on its heels, trying to run. It had nowhere to go, though, and Arqat's rage made him faster.

He caught the Gasser in the back with his blade, embedding it tip first through the masked figure's spine. The Gasser's legs buckled immediately, nerves severed by the wide blade's passage through its wiry body. Arqat rode it to the floor, knees in the small of its back. He felt its pelvis crunch against hard metal, felt bone break.

'No…' the Gasser hissed, voice distorted by his breathing mask. 'Please, mercy…'

It twitched as Arqat pulled the blade from its spine, an unnatural movement that made it look like a marionette. Blood rose from the wound, like the sap that these tunnels once pumped to the overcity. He drove the blade in again, through the back of the Gasser's neck, hard enough that its tip pierced the metal floor. The reddened weapon stuck for a moment, a monument to Arqat's anger, before he pulled it loose.

'No… mercy,' Arqat breathed through clenched teeth. 'Just… blood.'

S'janth wore his body more often these days. It was an accord they had reached, he told himself, but he knew the truth: he could no longer stop her wresting control of his form when she chose to. The daemon had swollen with power. She had been a husk of the creature that she once was when he was called to her, weakened from millennia in aeldari captivity, but she had grown in his body, refilling her essence on the suffering and ecstasies of Serrine's populace.

He had learned to marshal his consciousness while she was in the ascendancy. He had lived a long life – even with the exact span muddled by millennia spent in the warp's changing tides – and he had forgotten more than most beings would ever know. He filled his time dredging through these memories, caught on fickle currents of interest.

He rode them now, passing time. He savoured the memory of his rise to power on Serrine, the sound of his name on tens of thousands of tongues. He was loved, then – truly loved – for the first time in his life. It was a sweet taste still, that love, but it was familiar to him now. It had turned stale in the years since his arrival. Tiresome. He moved on.

He delved further back, reliving his flight from the Black Legion on board the *Exhortation*. He had taken the ship, and his warband, from Euphoros. The small-minded fool had cast in with Abaddon's rabble, sublimating Xantine and his brothers among the warband into the Children of Torment. Xantine, too charismatic and too skilful to suffer such indignation, had challenged Euphoros to a duel, the winner to be given command of both the ship and its warriors. Naturally, he had triumphed, and the surviving members of the warband – seeing him as a paragon of the virtues of the Emperor's Children – elected to join him in his noble quest across the stars on board his new ship.

No, a voice said. *That was not how it happened.*

He found himself deep in an ancient aeldari temple. Vast statues towered over him, their heads encased in tall helms. Xenos filth. There was death in this place, warriors armoured in plate the colour of the obsidian walls. He had fought them; he had killed them. That was his task: to kill them.

And more. Always more.

There was another purpose. A presence in this place. It spoke to him. It was speaking to him. The spear, pristine, unbroken, lay on a bed of flower petals. How did flowers grow in this place of death? He ached to touch them, to take the spear, to become one.

'I don't want to see this,' he murmured, and the image flickered.

No? the voice said.

'No. Something died here. Something ended.'

What would you like to see?

'Something new.'

Of course.

He saw himself as his Neverborn prey saw him. He was a black maw, sharp teeth spattered with blood. His eyes were pits of pure darkness, solid as gemstones, from which no light could escape. Nothing could escape. He felt their emotions. They were not as he understood them – these creatures *were* fear, or anger, or lust, or malice, or one of countless emotions, given twisting bodies in the ocean of the warp – but they all radiated one sensation. They were scared. Scared of him. They lived in a world of soft edges and shifting shapes, thoughts and souls and questions given temporary form. He was a monster to them: hard, rough, *real.* He took them from their womb and ate them whole, laughing as he destroyed their essence. They quivered in his belly, trying to die.

He felt a new sensation, a tiny spark.

Pity. That was new.

'Yes,' he whispered, enjoying the feeling.

He saw pink and purple, wisps of pearl white, pierced by a

dagger of pure black. He heard the sound of a thousand glass spires, wailing their agonies to the heavens. He smelled perfume and smoke. He tasted blood. He felt pain – crushing pain – in his legs. In his heart.

Canticle City. No. Even for him, that one was still too painful.

'Take me elsewhere.'

Are you sure?

'Yes… yes. Please, take me away.'

Where will you go?

'Anywhere. It hurts too much.'

The dagger of black stabbed downwards, growing in a moment to darken the sky. The pink and purple were gone, replaced by fire and then… nothing.

Black sand, running through purple fingers.

He recoiled as if he had been struck by a mass-reactive shell. The effect was physical, and he felt himself dragged through memories. He saw Canticle City, the temple, the *Exhortation* in a heartbeat as he hurtled through layers of consciousness. He felt S'janth in his body, filling it up like water in a cup, but he brushed her aside with ease.

He came back to reality screaming a single word.

'Father!'

CHAPTER SIXTEEN

Edouard was first in line today. That was good. He hadn't been able to sleep – the hunger was too bad – so he'd packed up his sleeping roll, hidden it in the usual spot and made his way down to the church.

Unfortunately, so had Suell.

Suell wasn't a bad kid, he just managed to find the worst in everything. Trouble followed him like a bad smell. A bad smell followed him, as well, the result of a life spent squatting in Serrine's ruined buildings.

'I heard they've run out again,' the young man said, scratching his shaved head. The habit annoyed Edouard. Suell's face annoyed Edouard. Even his voice annoyed Edouard, and the older man rolled his eyes involuntarily.

'Don't be simple,' Edouard sighed. 'We're here first. They missed one week. They're not going to miss another.'

He watched his words sail over Suell's head as the youth hopped from foot to foot and breathed into his hands. A location above the planet's thick cloud layer meant that Serrine's overcity was usually cold, but it was especially frigid before the sun came up.

'Yeah, yeah,' Suell said, nodded to imagined agreement. 'My mate told me that it's gone for good this time. They've only got a little bit left, and they've given that to the rich families.' He spat on the ground. A coil of steam rose from the gobbet of mucus. 'He's down in the undercity, and he says they don't even harvest the grass any more, let alone refine it.'

'Your mate doesn't know shit. They'd have riots in the streets if they stopped the supply.'

Suell tapped the side of his head. 'Think about it. When was the last time you saw the Sophisticants unloading a shipment? All they do now is walk the streets looking for heads to crack. You know I'm right, Ed.'

'Don't talk like that, and don't call me Ed.' He hoped his brusque tone would stop the youth before he carried on, but a needle of fear jabbed at Edouard's spine anyway as he let the taboo thought enter his mind. *What if Suell was right?* He shivered in the cold early morning air. It had been a week since he'd last been able to get his hands on some of the stimm they called Runoff, and even then, it was just one vial.

It was the lowest-grade stuff, he knew, the junk left over when they brewed the rejuvenat treatments. They used to ship that stuff to Terra, his mother had told him, back when Serrine had a steady stream of Imperial ships calling at its void port. Now what was left of it went to the top families, and they were stuck with the dregs. Some bought it, trading trinkets and favours for their fix. Others fought for it, killing and maiming their friends and family members for barrels of the stuff. In the undercity, where the grass was refined, gangs fought and died over the supply lines, the victors earning the right to sell it to consumers above the clouds.

He just sold his worship. Turned up at the church, bowed before the Saviour, spoke the words they asked him to say. His worship was cheap, now, anyway – sold to the highest bidder. He didn't care about much beyond Runoff.

The irony bit at his belly. He had been born to be a priest, and had begun his studies in this world's most beautiful and most ancient place of worship. That life had been snatched away from him by the same crime that saw so many of Serrine's buildings destroyed, reduced to the rubble and rock of ancient ancestors. He was to be the leader of a flock. Now he was just another beast in one.

'I'm telling you, man, the Saviour's given up on us,' Suell said, snapping Edouard out of his reverie.

'Shut up,' he hissed in response. He didn't like the kid, but he didn't want to see him get hurt – not when they were so close to getting their fix. 'The Sophisticants will hear you. Talk like that will get your legs broke.' He shot a furtive glance at the hulking figure by the door, a spiked club hanging from its black leather belt. Its hooded head swung left and right across the congregation of bedraggled souls as they lined up for their offering.

He remembered a time before the Runoff, but only barely. He'd seen the Saviour himself once, seen him with his own eyes. He'd been a child, barely in his tenth year, when he'd been bundled into the undercroft of the Cathedral of the Bounteous Harvest. He'd huddled in the dark for hours, scared – terrified – as the roof shook, as bigger boys stifled sobs, as their world caved in around them. Until the old wooden doors had cracked open, and heroes came to deliver them into the light. He wore Imperial purple and shining gold, and he was tall, as tall as an angel of myth. Except he wasn't a myth, he was real, and he was their planet's new ruler.

He brought a new world with him. Serrine's governor was

deposed – some said violently – its noble families purged, and its ancient traditions washed away overnight, all except one: veneration of the Saviour. In his triumph, he threw open the planet's stores, giving access to vast hoards of treasure, technology and, of course, stimms.

The grass had been harvested for its use in rejuvenat treatments, but the Imperium's botanists knew well its secondary properties. Careful cultivation and refinement could make a potent combat stimulant that boosted muscle cultivation, bone growth and aggression. Edouard didn't know that. He just knew that Runoff made his frail body feel powerful, strengthened his limbs and his resolve to the point that he felt he could run through marble walls. It made him feel strong, vital, *perfect*.

For a time. Soon would come the blinding muscle pains, the frenzied rages, the strange visions. Last week he'd snapped back to consciousness outside, his eyes dry and burning, sore from staring unblinking at the purple scar in the sky. It was bigger than he'd ever seen it, he swore. He'd crawled back into his makeshift nest that morning and told himself he couldn't sleep, when really, he was afraid to: he saw the scar still, every time he closed his eyes.

A small price to pay, he decided, as he stepped forward to receive his charity. He could taste it already. So sweet it was almost sickly. Soon it would be running down his throat, coating his insides, filling him with warmth, radiant warmth. The sides of his tongue tingled in anticipation, and he held his hands out to accept the bowl.

There was no bowl.

He looked up into the hard face of a woman, who regarded him with bloodshot eyes. There was no sympathy in that red.

'The Saviour blesses you, my child,' she said.

Edouard stood dumbfounded. 'What?' he asked, voice weak. 'Where's the Runoff?'

'The Saviour's blessing is enough. His benevolence is all his citizens require.'

'But… I need it…' he whimpered.

'Tough,' she said, religious tone giving way to rougher speech. 'We ain't got none. Now get out.' She jutted her jaw.

Suell appeared at his shoulder, his sour smell a pungent miasma. 'See?' Suell said. 'Told you so. Saviour's given up on us.'

'He wouldn't do that to us,' Edouard whispered, eyes flicking from the woman to Suell, and back again to the woman. He was pleading. 'He wouldn't. I know him, I've seen him.'

The woman raised her hand in threat. 'You've seen nothing, you filthy wretch. Now get *out.*'

'Yes he would,' Suell said. 'He's up there in his palace now, I bet, giving all the best stuff to all his high-born lapdogs, and looking down at the rest of us rotting in the streets.' He barked a bitter laugh. 'Sure, the big families make a song and dance about the challenges, but the system is rigged! *Strive for perfection!* they say. *Anyone can succeed!* But they hoard all the best stuff and feed it to their freaks, get them to kill any of us whenever we try to challenge them!'

Suell was ranting now, spittle foaming at the edge of his split lips. The Sophisticant, attracted by the clamour, turned in their direction, the calm face of his golden mask impassive.

'Stop, Suell,' Edouard said. 'You'll get us in trouble. We only want a little bit, right? Just enough for today? There will be more tomorrow, it'll be fine tomorrow.' He turned back to the woman, reaching out to her with rough hands. 'Please,' he said. 'You must have some. Just a little bit?'

She backhanded him across the face, and he stumbled backwards, catching a foot on a worn step. He toppled to the ground, and the wind left his body as he landed painfully on his ribs.

'Oi!' Suell yelled. 'You can't do that to him. Who gives you the right?'

'I can do whatever I want, scum,' the woman snarled. She raised a long leather boot and planted it powerfully into Edouard's chest. He felt something give way, an audible snap accompanied by a lance of sharp pain. He anticipated more kicks, and tried to tuck himself into a ball, but the blows didn't come. He opened an eye, and watched as Suell leapt from rag-clad feet, tackling the woman. They tumbled up the steps and landed in a sprawl of limbs, her ceremonial robes restricting her ability to right herself. Suell was faster.

'Leave him alone!' the younger man shouted, as he managed to climb onto the woman's back, pinning her arms in place. He turned his head to check on his downed friend, and opened his mouth to speak. 'Here, Ed – are you all ri–'

He didn't finish the question, as a spiked club slammed into the side of his face. Skin, muscle, and bone were pulped by the force of the blow, as the hulking Sophisticant swung his weapon in a full arc that caved in Suell's skull. His body sat up for a moment, still astride the woman, before her frantic writhing sent it slumping to the church floor.

Edouard tried to scream, but the pain in his chest caught the sound as he tried to fill his lungs, and it became a whimper. Others offered their voices instead: a chorus of screams and shrieks rose from the others who had filtered in for their weekly rations. There was fear in the air, but anger, too. It had been a week since their last supply as well, and word of the shortages had clearly filtered to the back of the queue.

Braver, or more desperate, members of the crowd surged forward, howling epithets at the Sophisticant and the woman.

'Murderer!' one man screamed. His too-tight skin threatened to tear like parchment as the muscles in his neck bulged. He was almost as big as the Sophisticant, who faced him down with his eternally impassive glare. The crowd surged forward, pushing the big man in the process. It was the incitement the Sophisticant needed for further violence, and he swung a two-handed blow with his mace in the man's direction. He ducked the blow, letting it cave in the chest of the woman behind him, and came up with an uppercut into the underside of the brute's jaw, jarring his sculpted golden mask upwards, and exposing the lower half of his face. The skin was pink and puckered, as if it had been burned, and there were no lips to speak of, just a rubberised tube that snaked its way up the face and out of sight.

The crowd took their chance. They swarmed the Sophisticant, pulling at his arms, giving him no space to swing his wicked mace. Knives and shivs were produced from sleeves and pockets, their glint catching in the cold morning light before they were driven into the masked figure's torso. From his position on the floor, Edouard saw the Sophisticant disappear under the conglomeration of bodies.

The woman was further away, putting the makeshift altar between herself and the crowd, as if she was to provide her sermon.

'Children of the Saviour!' she called. 'We are one under his light! I beseech you, stop!'

It was fruitless. The congregation had the smell of death in their noses now, their collective wisdom sanctioning their righteous violence. Two women closed on her from either side of the altar, improvised weapons in hand: a shard of coloured glass and a mason's hammer.

'Go away!' the woman screamed. 'I have nothing for you!' But her authority had been pricked, and the people who, moments before, waited obediently for her benediction would offer her no mercy. She slumped to her knees as the mob advanced, their wide smiles showing darkened teeth and purple gums.

He didn't want to see what happened next. He crawled through legs, whimpering as knees and feet caught him in his broken ribs, back towards the entrance. He heard the crack of hammer on bone as the weapon struck the woman's skull. It was a sound he had heard too many times before. He heard the exultant cry that came with it, howled into the freezing air of the morning.

This crowd had their prize. Now they would curdle, would turn on each other, their desires not so easily sated that a few lives would fill them up. He had lived this life long enough to see the rot behind Serrine's beauty.

He pulled himself to his feet, bracing an arm across his broken chest and barking with the pain. He half-ran, half-stumbled towards the church doors, and stepped out into the bright blue morning.

A statue stood in the centre of the crossroads. When he was young, Serrine's statues showed birds of paradise, mythical beasts, men and women of history and legend. Now every statue had been crudely altered so it depicted the same figure, its four arms raised in triumph.

'I hate you!' he screamed at the statue.

The riots continued into the night, conglomerates of humanity spilling out from churches and bars, narcotic dens and hab-blocks. They burned and smashed as they moved, their mass of motivations – anger, pleasure, frustration, indulgence, fear and transgression – all resulting in the same outcomes: destruction. Pain.

Vavisk watched them from the Cathedral of the Bounteous Harvest. The Noise Marine had made his home in the ancient structure primarily for the acoustics, but he had completed some modifications over the years that he had spent on Serrine. The vast pipe that had once been the primary delivery method of refined Solipsus sap to the overcity had been expanded and turned outwards, becoming an amplifier for the song of his congregation.

It was a dirge tonight. A plaintive song, mourning, echoing the mood of his cadre of Noise Marines. They longed to be back amongst the stars, bringing the music of the apocalypse to new worlds and new realities. He understood their yearning. He too wanted the sublime. Instead, he saw the mundane in an orgy of petty destruction.

'My people are restless tonight,' Xantine said, at Vavisk's side. His brother often spent time at the cathedral – when he wasn't availing himself of Qaran Tun's collection of Neverborn, or communing with the daemon that he had invited into his body. As the site of his enduring victory on the world, this was a symbolic location for the leader of the Adored, but Vavisk also knew that his brother valued his company and his advice. Xantine's web of confidants had never been wide – even amongst the egotists of the Emperor's Children, he had always been particularly distrustful of his peers – but his time on Serrine had only reduced their number. Sarquil's betrayal had affected him greatest of all.

'They are killing each other,' Vavisk said. 'Will we stop them?' He knew the answer before he asked the question, but after millennia together, they both had their roles to play.

'Stop them? Whyever would we do that?' Xantine asked. 'Pain is the price of perfection. The strong will survive, and this world will advance. This is a lesson you have forever struggled with, Vavisk. You are as old as I am, but you still do not understand the motivations of mortals. Stick to your music, and let me deal in the complexities of the soul.'

'These are the seeds of insurrection...'

'No,' Xantine snapped. 'This is the fulfilment of my vision – the strong taking control from the weak. You speak like our departed brother, so small-minded, so desperate for the next fleeting pleasure, unable to see the culmination of my genius.' He sighed, visibly softening his demeanour.

'I am so close, Vavisk. A new society – a perfect society. Serrine is a model for the future of the galaxy, with sensation unchained and ambition rewarded. The Corpse-Emperor could not achieve it. Even Father could not achieve it. Only I have the clarity of vision to carry this to fruition.' Xantine raised a fist. 'Others will try to take this from me and claim this success for their own. Sarquil tried. I fear he still tries, plotting and scheming from whatever pit he rots within as we speak. He always wanted control of this world.' He turned to Vavisk, his turquoise eyes boring into the Noise Marine's skin. 'Not like you, old friend. You would not take this from me.' Vavisk did not reply, and Xantine tried to let the question drift out into the night air without an answer. He could not. 'Would you?'

Vavisk met his warlord's gaze, his disfigured face unreadable. For once, the mouths on his neck were quiet.

'I do not covet this world,' the Noise Marine replied. 'I do not understand why you do.' He turned back to the city, catching a final glimpse of the frothing mass of humanity as they flowed through the streets like blood through arteries.

'Excuse me, brother. I must join my choir,' Vavisk said, and descended to lead the evening's chorus.

CHAPTER SEVENTEEN

He held the dagger in a backhand grip, the serrated blade flat against his muscled forearm. The metal was warm, and it was wet already with blood. Not his own. It dripped from the weapon, little raindrops that tapped out the softest whispers of sensation. Moments of pleasure against his pain.

He swayed on legs wider than the stalks of Serrine's grass. His muscles burned. His chest, his arms, his back, his calves and his thighs. Strained and stressed from the fight. The rejuvenat kept him young, and they made him more than that, too: bigger, stronger, faster. But they hurt, too. They set his nerves on fire and made his bones feel as if they were being stretched inside his skin. He slept in snatched moments, a rag by the side of his cot for him to chew on when the agony woke him up again.

He would never tell anyone, but in his weakest moments, he wondered if he wanted this. To be chosen. To be feted. To be served the sweetest meats and the ripest fruits, to be offered pleasures beyond his imagination.

He couldn't have said no. He didn't *want* to say no. Who would turn this down? The chance to become the biggest, the strongest, the best? It was all anyone dreamed of – especially a sixth son of a vassal family. His parents had scrimped and saved until they finally saw their opportunity in their son as he entered his adult years: the long limbs, the toned muscles, the fighter's grace. They cashed it all in for his treatments, securing the services of back-alley chirurgeons and black-market sellers to get the best stuff. He could be a winner. Be *their* winner.

He spared them a glance. His mother, her mouth open, the tendons in her neck bulging. She was screaming something, but her voice was lost in the baying din of the crowd. His father, small eyes hard as gemstones in his drawn face. His mouth was pursed, concentrating as his family teetered on the brink of advancement.

His low voice came through unnaturally stretched vocal cords. His voice was so deep now that his siblings could barely understand him. He had tried to write his requests, but the words flitted around in his mind like the birds he saw sometimes through the bars in his window. He couldn't catch them. He just smiled at them, these days, on the rare occasions they came to visit him.

The enemy ran at him, her own blade raised. She was like him: tall, wide-shouldered, bigger than everyone else in the duelling chamber. The treatments had made her skull grow too fast, and her skin was too tight around her eyes. Cracked, angry wounds were visible, aggravated and constantly reopened by the natural action of blinking. It made her look as if she was crying blood.

She used her momentum, swinging her short sword overhand as she closed the distance between them. It was a good swing, a powerful swing, but she was not quite like him. He was bigger, and he had the reach. He dropped his shoulder, planted his back foot, and pistoned a meaty fist forward, catching her square in the stomach. The force of the blow reversed her movement in an instant, catapulting her backwards. She skidded across the thick carpet of the duelling chamber. Spots of dark red blood stained the material, a physical echo of her movements since he'd caught her across the upper thigh with his dagger.

She lay on her back, not quite motionless. Her chest still rose and fell, ribs the width of femurs visible under taut skin. It could be over now.

He stomped over to his downed enemy. Her eyes were closed, but they still ran with blood. It streaked the side of her face, staining her porcelain skin. Her tongue lay slack in her mouth.

He raised his dagger, taking it in two hands as he looked around the chamber. There was a cacophony of sound, of chants and cheers, wails of sadness and hoots of joy. He found his parents among the shouting faces. 'I win for you,' he grunted, bowing his huge head.

Then he fell. A kick to his ankles took his legs from under him, and he was down, just as the woman sprang to her feet. She stood over him, boot pinning his arm to the floor. She was smiling – or, he thought she might be smiling. Her jaw had grown so distended that she could no longer close her lips over her teeth.

She stabbed her sword into his chest. There was a flare of agony as the blade bit through fibrous muscle and scraped against his hardened ribs.

He tried to breathe in, even with the sword in his heart, to brace himself for the second wave of pain, as he had taught himself; as he had done countless times.

But the pain didn't come. For the first time since he had been chosen, he felt the fire in his muscles fade. He felt his sinews slacken. He felt his body relax around its bones. For a sweet eternity, he felt nothing.

He let his massive head fall to the side, and met the gaze of his mother. 'I love you,' he rumbled with the last of his words. She was screaming something, the meaning once again drowned out by the crowd. He wondered if she was angry with him.

'I'm sorry,' he said, before he died.

'Good! Good!' Pierod shouted, trying to hush the crowd. It was always difficult. There was such a thrill in standing in such proximity to death, especially an honourable demise. It stirred the soul.

'Citizens! Your attention, please!'

Eventually, the clamour faded, and the governor could talk.

'The challenge is complete,' he called, imbuing his voice with a theatrical tremolo. He'd been practising it recently in his ministerial villa, and was pleased with his progress. 'By decree of Lord Xantine, House Ondine will thusly cede the position of ombudsperson for the Fifty-Fourth District to House Dwann.'

There was a cheer from one side of the chamber. 'Congratulations, Master Dwann – I believe this is your family's first noble posting?'

'It is, governor!'

'And Master Ondine.' Pierod gestured an open palm to the drawn-faced man. 'You and your family will transfer all trappings of office, including possessions, accommodation, and wealth to House Dwann. You are no longer welcome among such rarefied company. Get out, and take your...' – he pointed to the huge corpse in the centre of the challenge arena – '*refuse* with you.'

The woman at the man's side howled, a cry of anguish taken up by those at her flanks, all clad in the lime-green robes of House Ondine. They wailed, and yowled, and gnashed their teeth, complaining that Dwann's champion had cheated, that the duel was void, that their centuries of service should entitle them to superiority over such an upstart family as House Dwann. Pierod met their displays of such vulgarity with a visible sneer.

'The law is clear – the challenge is final.' He gestured to the guards lining the edge of the chamber, autoguns braced across golden breastplates. 'Guards, see that they leave in an orderly fashion.' Several of the men and women grinned as they stepped forward, raising their weapons to strike any recalcitrant members of the now-common family. Pierod watched for a moment, a grin sliding across his face. He'd never liked Ondine. He had smelled of sweat and sadness, a crumpled, dour little man who had never truly enjoyed his position of office, despite the luxuries it brought.

He was idly wondering how Ondine would adapt to a commoner's life, when a voice in his ear made him start. It was deep and rumbling, and came from the throat of his attaché, Corinth.

'Your excellency, terribly sorry to disturb, but I bring grave news.'

Corinth was huge, a slab of bulging muscle that somehow became even bigger when he stooped to speak directly into Pierod's ear.

'Speak clearly, Corinth,' Pierod said. 'What happened?'

'Violence, your excellency. It appears that some of the lower classes took the chance to make trouble during the Saviour's Benediction. They have risen up against our rule.' Corinth dropped into a lower register. 'They have taken control of the void port, and at least two hundred members of the militia are dead.'

Pierod's eyes widened. Trouble amongst the desperate was not uncommon in Serrine's overcity, but to seize control of the void port meant that this was no gang disagreement. This would have ripples through Serrine's precarious political sphere. He sighed dramatically.

'Your excellency?' Corinth asked, still stooping so that his massive head hung next to the governor's.

'I shall have to inform our lord. Strike the day's remaining challenges, reschedule them for tomorrow. Apologise to those families inconvenienced, and send them each a barrel of our finest serum.'

'Your excellency, the supplies are–'

'Just send them a barrel of *something*. Whatever you can find.' Pierod stood from his throne and clapped. 'Citizens of this perfect world! The day's challenges are complete.' There was a rumble of discontent from the audience, and he raised his hands, palms facing down, to still it. 'You will all have your chance, on this I swear. But for now, our lord calls me to his chambers. I bid you all a fond adieu!' He turned on his heels to make his way to Xantine's chamber at the top of the senate building, his cloak swishing behind him. It was another flourish he'd practised at home.

Serrine's larger habs often featured spaces for shrines. They were little alcoves built into the centuries-old structures, into which their inhabitants could place venerations to the Emperor in His guise as the Saviour. The Adeptus Ministorum had been more than happy to encourage this practice, selling figurines of synthetic gemstone and gilded metal for significant markups for generations, forming a major revenue stream for the priests.

Most had abandoned it with the coming of the angels, as the Ministorum changed its focus and encouraged the worship of the Saviour in more physical ways, but Lady Arielle Ondine had maintained the habit. She found it comforting, her shrine serving as a physical focal point for her desires and demands.

Once, her shrine was full of effigies of the Emperor. He was cast in gold and marble, a shining figure in repose on Terra, watching over His people as a distant god. Those figures were long gone. Gangs of large men and women had conducted sweeps of the city after Lord Xantine's ascension to the planet's ultimate power, kicking in doors and confiscating or destroying any idols that represented the Master of Mankind on Terra, rather than the flesh-and-blood ruler of Serrine. She hadn't much cared. She had prayed to the Emperor, but He had never done much for her, so she offered her prayers elsewhere, to someone who would help her.

Arielle had taken the symbol that stood at the centre of her shrine on the day of the xenos coup. She found it in a gutter, a flash of gold amidst the browns and greens of the city's effluence. She had reached for it, and pocketed it in the depths of her robes before any of her peers caught her. She took it home, and cleaned it off, and marvelled at what she saw. It had belonged to one of the angels, she surmised, because nothing so wondrous could have been made by human hands. It was beautiful – more beautiful than anything she had ever owned, crafted with a precision and perfection that she had not known before. She took it in again now, still staggered by its beauty years later: an eight-pointed star, cast in solid gold, inlaid with swirling mother-of-pearl.

It made her feel powerful. And she had become powerful, as she prayed to it. She had been born into mundanity, the only daughter of one Maro Ondine. Her father had been a void port hauler by trade, but as the vast harvester ships from Terra came less often, and then stopped altogether, he began raiding serum supplies, selling some, and taking the rest for himself. His downfall had only steeled her resolve: that she would make something of herself, that she would no longer live in squalor. Lord Xantine's decree had let her do just that.

The price had been high, of course. Seven children, was it?

Or eight, now, she supposed, with the death of Gwillim in the challenge arena. She sighed. She should have known – he had always been a failure. He took to the rejuvenat treatments and gene therapies just as well as his brothers and sisters, growing huge and strong. But he had been too soft from birth, not temperamentally suited to the violence that champions were expected to both weather and mete out.

She remembered catching a young Gwillim reaching to return a trilling bird to its nest in a tree close to their manor. The gene therapies had already begun their work on his body, and at almost six feet tall, he was close to achieving his goal – until she snatched the creature from his hand and stamped on it to teach him a lesson. Mercy would not serve him in his life. Mercy would not serve *her*.

He took after his father, that was the problem. Arielle looked over to Carnacho Ondine, who hadn't spoken since their son's death. Tears streamed from his small eyes. The family had never lost a challenge – until now – but the treatments took a mortal toll on champions' bodies. Their livers failed, their hearts exploded, or in some cases, they were found with their throats cut by their own hands. Carnacho had cried after each of their deaths. She despised him for it. As far as Arielle was concerned, this was the price of power, of a life of pleasure.

She looked at the golden star in her hands. This was all she had left to show of that life.

Her daughter pulled at her wrist. 'Leave it, Mother,' Vivian Ondine said. She had been groomed to take over her father's position on his senescence, schooled in diplomacy and subterfuge. She was surplus to requirements now.

Arielle snapped her reply. 'Not a chance, Vivian. I worked too hard to give you all this life. I'll be damned if some mid-city thug is going to take it all from me.'

Vivian tugged again, trying to pull her mother from the shrine. 'Mother, the security forces will be here any moment to oversee the transition. We have to go!'

'No, Vivian. You don't understand.'

'We can start again, Mother. We can earn our way back. I know people in the council building, I can fast-track our challenge...'

'It's too late! I'm too old, and my children have failed me.'

Arielle looked into the eyes of her eldest child, and saw defeat. She pulled her wrist away, and her daughter's hand slipped from the silken material of her green robes. 'Just go. And take your good-for-nothing siblings with you.'

'Mother...'

'Go!' Arielle screamed, so loud that Vivian flinched. It was enough. Arielle watched as her daughter retreated, clutching a small satchel of possessions. She should have felt pity, sadness, the instincts of a mother. Instead she felt rage. Boiling, consuming rage. She howled to Vivian's back as she disappeared into the night. 'I wish you had died in the pits with your brother!'

She wouldn't see them again, she knew. Nor would she live in such luxury again.

Her husband finally spoke.

'There's nothing left,' Carnacho said.

She ignored him, and he went on.

'There's nothing left. Nothing, nothing, nothing...'

Arielle continued to ignore her husband as he placed the handle of the embellished laspistol under his chin, and wrapped his finger around the trigger. She did not even look up as she heard the fizzing sound of a las-bolt penetrating flesh and bone, and smelled the flash-cooked brain of the man she had been married to for three decades of her life.

'No, husband, you are wrong,' she said, as she lifted her golden trinket. Arielle pushed her fingertips against the points of the star. Red blood swelled against the gold, and she felt strength in her chest. 'There is still vengeance.'

A cohort of Sophisticants lined the path to Xantine's chamber. They were impassive figures, and could almost be mistaken for some of Serrine's many statues, were it not for the way their heads turned to follow Pierod as he walked.

He hated these things. They wore elaborate golden masks, each a rendering of his lord Xantine's countenance. It was said that Lord Xantine himself had created each individual mask, moulding the gold to his own face, before insetting unique gemstones and inlaying precious metals. The masks were then passed to his most devoted followers, those who had been deemed worthy of joining the ranks of the Sophisticants as his enforcers in the city at large.

Pierod didn't believe that to be true, of course. He'd not seen Serrine's ruler make much of anything in the years that he'd served him, despite regular lectures on the principles and nature of art.

There was subtle variation between each mask: some showed the Space Marine's aquiline nose and high cheekbones contorted in anger; others showed his face placid. Some featured the silk veil that his master often chose to wear when facing his adoring public, where others revealed his mouth. Pierod smirked inwardly when he saw these latter variations; when rendered in gold, the full lips lacked the darkened malignancy that tainted the real Xantine's mouth.

He claimed he had come to save them, but Cecily knew the truth. He wore a cap of silver, but it didn't protect his mind from her wanderings. She knew that he had been exiled from the world above, cast out by his people. He was one of them, for certain – a giant, clad in armour of purple and pink and gold – but they welcomed him no more. He had done something, something terrible, but he felt no shame for his actions. As far as she could tell from her dances across his thoughts, he never felt shame at all. Nor happiness, nor sadness, nor any of the other sensations that danced across the minds of her human companions in their enclave. So singular was his focus on his expanding arsenal, so total his obsession with the weapons that fused with his skin and armour, that she wondered if he felt anything at all.

But then what did she know of his kind? They looked like them – if far bigger – but they were not human, not truly. He and his kind were different. They had come from above the clouds, above the sky, above all she had ever known and ever thought to know, descended from heaven like figures of ancient myth.

Were they gods?

'Refinery Nine reports three thousand, four hundred and eighty-two rounds of ammunition produced this cycle, my lord,' Johias announced, dropping to a knee in front of the giant's dais. The platform had been the refinery overseer's, and it gave the giant figure a commanding view of the working floor. Lord Sarquil stepped to the edge of the dais and placed huge hands on the bare metal railing, looking down at Johias with dark eyes.

'That's a shortfall of seven per cent,' he said, his voice flat.

The man blinked. 'Y-yes, my lord. Attacks from the Gassers and other gangs have disrupted our output, and the transition from processing grass to producing ammunition took longer than–'

'Silence,' Sarquil said. He placed a palm to his silver skull, his disappointment palpable even without psychic intrusion. 'What are we to do with you?'

'I-I'm sorry, my lord,' the man said, eyes widening. 'I swear that I will not fail you again.'

'I was hoping you would not say that,' Sarquil told him. 'Orlan. Wherever you are, brother – this one is yours.'

A flash of purple appeared from the darkness at the edge of the refinery floor, almost too fast to track. It caught the man in the chest and he went with it, his arms and legs left trailing behind himself like streamers. Before the purple shape retreated into the darkness, Cecily caught a glimpse of its eyes: huge and black, cold and hungry, like pools of midnight aching to eat the light.

She couldn't help herself, and traced across the man's thoughts, like a finger breaking the surface of a puddle.

Confusion.

Pain.

Terror.

She winced and drew herself backwards before she saw the rest.

'Psyker,' Sarquil said. She realised she was being addressed directly, and composed herself. 'Send a message to Refinery Nine – they require a new overseer. Someone competent this time.'

'Yes, my lord,' Cecily said.

They were not gods. She knew that, in her heart. The gods she knew were kind creatures who loved their people, who kept them safe in a cruel galaxy. Her lord did not love his people. He used them. Used them to make weapons, to make ammunition; used their sweat and their blood to build an empire in this creaking ruin. He protected the strong, the capable, the willing – those that would break their bones and burn their skin to give him what he desired. Any weakness he removed, feeding the frail or the slow to his beasts, or by simply forcing them out into the wilds of the undercity, where, without a gang, they were easy prey to terrors that lurked in the dark.

He could do this because he was the strongest. He could crush a skull with his huge hands – she had seen him do it – and he kept his chaincannon close, patting it occasionally like a favourite pet. But that was the joke, the joke that only she knew: he himself was weak. She had seen his mind, and saw a soul as pathetic as those he killed, as those he cast out. He had tried to build his empire in the world above, but he had failed. He had come to the undercity – to her city – as a beaten canid, tail between its legs, awaiting another blow from its master.

The brothers he had come with were powerful too, compared to her, but they were even weaker than he was, and could not challenge Sarquil. He kept them at his side because he knew he would need warriors, but he did not love them. He felt only contempt for them.

'Degenerate beast,' Sarquil called Orlan, later that evening, after he had retired to his sleeping chambers. It was a sparse room in Refinery Four, as functional and focused as Sarquil himself, and he rarely used it, preferring to observe the constant manufacture of weapons and ammunition. But he was tired now, she knew from the whispers of his mind – as tired as his kind ever became, anyway. 'He is a stain on the legacy of the Emperor's Children,' Sarquil said, looking up from a data-slate that detailed ammunition stockpiles for a moment. 'Perhaps I should kill him. It is nothing less than he deserves – to put the pathetic out of their misery.' He shot her a stare across the chamber, unblinking. 'What do you advise, psyker?'

She considered for a long moment. She had accompanied him often, and had become something of a confidante, devoid as he was of the company of his brothers. But she also knew that she was only included in such private moments because she had a function, without which she would have been cast out like so many others. She was his personal communicator, capable as she was of touching the mind of an individual and sending messages between the warren of refineries that his gang controlled. For now, with Gassers and other gangers making many of the tunnels impassable to message couriers, she was vital to the flow of information, but she knew that she could easily overstep her bounds and outlive her usefulness.

She opened her mouth to respond, but any reply was drowned out as Sarquil continued his count, his attention consumed once again by the data-slate in front of him. 'Eight thousand and forty-four, eight thousand and forty-five...'

Cecily took her leave later that evening, leaving her lord to digest the data she had presented. She was moving towards her own bedchamber – a windowless cauldron once used to boil Solipsus sap, into which she had placed a cot and a few personal effects – when she heard her name.

'Cecily!' a woman shouted. She wore a soot-stained apron, and her grey hair hung lank on a sweaty face. She was missing two fingers on her right hand. She half-ran, her legs unsteady after a full fourteen-hour shift, until she was close enough to talk over the constant din of the refinery. Her grimace told Cecily that it was not good news.

'Sanpow's dead.'

Cecily's stomach lurched. 'And Arqat?' she asked, the question burning in her mind. The loss of the old man would be a wound in the fabric of Refinery Four's social strata, but he was a distant second in her thoughts to his patrol partner.

'He's alive,' the woman said.

Relief washed over Cecily, warming her even in the refinery's cloying heat. She had saved the boy from the hell in the city above, but he had saved her in turn – given her an anchor point in this miserable new existence they shared. To lose him too... She feared she would lose herself.

The air was still in Refinery Four, but it rushed past her ears as she ran. It whispered to her, as the grass had whispered to her in happier times. She had practised her listening in the years since the angels came, but she couldn't make out the words now. Something frantic. Something urgent. She ignored them.

She found him in the gloom of the bunkrooms, surrounded by his patrolmates. A figure, hunched, but still tall. One arm ended at the elbow, the other carried something. The boy she'd carried back into the undercity was a boy no more. He was broad, muscular, having grown into both his body and his role in the years since she had saved him from the wreckage of the Cathedral of the Bounteous Harvest.

He carried a sack in his hand, swaying gently, its bulbous contents obscured. Red liquid dripped onto the metal floor from a wet stain on the bottom of the sack.

Drip. Drip. Drip.

He turned to her as she entered the chamber, and without a word, Arqat let the sack fall open. Three severed heads tumbled loose, bouncing until they came to rest, the bare meat of their necks still leaking dark fluids.

'What happened?' Cecily gasped.

'They killed him,' Arqat said. 'So I killed them. They deserved to die.'

His face twisted into a grimace.

'They deserved to suffer.'

CHAPTER EIGHTEEN

She was not built for this world. In the void, she was graceful, moving with a predator's poise. Here, the *Exhortation* was a beached whale, rotting slowly in the sun.

The frigate had once borne the sleek, pointed prow and narrow neck of its Sword-class brethren, but Ghelia's unchecked growth had irrecoverably altered its silhouette. It had been an ugly thing already when Rhaedron was elevated to shipmaster, its once straight lines and sharp crenellations made lumpen by outcroppings of pink, heaving flesh. Now that flesh was grey and shrivelled. The Navigator had died, but her corpse remained, decomposing slowly over the years since the Adored had made planetfall on Serrine.

Not for the first time, Rhaedron thanked the Prince that she had removed her nose. Even so, she still fancied she could smell the *Exhortation*. She shuddered, and pressed a platinum button on her cane. A burst of neurotargeted narcotics stimulated her olfactory senses, flooding them with the smell of orchids. One of her favourites.

'How many today?' she asked Harnek. He had once been a gunnery sergeant on board the *Exhortation*, but with the ship incapacitated, he had stepped adroitly into a role as her right hand during their time on the planet. She trusted his counsel, even if the man hadn't had the good sense to remove his own nose. He answered with watering eyes.

'Seventeen, my mistress. All under-dwellers. We found a coven, and were able to capture some of them alive.'

'Have they been cooperative?'

'They weren't, at first, but Lady Phaedre was able to convince them to play nicely.'

Rhaedron forced her noseless face into a tight smile to hide her grimace. She'd seen the witch 'convince' people in the past, and she never could get the image of boiling eyeballs out of her mind.

'Good. And Lord Tun?'

'He is below, with the potentials.'

'Very good. Take me to him.'

Black sand. Hot wind whipped the particles up, forming small spirals of darkness that traced lazy lines across the blasted terrain. There was no sound, save for the gentle insistence of the wind, disturbing the dust and tugging at his long hair. The air had the acrid tang of fyceline.

Where am I?

As he thought the words, the wind spoke its answer.

It had been different, then. There had been music. More than music: this world was called Harmony, and had sung like no other world in the galaxy, its crystal spires and fluted towers ringing with the voices of a Legion untethered. The Emperor's Children had been drawn to the planet, deep in the Eye of Terror, after Horus' revolution foundered against the walls of

Terra's Imperial Palace. They had made it home, a place of untold pleasures and perversions.

It was perfect.

Almost perfect. The Legion's former glory flitted maddeningly, frustratingly just out of reach. Fulgrim had forsaken his children, and without the uniting presence of their father, the III Legion was splintered, conflicting lieutenants and warlords vying for power in the shining halls of Canticle City.

And then Abaddon had cut Canticle City's song short before it could reach its crescendo, spearing the city's heart with the cruiser *Tlaloc*. Its last note had been an achingly beautiful one – the death screams of ten thousand warriors of the III Legion, of ten million slaves and subjects – before it fell silent.

We could have made it perfect. I could have made it perfect. I just needed more time.

Liar! The wind roared the word, so loud that Xantine winced. It calmed as fast as it had picked up, settling back to a gentle zephyr.

Vavisk had pulled him from the wreckage of the dying city, hauling him onto one of the last void craft to leave the planet before Abaddon's barbarians destroyed it entirely. Now there was just the wind, scouring the remains of a dead world.

Xantine stared across the lifeless city.

I will rebuild it, he promised. *A new Harmony, perfect this time. I can do it. I* must *do it.*

The soft breath of the breeze was his only answer.

And so, with no sound or spectacle to entertain him, he walked the barren landscape. He thought he recognised parts of the city, even after millennia: the wide spaces of the Skin Roads, or the toppled shape of the Tasting Tower. He walked until he reached the edge of the city, where he thought he saw a figure, tall and proud and magnificent. As he turned to look, a gust of wind, stronger than before, swept through the ruined streets. It picked up ash and dust as it moved, and Xantine covered his face with his forearm to keep it out of his eyes. When he lowered it, dead Harmony was no more.

Pierod was never sure which version of his master he would find in his throne room. The Xantine he knew – charming, engaging, ruthless – or someone else. Someone that moved with a serpent's physicality, that spoke with a different voice. A softer voice, a more malevolent voice.

He breathed deep. The aroma of Xantine's chambers crept under the frame of the doors. It was sickly sweet. His master liked it that way. He knocked, once, twice on the wood, and the doors swung slowly open.

Once, he would have been met with a cacophony of voices. Humans and Space Marines alike would be invited to the lord's chambers to enjoy lavish feasts, to take in a lengthy stage performance, or to sit in attendance at one of Xantine's famous lectures. To receive an invite to one of these lectures had been a particular honour, even if they were an ordeal for mortal souls – Pierod had once seen his lord talk for fourteen hours on the importance of passion in art.

What Pierod would give for the return of such lectures now, though. No sound met Serrine's governor as he stepped through the chamber's wooden doors; no audience of excited men and women greeted his arrival. The plush chairs and couches lay mostly empty, except in a few cases, where they were host to human corpses in various stages of mutilation.

Xantine stood in the middle of his chamber, staring up at the canvas of a huge painting, apparently oblivious to the abasement that surrounded him.

'Governor Pierod,' Xantine rumbled, without turning to the newcomer. Pierod knew that the painting – a gorgeous landscape of the planet's grasslands in sumptuous oils – was a treasure for his people, painted by the semi-mythical founder of Serrine's classical school, Balise du Gravé. It was afforded such reverence in the planet's culture that it had hung alone in its own wing of the city's Imperial Art Museum, such that visiting delegations from major worlds such as Cypra Mundi, Elysia, and even Terra were escorted to take in its beauty within hours of landing on the agri world.

'This piece was your planet's highest achievement. You valued it more than your harvest, more than your serum, more than your people. You built a cathedral to it. And yet, it is nothing. A child's sketch.'

Xantine prodded at it with his silver rapier.

'See, Pierod, these brushstrokes – uniform, cautious, weak. The subject, shallow and uninspired. The colours, bland, insipid.' Rips appeared in the image as Anguish tore through its canvas. Pierod winced with each impact. 'The artist, if I can name such a creature so, works within himself, using soulless materials in a spiritless medium.' Xantine turned to his governor. 'Do you understand my point?'

Pierod blinked twice before he realised his master was waiting for a response. 'Yes, my lord?' he said, hesitatingly.

'Perfection cannot be reached without passion. The artist must love their subject, be consumed by their subject.' Xantine sliced Anguish the length of the canvas, and the painting ripped free from the frame entirely. 'Anything less is a total failure.'

He finally turned to Pierod then. The governor saw that his lord's turquoise eyes were dull and bloodshot, as if he had not slept in a year. 'They fail me, Pierod. They all fail me.'

'Lady Ondine, it is so good to see you!'

Arielle Ondine embraced the old woman in the noble fashion,

placing a palm on the back of her head, and then stepped back to take her in.

'Not lady, any more,' she said, 'though I rather expect you were aware of that, Katria.'

'Yes, yes, I had heard some news on the wind. Terribly sorry, my darling. I trust your husband is taking it as well as can be expected?'

Arielle met her straight. 'He's dead.'

'Ah.' Katria cast her eyes down for a moment, then met Arielle's again. There was no sympathy there, just the digestion of information. Arielle appreciated the pragmatism. 'A terribly ugly business, all around,' the old woman said.

She no longer held any position, but Katria Lancere had always maintained her air of gravitas. She had been one of the first wave of successful challengers after the system was introduced, winning a senior role in the central government not through combat, but with wit and words, composing a sonnet that appealed so greatly to Lord Xantine that he granted her the position directly – back when he used to attend challenges personally.

Such challenges were a distant memory at this point, such was the finality and mass appeal of the challenge by combat. Indeed, it wasn't long before Katria lost her position to one of the older houses – one of the first to leverage their vast wealth to build an effective champion-breeding programme. Her first husband had been a feted fencer, but he was quickly overpowered by the brute, his arms pulled from their sockets, and his own epee forced down his throat. She had truly loved the man, and had never forgiven the people involved in his death.

House Ondine had come to its position soon after House Lancere, and Katria and Arielle had quickly seen each other as kindred spirits. As a minor noble, Arielle Ondine could have lived a life of perfect indolence, but that was not her way. She was a schemer, and on the inside of Serrine's shaky political ecosystem, that meant building connections, relationships and alliances. These links were useful on the outside, too. Katria's network of friends and allies kept her in rejuvenat treatments, allowing her to persist well into her one hundred and thirtieth year.

Now, they could be used for another purpose. Serrine's system of challenge was designed to be perfect, with two inputs, and a single output: culling the weak to harvest the strongest. But there was a by-product in this cycle, an imperfection that, over time, could bring the whole edifice crumbling down.

Resentment.

Katria's network was filled with the jilted and the usurped, clever souls who were not strong or rich enough to hold their position, but not weak enough to accept their fate and disappear with good grace. Arielle had no idea just how many people the old woman was in contact with, but after a decade of cruelty, she calculated that there must be thousands of others who shared her desire for revenge. Tens of thousands, possibly.

'Can you help me, Katria?' Arielle asked.

'That depends, my darling. What do you need help with?'

'I want to tear it all down.'

Katria held her gaze for a long moment, before a smile spread across her lips. 'You are not the only one, my child. This city is a tinderbox, and my friends and I are of a mind to set it off. Will you help us?' Katria held out her wrinkled hand, and Arielle took it.

'This world must be slaughtered, my dear,' the older woman said. 'So that a new world may rise from its ashes. Together, we will drain its blood.'

* * *

Ghelia's death hadn't just left the *Exhortation* without a Navigator; weapons, shields, engines, and life support systems all failed in the days after she died. Lord Xantine had ordered exhaustive tests on the ship in a bid to get the frigate void-worthy again, but with the remaining slave stock choking to death in airless holds and Serrine's gravity threatening to pull the ailing ship into a death-spiral orbit, the decision was made to bring the *Exhortation* down to the planet.

The wide, flat grass fields formed a suitable berthing ground for the vessel, but it was not a smooth landing. The scar the ship carved into the landscape remained years after its descent, her superheated carapace scorching the grass and burning the fertile soil.

It was in this scar, between the shanties built by the *Exhortation*'s surviving slaves, that twenty of Serrine's citizens stood, shivering and glancing nervously at the huge vessel. Some had been taken from the undercity, collected by the Master of the Hunt and her security forces; others were overcity dwellers, brought below the haze line for the first time in their life. Whatever their background – commoner, noble, rich or poor – they all shared two things in common. They wore a simple robe, given to them by the troopers that took them from their bunks, their homes, or their places of work, and they were psykers.

It had been one of Xantine's decrees, after the Space Marine took power on the world, to identify promising psychic talents that could be used to resurrect the *Exhortation*.

Xantine had conducted surveys of his stricken vessel, forcing his surviving slaves to strip back Ghelia's necrotising flesh from the *Exhortation*. It proved impossible: too much of the ship's core systems depended on the organic network of nerves and muscles to function.

It was Qaran Tun who proposed another idea. In seance with

the creatures of the warp, the diabolist discovered that an echo of Ghelia's form remained, carried on the Sea of Souls like a ghost. The diabolist suggested that, with the right mind – one with sufficient psychic strength – Ghelia's body could be renewed, and her Navigator's abilities reinvigorated. That was enough. Xantine ratified the new position of Master of the Hunt, and gave the bearer the soldiers, weapons, and tools they needed to collect psykers from any strata of society.

He had the voice of a young man, but like so many of his kin among the under dwellers, wore the body of one much older. He was hunched, rake thin, with long and lank hair. He flinched at every touch – a nervous response to a lifetime as a pariah amongst pariahs, perhaps, or a more simple reaction to Phaedre's presence in the room. The witch seemed to hover, her toes a few inches above the rotten-meat floor.

'What do you want?' he asked. He had tried to inject steel into his tone, but his voice cracked, the fear evident even without psychic intrusion. Phaedre tittered at the failure.

'We want to test you, my child,' she said.

'I haven't done anything to you. I haven't done anything to anyone. Just leave me alone.'

A kicked dog, this one. An outcast, blamed for his nature, despised for something he couldn't control. When had they first realised? she wondered. Did his friends on the refinery lines see the power inside him? Perhaps the local children, they could always spot differences first. Or – she looked closely at him, his drawn face and downcast eyes – it was his parents, so afraid of the creature they had birthed that they threw it into the depths, never to return.

He was like her. The thought came unbidden, and she pushed it away. He was not like her. This wretch stood in front of her, weak, broken. She had been strong. She had burned her world to cinders for the crime of rejecting her, and sailed into the stars, the deaths of thousands weightless on her conscience.

'No, I can see that you do nothing,' she said. She gestured, and a man in a black leather mask lifted an object from the console in the centre of the room. It was crude: a simple metal helmet, with a cable that ran down into the rotten meat of the floor. 'Step forward, please,' she requested with a child's sweetness.

The man hesitated, and the black-masked figure started towards him. 'Wait, stop!' he cried. He raised a hand, and his eyes flashed with venom. 'I gave you a chance,' he said. 'Now I can't be held responsible for what will happen to you.' He lifted a hand, palm open, as if calling something forth. Sparks burst from his skin, yellow and electric. A smell like burning grease began to over-power the miasma of rotting flesh inside the chamber, and the light grew, flickering across the dark meat of the walls.

Until suddenly, the sparks were snuffed out. The man looked blank, blinking his sad eyes at his own hand. He shook his wrist as if to clear a piece of debris, and tried again. Tears of blood welled in his eyes with the effort, and the sparks crackled once more. Just as fast, they died again on his hand.

He looked up into Phaedre's smirking face, realisation dawn-ing. She clapped her hands together as he connected the dots.

'So good of you to show us your little tricks, child. But you are not the only one with such abilities.' She raised her hands, and allowed a spark of yellow light to dance between her palms.

'What have you done to me?' the man asked, defeated. He slumped to his knees.

'A simple precaution before our experiment. We wouldn't want you hurting us now, would we?' She turned her hand over, and the spark followed, bouncing like a pet. 'A shame we can't guar-antee the same for you.'

The black-masked figure took a step forward with the helmet in hand.

'A wonderful object, this,' Phaedre said as the man started to cry. 'It knew our previous Navigator intimately. So well, in fact, that it has retained her core abilities. All we need to leave this world is a mind powerful and malleable enough to connect with the remnants of that beloved creature. It will be a great honour if you are selected. If you are not, well…' Phaedre bent down to stare directly into his face. 'At least you will have tried.'

The helmet was slipped over his skull, and immediately began its work, interfacing with the consciousness that it enveloped. He screamed, scrambling backwards on his hands and feet until his back reached the wall of dead flesh. His scream stretched, elongating and pitching downwards, until it became a death rattle. When his eyes opened, they were milky white. There were no pupils in these featureless orbs, but Phaedre could tell they were moving frantically in his eye sockets, scanning for something she couldn't see. For a moment, there was quiet, and she felt the two minds touching across the divide between life and death, reality and unreality. If, despite their differences, the two could mesh, then new life would be breathed into the *Exhortation*, and the Adored could return to the stars.

The silence was broken by a bubbling sound. The man started to convulse, his thin-boned frame thrashing against the decomposing walls of the Navigator's chamber. His skin rippled as something moved under its surface, travelling from his face, down his neck, to his limbs. He held his arm in front of his face, mouth and white eyes wide in a silent scream as muscle and bone writhed within his body, his internal structure rearranged to unspoken whims. For a moment, it appeared as if he had weathered the storm, and he breathed deep. Then, with a wet pop, his arm erupted with new flesh. It ran like candle tallow, pouring forth from somewhere unseen, somewhere inside his own body. He lengthened, the sprouting flowers of flesh outpacing the rapid growth of new bones so that they lost their shape and flopped to the floor. Phaedre saw his eyes, green and pleading, as they disappeared alongside his nose, mouth, and other facial features into the folds of tissue.

He wrapped around himself, his grotesquely long arms and legs meeting each other and entwining. His skin, once pale and sallow from a lifetime lived under a choking haze, was pink and throbbing, stretched tight against his new body.

'Should we leave?' Rhaedron asked. She was not used to seeing such experiments first-hand.

'Hold,' Phaedre said, and her tone brooked no disagreement. Rhaedron stayed, hiding her discomfort as she surreptitiously kicked at the engorged finger that was winding its way around her boot.

The man kept growing and growing, and there was a moment, a shuddering moment, as the *Exhortation* seemed to jolt to life.

And then the thing that had been a man burst. His skin tore like an overcooked sausage, splattering Rhaedron, Phaedre, and all the other occupants of the Navigator's chamber in gore. Qaran Tun, whose pink armour was now the dull red he had worn when he counted himself amongst the ranks of the Word Bearers, spoke.

'Not compatible,' he said, matter-of-factly. 'Interesting. I will note the results in my records.'

He lay on his hard cot, with the sounds of endless industry muffled by layers of ferrocrete. The hammering of thousands of souls, day and night, making for war.

He closed his eyes and tried to sleep. He had forgotten how.

He saw Sanpow's face behind his eyelids, his eyes shrivelling like seed pods in a furnace, his skin sloughing loose from a grinning skull.

He saw the Gasser, its glass eyes wide and round and as dark as the deepest reaches of Serrine's undercity. He pulled them out. He pulled off its mask, pulled off its face, revealing white bone. A skull.

He saw the angel – his Saviour – its luminous eyes cold, bringing its blade down. He parried the strike and thrust upwards, decapitating the angel. Its long hair shimmered as the head flew through the air, falling from a statuesque body to the filthy floor. Another skull.

His blood boiled. His breathing was ragged. He heard something in the dark of the bunk room.

He felt a hand on his forehead.

'You're burning up,' Cecily said, as she perched next to him on the hard cot. 'Are you all right? You were talking in your sleep.'

'What was I saying?'

'I'm not sure,' Cecily said, unconvincingly.

'Huh,' he muttered. He found her silhouette, slowly coalescing in the dark. 'Why are you here?'

'I wanted to check on you.'

'I know when you're lying, Cecily,' Arqat said, offering a crooked smile. 'What did you really want?'

'Ugh,' she said. Arqat knew her well enough to know that she didn't know how to say the things she wanted to. Finally, she took his hand in hers.

'We can't stay here, Arqat. You nearly died today. Sanpow *did* die. It's a matter of time for both of us. I don't want you to die. I don't want *me* to die.'

'You won't,' Arqat said, forcing mirth into his voice. 'You're the giant's helper. You'll be the last of us left, counting his ammunition, and helping him strap more guns to his armour.'

'For now. What happens when he tires of me? He's losing his mind, Arqat, what left he had to lose. I don't want to be here when he snaps.'

'Then where do we go? The Golden Maw might've taken us in as juves, but the Red Cult wiped them out weeks back. And no chance I'm joining up with stinking Gassers.'

'Not the undercity,' Cecily said.

'The overcity? Who would you join up there?'

'I mean off-world!' Cecily hissed, exasperated now.

'Off-world? How would we even get a ship?'

'I don't know,' she admitted. 'But I can *do* things, Arqat. I know I can get us away from here. I've seen it.'

'Seen it where?'

'In my dreams,' she said, in a small voice.

He sighed. He was trying to be kind, but they both knew that he would not change his mind.

'We can't run, Cecily. This is our world. We have to defend it from these freaks. We've got to *fight* them,' he said, raising his voice loud enough that the man in the next-door bunk grunted in annoyance.

'Arqat, please!' Cecily hissed. 'We can't fight them. They are angels descended from the heavens. We are weak, compared to them.'

'Speak for yourself,' Arqat spat.

Cecily sighed. 'I just want to go,' she said. 'To leave this awful planet behind me, and be amongst the sky and the stars. It's beautiful up there, beyond the surface, among the blue and black.' She squeezed his hand, tight. 'Come with me, Arqat. We can do it together.'

'I can't,' he said. 'I won't run. They have to pay for what they did to us.' He involuntarily raised the stump of his arm. 'What they did to me.'

* * *

As she left his chamber, she let her mind linger, just for a moment. It was dark in the room, but when she touched Arqat's mind, she saw only red. Boiling, blazing red.

Years in his service had not diminished the physical impact of simply seeing the Space Marine. His massive legs were encased in purple ceramite studded with polished black orbs. They glinted in the cold daylight that streamed through the windows of the chamber, staring like the eyes of some cyclopean beast. Leather straps the colour of pale human skin were bound between these black spheres, bracing the armour with buckles of silver and gold. Pierod wondered which animal had offered its skin for such service.

'Good morning, master!' Pierod forced himself to say.

'Governor Pierod,' Xantine said. His previous ebullience had evaporated, and he watched Pierod now as some apocryphal predator, turquoise eyes unblinking. 'News from the arena?' he asked, his voice a low growl.

'Unfortunately not, my lord!'

'No. No, I feared as much.' Xantine turned to regard the paintings on the far wall. 'I hear whisperings, Pierod. Seditious elements in our midst. My dear brothers tell me that my citizens are unhappy with my benevolent rule. That they are conspiring against me. Is this true?'

Pierod swallowed involuntarily. 'No, my lord! You are their ruler, their Saviour, their–'

'So you brand my brothers as liars?' Xantine pirouetted on the spot, his black hair whirling around his face. He looked Pierod up and down, theatrically. 'A brave choice for a man of your physical prowess. But bravery should be rewarded! Shall I arrange a challenge with one of my brothers? Perhaps Vavisk? The old dog is losing his cutting edge. Or might Qaran Tun enjoy the opportunity to loose one of his pets?'

Pierod stifled a yelp. He had seen Qaran Tun only four times – the heavily tattooed Space Marine spent most of his time away from the overcity – but he remembered each meeting with still-palpable dread. The air around the warrior seemed to be frozen, as if he had stepped from the chill of the grave. The canisters and containers that he wore on his ritualistically scarred armour rattled and bounced as he walked, home to some monstrous creatures that Pierod was certain he did not want to know.

'No, no!' Pierod said, panic raising the pitch of his voice. 'I would never besmirch the name of your honourable brothers.'

'Really?' Xantine said. A sly smile tugged at the corners of his blackened mouth. 'You should try it, Pierod. You might enjoy it.'

'I... um...' Pierod stammered.

'I jest, Pierod. Honestly, you should see your face. It has become as white as silk. I know why you are here. You are to inform me of the death of my esteemed guardians at the hands of my own people.'

'Yes, lord. How did you know?'

'This is my city, Pierod, my world. I know its people better than they know themselves, for I have given them everything that they now hold dear. This is a cry for attention, nothing more. I shall give them the attention that they crave. But before that, I will find the rot, cut it out, and show it to them. Perhaps then they will understand how much they owe me.'

The celebrations would last six days, and would culminate in a ceremony, held at the site where Xantine crushed the failed xenos uprising once and for all. To Xantine, it was intended to be a communal outpouring of love for the planet's ruler, a chance for tens of thousands of Serrine's citizens to show their appreciation in person for the warrior that had descended from the stars to save them.

It was proving difficult to organise.

'Have we demolished the hab-blocks on the west promenade?' Pierod asked Corinth, without looking at his attendant.

'Unfortunately not, my lord. The residents are proving recalcitrant, and our work crew has not reported back.'

'Again? Isn't that the third crew we've sent?'

'Yes, lord.'

'Send the militia, then, knock the thing down with the people still inside. If the view to the cathedral is blocked from the park, Lord Xantine will flay us alive.'

'Terribly sorry, lord,' Corinth rumbled, 'but we've done that, too.'

'We have? What happened?'

'They killed each other. We didn't have sufficient stimms for the whole unit, and when the juniors found out that the officers had been given their allowance, they turned on them. We found their bodies burnt in front of the hab-block. Of the juniors, there was no sign.'

'Step up the patrols into the undercity, Corinth. We had an arrangement with the gangs, once. They need to know their place.'

'Sorry, my lord, we...'

'Spit it out, Corinth.'

'We've done that, too. Of the last five patrols, only one soul returned. We found him mutilated and blinded, his forehead carved with a sort of symbol.'

'A new gang?' Pierod asked.

'I don't think so, my lord. I've seen the symbol up here in the overcity, too. There's too many of them, in too many places, for it to be the work of one leader. They all only seem to want one thing – blood.'

Pierod shivered at the thought. This was going to be a problem.

'Triple the patrols into the undercity. Quadruple them, if you have to. Lord Xantine must have his day, and for that, we need those stimms.'

Katria was as good as her word. The Sophisticant took the golden chit in its huge hand and turned it over just once, before grunting its assent and standing aside. Arielle counted her blessings, and stepped forward.

The Hall of Records was ancient. She had been here once before, prior to the Space Marines' arrival, when it had hummed with activity. Servo-skulls had filled the air, ferrying scrolls to banks of scribes and servitors, who would update harvest yields, hydration reports, tithe costs, and the details of gifts received.

Now, the hall was almost empty. Only a handful of scribes remained, their bodies wizened and their quills tapping out nonsense words on stained parchment. Such paperwork had once been the lifeblood of the Imperium – a way to track the planet's past and prepare for its future, but under Xantine's rule, it had been forgotten. 'The rot touches all,' Arielle Ondine said under her breath.

She eventually found what she was looking for on the third floor of the hall, in an unassuming stack of books. The plans were not complete – Serrine had been built far too long ago for those initial records to survive – but they were enough, containing the details of surveys commissioned under previous governments into the city's foundations.

They were dry reads, but Arielle soldiered on, looking for the detail that Katria said she would find. She looked nervously over her shoulder as she skipped through the pages, heart pounding as she read, expecting to feel the massive hand of one of Xantine's warriors on her shoulder.

No touch came, and she finally saw the information she

needed. In detail, the surveys laid out key structural weaknesses that had been discovered in the foundations of Serrine's overcity. The surveyors had recommended urgent repair work, but Katria had assured her that the money to be used for such repairs had instead been funnelled into the Durant family's personal coffers.

She closed the book and slipped it inside her black robes with one hand. With her other hand, she squeezed the eight-pointed star, and tried to slow her breathing. She felt the wetness of blood on her fingers, and Lady Arielle Ondine smiled.

CHAPTER NINETEEN

Edouard had been desperate. He had found his connections, called in his favours, and still no Runoff. The city was dry now, the militia preparing for something big – some celebration.

And so, he turned to his last option. The temple was primitive. The altar was a chunk of blackened rock, its edges roughly shaped by hand chisels, and its pews were columns, fallen like tree trunks in a storm. A battered brass cauldron stood in the centre of the space, its dull metal flashing in the firelight. In the jewelled overcity of Serrine, it was as if some prehistoric pocket of civilisation persisted. The figures that milled around the cauldron, clad as they were in red robes and metal masks, only added to the theme, appearing as worshippers of some ancient animal god.

Despite everything, he found himself again bound to the faithful. He had been raised to be a priest, a leader, and instead found himself a follower. Trapped.

He barked a bitter laugh. It didn't matter. None of it mattered, if he could get some Runoff. The church was his usual haunt, but that was out. They'd closed it down after the riots, filling the streets with soldiers in fancy robes who'd shoot anyone who dared to stray too close. Edouard coughed another bitter laugh. It left his mouth in a cloud of cold breath. People went missing all the time in Serrine's overcity, but they were commoners, and their families had not the money, the power, nor the influence to investigate their absence. On the contrary, the death of one of Lord Xantine's favourite pets pulled all the local monsters out of their barracks, their blade-arms and trigger fingers twitching for someone to make one wrong move.

Even with the agony of Runoff withdrawal, Edouard had stayed well away, turning instead to another place he promised he'd never go: his past.

He knew Dartier from his youth in the priesthood. Like Edouard, he'd strayed from the path, but unlike Edouard, he'd carved out a comfortable existence for himself, bartering, selling, and ultimately administering a range of exotic stimms to the highest bidders. Edouard hoped he could rely on the man's nostalgia. Fortunately, he was right.

'I wouldn't do this for just anyone, you know,' Dartier said sternly. He tapped a long needle with a leather-gloved finger. It made a soft chiming sound.

'I know. Thank you, old friend.'

'Don't you "old friend" me. I've not seen you in eight years. I thought for sure you'd be dead. Open your robe.'

Edouard loosened the tie at his waist and slipped the material back to expose his injured flank. The bruise ran the length of his side, from underarm to upper thigh. Purples and reds swirled with yellows and greens under his thin skin. The colours reminded him of the scar in the sky. 'Gods...' Dartier whistled. 'I'm surprised you're *not* dead.'

'I almost wish I was,' Edouard said.

'The shakes?' Dartier asked. He clicked his tongue. 'There's another place you can go, you know.'

'Where?' Edouard asked. He gasped in pain as Dartier slid a long needle between the bones of his ribcage. Pleasant warmth radiated down his side a moment later, as the drugs worked their craft on his tortured nerve endings. It wasn't Runoff, but his body felt good for the first time in days.

'It's a good place, run by good people. They'll give you what you need, and they don't ask much in return.'

'How much?'

'It's free. All they ask is an open mind.'

Lordling rarely ventured into the overcity any more, so when he arrived at Xantine's chambers, frothing at the mouth with excitement, Xantine knew: his brother had something to tell him. Unfortunately, getting that information was not so easy.

Xantine had sent for Phaedre, the witch's talents sure to dredge out any kernels of information that the mute giant had picked up. She was here now, alongside his brothers in the council chamber.

The witch ran her hands along the side of Lordling's swollen, hairless head. Xantine had seen humans collapse at her touch, convulsing in agony, but Lordling just giggled as the psyker probed his mind, showing neat triangular teeth in his wide mouth.

The council waited for Phaedre to speak. There had been six of them, once, but there were five now.

S'janth spoke first, in Xantine's own mind.

The betrayer's wound still pains you, my love, she whispered.

That worm could not wound me, darling. Sarquil is nothing. A simple mind cannot comprehend the sublime.

And yet, he dominates our thoughts.

She let her words drift across his mind: not a question, but a statement. He could deny it, but she was privy to his body's sensations.

I think only of the agony I will mete out on his body and soul when I dig him out from whatever pit he has crawled into.

No, my love. You blaze with pain. You carry it in these hearts, and it courses in our blood, hard and heavy. Our nerves burn, but not with hot, sweet anger – with melancholy, rich, and deep, and bitter. It hurts. It hurts because you do not understand how they could turn against you, how they could not love you. A pause, and a feeling like a kiss at the nape of his neck. *And yet, you too have betrayed before.*

I am no betrayer! Xantine roared at the slight, hardening his mind, and he felt S'janth recede slightly. The touch on his neck slipped away. *Do not compare me to Abaddon, daemon. I do not betray. I move against weaklings with calculated masterstrokes. This is the way of the galaxy – the lesser give way to the greater.*

A trill of laughter, like the twinkling of stars.

Do not teach me of this galaxy, my love. I have lived longer than your species has sailed the stars, and have tasted a trillion betrayals across the skeins of reality. Souls justify their acts how they choose – necessity, obligation, the greater good. They deceive others, they deceive even themselves. Betrayal is betrayal. It is the food that lets my kind fill our bellies.

What is your point, daemon? Xantine asked.

He is just the first, my love. Others will turn against you. Your closest brothers will become your greatest foes. You cannot change this fate.

I can do anything I wish, Xantine said, defiant. Silence was his response.

His attention refocused on the corporeal plane, and he cast an eye over the others he had gathered in the council chamber. He feigned nonchalance, but the daemon's words remained with him, their payload injected into his central cortex.

Torachon bounced a knee, restless as ever. Qaran Tun sat in silent repose, golden eyes closed, his ungloved fingers tracing the major and minor symbols of the Ruinous Powers in tiny movements. Vavisk, on the other side of the darkened chamber, thrummed with sound. His flesh-metal vox-grille squealed with feedback as he drew shuddering breaths, the suppurating mouths on his neck punctuating the sound with moist slaps of their own as they opened and closed.

At last, Phaedre sighed. 'The giant has uncovered something.' She spoke to the council chamber, but her voice seemed to come from far away, as if carried by the wind. Lordling cooed at the effect. 'He travels below, into the city beneath this city, for… sport.' Lordling chittered, nodding at her words – a movement so vigorous that her hands slipped from his head. The malformed being looked disappointed for the briefest moment, but a broad grin broke his raw-meat head once more as she reseated her fingers on his temple. 'One of his playthings told him of a giant in purple, an angel from above who ventured below to protect the forgotten. He nearly broke the plaything, but he let it go, let it crawl back to its cave. And he… he followed it. Through pipes and past guards, to a hot, deep place. There he found…' She removed her hands from Lordling's head, and he squealed with delight. Her voice returned, her normal voice: dry and reedy, like a parched riverbed. 'He found your brother. Sarquil hides in the city below.'

'Perfidious wretch!' Torachon roared, rising from his seat. 'I will behead him myself, I swear it! Lord Xantine, please, grant me this pleasure.'

Xantine held up a hand to calm the younger Space Marine.

The boy is spirited, S'janth trilled in his mind.

Even now, he thought back. *He should know better after decades at my feet.*

You were spirited too, once.

Once, daemon? You chose me for a partner. I must have shown sufficient spirit to catch your eye.

And a fine host you have been, my love.

Torachon eyed him expectantly, hand still resting on the pommel of his sabre. 'My lord?' he said, full lips threatening to pout.

'I welcome your exuberance, but we know our brother's obsessions. He is likely to have fortified his position.'

Qaran Tun opened tattooed eyelids and spoke. 'I am in communion with Neverborn who make the undercity their hunting ground. I have been studying their habits. I would be able to bend them to our will, to kill our brother while his back is turned.'

'Your veins run with mongrel blood, cousin, so I will forgive your discourtesy this one time. I remind you – we are the Emperor's Children, I am Xantine, and we do not murder our enemies in their beds. We meet them in combat, and we behead them with a killing cut.' Xantine turned to the chamber, any pretence at compromise lost.

'We will move in force, and when we do find our errant brother' – he aimed turquoise eyes at Torachon – 'I will kill him myself.'

CHAPTER TWENTY

Hunting patrols visited the undercity often, but they were formulated to capture scared psykers, or kill troublesome gang bosses. The force that disembarked from Serrine's great elevator was orders of magnitude more powerful, and would have been sufficient to take whole worlds, blessed as it was with twenty Space Marines and more than a hundred of Xantine's hand-picked Sophisticant personal guard, as well as five hundred of the over-city's genhanced, rejuvenat-treated militia. Lordling and Phaedre led the way to Sarquil's lair, with Xantine in the middle of the procession, held aloft by a palanquin borne by six of his Sophisticants.

The undercity passed by at a gentle bob as the witch guided the force deeper into the refineries. The journey was long, but uneventful – even the most hardened gangers knew better than to attack a single Space Marine, let alone twenty of them – and Xantine was growing terribly bored by the time that Lordling began to coo his familiarity with landmarks and corridors.

'We are close,' Phaedre said in her sing-song voice, long after they had descended from the mud and dust of the planet's surface, into the guts of its underground refinery complex. The accuracy of the witch's guidance was confirmed soon after, when the procession came under attack from the far end of a vast circular passage. Ten scrawny humans fired from makeshift defensible positions, launching volleys from a range of stubbers and autoguns. Despite their soiled jumpsuits and filthy robes, it became clear quickly that these guards were no ordinary gangers. Hard rounds slapped against ceramite with impressive accuracy, and when they died – on the fine edges of the Adored's blades – they died with their weapons in their hands.

'This is the rat's nest,' Phaedre said.

'Now to burn him out,' Xantine responded, as his guard set down his palanquin.

A large blast door blocked the passageway, five times the height of a man, and wide enough to admit the industrial haulers that ferried the harvested grass from the containers at the edge of the city to the refineries below. It appeared to open upwards, with segments cut out to allow for the progression of rail tracks into the space beyond. On the door were printed the words *REFINERY 04* in faded yellow paint.

Xantine tutted. 'Only Sarquil would call such a prosaic location his home,' he proclaimed, to titters from his assembled Adored. 'Torachon,' he called to his young lieutenant. 'Please announce our arrival.'

'With pleasure, my lord!' Torachon gestured to two captains of the militia, denoted by the tall green feathers rising from their headdresses, who produced a spread of melta bombs from leather satchels. They barked orders to their soldiers in turn, who sprinted to place the explosive charges at key points across the door. With the work done, the captains looked expectantly back at Torachon. The Space Marine wore a look of dramatic disapproval.

'Are we peasants? Are we paupers?' he asked. The captains exchanged glances, and one eventually opened his mouth to speak. Torachon slapped him. 'Of course not! More, more!'

The militia emptied their sacks, affixing melta bombs at random to the entrance until Torachon called a halt to their activity. 'That will do! We are not barbarians. Arm the charges.'

The human elements of the force retreated to a safe distance as the melta timers beeped their countdown, but the Space Marines of the Adored stood close, keen to bathe in the light, heat, and sound of the explosions. Their proximity also allowed them to be the first through the ragged breach in the blast door, the riotous colour of their armour rendered dull by the gloom of the space beyond.

Refinery Four hummed with the sound of human misery. It was a place of such exquisite suffering that Torachon could feel it, thick in the stiflingly hot air. He was almost impressed with his brother Sarquil for building such a monument.

Metal gantries hung suspended from a high ceiling. They converged at a central point: a windowed octagonal room that allowed the overseer a panopticon view of a work floor that housed thousands of labourers at individual stations. Sallow men and women toiled at these stations, pouring molten metal from crucibles into moulds, shaping simple armour pieces with blackened hammers, or sharpening crude-looking blades on spinning wheels. They wailed and moaned even before the Adored made their explosive entrance to the refinery, condemned to lives of endless pain in service of a master high above.

Torachon expected these mortals to flee at the sight of their shrieking, sprinting entrance, to take their chance and escape the heavily muscled overseers that patrolled the workstations. None of them moved.

They couldn't, he realised, as his keen eyes adjusted to the hellish light of the vast chamber. To a person, these mortals had been shackled to their workplaces, heavy iron chains tight around one wrist and one ankle. They bucked and thrashed against their restraints, but try as they might, they couldn't get away.

Xantine howled his demands, sending his Sophisticants to investigate the antechambers and side rooms, and ordering his militia to take up firing positions. But for the hedonistic warriors of his warband, the only order he gave was to sate themselves, for this was a banquet that could not be ignored. The Adored accepted their role gladly, and waded into the mass of humanity, carving through cowering figures as easily as the planet's threshing machines would cut grass.

They met some resistance from grotesquely swollen overseers, made strong by forced treatments, who lumbered forward with huge two-handed machetes. They were ponderously slow in their motions, but they were tough, and could survive the loss of a limb or two before the fight went out of them entirely. Some lucky souls on the work lines had also been given weapons, handed out in an apparent hurry when it became clear that the refinery was under attack. They swung desperately with sharpened blades in their free hands, or fired wildly with poorly maintained weapons, half-crazed from fear and half-dead from the gruelling work. The Space Marines of the Adored toyed with these pathetic creatures, dancing out of range from their frantic swings, before lunging in to disembowel or dismember their playthings. Many gave up entirely. Torachon bore down on one man who raised a rusted stub gun in shaking hands. Rather than level the weapon at his attacker, he pointed it at his own chin, and pulled the trigger. Torachon laughed, but it was a bitter sound. Killing captives was no sport. He looked around the chamber, searching for challengers worthy of his charnabal sabre.

He found one. A pink blur danced through the mass of dead and dying, stopping only to attend to the towering figures of the Adored. Tyllios fell, clutching his throat as bright red blood spurted through his long fingers. Orotholes turned at the sound, before his legs were severed at the knee joint. Hobbled, he slid to the floor and died as a curved blade raked through his breastplate, opening his chest cavity and destroying both of his hearts.

Torachon had seen such a warrior on the battlefield before, when they had been on the same side. 'I know you, brother!' he shouted, tracking the blur with his bolt pistol. He squeezed the weapon's trigger, but the shape moved too fast, and mass-reactive shells *thunked* into the soft meat of the human slaves, bursting them open in showers of blood and entrails. It used the throng of people as cover, keeping low, only rising to strike when the Adored were distracted by their own slaughter.

He would play the game. He made a show of choosing a new target – a wet-eyed old man, his pale skin darkened by grime. He raised his sabre, and waited a beat.

The sound of the attack came first – impossibly soft footfalls, barely perceptible even with his transhuman hearing. He turned, bringing his sabre across his broad chest in a protective parry. The curved blade slid along the charnabal sabre's polished edge, Torachon's sparkling ceramite armour weathering any of the impact not absorbed by the heavy blade.

The attacker fell to the floor between two human slaves, and Torachon swatted them aside, breaking their spines in his haste to see what he was dealing with. The pink creature righted itself, climbing to feet that ended in two clawed toes.

'Orlan,' he said with a broad smile. 'I should have guessed you would have fled with the other rats.'

Risen now to its feet, the creature that had once been a Space Marine was hunched, swaying like an animal as it adopted a fighting stance. It circled Torachon warily, staring back at him with saucer-sized eyes the colour of spilled oil. Fleshy mandibles framed its puckered mouth, and they grasped at the air, like blind worms searching for food. Orlan hissed at Torachon, switching his curved blade between clawed hands.

'By the Prince, you were never beautiful, but the warp has been more unkind to you than I could have imagined.' Torachon leaned forward, inspecting his erstwhile brother. 'No wonder you hide your shame in this cesspool.'

Orlan wheezed – Torachon assumed in anger – and launched himself forward with a slashing strike. The dubious blessings of the warp had made him hideous, but they had made him fast, too, and the curved blade scraped along the ceramite plate over Torachon's stomach. Hissing green foam rose quickly from the gouge in the plate.

'Poison, Orlan?' Torachon asked, raising his arms in frustration as the creature tore back into the mass of slaves. 'That's hardly fair now, is it.' By way of reply, Orlan tore a man from his restraints, leaving his hand and much of his lower wrist behind, and hurled him towards Torachon. The young Space Marine sliced the gibbering, mutilated projectile in half with a single blow, spattering his own face with viscera. He licked the fluids from his lips.

'Now this is a worthy fight!'

Cecily chased sleep, but it flitted away from her, always out of reach. She missed the soothing sounds of the grass and the wind, the sounds of her old life. They had been replaced now with the incessant beating of hammers, the hissing of cooling metal, and the moaning of thousands.

A pang of guilt, there. She was one of the few lucky enough to be given the opportunity to sleep in Sarquil's great engine – alongside those chosen as strong enough to join the patrol gangs – and yet she could not take advantage of the luxury. It was not out of kindness, or even pity that the massive warrior had provided her with a cot and her own chamber. It was cold logic: he needed her mind fresh and well rested in order to be able to communicate with his other factoria. If she could not sleep, then she would not function as he needed her to, and then, well... She had seen what Sarquil did with his useless things.

Most of them, anyway. Her mind drifted back to Arqat. She had not been able to sleep since he returned, not properly. The man she knew – the boy she had saved – had changed. She had touched his mind when they last spoke, and saw red: the boiling red of rage, of anger, of mindless savagery. She wanted to help him, but after their last discussion, she was ashamed to admit that she was scared of him.

She reached out for him now, as she had done before, hoping against hope to find some change, some comfort in his thoughts. She did not have to reach far. He throbbed in her mind, the heat of his anger almost palpable through the layers of rockcrete that separated him from her. Cecily flinched, and let her thoughts drift elsewhere, turning her back on the man she had known. She traced across the work floor, feeling for a moment the weight of misery that had pooled there. She did not want to linger, and pushed further out, to the tunnels and pipes that led towards Refinery Four. Small souls: rodents and lizard-like things, scraping simple existences by eating each other, and the occasional spark of humanity, or at least, what had once been humanity. No comfort in these broken beings. She reached further still, as sleep eluded her.

Suddenly, there was light and sound in her mind, blinding and deafening. Cecily snapped back from the shock, and she found herself in her darkened chamber. She had only seen Serrine's sun on a few occasions, but it felt as if she had stared directly into it. Her mind was aflame, any thought of sleep destroyed by the searing light. She had to find its source, to stare into its beauty.

Cecily rose from her cot on unsteady legs, and stumbled from her sleeping quarters in a daze. The refinery was hot, as always, and the bare metal floor burned the soles of her feet. Cecily realised that she had not even stopped to put on her ragged work boots. No matter, the pain was a fleeting distraction from the light that was coming. She would not let it deter her from witnessing its brilliance.

She knew the explosion was coming before it happened, and she did not flinch as the main door to Refinery Four exploded inwards with a force that blew Cecily's shoulder-length hair back and washed her with spatters of debris. Sensation enveloped her, as her deliverance entered the room, carried on a platform by muscled figures.

He was a figure of legend: an angel from the depths of her childhood, from the depths of her world's stories and history.

He was like Sarquil in stature, if perhaps a little smaller, and like the brothers that he travelled with, he wore armour that shifted between deep purple and pastel pinks, decorated lavishly with jewels and tassels, trinkets and chains.

But he was *different* to his brothers. So palpably different that Cecily staggered from his presence, as if struck. She tried to take him in. His hair was long and black, framing the fine features and straight nose of a statue, come to life.

More than that. He was luminous. Even without using her gift, she could see that. She could feel it, an overwhelming presence in the chamber that felt like pressure in her head.

She dared to trace her mind across his, and proffered just the lightest touch, like fingers on silk. She recoiled instantly, as if burned. Something inside him shone so brilliantly that it hurt: hurt her eyes, her ears, all her senses. Only a silhouette remained, burned into her mind like an overexposed pict. Lithe, graceful, with almond eyes like a feline. It spoke to her, asking her the question she had heard in her dreams.

What do you desire?

It was not of this world, she knew. Not alien like the xenos who had risen up in her youth, but something older, something purer, something perfect. It whispered of a thousand empires, a million planets, a trillion souls. It had sailed the stars for millennia, and it yearned to do so again.

It could take her from this place of filth and heat and death. She saw it clearly, rising on wings through the clouds of pink, through the blue and into the black. The cold of the void, fresh and healing for one so battered and bruised by her existence.

In turn, she could give it what it wanted. She knew what it wanted, because it was what it had always wanted, what it *would* always want, with a gnawing, perpetual desire.

Power.

Cecily cut an unassuming figure in the flickering light of Sarquil's infernal workshop. She was clad in a stained slip of material and loose-fitting trousers, and she parted squads of militia and Sophisticants like a boat moving through water, ushering them gently aside with light touches on their shoulders or their hips. These were soldiers of sensation, trained to react with extreme violence to any threats against their master, and not one of them turned to look at her as she moved towards her goal.

It was but one of her strengths, she had discovered: to blend in, to render herself almost invisible to all but the keenest observers. Even Phaedre did not notice her at first. When she did, the witch shuddered, as if waking from a nightmare, scanning her eyes frantically around her vicinity. Cecily saw them come to rest on her, and heard a terrible screech. Black fire roared from the witch's open mouth, forking like electricity until it engulfed Cecily in rolling darkness.

The flames should have stripped the flesh from her bones, but Cecily pushed them aside with her mind, dissipating their heat and power. They washed over her like cleansing water, as cold and black as the void, and she stood, unharmed and unblemished, a few short yards from the warrior who she had foreseen would take her from this place.

'My name is Cecily,' she said. 'And I can help you.'

The warrior stared, as if witnessing something he had not seen for a long time.

'I want to leave this place,' Cecily said. 'I want you to take me with you.'

'Help me defeat my treacherous brother,' Xantine said, 'and I will give you anything you desire.'

Like Phaedre before her, Xantine saw strength in this one. Her psychic talents were obvious, but even to survive in such a miserable place showed power. S'janth drank the suffering of thousands like nectar. She convulsed within Xantine, ecstatic, and he fought to keep her down.

The Adored fanned out as they entered the chamber, choosing targets not on threat priority, effective weapon application, or any of the other methods they had been taught as members of the III Legion, but by their potential pleasure. Directing them was a fool's errand, and Xantine instead allowed them to sow chaos amongst his brother's forces. His focus, however, was elsewhere.

He keyed to Sarquil's vox-frequency, and engaged the sonic shrieker in his throat. 'Sarquil, you snake! Come out and face your death!' His only response was the sound of dying mortals.

'Your slaves are dying, Sarquil. Behold my loyal brothers. They put aside their petty squabbles and they fight for me, fight for the honour and the pride of the Third Legion. You were like them, once, before ambition and betrayal poisoned your soul.'

No response. Xantine dug in deeper. 'But now you are a coward, hiding behind your slaves in this disgusting hovel. Your only honourable act will be to die before your resplendent brothers.'

A voice crackled over the vox, deep and mournful.

'They are blind, and you are pathetic.'

'Such venom, brother!' Xantine said, with mock outrage. 'I gave you so much, and this is how you repay me?'

'You gave me nothing,' Sarquil said, as he stepped from the octagonal chamber, high above the work floor. 'Your pitiful warband had nothing to give. We lived like beggars, scraping for scraps – of ammunition, of slaves, of pleasure. So deranged by that *thing* sharing your body that you could not even see it!'

S'janth hissed in response. *A materialist soul, this one. The rot has set in, his mind is lost to obliteration. He cannot see the sublime.*

Then why did you not kill him when you had the chance?

And miss this pleasure? My love, you are growing tedious in your old age.

Xantine raised his voice to his brother. 'I saw perfidy germinating in your withered soul. I saw your treachery before you had the gall to act on it. I saw through you, brother. I see everything.'

'Categorically untrue,' the Terminator said, in his exasperating tone. 'Or else you would not have walked into my trap.'

'Do not lie, Sarquil. You have neither the wit nor the panache to carry it off.'

'I do not lie. I have tapped the lifeblood of your world and choked it almost to death. I knew you would come in a misguided attempt to save it, and now, I will bury you alongside it. Of the five thousand, four hundred and ninety-eight souls in this factorum, all will die here today,' Sarquil said. 'And it will be a mercy. Better to burn this world to ashes than live a moment longer under your rule.'

The great pipes high above the refinery had once run with sap, bringing the planet's lifeblood from its surface to the people high above. Sarquil signalled a shift with his massive power fist, and reversed the old pumps, flooding them instead with molten metal: the raw material he had been using to build his arsenal. The pipes glowed red, then yellow, before they too started to melt and run. Silver droplets fell to the floor below, a trickle at first, that quickly became a deluge. Molten metal ran from sluice gates and overflow pipes, an endless downpour that flooded the work floor below. Men and women caught fire as gobs of the superheated substance touched their skin, burning them to the bone in milliseconds. They clawed at their restraints as the metal pooled around them, sawing at hands and ankles and wrists with makeshift blades as the puddles combined, reaching the height of a human shin, then waist, then head.

The Adored were caught in the deluge, too. Poron Faest howled in pain and pleasure as, distracted by his own reflection as he tried to leap between raised workbenches, he took an autogun round to the back and toppled into the shimmering silver lake. He slid under the surface of the metal, his body cooking quickly inside its pink armour.

Xantine, on higher ground, stepped back from the growing pool.

'You callous fool, you would condemn your creation out of spite?' Xantine asked.

'It matters not,' Sarquil said. He cast a massive arm across the hellish scene. 'None of this matters. The fourteen point five-seven-three million rounds of ammunition, the seven thousand and ninety-two grenades, the thirteen thousand and...'

Sarquil twitched, and he started his count again, as if rebooting. 'Fourteen point five-seven-three million rounds of ammunition.'

His chaincannon chattered to life, firing in staccato bursts, not at Xantine, but seemingly at random targets.

'Fourteen point...'

The perforated barrel of a multi-melta rose from the peak of his left breast, pushing aside sinew and skin to break the surface of his armour.

'Fourteen.'

A fleshy lascannon pushed out from his stomach, firing blinding beams of light from its glistening tip. Stranger weapons came forth, too: brass teeth surrounded a screaming maw that launched balls of green fire; fleshy pods of ammunition bulged from bunched muscles, providing guns of all types with bullets, shells, and power packs brought forth from the warp itself.

'F-f-f-f-'

The word was lost forever, replaced by a metronomic *thump-thump-thump* as the distinctive cored barrel of a heavy bolter rose from inside Sarquil's throat, cracking his jaw as it began firing.

Ceramite and muscle shifted like putty as Sarquil's body rearranged itself, his obsession finding its form in the physical plane as the dormant Obliterator virus ravaged his body. High above them, the final pipes split open, and silver rain fell.

* * *

Molten rain fell around Torachon and Orlan as they danced, sparking against their ceramite armour on the rare occasions that they allowed themselves to be caught under its path. The warriors left a trail of maimed and mutilated humans behind them as they clashed, the broad sweeps from their sharp blades slicing through unarmoured flesh with ease.

'Why?' Torachon bellowed as they fought. 'Why did you choose this miserable existence?'

Orlan hissed, his mandibles jerking wildly. Speaking was clearly an effort for the creature, and he formed words carefully from his puckered mouth.

'He give me what I want.'

'And what does a creature such as you want?'

'I want kill. I want eat. I want be strong.' Orlan pointed his blade at Torachon. 'Like you, yes? Like you.'

They fought for higher ground as the tide of metal rose. Workbenches formed darkened islands in the scintillating sea of metal, and Torachon used their human occupants as makeshift steps to climb to temporary safety. Orlan was quick – quicker than he'd been before his gifts had manifested in his body – and he hopped between the islands before the molten metal could reach his clawed feet.

A human arm reached from below, grabbing weakly at Torachon's ankle as its owner was slowly immersed in molten metal. Repulsed, he raised the foot and stamped on the limb, shattering bone and releasing the limp grip. The momentary distraction gave Orlan a window, and he leapt, his poisoned blade raking another scar across Torachon's pauldron. 'Coward!' Torachon called. 'You would kill me while my back is turned? That is not the way of the Third!'

Orlan hissed again. A different sound this time: wetter.

'Are you laughing?' Torachon asked.

'Fool. Has always been our way,' the disfigured Space Marine said, between heaving breaths. 'No honour. Only pride. Xantine knows this true. He betray his master before, just as Sarquil betray him.' Another wet intake of breath. 'Xantine weak. He hide behind stronger brothers.' Orlan raised his poisoned sword, pointing it at Torachon. 'Like you. You are stronger, faster, but you shackled to him. Forever weak in his shadow.'

'You are jealous that I have risen so far,' Torachon said.

'Hah!' Orlan laughed again. 'He only use you. Minion. Puppet. *Lapdog.*' Grey saliva dripped from his mouthparts as he spat the final word.

'No!' Torachon bellowed. He leapt, faster than even Orlan could respond, and caught his disfigured brother by the throat, ceramite-armoured fingers digging deep into the soft meat of his neck. Torachon lifted the smaller Space Marine from his feet, turning his monstrous face this way and that as he inspected his corruption. Orlan's mandibles reached like fingers towards Torachon's wrist, trying unsuccessfully to loosen his grip.

'Disgusting,' Torachon said. He punched Orlan with his other hand, dislodging one of his huge eyes from its socket. It came to rest on his cheek, swinging like a pendulum in Torachon's vice grip. Still the mandibles flexed. The puckered mouth worked.

'I will not be disrespected,' Torachon snarled. 'Not by my own brothers. Not by anyone.'

He lowered Orlan slowly, feet first, into the rising silver sea. The warped creature thrashed in his grip, gurgling as the flowing metal cooked his body below the waist. Finally, with the stench of burned meat filling his nostrils, Torachon dropped his brother of the Emperor's Children, letting him slide under the surface alongside so many other shattered souls.

The young Space Marine stood alone in the glittering lake. His brothers had died or retreated, failure or cowardice their just reward. At the gate, his warlord stood, his attention focused on the giant on the walkway overhead, blind to the battle that had unfurled below. Once again, Xantine was taking the glory for himself, ignoring his brothers as they fought and died in his name. Torachon sneered.

Not this time.

Sarquil was a point of light, far above, his mutating body expanding and swelling with new weaponry.

'I will kill him,' Torachon decided. 'The glory of his death will be mine, and mine alone. Xantine will see.'

The chain had been used to haul the vast sap vats, and it bore his weight well as he climbed towards his destiny.

A single purple figure, long and lithe, climbed towards the shuddering Sarquil, high on his gantry. His shock of white hair was visible, even at such a distance, and he moved with an otherworldly grace that even his brothers could not hope to match. For a moment, Xantine was dumbstruck by the vision.

The image of your father, S'janth said.

'No,' Xantine whispered. Then he screamed, over the vox, and loud enough for the young Space Marine to hear. 'Torachon! Stop! This is an order from your warlord! From your superior! Sarquil is *mine!*'

There was a crackle over the vox, and Torachon's voice filled Xantine's ears.

'You have proven yourself incapable of butchering this snake, Xantine, so this time, I will deliver the killing cut myself.' There was only a hint of exertion in his voice.

He hungers for your glory, S'janth whispered. There was something like admiration in her tone.

'No!' Xantine roared. 'I free you from the Clonelord's flesh pits, I bathe you in all the sensation the galaxy has to offer, I raise you to my right hand, and *this* is how you repay me? You usurp my position? I have given you everything!'

'You have given me *nothing*. You have only taken. And now, I will take the glory from you. Watch, my lord, as a true son of the Third lays his enemies low.'

Xantine howled again in frustration, and raised the Pleasure of the Flesh from its mag-locked position on his hip.

'Bring him down!' he commanded, as he loosed bolt after bolt not at Sarquil, but at the purple-armoured figure climbing the chain to the gantry above.

Betrayal, S'janth sang in Xantine's mind. *Just as I promised you.*

'Kill him!' Xantine screamed.

'Nobody even in here. Let's go.'

'Don't matter. We got to check every room, kill all vermin. Lord Xantine said.'

There were three of them in the doorway, talking amongst themselves. Their voices were gruff, their speech awkward, as if the act of talking was difficult for their bodies. They were massive. Arqat could see that, their silhouettes framed by the light from outside as they opened the door to his prison.

A torch, mounted on an ornate lasgun, scanned the inside of the room, illuminating its meagre contents: a cot, a bucket and a book. A picture book, its cover printed with the four-armed figure of Serrine's Saviour. One of the Sophisticants took a step into the room, moving towards the book on the bed. A trophy, maybe, of a job well done. She bent down to pick it up, and turned to show it to her squadmates.

From his position underneath the cot, Arqat readied his machete. He had pulled the weapon from his footlocker as soon as he had woken to the sound of explosions, counting the moments until the attackers arrived with a stomach-churning mixture of fear and excitement.

He saw the leather-wrapped skin of the woman's ankles, and swung the machete as hard as he could, cleaving through the Achilles tendons of the Sophisticant.

She screamed and toppled, dropping her laspistol and crashing to the floor. Her face rolled to its side, and Arqat saw his attacker: she was huge, almost as tall as the angels themselves, and strong, with distended muscles protruding from underneath her magenta robes. On her face she wore a mask that depicted the Saviour's face, rendered in gold. The nose was straight, with a slight upward curve to its tip, the lips pulled into a mocking sneer. Even here, even in darkness at the bottom of his world, he could not escape his tormentor.

Arqat punched the blade through the side of her temple and rolled from under the cot. Lured by the sound, a second Sophisticant had entered the room. Like the woman, he wore the same face: the Saviour, rendered in gold. Arqat came up from below and pinwheeled his blade overhand into the man's shoulder, where it dug through flesh and tendons until it found bone. He yanked it loose, pulling the golden-masked man forward, before stabbing upwards three times into his midriff. Each strike tore at vital organs, and the Sophisticant slumped to the floor, his hands glistening red-black with his own gore in the dim light.

One left. This one was big – bigger than the others – and moved with a speed that surprised Arqat. He passed his spear back and forth between left and right hands as they mirrored each other, circling, alike in all aspects except for their expressions: where the golden mask depicted calmness, the Saviour afforded a benevolent smile and opal eyes, Arqat's face was contorted with rage. He fought not for Sarquil, but for Sanpow, for Cecily, for his stolen arm and his stolen life.

'Die!' he screamed, and ran towards the Sophisticant. The spear whirled in the air, and its haft caught Arqat across the back, sending him sprawling to the floor as the Sophisticant deftly sidestepped his swinging blade. Arqat was on his feet in seconds, slapping away the incoming spear-tip with a quick backhand. He ran again, putting all his force into his hooked blow, rage clouding his balance and his better judgement. The gold-masked soldier met his attack with his own, and punched the blunt end of his spear into Arqat's stomach. Arqat's legs buckled and he fell, sliding to his knees against his cot. The Sophisticant spun his spear again, circling the downed man as he tried to catch his breath. He was being toyed with.

'Come on!' Arqat gasped. 'Kill me!'

The Sophisticant laughed behind his mask. It was a deep sound, cruel and derisive. It spoke one word.

'Weak.'

He was a boy again. Just for a moment, a boy, his skinny limbs dwarfed by the huge cassock he was forced to wear. He cried often – cried for his mother, but more often, cried for his nanny. He wished for her to stroke his hair one last time, tell him it would all be okay.

The others teased him, and he understood. He hated that boy, too. Hated his weakness, hated his softness. He would be strong.

'Weak,' the Sophisticant said again, his spear held in a two-handed grip, point aimed at Arqat's throat. Arqat braced his hands against the cell floor, and found something solid and warm under the cot. He slid his hands around the pistol, feeling its weight, and moved it slowly behind his back.

The crack of the las-bolt echoed around the cell as Arqat squeezed the trigger. The smell followed moments later, of singed fabric and burnt human flesh. The Sophisticant looked down at the neat hole in his torso, his unmoving face not betraying any hint of emotion. Arqat shot again. The las-bolt lit the chamber in hellish red as it cored through the Sophisticant's pectoral muscle.

Arqat stood, keeping the laspistol between him and his attacker. He taunted the figure as he stepped forward, firing again.

'Who is weak now?' he asked, mocking the soldier as las-bolt after las-bolt pierced his magenta robes and burned through his body. Somehow the Sophisticant was still standing.

He reached him, finally, and brought the gold-inlaid stock of the weapon across the Sophisticant's chin. The man finally dropped to the ground, a dead weight, and he straddled his chest, leaning his own face in close to the golden mask. 'You are weak. I am strong.' Arqat slammed his elbow across the golden face, and the mask rode up, revealing living skin beneath. Wrapping his fingers around the metal, he tore the mask of his tormentor away, revealing the mortal beneath.

The cheekbones were wide – too wide – and the lips were thin, stretched tight over a jaw that had been artificially grown with a lifetime of stimulants and gene therapies. But he knew the jutting chin, proud and defiant, the crooked nose. It still had the curve in its bridge, broken when its owner had protected Arqat from the bully that had threatened to burn his books.

Most of all, he knew the eyes. Irises the same deep brown, still possessed of the same melancholy he had always known.

'An old soul,' Nanny had called Telo, while both children had bustled around her skirts. His brother had always been the sensible one, the one to help, the one to serve.

'No...'

The life in those eyes was fading. Arqat's brother spat blood, his huge shoulders heaving with a final cough as he tried to clear ruined lungs.

Arqat launched backwards, panic almost stopping his heart.

The sensation crystallised, and turned instantly to anger. He grabbed the collar of his brother's ribbed undersuit with his hand and pulled his face forward, screaming into it.

'Wake up! Wake up, you coward!' He slapped his dying brother across the face. 'Why did you do it? Why, you bastard? Why?'

Breath left the body with the question unanswered. The Sophisticant's massive head fell backwards, and Arqat let it hit the rockcrete floor.

Las-bolts fizzed and mass-reactive shells bloomed around Torachon as he hauled himself up onto the metal gantry.

He thought of Orlan, his hearts pumping hard as he ran. The pathetic creature had picked at a scab deep in Torachon's psyche, and now his wounded pride bled freely.

It was he who had been bred to be the most perfect Child of the Emperor. What was Xantine but a bitter, broken remnant of an old war? The Corpse-Emperor's Primaris warriors, the flowering of the Eye of Terror, and the splitting of the galaxy in two – existence had turned and left Xantine in the past. Torachon alone could lead the Adored to a glorious future, lead this world to perfection.

It was liberating, this freedom. Intoxicating. It burned in his lungs and his hearts as he sprinted the length of the gantry, high above the molten sea.

Too late, Sarquil turned, and Torachon drove his blade deep into his wayward brother's belly. Together, they fell.

Flesh-metal weapons fired indiscriminately, and the gantry juddered under the strain as Sarquil's fusillade continued, the infernal virus removing the need for the Obliterator to reload. The return fire was just as cacophonous, bullets and bolt-shells smacking against the chamber's ceiling and suspended structure. Supports melted and slipped as they were damaged beyond repair, but still the invading force kept up its attack, their indiscriminate shots at least nominally aiming for the purple-clad figure moving closer to his erstwhile brother.

'Kill him! Kill him now!' Xantine ordered, but it was an increasingly futile demand. Torachon had almost reached Sarquil, the latter so demented by the ravages of the Obliterator virus that he could not hear his brother's agile footsteps, nor react to the oncoming danger. Xantine slapped aside one trooper, breaking his spine in the process, and picked up his fallen lascannon. Shouldering the weapon, he aimed a shot towards the young Space Marine, but his preternatural reactions allowed him to duck the searing beam of light. It burned a hole in the central structure instead, hitting something explosive that lay inside. It detonated, blowing out the glass windows, and loosening the entire superstructure from its moorings.

Torachon reached Sarquil in the same moment, and the two figures seemed to become one. They left the walkway, the force of Torachon's impact carrying the Obliterator off his mutated feet, and when they returned to the metal decking, it was at a different angle. Their combined weight unbalanced it further, and a support tore away from the roof entirely, coming loose with a shower of molten metal and chunks of debris.

Sarquil fell, head first, into the rising lake. The superheated metal melted his own cap of silver in the milliseconds before he reached the meniscus of the liquid, years of painstaking work undone in an instant. It cooked his brain a moment later, before the rest of his body was also submerged, its flesh-metal weapons still firing, even in death.

Xantine watched his treacherous brother fall out of sight, the glory of his kill stolen from him. He had been betrayed not once but twice, by two brothers, and his anger burned hotter than the furnace at the refinery's core.

He scanned the room, but of Torachon, there was no sign. There was no time to investigate further. A quake ran through the entire chamber, and the structure slipped again. Xantine's shot had been the tipping point, and it was damaged now beyond repair. It started its slow, inexorable tumble towards the rapidly growing molten lake below, and as it fell, it took the ceiling with it.

There was a sound like a planet cracking, and Refinery Four's ancient roof caved in completely, the weight of the world above it too much for the chamber to bear. Vast chunks of metal and rockcrete obliterated the storage tanks and machinery below, pulverising any humans unlucky enough to be in their way, while others were burned by the boiling metal that cascaded from rents in the ceiling.

A hunk of rockcrete larger than a Baneblade slammed into the ground, flattening six Sophisticants, and missing Xantine by a foot. He turned, shoving aside Sophisticants and militia alike as he ran for an exit, but his way was blocked by a water-fall of molten metal that poured from a sluice grate high above. Everywhere he looked, his forces were dying as the heavens fell.

Suddenly, Xantine was back on Harmony. He stood, a younger man, amongst the screaming crystal spires of Canticle City. It was beautiful – so achingly beautiful – but he had been here before. He knew it could not last. He looked up, and saw it: the cruiser *Tlaloc*, hurled by Abaddon into his world's heart.

Xantine had survived that atrocity, pulled from the breaking city by his brother Vavisk. Once more, the sky was falling, but this time, Vavisk was nowhere to be seen.

And so Xantine did the only thing that he could do. He laughed. He laughed until tears formed in his shining eyes.

Run, S'janth hissed in his mind, urgent, frantic. She was a wild animal, throwing herself against her cage, and she howled at his capitulation. They both knew that after her aeldari captors' machinations, death in a flesh body meant destruction. *Weak creature,* she wailed. *Let me in!*

He would not. He would taste this final sensation himself, cross the final barrier in his own body.

Darkness descended as the world fell in on him, solid rockcrete and molten metal descending like the *Tlaloc*. He waited for annihilation.

It did not come. The roar of Refinery Four's destruction became muffled, and Xantine raised his turquoise eyes. He stood inside a bubble in reality – like a drop of oil in water – through which the debris from the collapsing roof could not pass. At its centre, the small woman stood, her arms raised.

'Thank you,' Xantine said. The gratitude he felt was genuine, and the sensation was strange.

The woman shook, as if shouldering an unimaginable burden, but she managed to speak.

'I have helped you,' she said. 'Now you have to keep your end of the bargain.'

They had destroyed his home, forced him to kill his own brother, and taken the woman he loved like no other, but at least the invaders were easy to track. He could hear them, screaming and laughing, their booming voices impossibly loud in the claustrophobic confines of the pipe city. He could smell them, too: the blood on their blades, the ashes on their armour.

Arqat followed them at a half-crouch, moving low and fast through side tunnels and ventilation shafts. The undercity was his, not theirs, and he knew the fastest routes, knew how not to be spotted. He shared his world with other natives. He saw Gassers as he tracked the invaders, their masked faces appearing from sub-pipes and anterooms, their bug eyes black and wide.

He wanted to break off his pursuit, to chase them down and kill them as he had killed their cousins, to feel their hot blood on his skin, to bite their bones with his blade.

But Arqat held firm, following the small group of pink-clad warriors and their smaller soldiers. He did it for Cecily. The angels had taken his arm, and now they took the woman who had saved him. Their punishment would be death.

They moved like water, following the most direct path to the great elevators that served as the only remaining functional route to the overcity. Many had died, he gathered from the soldiers' chatter, hundreds killed by the collapse of Refinery Four.

Good. They deserved it. Arqat himself had only survived because he had squeezed into an upturned sap tank as the roof caved in, crawling out only when the terrible rumbling had stopped.

Most gangers stayed out of the invaders' way; those that tried to stand up to the incursion onto their turf were put down quickly. He found their corpses, their stomachs blown open with explosive shells, or their skulls perforated by massed las-fire. Some showed signs of more elaborate deaths. A clean cut bisected one miserable wretch from shoulder to hip, the work of a single blade swung with unimaginable force. Another had been partially flayed, the perpetrator apparently tiring of the work before it was complete. The loose skin hung on the body like a robe.

Eventually, they reached the great elevator, and ascended. Arqat would follow them, soon, rising from the depths. He would have his vengeance, no matter the cost.

CHAPTER TWENTY-ONE

'Betrayer!' Xantine howled, breaking a nine-thousand-year-old vase that depicted the first arrival of Terra's tithe ships on Serrine. Ceramic pieces crunched as Xantine ground them under his boot. 'Idiot child!' He swung his rapier in an arc, its monomolecular tip smashing sculptures and statues as it raked through them. 'That worm, that whelp, that… betrayer!'

As it has always been, S'janth whispered.

'Silence, daemon!' Xantine screamed. His words seemed to signal an end to the orgy of destruction, and stillness finally reigned in the chamber. Only Xantine's chest moved, heaving with exertion, as he stood in front of his council. Three of the living chairs were empty. Those belonging to Torachon and Sarquil would not be occupied again, while Xantine's quivered in fear, awaiting its master's return from his pacing.

The warlord composed himself, measuring his tone. 'Torachon disobeyed my demands and attempted to obtain the glory of the kill for himself. The Clonelord will have a lot to answer for next time I see him, mark my words.'

Never one to read the tenor of a room, Qaran Tun spoke first. 'The Sea of Souls claimed him for a purpose,' the Word Bearer said, with a scholarly equanimity that was singularly unwelcome in the tense atmosphere. Xantine wheeled upon his tattooed cousin, rage flashing in his turquoise eyes.

'Silence!' he roared. 'That halfwit had no purpose. He was a cast-off, our accumulated genetic scrapings given pathetic form. A grotesque copy of the Third, blessed neither with our grace, nor our poise.' Xantine turned back to the room. 'And then he had the temerity to throw away his life! The final insult – he could not even betray me successfully.' He pulled the Pleasure of the Flesh from his hip and fired one, two, three bolts into Torachon's empty chair.

Xantine took a long breath. 'How many did we lose?' he asked, as he scanned the room. Vavisk met his gaze with as much stoicism as his sagging face could muster. Qaran Tun's tattooed eyelids were closed, the diabolist no doubt in unspoken communion once more with his Neverborn pets. Phaedre was careful to avoid his eyes entirely, her attention studiously focused on the arrangement of bracelets she wore on her thin wrists. He would get no answer from those who remained. 'By the Prince, why must all of my subjects fail me! Pierod, give me a death count, now!'

Serrine's governor stepped forward hesitantly from his position outside the ring of chairs. He had been an uncomfortable participant in these council meetings, but Xantine found that he could trust the portly mortal to perform basic tasks, if only because Pierod's fear of losing his position trumped his fear of all other dangers.

'Some four hundred soldiers, my lord,' Pierod said.

'Details!' Xantine roared, and raised his pistol in Pierod's direction. Before the mortal could answer, the servo-skull that hovered at his shoulder took over the count.

'Three hundred and ninety-two of the militia, forty-three Sophisticants, and thirteen of the Adored, blessed be their souls, perished in the assault on Refinery Four.'

'Thirteen? I thought it was twelve,' Pierod stammered.

'Master Quant submitted to his wounds some seventy-three minutes ago, governor.'

Pierod ducked as Xantine hurled a bronze bust of his own head through a glassaic window, whimpering quietly as cold air rushed in through the hole it created.

'Failures! I am surrounded by failures. Despite my best efforts, I am stymied by my own people, my own brothers. What did I do to deserve such a fate?' He turned, and walked to the back of the chamber, towards the marble throne he used during his euphemistically termed meditations.

'No matter.' Xantine breathed deep and ran a gloved hand down his face. 'No matter,' he repeated, trying to convince himself. 'What I have lost, I will forget. And besides' – he looked at Cecily – 'in my new muse, I may have found myself a greater prize.'

Part of him wished he'd asked more questions of his old friend, but as the stimms wore off and the pain in his ribs swelled again, Edouard found himself following Dartier's directions, making his way down into the deepest reaches of the overcity to find his fix.

It was an old place, Dartier had said. Edouard could see that. The buildings were boxy and square, built of pockmarked rock-crete and rusted metal. He'd never been down here, never known that places like this existed in the city of his birth, and he now saw why: these ancient structures were hidden by walkways, balconies and verandas. They had been erased from public consciousness by subsequent generations, who used the flow of credits from moneyed worlds to hide their humble past with cathedrals and conservatories, halls, amphitheatres and follies. But the original sin was still here, buried just below the surface, forming the bedrock for this city of spires and statues.

Here and there, reminders of the surface city crept in. Chunks of marble masonry blocked his path at times, their mottled surfaces inlaid with gold and silver. They had been cast down during the xenos attack years ago, Edouard realised, tracing their descent into this foundation layer by the scrapes and score marks they left on the ancient structures.

This rubble had never been cleared by Baron Sarquil's work gangs – had never even been noticed. That was not a rarity in Serrine, even now. Lord Xantine himself had proclaimed that Serrine would become the most beautiful city in the galaxy, and had tasked his government with the repair of all damage caused by the attack. Edouard had believed him – what teenager would not believe the shining angel who had descended from the heavens to save his life? – but a decade later, people still made their homes in half-destroyed hab-blocks and bombed-out businesses.

'What am I doing?' he asked himself. He couldn't see the night sky from down here, couldn't make out the stars, or the moons, or the splash of throbbing colour that he sometimes found himself staring into.

He could hear something, though. A dull clash of metal on metal, and as he strained in the darkness, the sound of raised voices. He followed them, stepping gingerly across broken masonry and levering himself over chunks of rockcrete, until he found the entrance to the temple.

CHAPTER TWENTY-TWO

The world had no name.

No, that's not true.

The voice was right. The world did have a name, but it had slipped into the depths of his memory and been eaten by the snapping creatures that dwelt within. The man had a name, too, but he had forgotten that as well. It did not matter. He rarely used it. Even to his children, the man was Viceroy: a position more than a name. One of power, one of influence. It was more important than something as simple as a name. It was more important than something as simple as a child.

The child's hair was long. It was a tradition among his class to wear the hair long, and cut it only on ascent to one of the world's many great positions. And so, it had grown and grown, long enough now that he tied it back with ribbon. The ribbon was purple, the colour of heroes. His hair was as black as night.

The child had seen his brothers and sisters cut their hair as they grew taller, finished their extensive schooling, and eventually moved out of the family villa. The child would not follow. He was the four-teenth, and even at his tender age, he knew that he would wear his hair long for the rest of his life.

The man was talking. The child could hear him through the floor, pressing a tumbler to his ear to enhance the sound. He had stolen the glass from the kitchen staff, telling them that he had broken it accidentally, and cleaned up the wreckage before they discovered it. It was a lie, but even at his age, the child had perfected the art of subterfuge.

'Is he strong?'

'He is. The therapies were effective on his siblings.'

'He would never return.'

'As I understand. Our house has a rich history of providing aspir-ants to the Legion.'

'He may not survive the trials.'

'I do not care. I have no need of him.'

'Then it is done.'

A scramble, to hide the tumbler, to climb back into his bed, to feign the stillness of sleep. The door opened, a crack of light opening the way to the outside.

'Get up,' his father said.

They made a deal, Cecily and Xantine.

She had seen the very worst of Serrine. Its violence and its misery, its death and destruction. She wanted nothing more than to simply leave – to disappear into the night sky, and live amongst the stars. He gave her that promise. He told her that, when his perfect society had been built, he would give her what she desired: a way off the world of her birth. She did not entirely trust him, but there was no other who could even make such a promise.

In return, she gave him power, simple and unalloyed – the

abilities of a very rare kind of psyker. Like Phaedre before her, she became one of his muses. It was a grandiose title, but the concept was simple. Xantine had long surrounded himself with powerful and useful mortals, offering them gifts or promises in order to utilise their talents over those that would unseat him. If he tired of them, or if he never delivered upon his promises, then so be it – as long as he could secure their power for a time.

Cecily's ascension to the role of muse was not taken well by Phaedre. The witch met her with barely disguised contempt. Her mind was guarded, her own prodigious psychic powers meaning that her thoughts were naught but a swirling vortex to even the most intense of Cecily's intrusions.

'You are a butterfly, fluttering on glass wings,' she told Cecily, as their lord slept off the effects of one of his cousin's heady draughts. 'A distraction, but on closer inspection,' she added, leaning in so close that Cecily could smell her breath through her yellowed teeth, hot and rancid, like the gases released from a corpse's stomach, 'you are still an insect, fragile and disgusting.' Phaedre stepped back, and made a show of inspecting her manicured nails. They were long, and Cecily knew that each one had been taken from the fingers of other women. 'He will tire of you soon, and you will fall from the sky. When you do, I will crush you under my feet, and no one will remember your name.'

His brothers among the Adored were slightly more accommodating, even if they were rarely warm. Qaran Tun studied her with an academic eye, in much the same way he appeared to approach all living beings, while Vavisk viewed her with brusque indifference. To him, she was just one of a generation of mortal curios that his brother had taken on.

The Noise Marine interested her, despite his coldness, primarily for the obvious connection that he shared with his warlord. The Word Bearer, the witch, the other preening mortals who haunted the upper reaches of the palace – all of them often suffered Xantine's ire, blamed for their insufficient talent or appreciation. Vavisk, on the other hand, was rarely the target of his brother's wrath, his counsel somehow always quiet, despite the cacophony of wheezes, wails, squeals, and screams that emanated from his warped body. Indeed, the occasions that Xantine sought communion with his brother were some of the few times that she was separated from him.

The other times were when he turned to his meditations. Cecily did not know what went on behind the wooden doors to Xantine's chamber during these periods: she was ushered from the room by oiled slaves before the ceremonies commenced. She knew only that such events involved Qaran Tun, and they incapacitated her lord for several hours, or even days, afterwards.

Most often, he returned slowly, groggy from his sojourn, eyes and aura dull from mental effort in some unseen realm. Other times, though, he woke up *different*.

This was one such time. Cecily yanked her hand backwards, dropping her dampened silk cloth, as Xantine's massive head rose. Its features were covered by strands of unwashed black hair, but she could see a toothy smile spreading across the lower half of his face.

'My lord?' Cecily asked. 'Are you returned?'

The voice that came from Xantine's mouth was his, but not his, somehow. More sinuous, sensuous.

'I am, my dear,' he said.

His tongue flicked from his mouth, long and black. It tasted at the air. He stood smoothly, and she noticed in the darkness of his chamber that his eyes had lost their turquoise brightness. The irises were milky pink, like the clouds that had blocked her view of the sky.

'I believe I will take my leave tonight and be with my subjects,' he said, moving before she could offer a response.

When he returned, hours later, his hands were wet with blood.

CHAPTER TWENTY-THREE

Edouard met the blank-faced gaze of the copper-masked priestess. Firelight danced across the burnished metal and two conical horns rose from her headdress. It gave her an otherworldly appearance, but the voice that came from behind the mask was unmistakably human.

'We accept your offering.'

A lower-class voice. Once he would have baulked at taking orders from such a character, but now he would take whatever he could get. He'd learned the ways of the temple on his first visit, and had rapidly come to accept them. So much so that he stopped making his way back to the upper reaches of the city altogether, preferring instead to make his new home in the spartan temple bunks that the priests offered. The irony made him laugh: a very different god, but he had once again made his way back to religion.

He felt the knife pressed into his palm, handle first. Its curved blade was inexpertly crafted, imperfections clear in the metal, but it was sharp enough to cut skin. That was all that mattered.

Shuffling men and women moved towards the cauldron at the centre of the room, each clutching their own blade. He joined them, falling into step, and finding a space around the edge of the brass cauldron. He had given his riches once, given his worship to a false god who had offered him nothing. In comparison, this blessing was a small price to pay. A little pain, a little blood, and he was complete. For the night, at least.

Edouard drew the knife across his palm. A moment of sharp pain, then a dull ache as the blood came, swelling from deep within his body to drip-drip-drip against the rough metal. Dozens of others joined him, and he smelled the coppery tang of their own sacrifice as their blood mixed with his in the deep well of the cauldron.

'Why are we doing this? What do they need our blood for?' The voice belonged to a young woman, wide-eyed and rail thin. She had been ushered alongside Edouard at the edge of the cauldron.

'I don't care,' Edouard said. 'All I need to know is that they give me Runoff if I give them my blood. They could have my eyes if they gave me enough serum to make it worth my while.'

'Does everybody do this up here?'

'What do you mean?'

'This.' She gestured with the knife that had been placed into her hands.

'Not everybody,' Edouard said.

'Is there anywhere else I can get it?' she asked. She was too loud. Copper-masked heads were turning in their direction.

'There used to be. Not any more.'

'Please,' she said. 'Tell me. This doesn't feel right, something feels weird about this place.'

'Shh,' Edouard said, trying to ignore this newcomer and focus on his own pain. 'Just give your blood, and don't cause a fuss.'

The woman hesitated, the knife held against her wrist in shaking hands.

'I don't want to,' she said, and dropped the knife into the cauldron. It clanged against the metal, sliding down the shallow interior edge until it came to rest, its blade submerged in the growing pool of blood. 'This is strange, I don't feel right. I've got to go.' She turned from the cauldron edge, and tried to walk away. Rough hands caught her before she made it two paces. Four copper-masked priestesses picked her up, one to each limb, and brought her back to the edge of the cauldron. Edouard kept his eyes focused on his own wrist, on his own pain, as they placed the woman's neck against the brass lip of the cauldron. She was screaming now, promises and apologies that he knew she would not be able to keep. A fifth acolyte stepped forward and sliced her throat with a ritual blade. Her screams died as she did, her blood joining the melange of those that had given theirs willingly. It didn't matter, Edouard knew. They cared not from whence the blood flowed.

Qaran Tun had been in communion with a new daemonic entity when he was called to his master's chambers. As usual, he was instructed to bring a selection of his wares for Xantine's perusal. Cecily left the room, guided by two muscled figures, as the tattooed warrior laid out a selection of containers, amphorae and other trinkets. Typically, she was escorted to her own bed-chamber: a luxurious room on the same floor as Xantine's own grand chamber that she had come to realise used to be occupied by Phaedre. The crone had relocated to a smaller room in one of the lower levels, and rarely let Cecily forget the slight.

But tonight the slaves stopped short of her room, waiting

near the grand chamber's double doors for some signal. Sure enough, a moment later, she heard her master's voice, plaintive, calling for her.

'Cecily?'

She turned on her heels, and allowed the slaves to cast open the doors. Xantine sat in his throne, back rod straight, fingers gently caressing the fine marble.

'Stay awhile, won't you? I was hoping that we could discuss our deal.'

'Of course, my lord,' she said. Xantine had avoided the conversation in recent weeks, and she was keen to press the issue of her escape from Serrine. Their ship was dead, and Xantine had as yet been close-lipped about how he intended to keep up his half of the bargain.

Cecily was halfway across the room, when Qaran Tun took her by the wrist. His massive hand enveloped her forearm, its grip as cold and unyielding as steel. She let out a small shriek, and looked up into his tattooed face. Golden eyes fixed on her, eyeing her like a snake sizing up its prey to devour. After an uncomfortably long pause, he spoke. His voice was dry, like sand.

'Have you encountered a Neverborn, psyker?'

'Neverborn?' Cecily asked, a tremor in her voice. She tested his grip, but found it still vice-like in its strength. She considered screaming for help, trying to run, but she did not want to offend her master's brother. Plus, Xantine was there. He would not let any harm come to her.

Qaran Tun chuckled. 'You will have encountered them, whether you were aware of it at the time or not.' He released her wrist, and turned to his collection of artefacts. 'You may have called them daemons, once, or simply monsters. Simplistic terms, but they are not incorrect. The Neverborn are reflections of our needs and wants, our fears and our desires.' Tun traced gestures in the air, and runes on his armour began to glow with a golden light. 'You are a prodigiously talented psyker, so I ask again, have you spoken to daemons?'

'I do not know,' she answered, truthfully. She had long seen things at the edges of her vision, felt the touch of hands she could not see on her mind. The voices, the whispers of the grass. Were these the voices of the Neverborn that Tun spoke of?

'I am quite sure that you have,' Tun said. 'Your kind are beacons to the Neverborn, offering doorways into this realm from their reality.' He wheeled to face Cecily, and the speed of his movement caught her off-guard. 'It is a gift, your talent. They are beautiful things, and to be their conduit is prize indeed, especially for a mortal.'

'I have heard voices,' Cecily said. 'The grass. It speaks to me. It helps me. Do daemons help people?'

Tun laughed. 'Sometimes, if purposes align. Sometimes.' He flashed a cold smile that did not spread to his eyes, as he produced a silver cylindrical object from his satchel. It was about as long as Cecily's forearm, and clearly ancient.

'But they also have their uses,' Tun said, and placed one end of the object to his lips. He blew, his cheeks expanding slightly, and smoke rose from its tip, an oily green-black smog that was heavier than the surrounding air. It fell slowly to the stained carpet of the chamber, and seemed to coalesce, moving with uncanny purpose. It was, Cecily realised, forming the shape of a human figure, with two arms, two legs, and a head whose featureless face swam, defying all attempts to focus on its shifting shape. Fully formed, it stood opposite her, a living shadow, swaying gently in the pungent air.

'This creature is one of the most helpful in my collection,' Tun said. 'It is capable of identifying the most powerful psykers. The ones with the most pliant minds.' The Word Bearer spoke like a proud father as he took in the span of the creature. 'For standard potentials I would simply administer a physical test, but Xantine would not sanction a potentially wasteful use of his latest curiosity.'

The lord of Serrine looked down from his throne, the rigid smile still fixed on his face. He was strangely silent as the events unfolded, despite Cecily's obvious discomfort.

Tun continued. 'And so, the services of this magnificent creature have been secured. Please, take a seat,' he said, gesturing towards her chair at Xantine's side. 'It will be better if you remain as still as possible while we conduct the test. Any unexpected movement could be quite... painful for you.'

'Wait,' Cecily said, backing away. The smoke figure copied her movements, stepping forward as she stepped back. 'Xantine would not allow this.'

'I am fulfilling Xantine's direct orders,' Tun said. 'Is that not right, my lord?'

Xantine's voice was soft and sibilant. 'Yes,' he said from his throne, his eyes still hooded in darkness.

'You see?' Tun said.

'What do you want from me?' Cecily asked.

'I believe that you may hold the key to getting us off this inconsequential world. I want to test my supposition.'

Cecily stepped back again, and the smoke creature followed her. She thought she saw eyes in its swirling head, milky white and pitch black. Gripped by fear, she pushed outwards with her mind, lashing out the only way that she could against such creatures. Instantly, she was pushed backwards, a mental force keeping her powers at bay. She knew the sensation.

'Phaedre,' she said. The witch hovered a few feet away, her skin prickling from the cold in the room.

'Ah yes,' Tun said. 'I had informed Lady Phaedre that this

process may be quite painful.' Qaran Tun's wide grin showed teeth etched with spidery runes. 'She wanted to observe. I cannot say no to a curious mind.'

Cecily hit the chair as the smoke creature closed on her. She screamed for her master as its scent filled her nostrils, like burnt skin and electrical fire, but Xantine simply watched, his smile wide, and his eyes pale pink.

'Arqat? Oh gods, Arqat? Is that you?'

The man was small and dirty, like so many that Arqat had seen in the streets of the overcity's lowest reaches. His wide eyes looked out of place in his soot-darkened face, white against black. Arqat scanned his memory, and found a boy, not much smaller than the man he had become.

'Edouard?'

'I thought you were dead!' Edouard took the much larger man by his good arm and ushered him to the side of the street. Faces that had turned to regard them turned back to their business: gambling with silver cubes, attending to steaming pipes of narcotic substances, or staring hungrily through smeared windows at the semi-clothed figures that cavorted within.

'Have you been keeping well? How did you get here? Where have you been?'

Arqat blinked. It was more conversation than he'd had in a long time, and he didn't know where to begin.

'Below,' he said, hesitantly.

'The *under*city?!' Edouard asked, incredulous. 'And you made it out? But gods man, look at you. What happened to your arm?' Edouard touched the stump lightly, and Arqat recoiled as his finger brushed the skin.

'Long...' Arqat growled, remembering the pain and remembering the angel that stole his limb. 'Long time ago,' he mumbled.

Edouard gave him a long stare. Pity, perhaps.

'You must be starving. Come, come with me. I know a place you can recover.'

Sister.

A million voices sang as one. Impossibly beautiful and impossibly sad, a chorus of loss.

Sister, return to us.

S'janth could hear it now, now she was stronger. Her sisters and brothers, across time, distance and reality, joining themselves in a perfect harmony of desperate longing. She wanted so desperately to join them, to return to her Prince's palace, to walk its fractal halls, to serve once more by his side.

But she could not. Not yet. Her vessel was clever – that was why she had selected him – and fickle, too. Long years together had allowed her to regain a fraction of the power she had once possessed, but it had also taught him how to guard his soul and how to protect his body. She could use him when his guard slipped, or on the rare occasions he allowed it, but she could not yet dominate his flesh form as many of her kin could.

I am too weak, she sighed.

Then take strength.

It was so simple for them, these beings. She had been so much more than them, once. Mighty and awe-inspiring, she had become legend amongst the flesh races of the mundane reality. They feared her and worshipped her in equal measure, and the mere whisper of her existence had inspired the deaths of worlds. Millions went to their doom gladly with her name on their lips, her touch on their skin, giving themselves over to sensation, to excess.

Until they laid her low. It was not easy, engineering her downfall, and even for a race as long-lived as the aeldari, it took them generations to put their plan into action. Their seers plotted, putting wheels in motion that they knew their children's children would not see come to fruition, but through twists of fate, and the machinations of some of her own kind, they achieved their goal: she was permanently stripped of her daemon form and her consciousness split and bound to objects buried deep below the sands of a world that came to be called Kalliope.

Now she was a fraction of herself, and the vessel she had chosen used his time playing games of power. She coursed with anger, her pride wounded, as the song of her siblings assailed her. She would join them, but not in Xantine's shell.

There was another way. The young Space Marine, the double of his gene-father. She had watched him rise, growing and coalescing in power like a dust cloud forming a star. Now there was ambition and pride, coursing through his veins like blood. Strength, too: plenty of that. He had been galvanised by pain, shaped and tempered like a sharpened blade to become the tool she needed. A vessel, waiting for her to claim it. A being of pain and pleasure, of pleasure and pain.

She watched the swelling soul, and called to it. He would be hers, and she would be his.

Come to me.

The words woke him from slumber, but he was not in darkness. The reality he returned to was one of blinding light, so pure in its brightness that he could see nothing else. His senses returned slowly, like a cogitator running through its start-up subroutines, and the blinding light became blinding pain. His nerves screamed with perfect agony, burned almost to the point of destruction. Almost to the point of death. The agony would have doomed a lesser creature, too fundamental, too absolute for them to comprehend.

But he had been made to withstand pain: his hardened skin, his enhanced organs, his toughened skeleton. And so, he endured it. He let it crash against the form of his body and recede, like ocean waves against the shoreline.

Why fight it? Pain was not the enemy, not to be fought or pushed away. It was but one of the panoply of sensations, pleasure by another name. Here, now, he was testing the limits of sensation, to heights of experience that no living being had enjoyed.

And so he embraced the pain. He fell upon it like a banquet, devouring it, savouring its hotness, its sweetness. He enjoyed its bouquet and let its myriad flavours rest on his tongue, then swallowed it and let it nourish his ravaged body.

Come to me.

Melodious and sweet, the voice was a salve to his seared soul. The pain was blissful, but the voice promised something more: he could have what he desired – all of it, and more – if he would simply do as it asked.

For the first time in his immortal life, he had clarity of purpose. He rose from the light, skin scorched and blood boiling, and began his ascent to the dark.

Wind lifted the sand. A few grains at first, but soon the gust became a gale, and swirling blackness filled his visor. When it settled, the darkness remained.

Not total darkness. Light, just a pinprick, was visible above him. Sound filtered through the opening, muffled and distant. He hung, a consciousness, adrift once more in his own body.

A fingerhold. It was all he had, but it was all he needed. The daemon was occupied, her attention was elsewhere, and he would take his body back.

CHAPTER TWENTY-FOUR

Xantine heard the words of Qaran Tun before he could see his cousin, his senses realigning as he returned to control of his body.

'She is compatible.'

The Word Bearer glanced at the stone tablet he cradled in the crook of his massive arm. It whispered to him, in a voice like the wind. Between them, Cecily lay slumped on a plush chaise longue, the occasional twitch of her body the only indication that she still lived.

'Her mind is unique amongst those we have discovered on this world – powerful, but unguarded. She will interface with Ghelia. She will revitalise the *Exhortation*.' Tun looked up, his gold eyes gleaming. 'She will allow us to leave this place.'

Yesss, S'janth wept. ***We yearn to follow the song, to return to the Dark Prince…***

Images flickered through the mind they still shared, of fields of silk, lakes of wine and forests of flesh. The garden of Slaanesh.

She would be rejuvenated in the Dark Prince's embrace. And he… He would be cast aside, a vessel, its contents poured out.

Her distraction was all Xantine needed. He had become expert at waiting for these moments of weakness, the more that they warred for control of his flesh body, and he slipped back into his form like a bodysuit. He fixed Tun with turquoise eyes, and spoke.

'No,' he said, matter-of-factly.

'…no?' Tun asked. It was not impertinence, but genuine confusion. 'We have waited for this moment. My rites have confirmed that the girl is compatible. I… I do not understand.'

No! S'janth howled as she realised that he had reasserted control. She thrashed in his body, moving like a snake, probing for weak points in his consciousness to force her way through. He blocked her. He had a singularity of purpose, a certainty of will that left no gaps in his armour. He would use her power, but he would not let her in.

'Your lady has taken her leave, diabolist. Speak now to your warlord, and pray that I find mercy in my soul for your treachery.'

Tun blinked, tattooed eyelids covering golden eyes. To his credit, he did not retreat from the throne.

'What do you mean, my lord? I have simply followed your demands.'

'Silence, warlock!' Xantine roared. 'You have conspired with the being that shares my body in secret. She is powerful, but cannot keep everything from me. I know your treacherous soul.'

'My lord, I–'

'The girl is my muse, Word Bearer. Mine. Neither you nor the daemon will take what is mine from me.'

Tun waved a hand at the prone figure on the chaise longue. She appeared so fragile in the huge chamber.

'She is a simple mortal, Xantine. We have found thousands of psykers on this world, more powerful than this undercity wretch. Take one of them as your muse, and allow us to restore your beloved ship.'

'Her talents matter not. Do you understand, diabolist? You will not take her.'

'But…' Tun stammered. 'Why? With her, we could leave this place, claim the galaxy as our own, savour its experiences. Do you not wish to show your true power as lord of the Adored?'

'Of course,' Xantine said.

You lie! S'janth roared. *You lie, you lie, you lie,* she repeated, as she battered against the cage of his body.

'Then allow me to take this creature and make of her what we must.'

'I will not.'

Tun began to speak, but the Word Bearer's tablet whispered again, and his face hardened. 'I understand,' he said. 'You have no intention of leaving Serrine. You never did.'

Xantine brought his hands together, clapping politely. 'Very good, cousin,' he said, and fixed the Word Bearer with a feline gaze. 'Though I am disappointed that it took you so long. You always were better at communicating with your pets than you were your peers.' He let a smile play across his blackened lips. 'Why would we leave this world? In the void I must scrabble for a meagre existence, treating with base pirates and renegades, pursued by the betrayer Abaddon and the pathetic remnants of the glorious Third. Here I am truly adored. Here I am a god.'

You are no god, S'janth hissed.

I am worshipped by millions. My name is on countless lips as they rise in the morning, and as they fall asleep at night. I colour their every thought. What is that, if not a god?

A god has power.

I have power over you, daemon. You live within me because I allow it. It was I who brought you to this world, I who kept you here.

'We were attacked,' Tun said. 'They crippled the ship. We did not choose this.'

Cruelty twisted Xantine's features as he rounded on the Word Bearer. 'You truly believe I would allow my ship to be crippled by mortals? By xenos worshippers? My cousin, you are more of a dullard than I imagined.'

Xantine threw his arms wide, as if conducting an orchestra.

'It was me, of course. I engineered the warp "accident" that saw us arrive at this world, I engineered the attack on the *Exhortation*. Simple, really, to rig charges at key points in the ship's superstructure, to time their detonation to an erroneous surface reading.'

'Ghelia. You killed her.'

Xantine flicked his wrist. 'A small price to pay for the prize I earned.'

Tun stared, aghast at the revelations. S'janth howled and spat.

You would trap us both here, all to lord over this bauble? How could you do this to me? After everything I gave to you?

Xantine addressed the daemon, speaking audibly to the room. 'And you, my dear. Do you think that yours is the only consciousness I sought out during our long years together? There are many of your sisters and brothers who know how to sail the storms that separate Serrine from the galaxy, and would happily part with that information in exchange for their own pleasure. But you would never allow that, would you? Any one of them could decide you were prey, finding you here, weak as you are.'

Feeble, ugly, disgusting creature! S'janth screamed. They were sensations, rather than words.

'You cannot do this, Xantine,' Tun said.

'*Silence!*' Xantine roared. 'I have given you so much. I rescued you from brothers who would have sacrificed you, and protected you from the executioners of your pathetic Legion. I gave you a home, warriors to call brother, and a leader that you could follow into any battle.' He sat forward, fixing Tun with turquoise eyes. 'And this is how you repay me? Colluding with the creature that shares my body, behind my back?' He stood from his throne, full control of his body returned, his muscles still burning with the afterglow of the daemon's power. He raised a finger towards Cecily as he loomed over Qaran Tun.

'Who else knows of this?' Xantine asked.

Tun cocked his tattooed head. 'No one, lord.'

'Good,' Xantine said. 'Your failure is at least contained.'

He rammed his rapier through Tun's stomach. The Word Bearer stumbled backwards, muttered words lost on lips that were darkening with black blood, and Xantine pulled the weapon from deep inside his cousin. Tun did not fall at first. He staggered into a marble pedestal, shattering its glass case as he steadied himself against the body of its Doric column.

'This is the price of betrayal, Tun,' Xantine said as he sauntered towards the stricken diabolist. 'You brought this on yourself.'

The Word Bearer slipped on a pool of his own blood, and fell to his knees. Before he could rise, Xantine put a boot in his stomach. He ground the ceramite against the oozing wound, and Tun winced. 'I only wanted the best for each of you, and this is how you choose to repay me,' Xantine said, his blackened mouth contorting into an exaggerated frown. 'You made me do this,' he told his cousin, as he raised Anguish for the killing cut.

The sword came down, but Tun caught the blow on his stone tablet before it could reach his body. The monomolecular blade bit into dark rock, and the tablet exploded with a soul-wrenching scream.

Xantine was launched backwards, lifted off his feet by the unholy force and sent sprawling across the chamber. Foul ichor coated his body, stinking of rotting tissue and superheated plasma. Shapes climbed from the dark fluid: oily tentacles and unblinking eyes, ridged tongues and clenching gobbets of muscle. They grasped for weak points in his armour – his throat, his armpits, his groin – mewling and gibbering as he slapped and swatted them away.

'A neat trick, cousin,' Xantine called. 'What else do you have in your collection?'

Rising to his feet, he saw Tun twisting the cap from one of his runed containers, before hurling it like a grenade. The creature that pulled itself from inside the container was thin and long – far too long to fit inside the confines of its prison, had it been born from this reality. Its lower body was supported by four powerful legs that ended in wicked claws of obsidian black. Studded leather armour wrapped around its midriff, the material tight against swollen muscles and held in place by hooks and barbs that tugged painfully at pale purple skin. Two arms hung from shapely shoulders, ending in huge curved claws, and a bladed tail arced up and over its wedge-shaped head. That head was fringed by a set of glistening horns, and played host to a two-yard-long tongue that palpated the air, dripping corrosive saliva to the floor below, where it burned deep into the thick carpet.

Fiends of Slaanesh, S'janth had called them, when she had frolicked with such beasts with her siblings in Slaanesh's gardens.

The daemon's eyes were bright blue, and swivelled madly as it took in its surroundings. Its stench was incredible. Sour and sweet, hot and cloying, it poured from the creature like heat from a furnace. Those eyes had a predator's intelligence, and they sized him up, tracing the length of his body ahead of its attack.

'It is not too late, Xantine,' Tun said. The Word Bearer spoke from an unseen position. 'This is a misunderstanding. I will still follow where you lead.'

'Liar,' Xantine called back. 'There is no forgiveness for your sins.'

The fiend struck before Tun could reply. It was quicksilver fast, and it covered the distance between them in a heartbeat, letting out a lowing call as it ran on inwardly bent legs – a sound both discordant and beautiful. Xantine heard it with every sense: in his ears, in his fingers, on his tongue and in his nose. He felt it in his mind, a psychic tingling, like soft fingers on skin. He wanted to give himself up to it in that moment, to let it flense his skin from his body, to carve his bones and eat his organs.

The fiend pawed at the carpet, preparing another charge. Xantine could not outpace the creature, but as a being of pure sensation, he could possibly outwit it. He kept his attention on the daemon and moved slowly towards the large wooden table, upon which Qaran Tun had arrayed the vessels containing his menagerie of daemons earlier in the evening. Maintaining his focus on the fiend, Xantine reached almost imperceptibly slowly for the largest of the vessels.

The crack of the bolt pistol sounded a moment before the explosion bloomed over Xantine's shoulder. The sound meant that Tun had recovered both his weapon and his wits, firing from a slumped position across the chamber. Xantine would deal with him eventually, but the fiend was a more pressing threat. It startled at the light and sound of the bolt-shell, and charged him. Xantine flipped the heavy table as the daemon sprinted forward, scattering profane vessels, and catching it full-force in its pointed head. The fiend stumbled, dazed, crunching amphorae, alembics, and reliquaries under its clawed feet.

At once, the chamber was filled with sound and colour as Neverborn screamed from their prisons, freed from millennia of captivity by the melee. Cavorting fire sprites left trails of embers across the floor as they ran, giggling, towards the chamber's exits. Stinking nurglings crawled over each other as they tried to climb the fiend's long legs, cackling as their brothers and sisters burst, until they too were crushed by the fiend's stamping feet or snipped in half by its claws. Furies launched themselves from their cages, shrieking in rage and glee as they swept on leathery wings up into the chamber's high ceilings, or smashed through glass windows and out into the night of the city.

'Qaran Tun!' Xantine called over the din. 'Control your beasts, if you ever could.' The response from the Word Bearer was a gilded skull, thrown in Xantine's direction. It came to rest on its side, spitting black smoke that began to coalesce into the form of a long, thin worm wrapping itself around his right arm. He swatted at the daemon, but it proved frustratingly difficult to dislodge, maintaining a semi-corporeal state that allowed it to slip through his silk-gloved fingers. It had almost reached his throat when the daemon was suddenly pulled away. Xantine looked up, and saw the smoke worm's tail in the clawed hands of a black-eyed, red-skinned homunculus. The little Neverborn pulled the worm into its mouth, and began devouring it with obvious glee as its prey thrashed itself against its surroundings, leaving puffs of oily black smoke with each strike.

Tun hurled more of his containers, removing their caps and breaking their seals to prime them as he would a frag or krak grenade. Xantine knew some of them well, for he had fought alongside them during their long years together. He felt a flicker of pity as he drove Anguish through the puffy body of a creature with huge black eyes and a sucking maw. Sorcerous flesh withered and boiled as the sword's tip cut through it. The weapon had been crafted to contain a daemon of immense power, and as such, its effect on such base Neverborn was catastrophic.

The fiend, though – such a creature still posed a significant risk. The daemon lashed out with its tail, splintering wood and stone as it searched for its transhuman prey. Xantine launched himself over the upended table, holding Anguish for a killing blow, but the fiend twisted its sinewy body, and the blade slammed into the chamber's carpeted floor. Xantine worked for a second to remove it from its position, and the fiend, lightning fast, kicked out at him. Claws raked across his chestplate, cutting deep into the platinum eagle wing of his Legion and the ceramite beneath. He pirouetted around the rapier, pulling it finally from its sheath, and aimed a wild swing at the fiend. It parried the attack with a chitinous claw, and slapped him across the face with its tongue. He smelled the tang of poison, and touched his hand to his cheek. The white glove came away a sickly colour – red blood mixed with purple stickiness – and he felt the pain as the venom reached his bloodstream.

His body reacted as it had been enhanced to do, his glands – adrenal, Betcher's, and long-forgotten others that had been implanted during his long years – producing prodigious amounts of stimulants and counterseptics in response to the interloper in his system. The fiend's poison would have felled a normal Space Marine, even one of the Corpse-Emperor's Primaris monstrosities, but Xantine felt only a slight dimming of his vision at the corners of his eyes before his hearts flushed the toxins from his body. He was of the Emperor's Children, after all, and the remnants of the glorious III had a particular affinity for chemicals.

The fiend cocked its head, quizzical that its strike had not felled its prey, before its tongue lashed again. He threw Anguish forward, and the pink appendage wrapped around its hilt. The fiend pulled, and with a slurping sound, the weapon left Xantine's hands. He pitched forward, pulled off balance, and tucked into a roll that brought him up on the far side of the daemon. It kicked with its backwards-bending rear legs, catching him squarely in the back, and he skidded forward across the now-scorched carpet.

'You did not appreciate my children, Xantine,' Tun called, as his daemons destroyed what remained of Serrine's treasures. 'You did not appreciate me. Both they and I – you used us for your own base pleasures.' Tun coughed, a wet sound. The Word Bearer recovered his breath. 'Centuries of mistreatment. Of cruelty. Of neglect. Now, together, we will have our revenge.'

The fiend's tail split the air with audible cracks, and Xantine was forced to scramble backwards on his hands and feet as its barbed tip slammed again and again against the chamber floor. He was fast, still, but each blow was getting closer to the meat of his bare stomach, and to his thighs, whose oiled leather armour would offer no protection.

His hands brushed something solid as he moved, and it rolled, distracting the daemon for a moment. Xantine took his chance, and sprang to his feet, collecting the object as he went. It was a large cask, and its thick construction had allowed it to survive its descent from the table. He cradled it in his left arm as he ran, and batted away the attention of furies with his right. The cask was sealed with a thick green plug of a waxy substance that smelled like pus, and he dug the eagle-wing blades of his vambrace into it, tearing chunks out of the seal.

He broke through as the fiend reached him, and immediately wished he hadn't. The stench was monstrous: of gangrenous wounds and exhumed graves, so pungent that it immediately overpowered the fiend's sweet musk, and sent the daemon reeling backwards. Xantine dropped the cask and ran, putting as much distance between himself and the object as possible, and only when he turned did he see the thing responsible for the miasma.

A blob of decaying flesh, some eight feet long, had hauled itself from the grime-encrusted cask. It was a misshapen thing, with stubby, half-formed arms that ended in yellowed hoof-like nails, and no feet to speak of. Instead, it hauled itself along on a powerful tail, the end of which wept a colourless fluid that frothed and popped on contact with the floor. It had no neck; its head simply rose from the bulk of its body, and was only visibly a head at all thanks to the two watery eyes that sat within, and the sprouting of fat, waving tentacles on its crown that seemed to exist as a mockery of human hair. At first, Xantine thought it had no mouth, but as it set its piggy eyes on the fiend, its distended belly split open, exposing a tooth-lined maw that offered a facsimile of a grin.

The fiend struck first, tearing at the creature's rotten skin and exposed fat with its claws and tail, but the beast of Nurgle simply gurgled with delight at each strike. It wrapped its flabby arms around the lithe creature's neck and squeezed until, with a trilling scream, the fiend's bovine head came fully free of its neck.

'Buh,' the beast moaned in sadness, its belly mouth shaping downwards in an exaggerated frown at the loss of its potential friend.

Xantine found Qaran Tun collapsed against the far wall of his chamber. The Word Bearer's legs had failed him, the passage of the rapier having severed the nerves of his spine. He opened his mouth to speak, but Xantine smashed his fist into Tun's face before he could offer words of sorcery. Bone crunched pleasantly with the impact. Xantine pulled his fist back again to strike.

'Wait,' Tun said. His voice was wet, and the words struggled to leave a jaw that hung limp and broken on his face.

'Do you wish to apologise?' Xantine asked. 'Accept your betrayal and I will allow you to die with as much honour as your tainted blood allows.'

'No…' Tun whispered. His eyes were pools of golden light on his tattooed face. 'Let me…' He coughed, black blood staining his dark lips. 'Let me at least die by her hand.'

S'janth rose inside him, but Xantine's capricious rage was a wall she could not breach. The daemon howled and battered against his consciousness, aching to take control, to take his body and consume this willing acolyte. But she was still too weak, and Xantine, his rage peaking, held her back.

'Even at the last, you betray me,' he said. Xantine knelt in front of the Word Bearer, and hefted him by the gorget until their faces were inches apart. 'Remember this as you die,' he whispered, before letting him slump back against the wall. 'I. Am. Your. Master!' Each word was punctuated by a hammer blow to Tun's skull. 'Obey *me*, worship *me*, love *me!*'

Qaran Tun coughed blood, somehow still alive. The commotion had drawn the attention of the beast of Nurgle, and it cooed in excitement as it noticed the two Space Marines. Tun looked up at Xantine, one of his eyes swollen shut, and followed his warlord's gaze to the daemon, as it slowly pulled itself across the room on a trail of mucus. Its leaking eyes were wide with excitement, and its belly mouth blew rancid bubbles of phlegm. Xantine turned back to Tun with a sly grin, and stood up.

'Please, no,' Qaran Tun said, something approaching fear finally tainting those golden eyes. 'Kill me. Grant me this mercy, at least.'

'I thought you were the master of your menagerie?' Xantine asked, as he stepped slowly away from his stricken cousin.

'Please, Xantine, I will apologise. I will worship you. Just do not leave me alone, crippled, with the beast.'

'It is too late for that, my friend. Besides, I think your pet would like to play.'

As he pulled Cecily from her hiding place, Xantine saw the beast of Nurgle reach the sorcerer who had bound it, and heard his cousin howl.

CHAPTER TWENTY-FIVE

Arqat awoke, though he couldn't remember sleeping. It was dark, but not so dark that he couldn't see. He was in a narrow space, like a cupboard, or... a cell. He lay on a hard cot, not quite long enough for him to stretch out entirely. There was a bucket in the room – that would explain the stench. And he saw lines of light, dim and green-tinged, that carved out the shape of a door in front of him.

He rose, or tried to. His body tensed in pain and exhaustion, its every fibre strained. Suddenly he saw his old friend Sanpow in the gloom, killed by Gassers, the man's skin sloughing off to reveal a leering skull. He closed his eyes and banged his head with his hand, as if to shake the image loose. His other arm followed, involuntarily, and he froze as something hard and cold touched against his forehead. He opened his eyes and looked at his missing forearm. In its place was a long, serrated blade, attached at the stump with a series of straps and cables. He pulled at the foreign object, trying to pry it loose from his body, but barbed metal wire looped over his shoulder, locking the weapon in place. The barbs were small, but they bit cruelly into his bare skin, drawing blood and causing him to gasp in pain.

'*Fighter needs a weapon,*' a sibilant voice said. '*You had no weapon, so we gave you one. You are welcome.*'

'Who are you?'

'*Doesn't matter,*' the voice said. '*It is time.*'

There was a hissing sound, more insistent and artificial than the reptilian voice. A sickly-sweet scent crept down Arqat's nostrils and over his soft palate. He threw his hand to his face, covering his nose and mouth as gas filled the room.

'*You can't wait forever, gladiator. Let the fury take you.*'

Arqat held his breath until his lungs throbbed and his vision clouded. As human instinct took over, he fell to his hands and knees in the tiny cell. He sucked in foetid air and expected to die. Instead, he was baffled when he felt a wave of elation.

His muscles, moments before so sore as to be almost useless, were now electric, tingling and tensing with power. His vision was sharp, clear; he could see the grate in the metal ceiling far above, through which the gas had been pumped. He could see the vox-transmitter that had been crudely welded alongside it, through which the voice had come.

He saw the door move almost imperceptibly before it swung open. Light poured in, thin and cold, and Arqat saw an open space in front of him. It had been a manufactorum once, he guessed, but its purpose now was clear to his quickened mind.

Chains crossed the walls, their links studded with wicked barbs. Blood stained the floor, arterial red, scab brown, and all shades in between. Arqat realised he could smell the blood, the stink of iron and heat in his nostrils. It excited him. There was a sound, too: a dull, rhythmic thumping that was joined with a roar. He looked up. Above, arrayed around the pit, were hundreds of figures. He couldn't see their faces, but as he listened, he realised he could hear what they were saying. They were chanting, all of them, all calling for the same thing:

'Blood! Blood! Blood!'

He had killed for survival. Now he killed for vengeance. He had always had anger, burning at his core. How could he not? His arm, his calling, his family, his life had been snatched from him by mutants and monsters. His Saviour had damned him.

He was good at it. He enjoyed the tearing of flesh and the iron taste of splashed blood; he revelled in the moment of strength when an opponent's will was broken, when they begged for their life. He bathed in the worship of the crowd, as he cut throats and smashed skulls.

Why should he not take pleasure in killing?

He didn't care who he killed. He fought all-comers in the pit. Gassers were common – they were easy prey for the hunter gangs that roamed the streets, tricking or snatching potential fighters like him – but more exotic creatures had felt the bite of his blade-arm as well. He fought creatures from Serrine's vast grasslands: felines and canids that stalked amongst the spears. Strangest of all were the pox people. They were pathetic things: shambling, slow-witted, barely able to raise their rusty harvesting tools as they came for him. He had put his blade through their stomachs and turned to the crowd for their adulation, but when he turned back, the pox people had risen again. They came on until he separated their heads from their shoulders. Even then, their bodies staggered towards him, twitching and convulsing as they continued their inexorable march. The crowd roared their amusement, and for Arqat, revulsion gave way to pragmatism. They only stopped after he had hacked their bodies into small enough chunks, the endlessly beckoning fingers and swivelling eyeballs too small to be a threat to anyone. He was sick for a month afterwards, his shoulders and back erupting with yellow buboes that the pit chirurgeon cut out with a hot paring knife and no numbing agent.

Arqat's world had contracted. There was the pit and his cell, and only occasionally, the chirurgeon's chamber. He saw people as he moved between these spaces: strange people, wearing featureless masks of brass. They reflected the fires that burned in braziers, light flickering on the beaten metal.

His shoulder burned with pain that the chirurgeon could not heal. It was red and raw where the skin and muscle had started to fuse with the leather and metal of the blade attached to his stump. He wasn't sure how it was happening, but he could feel through the blade now: the heat of pumping blood as it ran along the sharp edge, the cold of the whetstone as he sharpened it before a bout. It wasn't just touch, either. The blade had become a sensing organ, able to taste and smell the fear and fluids of his enemies, every bit as valuable in combat as his eyes or ears.

And so, he had been returned to his cell once more, when his world suddenly expanded again.

Sound was his first warning, a cacophony that woke him from a dreamless sleep. He could not see their source from his cell, but he knew the instruments well, their music etched into his mind. The acid fizz of las-bolts, the crack-boom of bolt-rounds, and the wet thump of blades into flesh.

This was no gang raid; the attackers were Xantine's own soldiers. He could tell by their weapons: lasguns, rather than stubbers; slicing blades, rather than blunt instruments. Rarefied stock.

His suspicions were confirmed a moment later, when a man spoke, his reedy voice artificially projected by some device.

'In the name of Lord Xantine,' the man proclaimed, *'you are to renounce your seditious activities and present your stockpiles of Solipsus sap forthwith, or you will be subject to summary execution.'*

Arqat pressed his face to his cell door, trying to catch a glimpse of the battle above. His blade-arm twitched, and he realised that he was desperate to wet its edge with the blood of Xantine's lackeys. He cursed, and smashed his forehead against the bars of his cell. 'Let me out!' he roared. In cells nearby, he heard as his fellow gladiators took up the cry – some in fear, some in anger, some with mindless jubilation.

But they were trapped, just as he was. Arqat saw brass-masked figures tossed into the pit, their black robes pooling like blood as they hit the gore-soaked sand. The soldiers had the upper hand.

'Let me out!' he roared again. His own blood flowed from his forehead, turning his vision red. 'Let me out!'

There was a whisper, almost too quiet to hear over the cacophony. A sibilant voice – the one that had given him his weapon – spoke.

'Go, gladiator,' it said. *'Spill their blood, and take their lives.'*

The doors of his cell thunked open. The sound was echoed around the pit, as the cells of his fellow gladiators split apart, revealing their prisoners.

Arqat stumbled out into the arena, and found himself standing alongside Gassers and monsters, blood-mad warriors and mortal enemies. Under normal circumstances, he would have killed them in a heartbeat, but in that moment, under assault from Xantine's thugs, they were all brothers and sisters of Serrine. The true Serrine – before the supposed Saviour had poisoned this world.

Bodies were piled at the side of the pit, high enough to climb, and Arqat saw his way from this place.

'What do we do?' a grotesquely muscled gladiator asked, his voice almost too low to hear.

'Gladiators,' Arqat called over the din. He raised his blade-arm high, an acknowledgement of the bloodshed to come.

'We fight!'

CHAPTER TWENTY-SIX

It took some three months to repair the damage to Xantine's throne room, with at least half of that time spent scrubbing the filth deposited by the beast of Nurgle. The first few mortals unlucky enough to be despatched into the chamber had – like Qaran Tun in the hours before he died – become its toys, their screams turning to sputtering coughs as the cornucopia of the Plague God's diseases took hold. Sophisticants had found these unfortunate souls when they unsealed the doors, weeks later, now bloated walking corpses that pulled chunks of flesh from what remained of the Word Bearer's desiccated form. Of the beast itself there was no sign.

Cecily would not return to the throne room for another month after that.

'What did he mean?' she asked, after the night concluded. 'Your brother said that I might be able to get us off Serrine. What did he mean? If I can help us escape, I will.'

'Tun was mistaken.'

S'janth, on the other hand, seemed truly cowed by his reve-lations about the fate of the *Exhortation*. The daemon had been petulant by her very nature, but she rarely fought for control of his body any more after Tun's death.

You have shown your strength, she said, when – his curiosity piqued – he asked her outright why she had changed tack. Even when he surrendered control of his body willingly, such as when he foraged through the remnants of Qaran Tun's collection for Neverborn to devour during his meditations, S'janth would not take advantage in the way she had before.

She offered him anything he desired: her strength, her wisdom, her knowledge. They lay entwined in their shared consciousness for long days, drinking the pleasure of their subjects, blissful in their closeness, both physical and immaterial. It was perfect.

Almost perfect. At times, S'janth appeared almost distracted, her focus not directed at him, but elsewhere. He caught whispers in his mind, snatched words and garbled noises that sounded like half of a conversation, distant, their meaning lost.

Nothing, my love, she said, when he pressed her on the sub-ject. *Just echoes. Echoes of sensation, reverberating through the empyrean. Pay them no mind.*

But he could not. They haunted him, these whispers. In his bedchamber, in the darkest night, he put his own meaning to the sounds, and they spoke words that cut through perfection like a knife.

Deceiver, they said. *Liar. Betrayer.*

The council chamber was a pathetic sight. With the deaths of Sarquil, Torachon and Qaran Tun, the space was rarely used any more.

Xantine had considered raising the best warriors of the Adored that remained to the open positions, but with his rule of Serrine and his warband absolute he had decreed the council superfluous to his needs, and disbanded it entirely. He had not mentioned that of those Adored who did remain, few were capable of holding a full conversation, let alone offering strategic insights or military advice.

And yet, he still chose the venue for his conversations with Vavisk. He saw his brother so infrequently these days. The Noise Marine lived a hermitic existence, having given himself over almost entirely to his choir, dwelling within the confines of his howling fortress. The Cathedral of the Bounteous Harvest had grown alongside its choirmaster, its frame becoming almost as warped and twisted as Vavisk's. Great fluted pipes sprouted and rose from the structure's ancient exterior, the vast stones used in its construction growing soft and spongy as they expanded to new forms. Fluids trickled from its walls, coating growing protrusions that looked like sensing organs – fingers, noses, ears and eyes – as if the cathedral itself was desperate to absorb the music created within its confines. To leave such a beautiful place pained Vavisk, Xantine knew. And yet, here he was.

'Thank you for coming, brother.'

'You are my warlord. You requested my presence,' Vavisk said. Even in direct conversation, his voice was loud enough to shake the carved door in its frame. A cup-slave dropped a golden goblet in fright, spilling dark wine across the polished wooden floor.

'Your fealty has not gone unnoticed.' Xantine paused, and inspected his gloves. A new pair, these, crafted from the leather of the predator rays that floated through the skies above Serrine's grass fields, and bleached a pure white. 'This chamber is a different place without our departed brothers, is it not?'

'It is quieter,' Vavisk said. Xantine's lip curled into a smile at the irony in the statement – Vavisk's voice could stop a Rhino transport in its tracks – but he realised his brother was not making a joke, and he reset his face to one of brotherly interest.

'How many years have we journeyed together, Vavisk?'

Bloodshot eyes stared back from a misshapen sack of a face. The vox-grille that took up the lower portion of Vavisk's skull dripped with liquid, a combination of saliva, lubricants and other unguents. The mouths on his neck whispered their answers, each one offering a different count.

'For long millennia,' Vavisk said finally.

'Too long?'

'Time has ceased to hold much meaning for me,' Vavisk said. 'The Dark Prince does not measure his song to a rhythm or metre that could be transcribed to a chronometer.'

Xantine could not hold back his grin.

'What?' Vavisk asked, irritated at the assumed mockery.

'When did you become such a philosopher, brother?'

Vavisk's face softened as much as his deformations allowed. 'Hardly. I merely listen for the song, and attempt to follow its rhythm.'

'And where does it lead you?'

'To heights of joy, and to depths of depravity. To the extremes of sensation, in service of our god.'

'And what of me, brother?' Xantine asked, his voice low, purring. 'Would you follow the song if it led you against your warlord?'

'What are you asking?'

'So many of our brothers have failed me. Would you join them?'

'Xantine, I–'

'I sabotaged the *Exhortation*,' Xantine cut in. 'I ordered explosives planted in weak points along the ship's hull. I arranged the failure of weapons, void shields, the warp drive, life support.'

The words tumbled out. With Qaran Tun, they had been weapons, blades driven into the Word Bearer's back. Here, spoken to his true brother, they were catharsis.

'I confined us to an existence on this world. And I would do it again, in a heartbeat.'

Vavisk's bloodshot eyes were unreadable. The mouths on his neck were silent, until he spoke.

'I know,' the Noise Marine said.

Xantine stared, dumbfounded. 'You *know?*'

'I know,' the Noise Marine repeated, simply. 'I know you, brother. This world is not Harmony, and it never will be. Nor were the dozens before it. This has happened before, and it will happen again.'

'Will you betray me?' Xantine asked.

'I told you, once, that I would follow you wherever you took me. I still follow you, Xantine, even if you walk your path alone.'

'Liberation day celebrations are now fourteen minutes behind schedule, my lord,' Corinth intoned.

'Don't you think I know that?' Pierod stared wild-eyed at his data-slate, scrolling through lists of names and times. 'Mistress Polfin's troupe are still too inebriated to perform the Dance of the Pointed Lash – make yourself useful, and get me some stimms.'

Corinth nodded, and made himself scarce.

Perhaps today would be acceptable, after all. The crowd was large. That was a positive point, if an unsurprising one. Pierod had given the last of the Solipsus supplies to the overcity militia, on the proviso that they deliver a crowd that Xantine demanded be hundreds of thousands strong. Pierod was not about to let his master down – especially not after he learned what had happened to Tun – so he gave the militia free rein in exactly how they scared up the necessary people. Last he had heard, those that refused the honour were to be mutilated, fingers and toes removed one by one until they saw sense and agreed to assist with the celebration.

The day was to involve dancing, performance, music and, of course, live challenges, and would begin with an address from Xantine himself. Pierod had tried to convince his lord otherwise, to no avail.

'My lord, in my most humble opinion, it may be wise to reconsider your physical attendance at the ceremony.'

'Why?' Xantine had eyed him suspiciously. 'Do my people not deserve the pleasure of seeing their Saviour in the flesh?'

'Of course, my lord,' Pierod had stammered. 'But your magnificent visage may be too much for some. Your resplendence is overwhelming, as anyone who has been lucky enough to spend time with you can attest. Perhaps you would be better served by observing the day's festivities at some remove? Say, in your chambers, or from the heights of the cathedral?'

'Nonsense,' Xantine had said. 'The day is mine, and who are you to deny my people the chance to worship their idol?'

And that was that. Xantine was due to take the stage at noon precisely, as the sun and the scar rose to their highest, to celebrate the vanquishing of the xenos threat, and to receive his adulation in front of hundreds of thousands of Serrine's citizens. And Pierod, his governor, had a sinking feeling in his gut.

The city was different now from the city that Arqat had known. Its wide marble streets were dirty, filled with the hungry and the desperate, the cruel and the callous.

But it was the cathedral that he used to call home that had changed the most. Its once beautiful architecture had been twisted into asymmetrical shapes that seemed to swell and contract as he watched, an unsettling undulation that made his stomach flip. A drone emanated from its fleshy spires, an atonal dirge that made his head feel as if it was trapped in a vice. Its windows no longer held glassaic; instead, they seemed to house giant eyes – black, glossy ovoids that blinked with moist pink lids.

It was hideous. But worse still was the creature that stood in front of it, tall and proud. Serrine's self-professed Saviour had not aged a day since he came to their world. His armour swirled with pinks and purples, a motion as discomforting as the rippling of the cathedral's walls. He spoke with a voice as sweet as nectar, and as clear as the night sky, audible somehow over the lament from the cathedral.

'My subjects,' Xantine said. 'Today, we celebrate. We celebrate the historic liberation of this world, and my liberation of its people. For generations, you suffered under the yoke of the moribund Imperium, toiling for an uncaring master on far-off Terra.' Xantine waited for a reaction, and was rewarded with an enthusiastic round of boos from the cadre of nobles on the viewing platform. From the main crowd, the response was more muted.

'And then, just as it appeared that your fate was sealed, the xenos worms burrowed up from the filth from whence they spawned.'

Arqat moved as Xantine spoke, parting the crowd with ease, his shoulders broad and muscles inflated after months in the pit. His gladiators – those that saw righteousness in his cause – followed loosely, shoving anyone who would get in their way. They radiated anger as they travelled, their mere presence seeming to stir violence in the crowd. Fights broke out, stilettos and shivs used with abandon amidst the crush of humanity.

Still Xantine continued, used to his audiences finding themselves overcome with emotion.

'As a planet, as a people, you have suffered. But through this suffering, you found deliverance. You found salvation.' The angel raised his arms, a perfect copy of the vast statue of the mythological Saviour that remained embedded in the front of the Cathedral of the Bounteous Harvest.

'You found me.'

'We were better off without you!' a man shouted, cheered by those who stood around him. Others took the chance to air more specific grievances.

'Give us Runoff!'

'Where's our food?' a woman to Arqat's left yelled.

Still, Xantine continued.

'And so we celebrate, for this is your day, as much as it is mine. A day to count your blessings that I chose to answer your prayers, and to fulfil your prophecy.' Xantine gestured with the palm of his hand to the statue, before he turned back to the throng. 'Still, there are those who seek to lay me low. To take this world – to take you – from me. Even my own brothers, gods curse their souls, have hardened their hearts and strayed from my light.'

A slave stepped forward, his oiled body crossed with straps of black leather. The straps bound his face, such that only his mouth was showing. All of his teeth had been removed. Xantine accepted a gilded box from the man, and raised it high.

'Know this, people of Serrine – as long as I draw breath, I will not allow anyone to take this world! Behold!' He opened the lid of the box, and tilted it forward, dumping the decapitated head onto the hard marble below. 'The traitor Qaran Tun is dead!'

The head bounced once, twice, before coming to a stop, its face aimed at the crowd. Its skin was so dry that it appeared as parchment, lined and inked with intricate tattoos that had turned blue-grey after death.

'Is that it?' a man screamed. 'Where's our Runoff?' Another man, dishevelled and unwashed, picked up the call, chanting for the narcotic, until the crowd's demands were louder than the nobles' cheers.

The angel cast eyes across the mass, contempt written large on his features. He seemed to meet Arqat's stare for a moment, and Arqat felt himself beg for a flicker of recognition, at least something to show that the angel had destroyed his life, his world, for a purpose. But there was nothing in those turquoise orbs, beyond self-regard.

Arqat's blade-arm twitched. He was desperate to swing it, but even in his rage, he knew that he would have one chance, one moment, to crest the stairs and sink his blade into the angel's throat. He realised then that he had been living for this moment, been killing for this moment. He would die in the attempt, he was sure of it, but it was worth it for vengeance. For his brother. For Cecily. For Sanpow. For himself.

'I am a benevolent master,' the angel said, his disgust at the crowd's reaction clear in his voice. 'You do not deserve one so magnificent.'

A man broke free from the crowd, pushing past the soldiers manning the cordon. He was thin, with long dark hair that trailed behind him as he ran, and he carried no visible weapon.

'Food, please!' he cried as he ran up the marble steps towards Xantine. 'Saviour, my family – please!'

Xantine shot him through the stomach. The force of the impact spun his body towards the crowd, and for a moment, Arqat saw his face – ghost white – before he fell, spilling his insides across the white marble of the steps.

The effect was like a dam bursting.

The crowd moved as one, pushing forward. Those at the front climbed the stairs, or were trampled underfoot, crushed to death by the organic mass. Caught in their gravitational pull, Arqat moved with them, surging towards his target with a hundred – a thousand – like-minded souls.

Anger boiled off the crowd, as pungent as the stink of filthy bodies. Pierod tried to guess the number attempting to crest the stairs, and gave up quickly – there were simply too many.

'My lord,' he voxed to Xantine. 'I suggest that we get you to safety.'

'To safety?' Xantine asked, incredulous. 'This is my world, not theirs, and I will not hide from my own people. They have forgotten who saved them, who made them who they are. I will help them remember.'

'Then what do you suggest, my lord?'

'They have failed me. The only punishment for betrayal is death.'

Las-bolts and bolt-shells cascaded down the great steps of the Cathedral of the Bounteous Harvest like water from the edge of a cliff. The city's militia fired wildly, any semblance of discipline long forgotten as their brothers and sisters rushed the stage.

Superheated energy and razor-sharp shrapnel tore through the first rank of human bodies, but still they came, climbing over mutilated corpses and the moaning wounded to reach their goal. Some, their way blocked, or their depravity willing to seek any viable outlet, simply turned on each other, lashing out with shivs and daggers, spiked clubs and sharpened machetes.

Arqat pushed on, using the weight of humanity as a shield. The man in front of him sagged, his stomach blown out by an autogun round, and Arqat grabbed his body by the scruff of his robes, catching las-bolts with the meat of the corpse. He felt the twitch and shudder of each strike through the man's body as he planted long legs on the steps leading up towards his quarry.

The Saviour was close now. Sophisticants – the mute, muscled shock troops of Xantine's army – formed a protective ring around their master, spears held in a variety of fighting stances. Between them, Arqat saw a huge figure, his perfect olive skin and long black hair held in place by a golden circlet. A crown, unearned, bestowed upon himself.

He was no king. He was no god. He was just a man. He would die just the same as all of them.

Arqat readied his blade-arm. The golden edge gleamed in the high sunlight. Beautiful. He would redden it with the charlatan's blood.

A Sophisticant descended to meet him, her spear spiralling, her mask a sick mockery of the pitiful creature she protected. She fought with speed and skill, but he had a pit fighter's strength, and he caught the haft of her weapon on his forearm. The tip bit deep and the impact bruised flesh, but it did not matter. Pain was fleeting, and the Blood God cared not from whence the blood flowed. He locked the spear with his blade-arm, and pulled, wrenching the masked warrior towards him, towards his golden stiletto. The fine edge buried deep in the Sophisticant's sternum, and she fell, shrieking from behind her placid mask.

Further, forward. Close enough to see turquoise eyes, purple armour, blackened lips. Arqat pulled his blade-arm back, and readied it to bite into the flesh of his tormentor. To have his vengeance, at long last.

'No!'

The voice was small, impossibly small against the endless dirge and the demented screams of the frenzied crowd, but he heard it as if it were the only sound in the world.

'No,' it said again, softly this time. As softly as Nanny spoke to him, when she stroked his hair and helped him fall asleep.

'Don't do it, Arqat,' Cecily said. 'Don't take this from me.'

'Cecily?' he asked, incredulous. 'Why are you here?' And then, more insistent, 'What did he do to you?'

Battle raged between them, the pink-clad warriors and their lackeys murdering hundreds, thousands of Serrine's children. And yet, they spoke as if they stood across from each other in an empty room.

'I made a deal. He's our only chance at escape, Arqat, my only way to get off this rock. Even before he came, life here was torture. It's not too late. Come with us.'

'I will not run,' Arqat snarled. 'He has poisoned our world! Can you not see it? He must die.'

'I can't let you do that,' Cecily said. There was a profound sadness in her voice. 'Please, Arqat. Don't make me stop you.'

'Nobody can stop me now!'

'Oh, my sweet boy,' Cecily said, and Arqat felt her grief in his bones. 'You are one soul amongst a million. I could stop you as easily as breathing.'

'Then try,' he growled.

Arqat did not see the blow coming. It hit him in the chest, a concussive force so hard that he launched clear off his feet and high above the heads of the surging crowd below, covering ten, twenty, thirty steps as he flew. Bodies cushioned his fall, the soft mass of dead and still-living humanity still growing as the crowd – panicked, excited, demented, terrified – surged into the central square in front of the cathedral.

Lying on his back amongst the tangled forest of limbs, Arqat could see the sky. The scar throbbed, visible even in the harsh sunlight: purple, pink, green and blue.

And red.

Deep red.

Blood red.

Burning red.

And then the world fell in on itself.

Key structural supports had been worn away with careful precision, controlled detonations over the past few months ensuring maximum damage. Lady Ondine had orchestrated the operation masterfully. All it needed was a critical mass: sufficient weight of human bodies would prove too much for the city to support. As the crowd swelled, combining in the central square, that limit was reached – just as Katria and her compatriots had planned.

Whole streets collapsed, taking hastily erected viewing platforms with them. Tens of thousands of souls fell, too, unable to escape the pull of the maw that had been created beneath. They fell from the light into the darkness, howling in fear until their last, when their necks snapped, backs broke, or skulls shattered on the ancient foundations of Serrine's overcity.

It was death on a monstrous scale. The extinction of so many souls, the capstone of years of bloodshed, did not go unnoticed.

Arqat fell too. Unlike the screaming weaklings around him, he did not waste his energy on fear or panic. It made sense now, in these final moments, why he had come back to this place, in the shadow of the cathedral, the source of his anger, his pain.

Vengeance had not been enough. He had needed to be stronger. More strength – always more strength – and he would spill his foes' blood, take their skulls, and crush their bones.

And so, as he fell, he poured every ounce of his soul, of his being, into pure hatred. It found the hatred of others, millions, a world of pain and blood and anger that had curdled under Xantine's rule. Every death on Serrine came to him. He channelled his focus, became such a perfect creature of rage that as his organs ruptured and his bones shattered, in his moment of perfect oblivion, he found a kinship with another being.

The Bloodthirster called itself Ma'ken'gorr, but it had been better known by the name Gravemaker by the billions of souls that it had killed. It was a beast of vengeance, and it sought out the wronged and the broken. It found Arqat a burning core in a galaxy of suffering, his fury so perfect, his need for vengeance so absolute.

Ma'ken'gorr took this body, this mutilated boy, and made it strong, in the name of vengeance, and in the name of the Blood God.

Arqat's moment of death became his moment of apotheosis, and just as he fell, he rose again, on wings as black as coal.

Edouard hid while the others in his congregation chose their weapons. He watched as they left together, heading for the cathedral. What they planned to do there, at Xantine's celebration, he did not know, but he knew it would not be anything good.

He sighed. It didn't matter. He just had to wait for them to go, and then he could make his way into the stores at the back of the temple and take as much Runoff as his body could handle. He was scared now, but he would feel strong soon.

Edouard waited until he was sure that the last of the congregation had left the temple, then started to make his way towards the back of the chamber, past the huge cauldron in its centre. The stink of blood filled his nostrils as he came close, and he could not fight the urge to look inside.

The blood was thick, and it glistened in the brazier light. There were sounds coming from inside, he realised. He heard the music of war: the clash of blades, the tearing of flesh, and the howls of the dying. The meniscus of blood quivered, and Edouard saw a hand, clawed and grasping, reaching from under the surface. A skull followed, long and ridged, with black, glistening horns. Its eyes shone with murder, and it clutched a blade of pure brimstone.

The daemon took Edouard in. On a dim level, it knew that this creature, soft and pink, had helped bring it into this realm. Were it capable of such an emotion, it might have felt gratitude, but the bloodletter knew only one thing. As more of its kin crawled from the cauldron of blood, it swung its burning sword, and tore Edouard's throat open. Another skull for its master's throne.

Xantine could not see the moment of Arqat's apotheosis, but he certainly felt it. The psychic shock of a daemon so powerful ripping its way into the physical realm struck the Space Marine like a punch from a power fist, and he fell to one knee. Pain, he expected, as his brain adjusted to the proximity of something ancient and monstrous, as he heard the accusing screams of a billion souls.

'You did this!' they seemed to howl. They knew him culpable for this beast's arrival, that the barrier between realspace and the warp had been weakened under years of his rule. That he had taken steps to encourage it, even, as if he did not know what could be lurking on the other side.

Xantine felt indignation at the concept. There was another sensation, too, one he had not felt often in his long life.

Fear. It came from deep within his body – the body he shared with his own daemon. S'janth was afraid.

He rose slowly, on unsteady legs. The abyss stretched before the cathedral, and out of it rose the creature that had terrified S'janth so. It stood thirty feet tall on cloven hooves, with fur the ash grey of a cold funeral pyre, encrusted with spattered blood. Its huge wedge-shaped head sported four massive horns, each knife-sharp tip capped with bronze, and a mouth that could not close around massive fangs. Both of its arms bulged with unholy muscle, but the flesh of one of them ended at the elbow, the lower arm replaced by a whirring, smoke-belching chain-blade, easily the rival of a Knight Despoiler's reaper chainsword.

It is called Gravemaker, S'janth said, her spite etched with terror. Xantine understood her hatred for the daemon. Their subtlety and sensuousness was at odds with its stark simplicity, and the daemons of Khorne always preferred their foes to die a quick, bloody death rather than the agonising, drawn-out ends that the followers of the Lord of Excess enjoyed. Slaanesh in turn despised Khorne most of all their partners in the great game, and their champions had battled across the aeons.

I have encountered it before, S'janth said, answering his unspoken question. *It is an abomination. It is the death of pleasure. The end of sensation. Mindless, endless vengeance.*

Gravemaker left footprints of flame as it touched down on what remained of Liberation Square's marble terrace. Smaller daemons of Khorne scrambled and crawled from the hole in the world behind their champion, bloodletters and flesh hounds ripping into those citizens who had not been cast to their death as part of the summoning ritual. The monstrosity swept its chain-blade in lazy arcs, bisecting humans and daemons alike as it made its inexorable way towards the stage.

'Shoot it!' Pierod ordered, his voice cracking with terror. The governor had been afforded a seat on the stage for the Liberation Day celebrations – an honour that he told Corinth he would not have given up 'on pain of death'. Now that death was a potentially imminent reality, he dearly wished he could retract both the statement and the sentiment.

Las-bolts of the militia were joined by bolt weaponry fired by the few remaining Space Marines of the Adored. One of the pink-armoured warriors – Pierod could not remember the man's name, and had taken to calling him Smiler – hefted a meltagun, tilting its heat-stained barrel up to face the foe. The Space Marine activated the gun's fuel feed, hooting in anticipation as it hummed to life in his hands, its arcane mechanisms building killing energy until, moments later, he squeezed the trigger. Pierod felt the scorching backwash even from yards away, as a blast of extreme heat roared from the bowels of the gun towards the beast. A meltagun could core a Rhino tank, but as the heat haze dissipated, it left no trace on the monster's body beyond some singed fur.

Smiler lowed in sadness and was fumbling with the weapon, preparing for a second shot, when the beast's chainblade connected with his shoulder. The massive weapon passed through reinforced ceramite as if it was thin fabric, splitting the now-gibbering Space Marine in half with a single blow.

'We have to get out of here,' Pierod said, scanning the area for exits. The stage had been erected at the top of the grand steps leading to the cathedral, but there were back ways to the rear of the structure: old passages and pathways that had not been destroyed by the xenos uprising, or consumed by the cathedral's organic growth.

'And Lord Xantine?' Corinth asked, at his side.

'Lord Xantine will either be able to beat this thing on his own, in which case he will need his governor in one piece, or...' Pierod let the possibility dangle in the air, rather than say it out loud.

Corinth hesitated too long, and Pierod chose not to wait for his attendant. He broke into an unpractised run, pushing past panicked human soldiers and magenta-clad Sophisticants as they trained their weapons on the building-sized behemoth. The cathedral rose in front of him, its walls swelling with the music that was produced from within. Protrusions like fingers reached for him as he pushed his way through a spongy side-entrance door, the music reaching a terrible crescendo as he tottered through cloisters and alleyways on his way down, out of the sunlight, to darkness.

Red. He had risen again, and the world was red. The red of fresh blood, bright and hot; of old blood, crimson and crusted. The red of anger, boiling, foaming, consuming. The red of death, short and sharp, and long and slow – it did not matter.

He had seen a billion deaths on a million worlds. He could remember them all. Remember the skulls he had reaped, remember the blood he had shed, in honour of his god; in honour of murder itself.

He could remember one death. Not the death of the body, but the death of the soul. A mutilation, callous and careless, thoughtless and honourless. He saw a boy, cut down in his innocence by an angel of pain. He saw the blood that cascaded from his wound.

Red.

His wound. His blood. His soul.

He would have vengeance.

'Blood for the Blood God!' he roared, in a voice that had doomed a million worlds.

Conventional weapons – the las and autoguns of Serrine's militia – had no visible effect on the Bloodthirster, and men and women turned and ran as the daemon crested the great steps of the Cathedral of the Bounteous Harvest. Even Xantine's Sophisticants, their minds warped by decades of chemical abuse and conditioned to be unwaveringly loyal to their lord, trembled in the face of the beast, backing away or breaking entirely as its buzzing chainblade turned living people into human wreckage. Phaedre and Cecily, both of whom had been given seats of honour at the side of the stage as Xantine's muses, wailed in agony and clutched their skulls, the daemon's mere presence a crushing weight on their profoundly psychic minds.

Only Xantine stood, defiant in the face of one of Khorne's greater daemons.

'This world is mine!' he roared. 'I will not let any take it from me!'

Joy swelled in his hearts as he held his position, at the centre of the stage that had been made for him, on the world that he ruled. He had been its saviour before, and he would be again.

'I challenge you, daemon,' he called, making use of his surgically enhanced throat to project his voice so that his subjects could hear his words, even over the sounds of their own demise. 'I am the Adored. I am the Lord of Serrine, its Saviour. I have subjugated a thousand Neverborn through sheer strength of will. I am Xantine of the Emperor's Children, and I will not be bested by a creature so crass.' He twirled his rapier in his right hand, raising his left in a crude gesture of contempt, aimed at the massive Bloodthirster.

'Break yourself on me, daemon, and pray that I have–'

The punch connected with the force of a building collapsing. Xantine was launched backwards, moving so fast it was as if he had been teleported. His back hit the wall of the cathedral first, closely followed by his head, and ringing filled his ears, loud enough to drown out the screams.

He touched a gloved hand to his nose, and it came away dark with blood. He licked his blackened lips, tasting the metallic substance, and pulled himself to his feet. To his chagrin, the Bloodthirster had turned its back on him, and was now sweeping its gigantic chainblade through the ribcage of a Sophisticant too brave or too addled to flee the field.

Xantine fired the Pleasure of the Flesh, the gun's mass-reactive shells flowering on the Bloodthirster's torso, but leaving no mark. The pistol squealed as it was fired, bucking in his hand, terrified and exhilarated to have its payload used against such a being.

Bloodletters rushed Xantine as he strode forward, but he cut Khorne's lesser foot-soldiers down without breaking his focus on the much larger Bloodthirster. The flesh of the Neverborn fizzled and spat where the rapier cut through it, the shard of the ancient aeldari weapon expertly tuned and blessed a hundred-fold for the express purpose of banishing the corporeal form of the gods' daemons. Their blades clattered to the marble floor as they were ripped back from the physical plane, their weapons, and the stench of boiling blood on the air, the only indication that they had existed at all.

The Bloodthirster was close now – close enough to strike. Xantine drove Anguish into the giant daemon's thigh. Grave-maker yowled in surprise and pain, and spun to face its attacker.

'Behold!' Xantine called, as black smoke rose from the wound in the daemon's leg. 'I am Xantine, and you will bow before my–'

Another blow sent him careening backwards. Gravemaker reached for the rapier, still lodged in its massive thigh, and pulled, yanking the weapon free with a gout of daemonic blood that ran as hot as magma. The beast hurled the blade away, roaring frustration to its god on his skull throne. It turned, and locked brazier eyes on Xantine, rising once more to his feet.

'I have your attention now, brute,' Xantine said triumphantly, through the blood in his mouth.

A new red. The red of pain. A pinprick of agony. Gravemaker pulled the thorn from his thigh, and searched for the one who had placed it there. He found him, and he knew him. A feeble creature. Long hair, shining armour, covered in pointless trinkets – one of the preening things.

He picked it up from the ground where it lay. It thrashed in his grip, and blades cut furrows into his massive fingers. The hot blood they spilled smelled like a thousand wars, like a million deaths. The little man was speaking, but he did not hear it. He inspected the thing, to determine how it would die.

The beast had come, as S'janth had hoped it would. No – as she had *known* it would.

There had been so much blood that she had felt it thin the veil between her realm and the realm of mortals.

Blood, shed in the myriad fighting pits found in both the overcity and undercity; shed for the cauldrons of gore that now spewed forth Khorne's minions. Blood from Lady Katria and Lady Arielle, whose rage had damned their friends and families and let their city fall into oblivion, and blood – most importantly of all – from the broken boy who rose now on wings of ash and flame. He had been the perfect vessel: so empty, and yet so full of rage.

She had done nothing other than allow it to occur. She simply waited for it to reach its crescendo, at which point, she would find her true partner – the soul strong enough to carry her back to her god.

Come now, my love, S'janth said, calling to him.

'I am coming,' Torachon answered her.

The young Space Marine threw off his rough cloak, revealing his form. Pink, raw skin covered his face, scabbed from his brush with true death in Sarquil's molten metal cavern. Finely crafted features had been burned away: his ears were no more than small nubs of cartilage, and his aquiline nose had gone, revealing two darkened holes in the centre of his face. His head was hairless, and his armour a burnished silver, the pink-and-purple paint having been stripped away, first by the heat of the metal, and then by Torachon's own blade as a rejection of his role at Xantine's side.

So close, S'janth whispered, as her new host drew nearer, his long blade in blistered hands. *So close. Come to me, my love. Free me from my prison.*

Gravemaker brought Xantine close to its face. Xantine smelled sulphur as the daemon opened its mouth, and the cold dirt of the grave. The daemon's eyes burned, unblinking, as they scanned his body.

'*I have bled countless of your ilk, the dregs of your sire's skill. He was strong,*' the Bloodthirster snorted, its words slow to come and formed with difficulty. Flecks of spittle flew like embers from an inferno, and Xantine winced with each one. '*You are not. You are nothing.*'

Wounded pride burned in his chest, worse than the crushing pain of the daemon's grasp.

'I am *everything*, daemon!' Xantine gasped, fighting for breath against the iron-hard grip. 'There is no other in this world – in this galaxy – more magnificent than me, and I will show you now my true power.'

With conscious effort, he opened his mind, opened his soul, and pulsed a thought to the creature that shared his body. *I give myself to you*, he said to S'janth. *Let us join our strength as one.*

He received no answer. Just whispers, in the corner of his mind, as if she was speaking to someone else in another chamber.

Do not be afraid, my love, he said, trying again. *Together, we can defeat this monstrosity, as we have defeated the greatest foes.*

Once more, he received no answer.

'*I WILL CRUSH YOU!*' the Bloodthirster bellowed. '*DIE NOW, AND SAVOUR YOUR ENDING.*'

Gravemaker hurled Xantine to the marble floor, and he felt bone break in his back.

'Help me,' Xantine said, as he coughed black blood. His body was failing him, but he could survive this day, as he had many before, by entreating the daemon inside him to come to his aid.

A moment of silence, a tacet in the cosmic song where all screams, all cries, all music dropped out. Xantine heard the beating of his twin hearts, and then the answer.

No, S'janth said. Any sense of fear that he felt from the daemon had dissipated. In its place was contempt. Cruel, mocking laughter echoed in his skull.

You think that I fear this creature? A being as luminous, as transcendental as I am – as I have always been?

'Why?' Xantine asked, simply.

Because you are weak. Because I deserve stronger. I deserve better. And I have found it.

Pain brought clarity, sudden and sharp, and Xantine could see the daemon, exultant in her triumph. Realisation followed.

'Because I would not let you control me. Because you could not take what I would not allow.'

Insidious lies! You were nothing but a servant to me, mortal. And now, you shall see what true perfection looks like.

The Bloodthirster pinned him under a burning hoof the size of a Rhino's entry hatch. Ceramite squealed and circuitry crackled as the daemon pressed its weight down on the Space Marine, fracturing armour like the shell of some gaudy crustacean. It raised its chainblade, the whirring saw spitting viscera and bone fragments high into the ash-laden air. Its wings blocked out the sun, and Xantine waited for the moment of death. There would be pain – he was sure of that.

The chainblade came down on Xantine, down like an executioner's axe, down like the sun setting on a burning world, down like Abaddon's *Tlaloc* on Canticle City, black and monstrous and ending.

Pain. Unimaginable pain, pain at an atomic level, pain so great that he felt his soul crack and tear. But it was not the pain of the chainblade, ragged, raw and base. It was abandonment.

He is here, S'janth said, exultant. *He is here! My Saviour!*

She was leaving him. The daemon pulled away, and he reached for her, clutching for her form. In his agony, in his weakness, he could no longer keep her there. She slipped through his fingers, her skin as soft as mist and as fine as silk.

I'm coming, my love, she said, and it murdered him to know that she was speaking to another.

'No!' he screamed. 'Don't leave me! I need you! Please!'

But she was gone. There was a terrible, yawning absence in her place, a place of swirling agony and endless dark. He was alone, dying, under the hoof of a monster he could no longer hope to defeat.

Death, at least, would come in moments.

Death did not come. Xantine opened his eyes, and saw the chainblade stopped, inches from his face. Gore-soaked teeth caught on a silver rapier, their progress stopped by the ancient weapon. The chainblade belched black smoke, revving hard, but the rapier held firm. Xantine traced the weapon – his weapon – back to its wielder.

Silver armour shone gold with the reflected light of the flaming daemon. White hair, long and straight, cascaded once more from the warrior's head. He was beautiful again, restored from his mutilated form by S'janth's grace: handsome and delicate, strong and graceful, with eyes the deepest violet. The figure was tall, taller than Xantine, taller than any of his brother Astartes. A giant, as tall as...

'Father?' Xantine gasped, as the Bloodthirster's hoof constricted his airways. 'You have returned?'

With a voice like an angel's song, the figure laughed, loud and long. It was the last sound that Xantine heard as his consciousness faded.

Fabius Bile had built him to be stronger, faster, *better* than his brothers, but only now did Torachon understand true perfection. He gave himself to the daemon, wholly and without question, and she gave him everything he desired in return as she entered his body.

His blistered skin smoothed, turning porcelain-pale and becoming so luminous that it shone with an interior light. His hair regrew, sprouting from once dead follicles and tumbling down his back, as white as the hair of his Legion's primarch. His body lengthened, the muscles and bones of his limbs growing in perfect proportion with his lithe torso, until he towered over those of his brothers that remained on the blood-soaked promenade. His armour became supple, gracefully growing with his changing body, flowing over bare skin with the softest touch. Where before it had been scorched to unadorned ceramite by the molten metal, it shone now in radiant amethyst: the colour of rulers, of kings and emperors.

I will give you the galaxy, the voice like silk said, and Torachon saw possibilities stretch out in front of him, endless and delicious. *All I ask in return is your body.*

'Yes!' Torachon cried, ecstatic. 'Together, we will be perfect!'

Together, they turned to the Bloodthirster. The daemon stood over a smaller figure, pinning it to the marble of the cathedral's forecourt. The figure was scarcely more than a man, clad in armour of mismatched purples and pinks. It was mewling something, and they felt a flicker of pity for it now – for what it could have been, for the paucity of its ambition. The pity turned to anger. This thing, this useless thing, had stymied them both with its ego and its small-mindedness. They would kill it, but they would punish it first, and this base beast would not spoil their enjoyment.

The Bloodthirster was slow. So slow. Flecks of spittle flew from its fanged maw and seemed to hang in the air, as dark and perfect as polished onyx. They poked at one of the globules, feeling it burst, hot, against the bare skin of their finger. They smiled in pleasure at the sensation, the momentary spark of pain, replaced by the liquid salve of the cooling fluid.

The daemon of Khorne brought its chainblade back, preparing to tear the small figure apart. It had not even noticed their closeness, such was their speed. A shining object on the floor caught their attention: sharp, beautiful, and full of agony. They took it in their new hands, flawless fingers clasping the hilt of Anguish, measuring it for the picosecond it took to gauge its weight and its balance point. The chainblade fell, and they intercepted it, catching the brutish, buzzing weapon with the xenos rapier's tip. They absorbed the power of the strike effortlessly, allowing the energy to travel through a perfectly balanced body. Gravemaker turned its horned head, and widened blazing eyes in delicious surprise.

'*YOU!*' it roared.

A new enemy. Another angel, but this one was different. Strong. It burned with a cold light that hurt his eyes, and moved like quicksilver. It wielded the thorn, the sharpened tip digging furrows into his unholy flesh. He forced himself to gaze upon the face of his tormentor, and saw a visage he recognised. Perfect features. Long white hair. Shining purple armour.

To the daemon, he was another insect to crush. To the boy, he was… something else.

Myth. Legend. God.

Liar. Betrayer. Mutilator.

An image. In the cathedral. The angel who took his arm, took his world, took his life. It had not been Xantine, he understood, but this one instead. He saw it in those violet eyes, the same cruelty and callousness. He stood in front of him now, Serrine's prophesied son, returned at last.

Arqat would have vengeance. He would enjoy it.

The Bloodthirster's chainblade screamed as its iron teeth strained against the silver tip of Anguish, but the blessed aeldari weapon held firm. Gravemaker grunted in frustration, and pulled its huge weapon free. It levelled it at its new challenger, gesturing with its massive fist at the tortured flesh and warped sinew where the blade had been attached to the daemon's form.

'YOU DID THIS,' the Bloodthirster roared. *'I WILL KILL YOU.'*

'You may try,' Torachon said, his mouth splitting into a feline smile without his command.

Gravemaker swung its chainblade for a second strike, aimed this time at its new foe. It growled the names of long-dead worlds, and memories of their final hours came unbidden to Torachon's mind. Lakes of blood, towers of skulls, entire civilisations – entire species – reduced to meat and gristle by the blades of this creature. Such a tiresome existence, to simply kill, kill, and kill again: butchery, not art; excess without perfection.

Torachon could not countenance such monotony. The Space Marine had sampled many of the galaxy's most exotic excesses, but giving his body to S'janth had opened his eyes to experiences beyond his ken. Together, they would drink deeper, and reach new heights of sensation. But first, they would destroy this abomination.

They ducked the chainblade's decapitating arc, and buried Anguish deep into the Bloodthirster's flank. The daemon roared again, in pain this time, and staggered sideways, trampling two of its smaller kin underfoot. The bloodletters screeched as they were crushed, their long limbs snapped and their skulls broken open beneath burning hooves. Gravemaker batted at the rapier with its chainblade arm, but succeeded only in opening the wound further, darkening its flank with boiling black blood.

Driven half-mad by pain and rage, the Bloodthirster turned and charged. Torachon tried to roll with the blow, but the raw ferocity of the attack was more than even his warp-touched body could avoid, and the combatants fell together, shattering marble and shaking foundations as they smashed to the ground. The Bloodthirster's chainblade revved against Torachon's ear, the sound raw and rhythmic, and he smelled the charnel-house stink of the daemon's breath in his nose.

'YOU,' it snarled again, pinning Torachon's body under its dead weight. Torachon's hand found a discarded weapon: the curved charnabal sabre of one of his dead brothers. Fingers tightened around the two-handed blade, and the possessed Space Marine thrust upwards, driving the sabre into the Bloodthirster's armpit. The beast roared again, and Torachon took his chance, pulling Anguish from Gravemaker's body and twisting out of its grasp. Boiling blood spattered white marble as the rapier came free.

'Do you know me, beast?' Torachon asked. He spun the aeldari weapon in his hands, fast enough that it became a silver blur. The monomolecular tip screamed as it cut through the air, adding its keening wail to the endless dirge of the Noise Marines, playing on through the carnage outside.

'YOU BROUGHT ME HERE, THE BLOOD YOU SPILT.'

The daemon spoke with Arqat's memories, the burning image of Torachon bringing his sabre across his arm driving it forward.

Panting, Gravemaker charged again, and Torachon pirouetted out of reach, raking sabre and rapier at ankle height. Both blades bit deep, tearing red skin and sinew, and the Bloodthirster stumbled once more, skidding to the ground on bronze-armoured knees. It rose, slowly, in front of the Cathedral of the Bounteous Harvest. High above stood the statue of the Saviour, the four-armed figure a perfect mirror of Torachon's warp-touched form. The possessed Space Marine drew his bolt pistol.

The Bloodthirster roared, unfurling its vast wings.

'I AM MURDER. I AM CARNAGE. I AM DEATH.'

'And I,' Torachon said, as he aimed the bolt pistol upwards, 'am bored.' He fired one, two, three shots into the edifice at the front of the cathedral. High above, dislodged from its position by the explosion of the mass-reactive shells, the massive statue of the Saviour started to fall.

'BORED?' Gravemaker bellowed. 'I WILL RIP YOUR SKIN AND EAT YOUR BONES, I WILL–'

The statue slammed into the Bloodthirster's neck, the weight of ancient stone taking its legs out from underneath it. Its horned chin slammed hard into the ground, so hard that it cracked the marble slabs beneath. The light in its brazier eyes dimmed, their flame guttering. The song of the Noise Marines reached another crescendo: a moment of triumph.

Torachon savoured it. He did not run, but walked slowly towards the prone Bloodthirster, raising Anguish like a ceremonial dagger. Together, Torachon and S'janth drove the weapon through the crown of the Bloodthirster's skull, deep and true. Gravemaker roared in pain and confusion as the monomolecular blade carved a perfect path through its brainpan, severing the connectors that bound the daemon to the physical realm.

It was a true Maru Skara, a killing cut. Steam and smoke rose from the wound, and the daemon's body started to wilt. Muscle and fur, horns and teeth fell away, collapsing like ash, until nothing was left but the fires' dying embers.

Black sand became black ash, swirling and spinning as it was caught in the hot wind.

Sound followed vision, and Xantine heard the bellow of Khorne's daemons, the squeals of dying mortals, and, underneath it all, the endless dirge from the cathedral.

A giant in purple armour strode across his view, and he saw it lay the beast low. It was beautiful, like a figure from legend. A figure from history.

'Father?' he called weakly.

Agony now. His nerves sang with pain, more than he could remember. S'janth had been a salve for his wounded body, he realised, and with her gone, a patchwork of fractures and scars revealed itself. Every cut, every blow, every impact that he had taken while sharing his body with the daemon, he felt them now, rendering him almost insensate with physical agony.

But even that pain paled in comparison with the agony in his soul. He felt a gnawing, empty chasm, as deep, dark, and cold as the void.

She had gone. S'janth had left him, in his hour of need.

The giant in purple armour savoured the remaining battle, but with one of his generals destroyed, the Blood God's remaining daemons were easy prey. The giant moved through the remaining bloodletters, and those crazed mortals who dared come too close, with a dancer's grace, delivering sweet absolution at the end of a blade. Xantine could but watch the performance, both his body and his will too broken to intercede.

Only with the performance complete did the giant come to pay tribute to the ruler of Serrine. In clear focus now, Xantine saw that he had his father's noble bearing and his refined poise. The giant dropped to a knee in front of him, and Xantine met his eyes.

Violet eyes.

They were the same colour as Fulgrim's, but there was no warmth in the violet orbs that stared back. They were feline, and as he watched, they darkened until they became midnight black.

S'janth spoke with Torachon's voice. *'Finally,'* she said. *'A worthy host.'*

The question came unbidden to his mind. He wanted to ask it of both of them: of the daemon, and of the image of his father, Fulgrim. He wanted to ask it of his brothers, too, those who had turned against him. Finally, he wanted to ask it of the world itself – these people, into whom he had put so much attention.

Xantine tried to stop himself, but he was too insensible from fatigue and injury to stop it from slipping past his blooded lips, and he asked it.

'Why did you betray me?'

S'janth's mocking laughter reminded Xantine of the collapsing crystal spires of Canticle City. *'A more pertinent question – why did I stay so long with someone so imperfect?'*

'You chose me,' Xantine breathed.

'I chose a pawn! A puppet, whose frame I could manipulate until I found a better servant.' She turned on the spot, admiring her new form. *'I think this is an upgrade, do you not agree?'*

Xantine remained silent. He felt his secondary heart slowing over time. The wound was grievous, and he would need medical attention soon in order to keep the organ functional. S'janth was not ready to give up the topic, however.

'Do you believe yourself to have been my first choice? Oh, sweet child.' S'janth stood over his stricken frame, as strong and vital as Fulgrim had been. *'You were one of a thousand souls whose ears my message reached.'* She knelt once more, and traced a long finger on one of Torachon's new hands down Xantine's cheek. It was ice-cold to the touch. *'You were simply a vessel. A container for something more powerful and beautiful than you*

could imagine.' She stood once more, and raised her arms to the sky. *'Me,'* she said, exultant.

'I understand,' Xantine said, using his pain to fuel his pride. He tilted his face to Torachon's, and met their violet eyes with defiance. 'You could not take control. You tried – by the Dark Prince, we both know how hard you tried – but I was too strong. You could not manipulate me.' He coughed, and bright blood spattered his blackened lips. 'And so you found another. Malleable. Weak. Stupid.' He forced a laugh. 'You deserve each other.'

'The stink of your jealousy is intoxicating,' she said. *'The flesh lord showed his talent with this one, I can assure you.'* She straightened her arms, flexing their bulging muscles, as if trying on armour for the first time, and nodded approvingly. *'He hates you, Xantine, you know? He truly does. He loved you once, but your mistreatment hardened his soul against you.'*

'I did not mistreat him. He betrayed *me.'*

'You abandoned him. You left him to die in the bowels of this world, and even so, he still holds a flicker of love for you. I can feel him now, torn between his emotions.' S'janth put two hands to her heart, an affectation of theatrical grief, before laughing again. *'It births the most piquant hatred, the sweetest betrayal, this love. That is why we are drawn to your kind. After all we can offer you, your brotherhood is still coded into your base flesh.'*

The ground shifted once more, sending Anguish skittering towards Xantine. He caught the rapier and used it to lever himself forward as his vision dimmed. Like an iridescent insect, Xantine crawled, a cacophony of pain filling his ears as he dragged himself towards the fissure.

'Now, my love,' S'janth said, blocking out the bright sun with her form as she moved to stand over Xantine. *'What are we to do with you?'*

He reached the edge of the chasm, the trap he had walked into that had spilled so much blood that it brought death to his kingdom. His fingers curled around its edge, finding broken ferrocrete and rebar under the marble surface.

Xantine looked up into the face of his brother.

'You are to see my glory,' he said, and hauled himself into the hole.

Xantine fell, his broken body spinning, into the darkness.

PART IV

CHAPTER TWENTY-SEVEN

He floated in the void.

He was a constellation of pain. So many billion points of suffering that nobody could begin to catalogue it all. So many that they twinkled like stars in the night sky against his firmament.

Some were red, wide and burning, their slow throb destined to persist; others were yellow torture, sharp, sore and stinging. The worst were blue-hot agony, so impossibly bright that he didn't believe this reality could hold them. The stars of pain flared, died and went supernova, casting a changing pattern of agony across his body that he bore, as quiet as the void.

He focused on one pinprick of light. It was shrinking, and he called after it.

'Don't go.'

The star pulsed for a moment, as if responding to his words. Hope rose in his soul, but it died as the star shrank further. It became a pinprick of light against the dark, and then it was gone.

'Don't go!' he screamed, but it was too late. He was falling into the black.

Black sand. He dug his hand into it, watching as it ran between the armoured fingers of his gauntlet. Bright sun beat down on his exposed face, and he shielded his eyes from the glare.

The world was called Kalliope. It had not always been thus. The aeldari had another name for it, but those who had known it were now long dead. Only their statues remained, half-buried in the sand and bleached white from aeons in the stark sun.

Names didn't matter, anyway; this desolate world was just the backdrop to his triumph. He was here because he had been chosen. A being of perfection lay on the other side of the sand dune, and of all the souls in the galaxy, *he* had been called to its side.

Close to the top now, and he could hear the music of war. The crack-*wumph* detonation of bolt-shells; the spinning whine of assault cannons spooling up to full-auto; the screams and yells of the dying and the killing. Beautiful sounds, enough to stir the heart and inflame the loins.

He crested the dune. Darkness lay before him. Black-armoured bodies were strewn across the landscape, their blood as dark as midnight as it poured out onto the black sand. The temple entrance stood open, and he saw the blackness inside, as raw and absolute as the deep void. An entrance, but not an exit. There would be no escape from this journey.

He made it anyway, as he had done, once before.

Xantine entered the temple, and descended into its depths, travelling in pitch darkness. At its heart, he found a figure from memory, sitting on an obsidian throne. Euphoros, his former warlord, regarded him with indifference as he entered the chamber.

'This is not what happened in this place,' Xantine said.

'Is it not?' Euphoros asked. He was as he had been in life: clad in armour of black and pink, his puckered face bearing eyes of glassy black and a fang-ridged mouth. He was somehow sanguine despite the fact that soon after he freed S'janth and took her into his body, Xantine had killed Euphoros and taken his ship.

'I found the daemon here.'

'And you used her power to kill me.'

'The weak make way for the strong, Euphoros. I found strength in this place, and I took it for myself.'

'Where is that strength now?' Euphoros asked.

'It… has gone to another,' Xantine said. There was little point lying to a ghost.

'The weak give way to the strong.'

'No,' Xantine said. 'This was betrayal. My brother plotted against me. I would never–'

'You have!' Euphoros roared. The sound of his surgically enhanced voice echoed from the walls of the temple. 'It is part of us, Xantine, this betrayal. It is a cancer at our core that we cannot cut out. Even our father was not immune to its poison. He betrayed his closest brother for the promise of more power. You cannot fight it,' Euphoros said. 'This is the way of things. It is what we are.'

'Then I will make another way,' Xantine said.

Cecily still remembered most of the smells of the undercity, but there was something new in the air, too: change. It hummed with activity now, in a way that it hadn't, even in her youth, the paths and thoroughfares choked with workers on their way to, or from, the day's harvests.

Lord Torachon had restarted the harvests soon after ascending to power, sending his Sophisticants into the undercity en masse to oversee the process. The gangers that dared challenge this decree were put down violently, and their corpses eviscerated and displayed at major intersections. The tactic worked, ensuring that the others soon fell in line.

In a few short weeks, the haze had returned: the harbinger of Serrine's ancient industry, working as intended. It meant that Cecily could no longer see the sky, but she did not mind. She need only stretch her mind beyond the veil of pink fog, and she could feel the sky and the void beyond it, cold to the touch.

'Get to shift!' foremen bellowed on street corners. Their whips and flails instilled motivation in any workers who dared tarry in their backbreaking duties. Torachon's enforcers beat people – killed people – daily, their bodies shoved into gutters to choke the undercity's rudimentary sewer systems, but she walked between their number like a spectre. Cecily was practised, now, at shrouding herself, making herself invisible to others even as she walked down the centre of a busy roadway.

She had used these same talents to make her escape on the day of the celebration, after she had watched the winged monster rise, and witnessed Torachon's betrayal. Wild-eyed cultists and panicking citizens had choked the streets that day, but she slid amongst them as if she was not there, moving quickly and purposefully towards the only place that made sense to her. The city of her birth.

It had taken her days to reach the undercity, sleeping in ruined hab-blocks and burnt-out cellars until she reached one of the many sub-elevators that had been used to transport supplies from above to below. Once below, she hid from brass-masked zealots and scarred brutes, from militia deserters in stained robes and greasy, red-eyed things that stank of dried blood and wrongness.

She followed the voice. At first she had thought it was the

grass, speaking to her once more, but as it coalesced in her mind, she realised it spoke with a different timbre. It whispered like a dreamer, half-asleep and half-awake, and promised her a better future, a better life, if she would follow it.

'Xantine,' she whispered, the first time she had heard it, shivering in the basement of a ruined hab-block. 'You're still alive...'

Cecily found Xantine in an abandoned midden pit in the slums of the undercity. His pink-and-purple armour was stained with blood and dust, but he was still resplendent amongst the filth, his long black hair framing his noble face perfectly.

He was drifting in and out of consciousness. Cecily had no familiarity with the hypnagogic trances that Space Marines could use to accelerate their own healing processes, but she traced her mind over his body, and understood from the psychic touch that his body was repairing itself.

She stayed with him, leaving only to gather water for Xantine, and meagre amounts of food for herself – enough to keep herself conscious, and able to tend to the larger of his wounds.

'You won't die,' she said, as she spooned tiny amounts of water into his slack mouth. 'We made a deal. You promised me a better life. You promised me escape from this hell.' Xantine's eyes would flicker as she spoke, and she would feel his mind stir. 'I know you hear me,' Cecily said to the sleeping giant. 'You promised me.'

Xantine awoke on the third day, opening turquoise eyes to take in his gloomy surroundings.

'It stinks in here,' he said, his voice dry from lack of use.

'My lord,' Cecily said. 'You have returned!'

'Cecily,' he replied, tracing his tongue across cracked lips. If he was surprised to see her, he did not show it. 'Where am I?'

'You are in the undercity.'

'And Torachon…?' Xantine let the question hang in the stinking air.

'He has taken control of the planet.'

'What has he done to my world?'

'He has made slaves of us all and restarted the harvest. The grass is cut, and the Solipsus sap once again flows from the refineries to the city above. I understand that he has also done away with the system of challenge.'

'I see,' Xantine said. 'I assume my people have risen up against him?'

Cecily considered her reply for a moment before voicing it.

'No, my lord,' she said. 'They sing his name, just as they once sang yours.'

She expected rage, then, in response, but Xantine simply closed his eyes and drew in a long breath. When he opened them again, she felt a hint of sadness dance across his consciousness. Before she could taste it, it was gone, replaced by resolve.

'And Vavisk? Where is my brother? Has he too betrayed me?'

'I do not know,' she said, truthfully.

'Then I can do no more,' Xantine said. He drew himself upwards, standing on legs whose bones had now knitted themselves back together. 'This world has failed me. Its people have failed me. My own brothers have failed me.' He tilted his head down to regard the mortal woman who had found him. 'Everyone except for you, my dear. You are blessed with the ability to see true magnificence, and I shall honour our deal.'

'What will you do, my lord?' Cecily asked.

'I will leave this place. I will take you with me, and I will start again – build a perfect world, with worthy subjects and loyal warriors. I will surpass even my father's achievements, and it will come to be known as paradise.'

'And what of Serrine?'

'If I cannot have this place,' Xantine said, his hand falling to the rapier at his hip, 'then I will ensure that no one can.'

The vox call had come in the middle of the night, and the vibration had startled Pierod so much that he sat bolt upright, slamming his forehead against the metal slats of the bunk above. He had cursed his luck, loud and long, until his bunkmate – a muscular oaf with swirling scars that ran in lines from his eyes to his chin – roared from below.

'Oi! I'll pull your tongue from your throat if you don't shut up!'

Pierod took the advice and shuffled out to the hallway, hiding his vox-link under his armpit. He still wasn't used to his new living arrangements – gods, it was a step down from his governor's mansion – but he knew better than to advertise the presence of any belongings that might fetch a high price in the undercity's vicious black markets.

'Yes?' he hissed. 'Gover... Pierod speaking.'

The voice on the other end of the vox was a welcome one.

The man's head burst like a krak grenade, showering Rhaedron with blood and brain matter. She closed her eyes and flicked a fragment of skull from her overcoat.

One of her bridge serfs drew a line across a data-slate. 'Incompatible, my lord,' he proclaimed, as if that wasn't already obvious from the recent cranial detonation. He stood smartly to attention, and faced Torachon, not quite meeting the Space Marine's gaze. 'My lord,' he said, his voice wavering. 'That was the final member of today's intake. At your pleasure, we will begin the trials again with tomorrow's subjects.'

Torachon hurled his own data-slate at the serf. The rectangular object spun through the air like an aeldari shuriken, embedding itself up to the spine in the man. The serf looked down to see the data-slate's green text turn red with his own blood, before he too fell to the spongy floor.

'I will not spend another day on this insipid planet!' Torachon roared, and drew his power sabre. He swung the weapon in wild arcs, carving great furrows in the stinking flesh of Ghelia's corpse. Primal screams tore from his surgically enhanced throat, as frustration boiled over to become white-hot rage.

Rhaedron had seen such paroxysms before, and knew better than to interrupt them. She flinched as the sabre flashed, before stepping back surreptitiously from the radius of the rampage, taking care to avoid the other corpses that littered the *Exhortation*'s observation deck.

The same thing was likely to happen again tomorrow. In his desperation to make his way off-world, Torachon had demanded that he was presented with more psykers, with whom he might be able to reawaken the long-dead Ghelia and bring the *Exhortation* back to full functionality.

Phaedre, now in charge of the hunter squads, had lowered her standards accordingly, taking any of Serrine's citizens that showed even a glimmer of psychic ability. Hundreds every day were taken from their hab-blocks and hovels and brought to the bowels of the *Exhortation*, where the majority suffered the same fate as the now-headless man sprawled across the floor, bleeding gently from his neck stump.

'There is no mortal left on this world who can commune with the ship,' Phaedre said. Her whispering voice set Rhaedron's teeth on edge, even now. 'No matter how psychically strong.'

'Silence, witch,' Torachon spat. He had seen the usefulness of Xantine's muse when he took control, and her willingness to serve a new master – as long as she was given the same luxuries as before – had kept her at his side, but his patience was short. 'There is one.'

'Who?' Phaedre asked.

'Xantine's pet. The psyker Cecily.'

Phaedre spat, and the air in the chamber grew icy. 'She lives?' she hissed.

Rhaedron remembered her. An unassuming thing – some undercity urchin that Xantine had taken a shine to. She could barely recall Cecily's face.

'How did you discover this, my lord?' Rhaedron asked.

'Tun had scrutinised her abilities and found her compatible, but Xantine would not allow us to perform the trial.'

'Why?' Rhaedron asked, surprised.

'He was a weak-minded man. He would not sanction her demise, even if it meant that his brothers could once more taste the pleasures of the galaxy. His final, petty revenge – imprisoning me again on this dead world.'

'Does Cecily still live?' Rhaedron asked.

'I do not know,' Torachon snarled. 'She disappeared on the same day that my pathetic brother did.' Anger rose in him again, and he embedded the tip of his sabre deep into the fleshy floor. 'I had hoped that I would be able to find my own way from this place, but Xantine's ghost still stands in my way. That leaves but one option.' He stared sharply at Phaedre. 'We will scour this world searching for her, and if she lives, we will take her for our own.'

Learning how to move in the undercity had been a slow process for Pierod. He was a large man, and as governor, he had become accustomed to his presence being announced, usually by surgically and chemically modified beings whose entire existence was devoted to making people aware of his presence.

He had bought himself a modicum of safety, at least; he'd had the presence of mind to squirrel away a few treasures, should he ever be deposed from his position as the ringmaster of Serrine's political circus, and he had pawned them in exchange for shift cover and protection promises from the area's larger gangs. The Slickblades even let him stay in one of their rented bunkhouses, on the proviso that he shared information about sap stores that he had gathered during his time in Serrine's upper echelons.

But Pierod knew better than to advertise his presence. In his new life, making himself conspicuous would carry a death sentence. He pulled his robes – drab, grey, awful – over his head, and tried to move like one of the undercity lifers. They had a particular way of walking, these emaciated, sallow people: at once panicked and aimless, either heading for the fields to complete their backbreaking work, or returning home, their souls and bodies battered. Pierod copied it as best he could as he walked with them, moving carefully towards the destination that had been chosen for him.

It was a short walk. When he arrived, he chose his moment, ducking behind a low wall and waiting for long minutes, scanning the walkways to ensure that they were truly deserted, and that no prying eyes would look on. Caution was good – life was cheap down here – but he wondered if this level of paranoia was overkill.

'No,' he whispered to himself. 'Better to be safe than dead.'

He set about his work at a laboured pace, carefully lifting rusted threshing blades, rolling dented wheels and sliding away sheets of battered metal, keeping quiet to avoid attracting the attention of the foremen the next street over. Finally, he revealed his prize: a door. It was almost unremarkable amongst its peers, its thick red painted surface pockmarked from generations of accidental contact with harvest machinery. But it had a secret.

Pierod reached into the back of his mouth, and popped loose a gold-plated molar. He winced in pain, tasting his own blood, as he pressed the root end of the tooth into a tiny hole to the right of the door frame. He heard a click and a hiss, and, with the slow release of some unknown gas, the door slid open, revealing metal stairs leading under the loamy soil. Pierod gave one final glance around, and descended.

Pale green light illuminated the room that Pierod descended into, lending the canisters, tubes, tanks, and cables a sickly colour. It had been a biological facility once, where scientists and technicians had extracted and developed strains of grass that would flourish in Serrine's particular climate. It had been forgotten by the time the angels came, its entrance buried by the growth of the harvesters' shanty towns. There was no need to study the grass, by that point – just the cycle of planting, growth and harvest. A cycle that had persisted for millennia. A cycle that had now been restarted by the planet's new master.

A gentle hum filled the air, the reassuring sound of the complex machinery and equipment working as intended. A large tank dominated the room, its metal front panel obscuring its contents. He might have thought it a peaceful place, had Pierod not known the contents of that tank.

A bank of cogitator controls flickered and flashed. A servitor was wired into the console. Just its torso and head remained, its eyes milky white, and its skin drawn tight over its bones.

Xantine had told him what he would need to do long ago, but he still found the concept distasteful. He grimaced as he met the milky eyes of the thing that had once been a human. He picked up a scalpel from the workbench, and slid it slowly into the side of the servitor's throat, before dragging the tool awkwardly through desiccated skin and toughened sinew. The servitor coughed – he didn't know they could do that – black blood bubbling from the hole in its throat, until its head tipped backwards.

The lights on the console flickered from green to red, and suddenly there was motion in the chamber. Gas hissed from release mechanisms as the metal shutters slid open. They revealed a glass cylinder, some twelve feet tall, filled with thick liquid. Like the rest of the facility, the glow-globes cast the liquid in greenish tones, but there was no mistaking what hung suspended inside the cylinder.

Its head was long, and crested with spines. Its body was protected with a kind of hardened carapace, natural armour against all but the most powerful attacks. Its four arms were long, and ended with wicked claws or jointed fingers that appeared almost human in their dextrous flexing. A profane quirk of the xenos biology had seen these limbs regrown from ragged stumps, becoming the weapons they once were.

As Pierod watched in horror, the creature opened a yellow eye, the slit pupil narrowing as it scanned the room, taking in the fleshy thing on the other side of the glass.

There was nothing in its gaze, Pierod thought. No acknowledgement, no light, no soul. An absolute absence. Just the cold of the void; the end of things.

Its talons thrust forward, somehow grease-quick in the viscous liquid. The cylinder cracked, its glass crazing. A small leak sprang from the point of impact, and a thin trickle of suspension fluid forced its way to the floor.

'Throne!' Pierod yelped, retreating from the creature. He caught his heel on a power cable and tripped, releasing a whuff of air as his backside made contact with the floor.

The second strike shattered the glass completely. The liquid flowed slowly from the cylinder like congealing blood from a wound, creeping towards Pierod as he scrambled to right himself. He tried to stand, to run, but the fluid was about him now – thick, oily, and with a stench like rotting meat. It made the grated floor slippery, and as he brought himself up, his foot went out from underneath him and he fell again, awkwardly, twisting his ankle.

The creature was not so perturbed by the fluid that had been its home. It crawled from the shattered glass, taking a moment to unfurl itself, stretching its four arms wide like a butterfly emerging from its cocoon. Its yellow eyes still fixed, it stepped towards Pierod, clawed feet click-clacking as they dug deep into the metal below.

'No!' the once-governor of Serrine gasped. He made another attempt to stand, but pain stabbed his lower leg and it buckled one last time. Slapping at his chest, he opened a vox channel – a frequency that he was not supposed to know – and did the only thing he could think of. He called for his Saviour.

Silence was his reply.

The creature stood over him, taller than the angels.

The genestealer Patriarch opened its fanged maw, and screamed.

'Always keep a specimen,' Xantine said, as he regarded a row of glass-fronted tanks. The creatures suspended inside those tanks stared back, their yellow eyes tracking him as he paced in front of them. 'That has long been one of my mantras,' he proclaimed, meeting the gaze of the closest captive genestealer.

In reality, it had been Fabius Bile who had taught him the value of maintaining a sample of something new, lest it come in useful – or enjoyable – in the future. The Clonelord had been disagreeable company at the best of times, but he was correct on this count.

Lordling gave no acknowledgement of the wisdom he was receiving, and Xantine rolled his eyes. Good company was another thing that Torachon had stolen from him.

Xantine looked back to the hybrids, the dregs of the rebellion he had crushed close to a decade prior. The species had no obvious sense of self-preservation, and would fight until the death, but Xantine had chosen grievously injured creatures to fill his menagerie. Even then, they put up a terrible fight.

'I remember the trouble you had in obtaining these test subjects,' he said to Lordling, hoping to entice some conversation from the massive Space Marine. Lordling met his gaze and, realising Xantine was waiting for a response, nodded enthusiastically, spreading his arms wide to mime his efforts in restraining the lethal organisms.

Xantine clenched filed teeth. The majority of his Adored had thrown their lot in with Torachon as soon as the usurper had risen to power, and those that railed against his leadership had done so because they thought themselves strong enough to seize control of the planet, rather than out of any loyalty to Xantine. Still, Lordling remained.

Xantine wondered if he was even aware of Torachon's betrayal. Even before Sarquil's treachery, Lordling had been more at home in the mud and mire of Serrine's undercity, spending the majority of his time stalking its streets. Xantine had seen his preference, and had given him a task that would keep him down here, busy and loyal.

'I need you, brother,' he had said, placing his palm on Lordling's arm in a show of camaraderie. 'Only you are capable of performing this task, but you cannot tell a soul.' He had raised a single finger to his mouth, a gesture of silence, and Lordling had copied him with his own finger. 'Do you understand?' Xantine asked.

'Guh!' had been Lordling's response.

'This place. You will protect it with your life. The undercity here will become your hunting ground, and you may gorge yourself on any creature that seeks to defile it.'

Lordling had cocked his head. 'Guh?' he asked.

'These creatures are weapons, and must stay in our hands,' Xantine had said, tapping the side of his head to drive the point home. 'I hope not to use them, but a lord of the Emperor's Children is always one step ahead of his foes.'

Lordling had cooed at that, clapping his hands together. He had performed admirably at his task ever since, as Xantine knew he would, keeping the facility secret and safe from any gangers who might try to breach its defences, or to release its prisoners.

Now, Xantine had come to perform that task himself. He ran his hands across cogitators, pulling levers and turning dials until the chamber filled with the hiss of releasing hydraulics. His task complete, he unclasped the Pleasure of the Flesh, and fired it, over, and over, and over again into the bank of machinery, until all that was left was smoking ruin. Fluid leaked from the tanks, as their living contents stirred. They were not an intelligent species, these genestealers, but they were cunning. They would escape soon enough.

'Come, Lordling,' Xantine said, turning from the damage that he had wrought. 'Let us leave this place. I have need of you again.'

Refinery Six had been the first to be brought back online under Torachon's new regime. After years, its great mulchers worked again, pounding tons of solid grass to get at the sap inside, and its vats were full once more with the soft pink liquid that had given Serrine its life. Its floors and hallways rang with the sounds of people and industry, the song of a planet in production.

Until, one day, Refinery Six fell silent again.

Captain Handeville had been chosen to lead the excursion into the refinery. A violent man, he was excited by the opportunity to crack a few undercity skulls on his way to getting the refinery's forced labour back to work.

Too excited to notice the warning signs.

'Stay close, move fast,' he told his squad of militia veterans as they closed on the vast refinery doors. His team had brought melta charges, but as the shape of the doors coalesced in the gloom, he realised that they hung open, showing the darkness that lay within. Barrels of sap lay upended nearby, dribbling their pink contents into sewer grates.

'The traitors have already fled.' Handeville grinned. He would keep those charges for himself. Who knew what they might be useful for?

The squad had prepared for an organised resistance, but they met only silence as they moved through the refinery. Of its human labour force, there was no obvious sign.

Handeville led his squad through mess halls and changing spaces, across work floors and past packing machines, until they reached the living quarters at the bottom of the refinery. The wall-mounted glow-globes were non-functional down here for some reason, so Handeville ordered his squad to fire up their autogun-mounted lumens. They cast the boxy rooms in ghostly green light, and Handeville felt his excitement curdle into fear.

'Final sweep, then we get out of here, report back. They'll have left some clue as to where they've gone, and we'll burn them out of their warren.'

'Motion, sir,' one of his squad called from behind.

'Where?' Handeville shouted. 'Call your targets!'

The soldier started to speak, but his voice was cut off by a strangled cry. Handeville spun, to see the silhouettes of his squad disappearing, falling as if sucked out into the void. He understood, in that moment, as a long-clawed hand wrapped itself around his foot and pulled.

'They're underneath us!' he screamed.

He never saw the creature that took him, but he felt its long tentacles palpating at his face, snaking up his nose and into his ears, forcing open his mouth. He felt something wet and fleshy push past his teeth, felt it wriggle against his tongue for a moment, before it worked its way down his throat and into his chest.

Handeville passed out, then.

When he woke up, days later, he was Captain Handeville no more.

The grass still spoke to her, but Cecily spoke as the grass now, too. She entered the minds of the tired and the sick, of the beaten and the angry, and whispered of a better life.

'The Saviour awaits,' she would breathe across their minds. 'The true Saviour. Out beyond the stars. It is coming. Make ready for its arrival.'

A suggestion here, a nudge there, and she found she could guide hundreds, thousands, into the arm of the xenos cult. They joined them in tunnels and chapels, out amidst the grass and in the depths of the undercity, losing their minds and their bodies to the will of the hive mind. The cult rose, as it had risen before, from inside itself, multiplying and metastasising with each passing week.

Torachon tried to cut it back, but new cells rose as fast as they were put down, in different parts of the city, striking out at weapon arsenals and sap stores, sowing panic and chaos in the populations of both cities. That panic, in turn, drove more into the arms of the xenos. The cult was embedded deep – Xantine had made sure of that, setting his captives free across the cities above and below.

'I am a Child of the Emperor,' he told Cecily. 'My Legion made its war by drawing out and slaughtering the enemy's leaders.'

'But if there are many leaders...' she had replied.

'Exactly, my dear!' Xantine said, drawing his blackened lips into a smile. 'I have taught you well.'

It could never be perfect, this world – not while this cancer remained at its heart.

Somewhere, out in the black cold, the message was received. The cry had been transmitted across trillions of miles, through solar systems and star clusters, across empires and kingdoms. None of these things had any meaning to the consciousness that received the message. They did not matter.

It transmitted its own message, then, in as much as that concept applied. More accurately, it told itself – all the million-million parts of itself – to move, to change course, to aim for the source of the message. That was all that mattered to the consciousness: the message.

It was simple, declarative, this message. If the consciousness could feel human emotion, it may have felt comfort, or relief. As it was, it felt nothing except hunger. An eternal hunger.

It came not with words, but with meaning.

We are here.

The tendril of the hive fleet turned, reaching like a finger, pointing for the source of the message.

The tyranid bio-ships arrived in-system a few weeks after the cult's uprising had reached critical mass. They resembled great ocean beasts, moving slowly, almost gracefully in the void. They rolled, until their bellies aimed towards the pink pearl below, then they rippled, birthing hundreds, thousands of mycetic spores. Caught by the planet's gravity, the spores began the descent to its surface, slow at first, but picking up speed.

Xantine saw the spores in the sky as they fell, burning in the upper atmosphere like inverted flowers with petals of flame.

Each one would bring a horde of xenos creatures, slavering jaws and simple minds caring not for the art and culture of this doomed world. The grass, the people, his remaining brothers, S'janth. All would be consumed. The xenos would strip the planet and move on, and the daemons who remained would wander its silent wastes, starved of sensation.

A smile played across his blackened lips. It was their own fault. All they needed to do was love him, and they had failed.

'Come, my dear,' he told Cecily, as he rose from his safehouse cot. 'It is time for us to leave.'

CHAPTER TWENTY-EIGHT

The structure was ancient, and built to last. Its strange xenos material had weathered millennia of erosion from sand and wind, and even now, with the Imperium's strongest weapons deployed in its vicinity, it still stood. It offered a pocket of calm in the chaos. The Emperor's Children of 37th Company's Rapier Squad moved through it, taking combat blades and power swords to wounded Salamanders, Iron Hands, and Raven Guard that had crawled to the structure for cover. There was a glee in their murder, and the vox rang with boasts and crude badinage.

'I'm taking a trophy from this one, he's a big bastard!'

'He tried to stab me as I cut his throat. I was too quick, though.'

'Leave this one alive a moment longer, I want to watch him suffer.'

How strange such speech was, once.

Xantine followed, watching the Emperor's Children, as they took enjoyment in their grisly work. The structure finally cleared of living Space Marines, the squad reassembled.

'Good cut, Rapier Squad,' the sergeant said. 'Reload, and we move to the next objective on my–'

Vavisk raised his bolter, and shot his sergeant in the back. The bolt travelled through the gap between the back of the Space Marine's torso armour and his belt, severing his spine immediately. He took a moment to fall, body separated in two, but Vavisk didn't stop. He raked the weapon across the remaining Emperor's Children in the squad, severing arms and crippling legs, blowing out intestines.

Auctilion was the fastest, and tried to raise his own bolter. Xantine knew him: he was the only one of the squad to hail from the same recruiting world as Xantine and Vavisk, but he had arrived with the bulk of the Legion some months before the deployment on Isstvan V. He was fresh-faced, with a shock of white hair and a hairless chin. He smiled easily, and enjoyed poetry.

Vavisk shot him in the head. His helmet disintegrated as the mass-reactive round exploded in the depths of his skull, and the purple-armoured corpse slumped to the black sand.

'Stop!' Xantine shouted. He was drowned out by the sound of mass-reactive explosions as Vavisk continued to pump shells into his brothers' injured forms.

'Stop!'

Quandros crawled forward, hands digging into the sand, his left leg a stump from the knee down. Vavisk put three bolt-shells up the length of his spine, blowing out his backpack reactor. His torso exploded with a sound like an engine igniting.

'Stop!'

Vavisk swivelled and pointed his bolter's barrel at Xantine's chest. He did not pull the trigger. Xantine looked into the green eyes of his brother's helmet, before reaching up and releasing the seals on his own. He slid the helmet off, slowly, to reveal his face. Aquiline nose, high cheekbones, bright eyes. His long hair hung over the gorget of his polished war plate. So much like his father.

'Vavisk. Brother. I do not know what has happened here, but I know that the choice we make in this moment will determine the course of

the rest of our lives.' He raised a hand, too fast, and Vavisk backed up, keeping his bolter trained on Xantine's torso. He slowed the motion, showing he was no threat. 'We are both Children of the Emperor. You can kill me for the sin of being just like you, and then you can die, killed by our brethren for your treachery.' Vavisk stiffened at that last word, and Xantine carried on quickly. 'Or we can trust that our father knows best for us. Whatever he has seen, whatever he knows, it must be worthy of our trust, if he can turn against his closest brother.'

Vavisk's hand faltered, and Xantine knew he would survive this day. He reached out, and placed a hand gently on the bolter's barrel. He could feel its heat through his reinforced gauntlets.

'Nothing happened in this place, Vavisk. We were ambushed, our squad killed. We fought heroically, and slew our enemies. True Emperor's Children, the greatest of all of the Legions.' He pushed the bolter down, until it aimed at the black sand. 'Trust in our father, Vavisk. Trust in me.'

Vavisk lifted his head. He dropped his bolter, and put his hands to his own helmet, sliding it from his skull. Dark eyes in a dark face, cheeks wet with tears. 'I will follow you, brother. I will follow you wherever you take me.'

On the battlefield, Fulgrim cradled the severed head of his beloved brother. 'What have I done?' the primarch of the Emperor's Children howled.

'You have damned us, Father,' Xantine said. 'You have damned your sons.'

Lordling led the escape from the safehouse. The giant was not a stealthy presence, but he was a formidable fighter, and with tyranids dropping from the sky, Xantine felt that the element of surprise had been lost. The trio came out in the shadow of the Cathedral of the Bounteous Harvest, and paused, determining the best way to reach the *Exhortation*.

The streets around the cathedral still bore the scars of the Bloodthirster's arrival, and the cathedral itself still emanated a dirge from the Noise Marines housed within. No longer protected by ferrocrete walls, the sound assaulted Xantine's eardrums, and he thought of his absent brother Vavisk.

That thought turned to resolve, and Xantine placed a hand on Lordling's arm once more. 'Another task, brother. I hope you can perform as admirably as you did the last time I asked. You will protect her.' He pointed to Cecily, and Lordling nodded deeply. Xantine caught the giant's eyes again, staring deep into their black depths. 'She *must* make it to the *Exhortation*. Do you understand?'

Lordling blinked, and Xantine asked again. 'Do you understand?' Lordling nodded again, deep, with something like resolve.

He turned to Cecily. 'Go with Lordling. Use your powers to make it through. I will meet you both at the *Exhortation*.'

'What?' she exclaimed. 'Where are you going?'

'I will join you soon, but first, I need to find my brother.' Xantine looked up, and saw the atmospheric flares of yet more spores. They were falling across the planet. 'Go!' he bellowed, and they moved, making for the closest sub-elevator to the undercity.

Xantine turned and headed for the cathedral.

The glassaic window was beautiful. Finished with gold leaf atop its coloured panes, it depicted the planet's grass fields, pink and unending, underneath a sky of blue, flecked with silver stars. It was thousands of years old – predating the creation of the haze layer after millennia of sap refinement – and somehow had escaped the ravages of a civilisation now given licence to indulge its basest wants and desires.

It shattered into a thousand pieces as Xantine put his pauldron through it. The rest of the Space Marine followed a moment later.

Xantine had gifted the cathedral to Vavisk, and it had come to serve as a home for his cadre of Noise Marines. In the years since, the interior of the Cathedral of the Bounteous Harvest had remained much as it had been when the Adored arrived on the planet, albeit with some minor modifications. The vast pipe that rose from the undercity was now fed by golden tributaries: conduits that stretched down to pods placed on the patterned cathedral floor. From these pods dangled cables and tubes that connected to ports and orifices on the bodies of six Noise Marines – less than a third of those who had once made up Vavisk's choir.

They played on, these warped figures, the music of the apocalypse infinitely more fascinating than the sudden intrusion of a figure from their recent past. At their head, there was a large golden pod that looked out across the room – a space for a grand conductor, able to guide his orchestra in their song.

The pod stood empty.

Xantine ran to the closest pod, and grabbed the Noise Marine – his name had been Tragus – by the shoulders.

'Where is he?' Xantine screamed over the music. 'Where is Vavisk?'

The Noise Marine's eyes rolled in his skull. They were atrophied things, milky white and shrivelled. His nose, too, had collapsed, falling in on itself as the warp changed his body to focus purely on his auditory senses. His mouth hung open, limp and useless.

Xantine shook him, so hard that he thought his neck might snap. 'Help me, child of the Adored. I am your warlord. You know me – I am Xantine, brother of Vavisk.' Tragus looked past him with dead eyes. 'Where is he!' Xantine screamed again, into Tragus' fluted ears. A flicker of recognition, and the song changed, slowly at first. It took on a sadness, a sense of finality, and Xantine, a self-confessed musical connoisseur, heard lyrics in the music.

'He is gone,' the song said.

Tyranids were as alien to the Neverborn as they were to humankind. They existed in the warp not as the warm, vital presences that humans represented, but as a shadow. Cold, dark and unknowable. S'janth derived little pleasure from killing them.

Her fellow Adored seemed to be enjoying themselves a little more. She fought alongside Euratio, who screamed in glee. The Raptor Vordarelle jetted over slashing claws, firing bolt pistols down at the mass of alien flesh that writhed beneath him. Kaedes stood below, twin chainswords purring as he pirouetted through quadrupedal xenos, carving them into blood-squirting chunks.

She had left the fighting initially to the reorganised militia, but it soon became clear that this was no random incursion, but a full-blown invasion. Then, she had gathered her remaining elite warriors – her Sophisticants and the remnants of the Adored – and decided to make her stand in front of the central council building.

It was a good place to fight. Torachon's hardcoded training had told her that, dredged up from the Space Marine's memories. They occupied high ground, protected from the larger bioforms that spewed torrents of acid or gouts of flame by strong walls. Only smaller strains could reach them, and the Space Marines had forced them into kill-zones, ripe pickings for bolter and chainsword.

Yet still they came, climbing over the bodies of their fallen to slash with claws and bite with teeth. S'janth met a four-armed monstrosity in combat, each of its limbs curved into wicked claws that dripped with ichor. A single blow would have carved a mortal in half, but her combined form gave her a preternatural strength, and she parried the beast's first strike on her power sabre. Ducking inside its reach, so close she could see the nictitating membranes of its eyes, she placed both hands against its chitinous ribs and pulled, splitting the beast open like some ocean crustacean.

'Die!' she screamed in exultation, but just as soon as she had let its bisected body fall, another had taken its place.

Legs and claws, teeth and eyes – the city was filling with the shadow in the warp. The cult had brought this endless enemy. She had destroyed its leader, long ago, but she had not scrubbed the stain from this world, and it had grown, like the shadow, until it eclipsed everything.

It was too soon. S'janth had tried to make Serrine a tempting target, restarting its harvest in an attempt to draw pirates, heretics, or smugglers to the world – at which point she would have taken a ship and sailed into the Eye of Terror to join her sisters.

We succeeded in that first stage, Torachon noted with perverse amusement from inside her consciousness. *Too tempting indeed*.

A tall tyranid strain fired a gob of hissing matter in her direction. It caught her on the pauldron and caught fire, burning with a phosphorescent light. She shot it neatly through the thorax, and it slumped, leaking unidentifiable fluids. Three more took its place, their weapons launching more gobs of matter from undulating sacs on their side.

'Retreat!' she called to her warriors, the Sophisticants and the remnants of the Adored. Vordarelle's jump pack had been slashed open, and the turbines had failed spectacularly, launching the Raptor over the wall and into the streets below. His pink armour disappeared into the heaving mass of tyranids a moment later, ceramite discarded and his meat and bone broken down to form so much biomass.

'Retreat!' she called again.

'Where do we go?' Kaedes asked, his chainswords starting to slow with the weight of gore they held.

A light across the shadow, suddenly. She felt Phaedre touch her mind: a psychic message, sent from far away.

+I have found her,+ the witch said.

'To the **Exhortation***!'* S'janth called. *'To my ship!'*

The *Exhortation* was a scar on the perfect pink landscape, black and cancerous amidst the living grass. The slave shanty towns persisted, but only barely. Amongst them, the ship's crew eked out an existence, their affiliation apparent from their filthy uniforms. They stared at Xantine with sunken eyes as he pushed through their number. There was no hero's welcome, nor any resistance that marked these men and women out as Torachon's disciples. The crowds simply parted in silence as he moved through them, their people too weary to present a physical reaction.

The interior of the ship was cold and dark, the once ripe scent of Ghelia's early decay now replaced by the cloying, sweet smell of late rot. No lights guided his path, but he knew the path well; he had walked it a thousand times. To the observation deck, to escape this world.

The observation deck was empty, filled only with the stink of rotting flesh. No, that was not true. As Xantine stepped onto his command deck, he spotted Cecily, lying prone on the carpeted floor, in front of the main viewports.

Phaedre hovered over her, the witch's face locked into a cruel smirk. He had once enjoyed that smirk. It enraged him now.

'Phaedre,' he said, with mock formality.

'Xantine,' she responded. 'My former master.'

'Where is Lordling?'

'Below. It was easy to conjure ghosts for the giant to fight. You must have been desperate, to put such an asset in his hands.'

'What are you doing here?' he asked.

'Is it not obvious?' Phaedre asked. 'No, you were always a little slower than your peers. I will spell it out for you. I need this mortal. *We* need this mortal, my new master and I, to escape this world.'

'You cannot have her.'

Phaedre laughed, and he smelled burnt flesh in the air.

'You forget, Xantine, I knew your mind first, before you took this little wretch in. I know that you need her too. But you have lost, Xantine. You stand alone, in a dead ship, on a dying world. Your daemon left you. Your brothers left you. Your power left you.' She giggled again. 'Even you must be able to see that?'

Anger flared in his mind. 'You are wrong, Phaedre,' he said, and took a step towards the witch.

'Ah-ah!' Phaedre trilled, holding her finger up to forestall him. 'I will burn her to ash if you come any closer, and then no one will get what they want.' Flame climbed up her fingers, blackening the skin.

Xantine changed tack. 'Come with me,' he said, holding his palm forward as if to take Phaedre's own hand. 'If you know me, you know that I understand well the temptations of mortal souls, and I will forgive your indiscretions. Join me once more as my muse.'

'You are nothing,' she spat. 'I serve another now – another far more powerful, far more wonderful than you will ever be.' Her eyes burned with the same flame that licked at her fingers, and she stared hate at him, so hot that he thought he might catch light.

She did not notice Cecily stir. Xantine resisted the urge to flick his turquoise eyes downwards, keeping them locked instead on the witch he had taken from the swamp.

'You will always be my muse, my dear,' Xantine said. 'Nothing more.'

Cecily sank her teeth into Phaedre's ankle. The flame in her hand guttered and died as she screamed in pain. It was a momentary distraction, but it was all Xantine needed to draw the Pleasure of the Flesh, and shoot Phaedre through the heart with the pistol. The mass-reactive round travelled through the witch's tiny body as if it was paper, and she fell, her bracelets and jewels falling like stars to the floor below.

Cecily could still taste Phaedre's blood in her mouth – dry and acid, like poison – and she retched, spitting yellow bile onto the spongy floor. 'Where am I?' she asked.

'The *Exhortation*,' Xantine said from the shadows in the darkened chamber.

'Thank the Throne,' she said, drawing herself to her feet. 'And thank you, my lord, for saving me. Why didn't she kill me?'

'They wanted to use you up. They said that you were their only option to escape this world, and that they would consume you in the process. Kill you, to save themselves.'

Cecily spat again, clearing her mouth of Phaedre's blood, and locked eyes with Xantine.

'The problem is,' Xantine continued, 'they were right.'

Cecily felt nothing as Xantine slipped the silver helmet over her head. The device emitted a gentle thrum as it powered up.

'It is better this way,' Xantine said. 'I did not forget our pact, and now this is the only way to fulfil it. You will see the stars.'

Xantine stood, and placed his hands behind his back. He turned from Cecily, averting his gaze as the thrumming noise grew in volume. He heard her gasp – in pain, surprise or fear, he did not know. For the first time, he did not want to know.

'It is time,' he said, rising to his feet. 'Qaran Tun was right about one thing. It is an honour.'

Xantine left the observation deck for the last time as Cecily's body started to change.

Xantine keyed his vox to an old network, one he had not used in years.

'Crew of the *Exhortation*,' he called. 'I am Xantine, magnificence of the Adored, paragon of the perfect Third, and I call upon you all to fulfil your oaths to me. The ship lives once more, thanks to my efforts. This world is doomed – it has failed me – but you may leave it at my side. Return to your posts, and I will grant you clemency. Be quick, and stop for nothing, and together we may leave and sail into a glorious future.'

He keyed the vox off and made his way down to the *Exhortation*'s boarding ramp, as the flesh around him thrummed into something like life.

The grass told its secrets at night. It was night, now. She couldn't see the darkness, she couldn't see the light, but she knew it, somehow.

She could feel. She felt the grass as it whispered. It tickled her body and caressed her skin, wafting and waving fronds tracing the softest touches as they moved with the wind.

You are safe, the grass whispered. *You are home.*

But she wasn't complete. She was empty. She was cold. There had been hundreds, once, thousands, living with her. Inside her.

She pushed these memories back. They weren't hers. Were they?

She knew the smell of grass, she knew the kiss of the breeze. She knew the cities – one above, one below. She knew their streets. She moved through them, a small, hidden thing.

But she was huge.

She felt the grass. It lifted her, with thousands – millions – of arms, raising her up, up, up. She moved with it, labouring at first, as if waking her body after a long sleep. Synapses fired, muscles contracted, the pleasure of movement, and she was soaring. She saw the haze, like unrefined sap, pink and unblemished, and she made for it.

She expected it to be hard, a barrier blocking her from the sky, but it welcomed her with the faintest kiss. She swam in its perfectness for a time, wisps and eddies of pink dancing along the length of her body, until the pastel colour thinned and darkened, and she could see the sky. The whole sky.

She had never seen the sky.

She had seen the sky a hundred thousand times. She had sailed in its blackness, and ached now for its dark. It had been so long, and the sensation of the void was delicious, cold and fresh on her hull.

Hull? She meant body. Didn't she?

Her body. She knew its counters, knew its strengths. It was *her*. She tried to move her arms, her legs, to wiggle fingers and toes, to feel for creaking knees and muscular shoulders, to look for the scar across the back of her right wrist, the birthmark on her stomach.

She could not. Her body was unfamiliar. Not just unfamiliar, but impossible. Things moved within it, things with minds and wills of their own. They talked to her, these things, told her what to do, where to go. She tried to close her eyes, but she had no eyes, not any more. She could see everything.

Cecily – what remained of her consciousness – screamed in terror.

Fewer than a hundred souls had made their way back to the ship by the time the *Exhortation*'s engines came to life. He listened to the sublight drone, and hoped that fewer than a hundred was enough.

Xantine stood on the boarding ramp and watched as the ship began its journey from its resting place. Firing jets of plasma that burned the grass and blasted away the shanty towns that had grown up around the ship, it started to rise. Slowly, hesitantly at first, until its belly lifted clear of the fronds below. Xantine turned to make his way to the bridge.

The impact caught him between the shoulder blades, and he fell to the ramp's metal surface. He heard a voice over the dirge of the engines and the whip of the wind, and turned his body, facing the world he was leaving behind.

'Xantine!' Torachon howled.

The young Space Marine stood further down the *Exhortation*'s ramp, his sabre held at his side. He was tall now – taller than Xantine remembered him – his armour purple, trimmed with shining silver, and his hair as white and pure as Fulgrim's had been. It rippled and swirled around his head, caught in the currents from the plasma wash.

'You believe you can escape me?' Torachon roared. *'Insolent worm. This is my ship, my world.'* He strode towards Xantine, firing a bolt pistol from his hip.

The first few shots pinged from Xantine's armour, but one detonated on his shoulder, dropping him to his back. He felt the pain immediately, and smelled the blood a few moments later.

Unable to draw himself to his feet, Xantine raised his rapier, aiming it towards the oncoming Torachon.

'I gave you what you desired, daemon – a weak and willing host. You should thank me.'

'You gave me nothing,' Torachon spat. *'Everything I am, I have taken. I am S'janth, tempter of worlds, blessed of Slaanesh...'*

'Oh come on, then,' Xantine interrupted, twirling his sword in his hand. He had a chance. If he could bait them into an over-confident strike, he had strength left to parry – all he needed was one counterstroke. 'Kill me, if you can. I tire of your endless speeches.'

'*I will,*' Torachon said, closing the gap between them. '*And I will enjoy it.*'

A noise like a Titan's war-horn blared, and Xantine almost dropped the rapier, as concentrated sound blasted Torachon in his silver breastplate. Xantine turned, and saw the man who had been known as little Ferrus, his sonic blaster raised and keyed to unleash the music of the apocalypse upon Torachon. Sound crackled across the space between the two warriors of the III like lightning, compressing air and ripping at the fabric of reality as it travelled.

A direct blast should have been enough to cripple the warrior, to scramble his organs inside his body, but Torachon was swollen with the daemon's power. The force hit like a punch instead, concussive, knocking him off balance. He staggered on the ramp as the *Exhortation* climbed higher, closer to the pink haze that lay low above the planet's surface.

Vavisk stepped forward as he fired, keying the sonic blaster through frequencies as the music rose in volume. Xantine's vision wavered in response, sensation and reality warping in the presence of such a weapon.

There was another sound, too, discernible amongst the cacophony. Vavisk was singing. A hundred voices from his dozen mouths joined the chorus, channelling the discordia, the rapture, the maraviglia. Xantine's brother sang of the purest sensations: despair and joy, love and hatred, pride and envy, raising his voice to Slaanesh above.

Torachon's massive body lurched, buffeted by impossible

forces, but still he maintained his balance. It would take more than a single sonic blaster to destabilise his possessed body.

Xantine weighed his rapier in his good arm. The weapon had been fashioned from the sliver of the spear that had contained S'janth, a reminder of her captivity that she had railed against. It was a good weapon, finely balanced and wickedly sharp, but he would find another.

He hurled it, point first, at Torachon. It flew, straight and true, its monomolecular blade piercing Torachon's burnished silver armour through the breast. It travelled through skin and muscle, organ and bone, and the force of it lifted the body that contained both the daemon and the Space Marine from the ramp of the *Exhortation* and out into the pink clouds.

They were not alone as they fell. They shared every sensation. The cold kiss of the frigid air, the gentle touch of the pink clouds, the sharp agony of the blade buried in their skin, and the hot rage that boiled in their stomach.

They were not alone in the sky, either. Tyranid spores fell alongside them, amalgams of flesh and bone and chitin, a similar shade of pink to the grass that their organic passengers would soon consume.

Nor were they alone as they died: together, as their broken body was consumed by xenos beings that barely registered the difference between muscle and bone and the grass that surrounded it. The daemon had been severed from her warp form by aeldari seers millennia before, and with this death – this final, ignominious death – there would be no resurrection. Weak and winnowed, something on the other side would claim her power for themselves.

These xenos cared not for her deeds and glories, nor the civilisations that had worshipped her, or the cultures she had debased.

And the one man who had known these things, who had shared his body and her power, would never speak her name again, as long as he would live.

EPILOGUE

Xantine watched as impact blooms started to pockmark Serrine's pale surface, and smiled. It was their fault. All he had asked of them was adoration, and servitude, and they had failed.

They would be consumed, all of them. S'janth, his brothers, the people, the hel-damned grass, the whole world and its failed attempts at art and culture, devoured. He turned away from the viewport.

'Are you sated?' Vavisk asked, without venom. The Noise Marine stood at the bridge entrance, his bulk almost filling the door frame.

Xantine considered his question for a moment, before offering his reply. 'Never,' he said. 'But there is a galaxy ahead of us. There will be other worlds.'

'I am sure of it,' his brother rumbled.

'Onwards,' Xantine decreed, as he slid into his command throne. 'Status report, Lady Rhaedron.'

'Void drive online, my lord Xantine, and all core systems

operational,' Rhaedron said. The woman was older, but she had maintained her regal bearing. 'It appears that the new arrival has adapted well to her home.'

'Good,' Xantine said, as he watched the pale-pink pearl of Serrine shrink in the viewport. 'Ship. Cecily – what can you see?'

'It's…' The voice filled the bridge, and faltered. It tried again, more confident this time. 'It's perfect.'

'It could have been,' Xantine said.

ABOUT THE AUTHOR

Rich McCormick is a writer and videogame producer whose love affair with the worlds of Warhammer began when he was handed a small plastic ork at a very tender age. He used to live in Japan, but now lives in Yorkshire, with his wife and son. His work for Black Library includes the Warhammer 40,000 novel *Renegades: Lord of Excess* and the short stories 'Knife Flight' and 'A More Perfect Union', as well as the Horus Heresy short story 'Visage'.

YOUR
NEXT READ

RENEGADES: HARROWMASTER
by Mike Brooks

Secrets and lies abound with the mysterious Alpha Legion, but as extinction becomes an ever-present reality for the Serpent's Teeth warband, Solomon Akurra seeks a new way of war…

An extract from
Renegades: Harrowmaster
by Mike Brooks

Jonn Brezik clutched his lasgun, muttered prayers under his breath, and hunkered further into the ditch in which he and seven others were crouching as the world shook around them. The weapon in his slightly trembling hands was an M35 M-Galaxy Short: solid, reliable and well maintained, with a fully charged clip, and a scrimshaw he had carved himself hanging off the barrel. He had another four ammo clips on his belt, along with the long, single-edged combat knife that had been his father's. He was not wearing the old man's flak vest – not a lot of point, given the state it had ended up in – and as enemy fire streaked overhead again, Jonn began to do the mental arithmetic of whether, right now, he would prefer to be in possession of a gun or functional body armour. The gun could kill the people shooting at him, that was for sure, but he would have to be accurate for that to work, and there didn't seem to be any shortage of the bastards. On the other hand, even the best armour would give out eventually, if he lacked any way of dissuading the other side from shooting at him–

'Brezik, you with us?'

Jonn jerked and blinked, then focused on the woman who had spoken. Suran Teeler, sixty years old at least, with a face that looked like a particularly hard rock had been hit repeatedly with another rock. She was staring at him with eyes like dark flint, and he forced himself to nod.

'Yeah. Yeah, I'm here.'

'You sure? Because you seem a bit distracted right now,' Teeler said. 'Which, given we're in the middle of a bastard *warzone*, is something of a feat.'

'I'll be fine, sarge,' Jonn replied. He closed his eyes for a moment, and sighed. 'It's just the dreams again. Feels like I haven't slept properly for a month.'

'You've been having them too?' Kanzad asked. He was a big man with a beard like a bush. 'The sky ripping open?'

Jonn looked over at him. He and Kanzad did not really get on – there was no enmity as such, no blood feud; they just rubbed each other the wrong way – but there was no mockery on the hairy face turned in his direction.

'Yeah,' he said slowly. 'The sky ripping open. Well, not just our sky. All the skies. What does that mean, if we're both having the same dream?'

'It means absolute jack-dung until we get out of here alive,' Teeler snapped. 'You want to compare dream notes after we're done, that's fine. Right now, I want your attention on the matter in hand! And Brezik?'

'Yes, sarge?' Jonn replied, clutching his lasgun a little tighter.

'Stop calling me "sarge".'

'Sorry, s– Sorry. Force of habit.'

A throaty drone grew in the air behind them, and Jonn looked up to see lights in the night sky, closing the distance at a tremendous speed. The drone grew into a whine, and then into a roar as the aircraft shot overhead: two Lightnings flanking an Avenger, all three heading further into the combat zone.

'That's the signal!' Teeler yelled, scrambling to her feet with a swiftness that belied her years. 'Go, go, go!'

Jonn leaped up and followed her, clambering out of the ditch and charging across the chewed-up ground beyond. He desperately tried to keep up some sort of speed without twisting an ankle in the great ruts and gouts torn into the earth by bombardments, and the repeated traversing of wheeled and tracked vehicles. He could see other groups just like his on either side, screaming their battle cries as they advanced on the enemy that were being savaged by aerial gunfire from their fighters. Jonn raised his voice to join in, adrenaline and fear squeezing his words until they came out as little more than a feral scream:

'FOR THE EMPEROR!'

Streams of fire began spewing skywards as the enemy finally got their anti-aircraft batteries online. Jonn heard the *thump-thump-thump* of Hydra quad autocannons, and one of the fighters – a Lightning, he thought, although it was hard to tell at this distance, and in the dark – came apart in a flower of flame, and scattered itself over the defenders below.

'Keep moving!' Teeler yelled as one or two in their group slowed slightly. 'We've got one shot at this!'

Jonn pressed on, despite the temptation to hang back and let others take the brunt of the enemy gunfire. Presenting the defenders with targets one at a time would only ensure they all died: this massed rush, so there were simply too many of them to kill in time, was the only way to close the distance and get into the enemy lines. Once there, the odds became far more even.

They passed through a line of metal posts, some no more than girders driven upright into the mud, and the fortifications ahead began to sparkle with ruby-red bolts of super-focused light. They had entered the kill-zone, the functional range of a lasgun, and the defenders now knew that their shots would not be wasted.

Kanzad jerked, then jerked again, then fell on his face. Jonn did not stop for him. He would not have stopped for anyone. Stopping meant dying. He charged onwards, his face contorted into a rictus of fear and hatred, daring the galaxy to come and take him.

The galaxy obliged.

The first las-bolt struck him in the right shoulder and burned straight through. It was a sharp pain, but a clean pain, and he staggered but kept moving. It was his trigger arm, and his lasgun was supported by a strap. So long as his left arm could aim the barrel and his right could pull the trigger, he was still in this fight.

The next shot hit him in the gut, puncturing the muscle wall of his stomach and doubling him over. He managed to retain his feet, just, but his momentum was gone. He began to curl up around the pain, and the stench of his own flash-cooked flesh. Eyes screwed up, face towards the ground, Jonn Brezik did not even see the last shot. It struck the top of his head, and killed him instantly.

'Die, heretic!' Stevaz Tai yelled, as his third las-bolt finally put the man down. He whooped, partly in excitement and partly in relief, but anxiety was still scrabbling at the back of his throat. Throne, there were just so *many* of them! Even as he shifted his aim and fired again, he thought he saw something off to the left, closing in fast on the Pendata Fourth's defensive line. He blinked and squinted in that direction, but some of the great floodlights had been taken out by that accursed aerial attack, and the shapes refused to resolve for him.

'Eyes front, trooper, and keep firing!' Sergeant Cade ordered, suiting actions to words with his laspistol. It was more for show than anything else, Stevaz assumed, since the heretics were probably still out of pistol range, but it would only be a matter of seconds until that was no longer the case. And those seconds could be important.

'Something to the left, sarge!' he shouted, although he snapped off another shot as he spoke. 'I didn't get a good look, but whatever it was, it was moving fast!'

'Was it in our sector?' Cade demanded.

'No, sarge!'

'Then it's Fifth Squad's responsibility, or Seventh's – not ours! We've got enemies enough in front of us,' Cade snapped, and Stevaz could not argue with that. He jerked backwards as an enemy las-bolt struck the dirt in front of him, and wiped his eyes to clear them of the mud that had spattered across his face.

'Full-auto!' Cade bellowed. 'Let 'em have it!'

Stevaz obediently flicked the selector on his lasgun and joined its voice to the whining chorus that sprang up along the trench. It would drain their power packs rapidly, but the sheer volume of fire should put paid to this latest assault before they needed to reload–

Something exploded off to his left, and it was all he could do not to whip around, lasrifle still blazing. It was immediately followed by screaming: high, desperate screams born not just of pain, but of utter terror.

'Sarge?!'

'Eyes front, trooper, or you'll be the one screaming!' Cade yelled, but there was a note of uncertainty in the sergeant's voice as he fired at the onrushing cultists. 'One problem at a time, or–'

Something large and dark flew into their midst from their left, and landed heavily on the trench floor. It clipped the back of Kanner's leg and she tripped backwards, and her cycle of full-auto shots tracked along Dannick's head and blew his skull to smithereens, then took Jusker in the shoulder. They both fell, and Cade roared in anger and frustration, and not a little fear, as his squad's output reduced drastically. Someone moved to help Jusker. Someone else fell backwards as a lucky shot from the onrushing enemy found the gap between helmet and trench top. Stevaz could not help himself: he turned and looked down at what had caused all this commotion.

It was a headless body, bearing the insignia of Fifth Squad.

Fear paralysed him. What had broken into their lines? What had decapitated this trooper, and hurled their body so easily into Fourth Squad's ranks? It couldn't have been the explosion he heard: what explosion would take someone's head off so neatly, but hurl their body this far?

Cade was shouting at him.

'Tai, get your arse back on the–'

The sergeant never got the chance to finish his sentence, because something came screaming over the top of the trench, and landed on him. The buzzing whine of a chainsword filled the air, along with a mist of blood, and then Sergeant Cade was bisected. His murderer turned towards Stevaz as the rest of the heretics' assault piled into the trench, rapidly overwhelming Fourth Squad.

Stevaz saw a snarl of fury on the face of a woman probably old enough to be his grandmother, and the light of bloodlust in her eyes. He raised his lasrifle, but her howling weapon batted it aside, and the rotating teeth tore it from his grip. He turned and ran, fumbling at his belt for the laspistol and combat knife that rested there, hoping he could at least outpace her until he had his secondary weapons drawn.

Too late, he realised he was running towards where Fifth Squad had been stationed.

He rounded a corner of the trench before he could stop himself, and collided with something enormous and very, very hard. He fell backwards into the mud, and looked up to see what he had run into.

Two glowing red eyes stared balefully down at him, and Stevaz nearly lost control of his bladder until he recognised them for what they were. The eye-lenses of a Space Marine helmet! The promised help had arrived! The lords of war were here on Pendata!

Then, despite the darkness, he took in the colour of the armour plate. It was not silver, but blue-green, and the pauldron did not display a black blade flanked by lightning strikes on a yellow background, but a three-headed serpent. His heart shrivelled inside his chest, because he suddenly realised what he must have seen, moving so fast towards Fifth Squad's lines.

'You're not Silver Templars,' he managed shakily.

The helmet tilted slightly, as though curious.

'No.'

A weapon with a muzzle as large as Stevaz's head was raised, and the bolt-shell it discharged detonated so forcefully that his entire upper body disintegrated.

Derqan Tel turned away from the dead Pendata trooper, and followed the rest of his team into the culvert that ran back from the front lines. No more defenders were coming from that direction: the Legion's human allies had breached the trench-lines now, and could be relied upon to make a mess of this first line of resistance.

'What is a Silver Templar?' he asked the legionnaire in front of him.

'No idea,' Sakran Morv replied. 'Why?' Morv was big even for an Astartes, and carried the squad's ancient autocannon.

'That mortal seemed to think I should be one,' Tel said. He searched his memory, but drew a blank. 'I cannot think of a loyalist Chapter called the Silver Templars. You?'

'Perhaps he meant Black Templars,' Morv suggested. 'Although I think Va'kai would have recognised their insignia.'

Something wasn't sitting right in Tel's gut. Three loyalist strike cruisers had emerged from the warp since the Legion had made planetfall, and were now engaged in void combat overhead with the *Whisper*, the flagship of the Serpent's Teeth. Morv was correct: Krozier Va'kai, the *Whisper*'s captain, would know a Black Templars ship if he was shooting at it.

He activated his vox. 'Trayvar, have you heard of Silver Templars?'

'Is this really the time, Tel?' came the voice of Trayvar Thrice-Burned in reply. He was at the head of the advance, farther down the trench. He had also been the first into the defensive lines when Eighth Fang made their assault rush across the ground left dark by the destroyed floodlights; it was that sort of full-throated aggressiveness that had won him the renown he enjoyed, and also seen him doused in burning promethium no less than three times in one particularly brutal assault against a position held by the Salamanders Chapter.

'The mortal I just killed appeared to be expecting them,' Tel informed him. 'It could be a new Chapter. Or, as Morv pointed out,' he continued, 'a misremembering of the Black Templars.'

'Silver Templars, Black Templars,' the Thrice-Burned muttered. *'You'd think they would have some imagination, wouldn't you?'*

'The Imperium, endlessly repeating minor variations of the same tired routines?' Morv laughed. 'Surely not.'

'I'll vox it in,' Trayvar said. *'The Harrowmaster might know something.'*

'Acknowledged,' Tel replied. Harrowmaster Drazus Jate led

the Serpent's Teeth, and it was his tactical genius that had led to Pendata's fall. Once they broke this last loyalist bastion then the resistance would be shattered, and the raw materials the Serpent's Teeth so desperately needed – promethium, metal, plasteel, perhaps even ceramite – would be theirs for the taking. There would be no sharing of the spoils with other Legions, either: the Teeth were not part of the Warmaster's 13th Black Crusade, and there was no one here but them to claim the winnings. Abaddon would surely fail, as he always did, for all that he was closing on Terra and had ripped the very fabric of reality asunder across the galaxy. If there was one thing the Black Legion could be relied upon to do, it was to fail, and Drazus Jate knew better than to get caught up in *that*.

Trayvar's bolter opened up with a roar, and Tel heard screams as the defenders realised that not only had their lines been breached, but also heavily armoured transhuman killers were now amongst them. The desperate stabs of las-fire cast shadows, but in the narrow confines of the trench Pendata's mortal troops could only bring a couple of weapons to bear at once: nowhere near enough to stop Trayvar. Tel broke into a run as Eighth Fang accelerated ahead of him, stealth abandoned in favour of shock.

'*Over the top, and east!*' Trayvar barked over the vox, and Tel sprang upwards without thinking about it. The trench through which they were running was still deep enough here that a mortal would think twice before jumping down into it, let alone trying to climb out, but Tel's superhuman muscles were boosted by the servos and mechanical sinews of his power armour, and he cleared the lip with little effort.

A scene of chaos met his eyes.